THE GAME IS ALTERED

MEZ PACKER

Tindal
Street
Press

First published in 2012
by Tindal Street Press Ltd
217 The Custard Factory, Gibb Street,
Birmingham, B9 4AA
www.tindalstreet.co.uk

A CIP catalogue reference for this book is available
from the British Library

ISBN: 978 1 906994 31 0
Ebook: 978 1 906994 86 0

This book is dedicated to
Alan Turing, 1912–1954

Fun and Games in the Garden

The smell of the flowers transports Lionel for an infinite moment, from now to another life, but then he's back with a corporeal thud. In his body. Hiding in the bushes. He can feel his heartbeat in his throat, excitement and a little fear, and he's peering through the gloss of the laurel. Even in summer it smells damp in here, in the shrubbery. This is where Mordecai pees, he thinks; along with the damp there's an ammoniacal tang coming up from the earth. He wishes his cat would come back. Mordecai has been missing for days.

But quiet. Here they are now, his brothers. He watches as they proceed through the arch that marks the boundary between here and the kitchen garden. Ben appears first, looking fiendish and satisfied, lashing the air with a willow whip – *whooish, whooish*. He's stripped the branch to a supple, creamy switch. Now James comes and stands framed in the arch and the whole scene is like a painting. Look how the older boy's adolescent posture is captured. Look at his thick neck and downy chin. The angry weight on his brow. James will take his frustration out on Ben if they don't find him and Lionel feels a stab of pity for the younger boy.

'Sshh.' James strikes a new pose; eyes fixed hard on his brother for a second before scanning the bushes for movement.

The boys consult briefly; they're still a way off and Lionel strains to hear what they're saying. But now James is creeping up one side of the garden while Ben takes the other, signalling like Red Indian scouts. They're sure to find him.

An urge to pee overwhelms him and he thinks of Mordecai again. He must not move, not now or the game will be up, so he grits his teeth and squeezes his eyes shut until his thighs flush hot with resistance and the pee is forced back through the jumble of tubes he knows are coiled up inside him.

The shrubbery is backed by a brick wall and several tall trees. Further along there's a trellis that supports a crop of wilting roses. Look how fragile they are with their heads hanging, dying of thirst. Lionel wonders if his pee would give them new life and he imagines their roots sucking moisture up through their stems, pumping along veins and capillaries, engorging their petals – the way butterflies' wings unfurl when they fill up with blood.

Come on now, forget the sad roses, forget butterflies, climb the trellis, shin over the wall and into the meadow. Courage, he needs courage. Ludi has courage. If Ludi were here he would pull his sword from its scabbard and come out of the bushes yelling, heroic – fearless character that he is. He'd get James and Ben by their scruffs and knock their blocks together, show off the strength of his muscles. Oh yes. But then Ludi has special powers while he has none. He takes a preparatory breath. He's got to be brave.

James, bathed in sunlight, has made a visor with his hands and is peering through the windows of the tool shed at the opposite end of the garden. Ben stands a little way off, examining the length of his willow whip, holding the tip in his fingers then releasing it, watching as it arcs in the air above his head. This is the time to get out of here, right now while they're focused elsewhere. But he can't move; he feels heavy and listless.

Listen. Not far away someone is singing in the meadow. It has to be Lilith. Lionel imagines his sister, sweet little thing, wandering through the tall grass and the buttercups in her favourite red dress, *tra la la*-ing; innocent. Yes, it's definitely Lilith, he knows that voice; he knows the song. They learned it together. He closes his eyes so he can picture her in more detail – a profusion of wild flowers surrounds her, the trees strew the ground at her feet with their blossom. The whole world is a frame for her loveliness.

Enough of this, move now. His body tenses. Time for action. But as he teeters, about to commit, a dark shape plops into the leaf mould at his feet making a small noise on impact. He looks up through the branches where the sky stretches away to an empty blue, but on the ground is a fledgling crow. One wing is bent at an awkward angle and its beak is open in a wide, silent cry.

James has homed in on the disturbance, quick as an animal.

'Lionel,' he tests, drawing his name out in a theatrical, questioning tone. 'Is that you in there? Are you hiding in the bushes again? Come out, come out wherever you are.'

Lionel's body burns with the effort of staying completely still.

Ben, stalking across the lawn, follows his brother's lead; they both have a gleeful angle to their heads like the hounds old Jackson keeps on the farm down the lane. Tails up, eager at the horses' fetlocks. Lionel's seen them slavering, circling a fox. He crouches for the crow and folds its wing gently against its body. It shivers in his hands and the vibration is quick and marvellous; it's how the earth feels sometimes when he lays his hands on it. But there's no more time to think and he starts off, hacking through the shrubs, dead wood striping his shins and his arms.

When he reaches the trellis he pushes the crow under his jumper and begins to climb – rose thorns and splinters tear at his hands. Wilting petals caress his face. The trellis creaks and shifts, but it doesn't come away although he slips twice, unable to get a toehold on the overgrown frame. He can hear James swearing, instructing Ben to 'just grab him, that's it, get his leg'. And the childish grunts of exertion as the smaller boy advances through the bushes under orders.

Lionel reaches the top, panting, feeling along the copingstones to get some purchase so he can pull himself over. The crow stirs in his breast – only a flutter – and he doesn't want to crush it, so he stops and sets it carefully on top of the wall. It tests its wings, hops – once, twice – and drops into the buttercups – to freedom.

The singing in the meadow has stopped. It's his fault. He shouldn't have caused this commotion. He looks for Lilith, to reassure her. He has a view through the tallest branches of the laurel, to the house in one direction, and over the wall in the other, but he can't see her. The crow has taken cover – clever thing. And here are the buttercups clothing the meadow on both sides of the river – a whole golden legion – and he struggles to hoist his leg over the top. The possibility of escape is unbearably sweet, almost disabling.

There's a comforting heat to Ben's hands when they grip his left ankle, but Lionel doesn't look down – looking down would be like defeat. He feels his trainer come free and Ben's hands are joined by others, grasping his calf and his haunches. The weight of his brothers like pack dogs at his waist, then on his shoulders, gives him an affinity with the wildebeest and the zebra he's seen on TV, brought down by hyenas. He understands the bland moment when an animal can do nothing but submit to destiny, when resignation replaces the instinct for survival.

Fear turns to warm release.

'Gotcha, you little brown shit,' says James.

'Ugh, look.' The younger boy's voice is piqued with disgust. 'He's wet himself.'

There. He's watered the roses.

It's only a game.

Years Later:
Connections in the Rain

'Look down there, Lionel. That is exactly what I'm talking about.' Lionel joins his sister at the window. 'People are so *programmed* – see! Like bloody machines.'

Lionel's flat is on the first floor, above Saeed's Grocery, and since he moved in he has watched the comings and goings on Milk Street the way other people goggle at their screens. Lilith's right: people do the same things over and over, repeating their tasks in an infernal loop. They almost never look up – he's noticed that too. The world might as well be two metres tall. The commuters, off to the railway station day after day; the women in saris with their pull-along trolleys, dragging toddlers behind them; the men in pakol hats sitting on crates on the pavement chewing qat – they all stare straight ahead or at their mobile devices. Only the working girls scan the street when they come out at dusk, but, still, they never look up. They never see Lionel.

He presses his temples, concentrates on a tall man in a white djellaba on the opposite side of the road and begins to hum.

'Lionel,' Lilith says, using her exasperated voice. 'You're doing that *thing* again.'

'I'm using my mind to make them look up here.' His body vibrates with the effort. 'I want to see if anyone can *feel* me.'

'I told you.' She flops onto the sofa. 'No one can ever *feel* anybody that way. Besides, you'd shrivel up if someone caught you doing all that psycho-bullshit. You'd hide.'

'No, I wouldn't.'

'Yes, you would; you'd curl up on the floor.' She does an impression of Lionel, foetal and shivering. 'Jesus, you can barely look anyone in the eye, except me.'

Lionel bites his lip. He thinks of Lilith as his real sister, even though he was adopted after *the boys* – before she was born. They're total opposites, but she's the only one he talks to now they've grown up and none of them have to pretend to be siblings. Lionel loves the way she chain-smokes and swears and trots off the slang that the *cool* people use. He loves it when she bursts into his flat – the way she did today – and dances round the room singing his name. Lilith is so present and connected to the world. She goes barefoot in summer and walks along walls instead of the pavement. Sometimes, but not often, she'll hold his face and kiss him, full on the lips, and call it a 'smoochie'. It makes him blush to his bones. When Lilith is at her best it feels like his blood is fizzing. He feels like a real human being.

But Lionel is careful not to upset or disappoint her. He doesn't argue when she admonishes him for being passive. He rarely disagrees when she bangs on about politics, or sneers at the 'sad lemmings' doing as they're told without question. And he would never tell her about his recurring dream – the one where he cracks his head open and a group of children run to help him, but draw back in fear because a portion of his skull has fallen away and there are cogs and wheels inside, whirring and ticking. Not human, but robot. The dream is a sure sign that he's a mechanical thinker and Lilith despises mechanical thinkers.

Too much disappointment sends Lilith into a 'bleak phase'. He can tell she's on the edge of one now. It began last week when she slapped the man in the club. They were there together, brother and sister, on a rare night out. Lionel watched from the other side of the bar as she caught the man's face with a right-handed swipe – *smack*. Everyone around her gasped and froze, waiting for the next thing to happen. The man came at her with the force of a bull from a bucking chute. He was a little man, oriental, but his companion – an Incredible Hulk of a character – had said, 'Not here, H, not now,' and struggled to restrain him.

Lilith stood there, cocky as you like, showing both men her middle finger with a snarl face on. Fearless, utterly fearless. She winked at Lionel and put a burlesque swing in her gait, as she flounced back to their table.

'What larks!' she drawled, vamping it up, lighting a cigarette as if it was all a game. But she wasn't smiling. 'Notice how the poor sod could only do one thing in response to that slap. No choice, you see. Pre-programmed.'

Lionel's heart was going full gallop. There was no point asking what had made her hit the man. She'd shrug, as usual. 'Rattling the cage, brother; just rattling the cage.'

When Lilith gets crazy he's never sure what to do.

'At least you're not plugged in twenty-four-seven, not like some of those androids down there.' She's yawning now, drifting off as she speaks. 'At least you live in the real world most of the time.'

Lionel scowls at the sky, trying to work out if it has been raining all week or just today, his day off after three straight shifts on the helpdesk. *Look into the camera and then key in your password. What appears to be the problem?* Days blur into weeks, especially when he's on nights.

The downpour is pitiless. One great, judgemental cloud presides over Milk Street and over the Georgian edifices that flank the one-way system to the sprawl beyond. Further off, a crease in the land channels the sullen flow of the river to some distant sea.

Buddha lies limp along Lionel's arm, one paw dangling, head flopped to the side. Lionel strokes him with lavish, sweeping movements and the cat responds with a grateful twitch each time he makes contact.

'If someone looks up at me now, Buddha,' he says, holding his head at an imperious angle and staring down his nose at the street, 'they'll think I'm a Bond villain.'

Stoic pedestrians dash through the spray. They don't notice the girl walk out from the alleyway next to the health centre. They don't notice her fists pushed hard into the pockets of her bomber jacket, or her hair plastered flat to her head. Lionel sees her immediately and watches her closely as she crosses and recrosses Milk Street. Her face is wild and strangely illuminated.

'Well, Budds,' Lionel whispers into the cat's ear. 'She's not pre-programmed, is she?'

The girl screams suddenly at nothing, although Lionel can't hear her through the closed window. In the middle of the road, in the path of traffic, the girl stops. She doesn't trip or stumble, she simply pulls up sharp – as if she's remembered something crucial – and touches her hairline and remonstrates with herself.

'Look at that.' Lionel laughs.

The girl is oblivious to the screech of brakes and the blaring horn as a car skids at an angle in front of her. Lionel stops stroking Buddha. It's going to hit her, he thinks, and he takes a step forward at precisely the moment the bumper kisses her shins.

The girl doesn't flinch or notice the comic-book fist that shoots from the driver's window. She walks to the pavement and stands there, not serene, just silent, glowering at the rain marching in the gutter. The girl is in another world entirely.

Lionel's breath makes circles of steam on the glass. The rain comes in sheets and slicks the girl's hair to the sides of her face. Water beards her chin. She closes her eyes, yielding to the rain, to whatever has brought her to Milk Street. She's unbelievably still, almost frozen.

Lionel rests his forehead on the window. 'Look at me,' he says. 'Go on. Look up here, at me. I bet *you* can feel me.'

The girl can't possibly hear him, but as soon as his words condense on the glass her chin jerks up and she opens her eyes. There's nothing accidental about it, no searching around, no random glance at one window then another. She looks directly at Lionel. Only him. She is as beautiful as an anime character from one of his games: a porcelain-doll face of ideal dimensions, a slender oval, wider at the forehead, delicate at the chin and huge, pellucid eyes that send blue beams of energy from her to him, bridging the filth of the street and the grime of the day. Her gaze is so fixed and intimate that Lionel holds his breath, afraid that the tiniest movement will break the spell. If only he could remain here in this moment. But the traffic gets louder and the hum of the desktop unit becomes an insistent whine, the heating system burbles and clicks and he hates the world for being noisy and complicated, for drowning out his quiet link to this heart-stoppingly beautiful anime girl. And Buddha meows, his loudest meow in weeks. Lionel gasps and the girl breaks his gaze with a slow, reproachful blink. Without looking back, she turns down the alley she came from. Shadows fold over her.

Parts of Lionel's childhood are lost to him. He has some static, colourless memories, black and white images of people and places. A few early events are more vivid – a trip to the seaside, his cat disappearing, his first day at primary school. Occasionally he's visited by dreamlike sequences – meadows and golden sunsets and dandelion clocks dispersing gossamer seeds to the breeze – but they lack substance. Only the computer games he's played since boyhood are truly animated, but then he's catalogued every one of them. Every level is digitally archived.

A documentary he once saw claimed that few people remember much from before the age of five, and this comforted Lionel at the time. But now he considers his whole first decade to be more of a story than a life – embellished by anecdotes, supported by snapshots – but not fully recalled, not 'in there'.

Lionel knows this much: his parents, Judy and David Byrd, adopted him and brought him to live in rural England after their tenure with a Christian charity in Kenya came to an end. Orphans of European-African heritage were likely to suffer additional disadvantages and David was proud to have rescued Lionel from Africa's 'cruel vicissitudes' (he had a preacher's way with words). The Byrds already had two natural sons – Ben and James. Lilith was born the year after their return.

If Lionel hadn't been such a clumsy and difficult child (there was an early but erroneous diagnosis of dyspraxia), things might have been different. But when he was ten he fell off a cattle bridge not far from his home, and spent weeks in hospital. It was a difficult time for everyone, he's been told – a nail-biting fortnight of forced sedation followed by a month in recovery. But in the end it was nothing that 'wouldn't mend'.

Lilith, unlike Lionel, can detail the past with the minute obsession of a historian or a therapist. She believes the head trauma of the fall disabled parts of his memory. He doesn't argue with her, but he's not so sure. Lionel can recall everything after the accident – David's bedside vigils, Judy's unspecified 'breakdown', the hushed conversations. The tears. And he remembers that when he was discharged David took him to his Aunt Rachel's to convalesce away from the chaos of family life.

From there he went directly to Cranbrooks, his boarding school, which had already been arranged for that term, and he never lived with his adoptive family again. David visited regularly, but Judy rarely came. An arrangement which was 'all for the best'.

Lionel bears no malice. He's grateful to have had a second chance, grateful his parents 'rescued' him and that Aunt Rachel mopped him up without question. If he had stayed in Kenya he would never have been to university or have had a flat of his own, or a sister called Lilith who loves him. And, although much of his early childhood is a strange waft of impressions, he is occasionally gripped by a hard-edged recollection that reaches out to him through the blur. One day, he hopes, he might have a chronological account of himself. In the meantime, he's content.

One thing that does stand out in his memory from before the accident is Mr Barber's shop.

'There is a barber for white boys,' his father had explained, 'and another for boys with hair like yours.'

Every six weeks, while his brothers were having a white boys' haircut, David would take Lionel on the train to see Mr Barber. It was a long journey but Mr B's was the nearest black barber to their village. A trip to Mr Barber's was like visiting a foreign country: the black men, the patois, the smell of the special coconut hair cream, the nips of rum taken on the sly. Lionel happily digested it all and was quickly native in the barber's domain.

Mr Barber is the main reason Lionel took the flat on Milk Street. The area felt safe and familiar despite being run-down. The shop is opposite the railway arches; left of the junction where Milk Street bisects the High Street. Here the railway bridge darkens the inter-section and pigeon guano slimes the pavement in streaks of grey and white. The barber's sign reads GENTLEMAN'S CHOICE and in the window are pictures of black men wearing suave smiles, showing off immaculate hairstyles that are ridged like tyre-tread and shining with grease. The pictures have been there for ever and their edges have curled and gone yellow.

The shop attracts a clientele of ageing West Indians who still wear trilbies and pork-pie hats and who call the barber 'Barber', though they underline the word with a quick dip of their heads and a note of deference in their voices. The younger men show their respect by calling him 'Mr Barber'. There's no Mrs Barber, no sounds of domesticity from the upstairs flat, no one asking what the old man would like for tea or prompting him to fulfil his household duties. Mr Barber insists that he likes the single life.

'I don't need no woman to nag me, nor pickney to worry about,' he says.

Mr Barber used to shut shop early on a Saturday so he could play slap-domino and drink a 'lickle drop' with his friends. But recently he's been keeping himself to himself.

'I'm feelin' me age,' he explains, if he's asked.

The old man has begun to grind his teeth even when his mouth is empty and there's a slight tremor whenever he turns his head. He's become rather thin in recent months, too, and his skin, the colour of spiced rum on his forearms, has dried out, become as thick as jerky. But Mr Barber is still dapper. He keeps his shoes shined and his hair pomaded.

Four men, damp from the rain, wait their turn as Mr Barber clips frizz from the neck of a dozing customer. The single barber's chair dominates the room. Hard-backed reception chairs and a sofa made of ruined leather provide spectator seating. Today, miniature 3D reflections dance in the customers' eyes as they absently watch the wall-mounted screen.

'Breaking news,' says the anchor. 'We're going *live* to our reporter on the ground.'

The remote control has been lost for months and Mr Barber has never got the hang of the voice commands, so a tall Jamaican stands to use the touch controls and adjust the volume. The reporter hesitates for a moment, scriptless, before describing the pandemonium going on around him. Missiles, aimed towards the camera, jump right into the barber's shop. The demonstrators have their faces covered and sousveillance cameras mounted on the sides of their Spex. These days everyone films everyone else.

'*Yes, John, demonstrations have gone ahead outside several transit camps . . .*' The reporter and a couple of the customers flinch as stones and projectiles whizz towards the camera. '. . . *And there are reports coming in of an explosion near the port at Dover.*'

Eventually the reporter hands back to the studio, where the anchor goes on to list three cities where there has been civil disorder. 'Activists "bussed in" by radical groups opposed to the Migration Bill have had running battles with border control units and right-wing organizations. Armed police have been struggling to contain the demonstrations.' The anchor has a special expression that denotes concern. 'Human rights commentators have accused western governments of precipitating the unrest by supporting developing countries during the redistribution, while community leaders up and down the country continue to condemn the government for what they say is an "inexorable flow of refugees".' The anchor drops his concerned look and pulls his factual face. 'It's estimated that twenty-five million people have now been displaced since land was appropriated for replacement fuel and solar development.'

These pronouncements are coupled with library footage of refugee children crying grubby tears in close-up.

Lionel is only half listening. He tries to avoid the news, but he's forced to watch on the 3D displays installed on buses and trains, or in his flat when Lilith comes to visit – and he feels coerced into thinking about things that have nothing to do with him.

Lilith always tells him, 'It's got everything to do with you,' but then Lilith has an opinion about most things. Drugs, technology, consumerism. But mostly she's preoccupied with their family and politics. She'll say, 'When are you going to find your real family?' or 'What do you think about the government's migration and transit policies?' or 'How can you bear to see people, like you, being forgotten or abused?' or 'Don't you realize the girls who work at the health centre have been trafficked – slaves, brother, right under your nose?' and 'What are you going to do about it?' *What are you going to do about it, Lionel?*

Action. Lilith always wants action. He doesn't know how she got to be so fanatical. He can imagine her adolescent fervour – the marches, the sit-ins, the pro-migration vigils – but he wasn't there to see the transition from child to adult for himself.

The dozy man gets up with a grunt and Mr Barber flicks hair from the chair with a towel.

'Come now, Lionel, your turn.' Mr Barber lowers the seat with the foot pump. 'You want the usual?'

Mr Barber knows all the styles, although he draws the line at cornrows or braids – that's women's work – and he frowns at the mention of fashion. Men should be smart and flawlessly groomed, according to Mr Barber. But recently, in the city, Lionel has noticed a number of black men with small dreadlocks that have been shaped into a jagged, swept-back style. He knows Mr Barber won't approve, but he has decided to grow his hair like this. He's trying to be more appealing for his sister's sake. If he keeps his old-fashioned crop Lilith will plague him.

'You're twenty-eight, for God's sake,' she'll pout. 'You're tall and handsome, but look at you! You look middle-aged already. You need to dress younger, update that nerdy style.'

He tells her he'll change when he's ready; besides, he's happy with the way he looks. And if he didn't come to Mr Barber's he'd miss the old Jamaican's companionship. GENTLEMAN'S CHOICE is not something he wants to give up.

The tall customer turns the volume down and someone brings out a stack of paper cups and a bottle of Wray & Nephew. The barber, bolstered by this gesture, recaptures some of his former energy and takes lip-smacking swigs as he lectures his customers about 'the world gone bad' and 'everybody with power to mek a change jos staring at them belly button'.

'This is the problem,' he says, stabbing the air with a comb. 'They all want to come here 'cause they own countries are done for, and who can blame them? But *H*ingland just fill up, fill up. It cyaan handle no more.'

His customers murmur their assent.

'You'd think with all a these people, business would pick up. But the High Street's gone rotten to blousebait, with everyting on-the-line. The *h*internet.' He pronounces the word with disdain and juts his chin towards the street. 'All a this used to be proper shops. There was a hardware store where that taxi rank is, and a newsagent next to that, where the all-night café is now. You don't get newsagents like that no more. Nope. It's virtual everyting. Don't get me started 'bout that health centre there neither.' Mr Barber shakes his head, describing it all as if his customers have come from far away and not witnessed the changes first-hand.

'At least the profession you in is safe, Mr Barber,' says the tall man. 'Man a man cyaan Google no haircut.'

'A'right!' Mr Barber slaps his thigh, his customers hoot along with him and everyone has a top-up of rum as they sound off about 'government' and 'society gone mashup'.

Lionel says little and soaks up the atmosphere. Several shops have been boarded up or had steel mesh installed across the windows since he moved to Milk Street. Some shop owners have stopped letting people inside, instead making customers queue at the window while an assistant collects the orders and a camera keeps watch. Everyone knows the health centre is a brothel, but the police do nothing and Lionel has noticed men and other young girls besides the beautiful anime girl skulking down the alley that leads round the back. Maybe it's because it's been a long winter, but the theft of the cheery sunburst that once advertised the Caribbean bakery has made the neighbourhood feel even more miserable and deprived.

Lionel fixes his eyes on the low table covered in ancient magazines and keeps very still while Mr Barber finishes off, shaping the hair round his ears.

'Yep, everyting gone mashup,' repeats Mr Barber, adjusting his false teeth with an adept flick of his tongue.

A mass of tiny curls lies on the floor and Lionel realizes he forgot to ask Mr Barber to twist his hair into the new shape. Perhaps Lilith won't notice. Perhaps his clean-cut crop will come back into vogue.

Outside, the rain has finally passed over and a layer of thin cloud sifts powdery light onto the street. It feels as if winter might be loosening its grip, just enough to stimulate a longing for spring. Lionel fancies the air carries the smell of blossom or sap and he jumps up and down a few times and shakes his limbs out, feeling athletic and lively. When he comes to the health centre he stops. The neon sign on the wall flashes hot pink and blue – ADULT HEALTH MASSAGE. Along the alley he can make out several crates of empties and a lean-bodied rat twitching its snout at a bin liner.

'Hello,' he calls.

The rat scampers off as his voice echoes back.

There must be a door further along, but he can't see past the shadows. He could go down, find the door and ask after the anime girl. *Action, Lionel.* Other men cruise down there all the time, but he suspects that paying the health centre a social call is not the kind of action Lilith keeps suggesting. He crosses to his side of Milk Street.

The flat smelled strongly of curry when he first moved in. It didn't bother him, but he was surprised it was so pervasive. He stopped noticing after a few weeks, but he knows it's still lurking because Lilith turns her nose up whenever she crosses the threshold, although she doesn't mention it any more. Previous tenants left various other things behind, including a silk wall-hanging of the Golden Temple at Amritsar, a stone statue of the Buddha (which he took as a good omen), and a large wooden box that he uses for storage.

The front door opens directly onto the living room where there's a sofa, a desk and a wall packed with old disks containing software he's written. Most of the disks contain his library of thousands of hours of recorded gameplay. All his computing – online now, in the cloud – is done from a modified Google terminal with no storage or processing power of its own, but he archives important files on two superdrives that sit on his shelves and wirelessly back up his work. Everything else is copied to his server, USA, or to his handheld device. Still, he holds on to the disks. They make the room look lived in; they make it look as if he has a full life, he thinks. A few other prize possessions – antique computer parts, character outfits he's collected, three or four 'classic' weapons – are stored away. Recently he bought a scimitar from an auction domain. 'Decorative' the caption said, 'not a weapon' (a typical e-merchant disclaimer). But the scimitar came with a leather sheath and is an exact replica of the ones used in *Saracen's Creed II*. Lionel keeps it with his other gaming paraphernalia under the bed. One day he'll dress up and go to a fantasy convention instead of just surfing the forums. It would be good to meet other people like him.

Lionel logs on, accesses his personal domain, and navigates to his new game, *CoreQuest*. He feels his brain shift to automatic. The relationship between man and technology is elegant and simple. Lilith says the human race has already relinquished too much of its power to machines, but he considers this to be a blessing. The moment he thinks of his sister his Google handheld vibrates and plays Lilith's theme tune. Vivaldi. Spring.

'You're there,' she says.

'Of course.'

'I've tried you three fucking times.'

'Sorry. I left my mobile at home. I was catching up with Mr Barber.'

'That old man. I told you not to go to him, Lionel, he's useless. He makes you look like a Christian. And since when does anyone go anywhere without their Google?'

He says nothing.

'Hello?'

'I'm still here.'

'Well, speak to me, for God's sake, I'm not getting a video feed.' She's definitely in one of her bleak phases.

'You sound cross,' he says.

'I'm livid that's why. I'm stuck down here and I can't get back.'

'Where are you?'

'Plymouth – the wet flange of England – I hate it. There's been a bomb scare or something and I'm stuck here for the night. The trains are all cancelled and I can't hire a car. I've offered credit – I've even offered the delights of my body.' She laughs emptily. 'I must be losing my touch.'

'What are you doing in Plymouth?'

'Work, you know, boring.' Lilith never likes to talk about work. 'Look, can you call Judy for me? I'm supposed to be going round there tonight and I can't get through. Network overload I reckon.' She snorts. 'New Digital Epoch, my arse.'

'You got through to me. Can't you call her?'

Lilith groans. 'Lionel, please. She'll keep me on for ages. I'm exhausted. If you call it'll only take you two minutes. Mum never knows what to say to you.'

Lilith's right. Telephone conversations with his mother are always stilted and uncomfortable. They begin with Judy saying, 'Oh it's you,' in her breathy, disappointed voice, even though she knows it's him on the line. After all, it was Lionel who set up her caller preview and video display.

'Lil . . . don't make me.'

'Please.' Lilith is getting wound up. 'Lionel. Do this one thing.'

He massages his forehead with the heel of his hand. 'Uh huh.'

'Promise me, Lionel. You never call her.'

'I'll call.'

'Mwah. Lionel, I love you, you're a star.'

When Lilith gets her way he's a star or a darling. He knows it's all lather, but still he gleams when she praises him.

'Oh, by the way . . .' He hesitates. Lilith must not be goaded in a bleak phase. 'Er, it's okay. It's nothing.'

'Tell me.'

'It's just, well, I made someone look up today.'

'Sorry?'

'On the street, I made someone look up at the window, and you said, the other week, no one would ever look up. That's all.'

'Well, *boom*.'

'Boom?'

'I mean, good for you, Lionel. Perhaps there's something in that psycho-bullshit after all.' She's being genuine.

He laughs. 'You mean psychic. I'm not saying I *am* psychic, it's just that not everyone's pre-programmed, eh, sis? We're not all robots.' Is he pushing this too far?

'I never said you were a robot, Lionel. That's your own little paranoid fantasy.'

Her insight troubles him. 'I'm not paranoid.'

'Yeah. Right.'

After she's rung off, Lionel tries to work out how his sister has managed to manipulate him again. His adoptive mother is such a chore. He can't speak to her without feeling anxious. After years apart, David's illness has forced them to reconstruct their relationship. Judy had the best intentions – he's sure – and perhaps it's because Aunt Rachel was such a cosy and attentive surrogate that he feels ambivalent about being rejected by her. And then there's Judy's nervous breakdown. Her vulnerability. But still, she's a difficult character and since David became ill they've had no choice but to see each other. Lilith knows all this and yet she insists on orchestrating additional contact.

Lionel pulls his shoulders back and pushes his chest out. Perhaps Lilith's right – Judy is his legal mother, after all. But Lilith isn't always right. He made someone look up today, didn't he? And he didn't hide. *Boom.* He forgot to tell Lilith about not hiding – he didn't duck below the windowsill, or quiver, or turn to dust. The beautiful anime girl looked at him and he looked right back. They had a connection. He taps his top lip. Perhaps he should go to the window right now and see if she is out there again. He's half out of the chair when *CoreQuest* pipes its tempting intro and he settles back, fingers running expertly over the SensePad.

CoreQuest is the new, online role-playing game by Castalia, with 'superfast 3D, 360° graphics', 'optional olfactory settings' and 'awesome TouchSense™ controls'. No product placements or advertising – guaranteed. It was his supervisor, Pema, who sent him a 'free for a month' discount code and now he's hooked.

The game realm won't permit custom-built avatars, but over the years Lionel has learned how to circumvent the protocols by hacking the game server and uploading his own avatar at source. It's not strictly legal, but he can't see how it hurts anyone. It simply means that, in every game he plays, he can be the same character – Ludi – the avatar he's designed and perfected over years of dedicated gaming.

Ludi is imposing and muscular. A He-Man with chiselled biceps and sculpted calves, whose wraparound Visor hides eyes of deep blue. But his beauty is deceptive. The valiant angle of Ludi's cheekbones, the golden hair that falls in Greek curls to his shoulders, make Ludi look godly not brutal. But he's ruthless. A quick *swish swosh* with his scimitar and Ludi's enemies fall in their hundreds.

This time the game servers have proved tricky to hack. Even though Lionel followed the instructions on the forum, his test avatar got snarled up during upload. But tonight, with some fancy footwork and the plug-ins his supervisor sent him, he'll finally sneak Ludi into the game. Before he begins he stretches his arms above his head and arches his back. All the joints in his spine ripple and pop. He is bone and sinew, flesh and blood. He's human. He is. But he should exercise more. Try and leave the flat more often, not spend so much time playing games. Tomorrow, he thinks, I'll track down the beautiful anime girl. Tomorrow.

He slaps his cheeks with both hands, picks up his Google and calls Judy.

@GameAddict (#23756745): 23:2:27

Log in, pop on your Spex or fire up your three-
sixty screen and in a second you'll pass into
another dimension. Actually you're broken into
a zillion digital pieces – catapulted through
space-time, bounced off satellites and flung
back and forth through oblivion. The bits reform
and you're reborn on the Game Layer. It's
another you – a better you by a mile – traversing
new worlds in the blink of an eye. It doesn't
matter that your flat's empty and there's no
food in your fridge or that none of your neighbours know you exist. It's carefree adventure
you want, and you can have it at the touch
of a button.

Level 1: Upload

Drufus Scumscratch was the name of the Mutant that found me, or so I discovered much later, tho there was no way to miss me since I came hurtling, meteor-style, and belly-flolopped into the square – innard-juice leaking all over the cobbles. Unseen mitts turned me onto my back.

The Mutant – snot-bubble snout, fish-eyed in my Visor – said, 'Did you see that? The Reject fell out of the sky like a *blazer-ball*,' and I could smell roast meat (me) and marsh damp (Drufus) competing for smell space.

As I came half conscious, all manner of WeirdFucks de-blurred in the background, fanning out behind Drufus. They were awestruck, cooing and farting and scratching their wart-arses as Drufus made search of my knapsack. It was a Harridan, old as a fossil, who summoned the courage to poke me. She scuttled up matter-of-fact, dugteats swinging, and pushed a gnarled digit hard into my goolies, not once, but three times.

'That usually wakes 'em,' she cackled.

I didn't move. Couldn't feel anything. My body was paralysed – half burned from the speed-heat of entry – and all I could do was soundlessly intake it all.

'A NoHoper – 90/10. Pah! He'll be crash-mode before nightfall,' said the Harridan and limped off, stage-left.

Drufus stroked his jowls, frowning. His bad eye, all-cataract, seemed to see into the future. 'We can't leave him here,' he said drily. 'Help me carry him back to my lodging.'

I wished I could encourage him, but even my speech centre was blown. I was heading for crash-mode – good and proper – preparing to re-enter the Void. Still, I was cogitating some on the new dimension I'd landed in when the WeirdFucks shuffled sideways and cleared a path to the edge of the square. I could spy market stalls, higglers and lazy mange-dogs all round me. Only Drufus dug in, but he was trembly and his lips dribbled slime on his belly. I discerned he was wrathful and shit-bricking, both. A long-leggedy, black-clad, Nubian hottie of PornDreams stepped, foot over foot, down the path that was made.

I took her in from a distance and Drufus said quietly, 'If you can hear me, Reject, then listen. She's an Eroticon, bad Pussy on leg-stilts. Got more flesh-moves than a GrindSiren, but she's hardcore. Fix that in your nog and soonish. You'd be better off Void than risk your goolies on her.'

Slightly concerned by the Mutant's obsession with goolies I watched as he bowed to the creature. His lips dangled so low they actually scraped on the cobbles.

'Mata Angelica,' he said, very caustic, keeping his good eye on her mons quite by accident.

She said nothing, but pointy-stepped round me, cat-wise, sniffing the singe on my skin and my hair.

'H-he's a Reject. NoHoper,' stuttered Drufus. 'I'll take him till he crash-modes. Better than making a mess of the square.'

Mata Angelica soft-stared me over, stroking my hair. 'Strange. I'd say he has the same Creator as the Sylph, wouldn't you?' She shot Drufus a look as the WeirdFucks all mumbled sheepish. They, not I, knew the significance of the Sylph. 'But he's a Reject all right.' She paused and took a big noseful of my body scent. 'Tho I'd say a Hoper – 60/40.'

She cast her eyes round the crowd and the WeirdFucks all clapped as if her pronouncement alone had just saved me.

Drufus knuckled his snout. 'I wouldn't know 'bout the Sylph, Mata Angelica. All I know is, his tubes are all over the floor. He'll be in crash-mode in a couple of clicks – plain as pie.' He indicated the swill all around me.

He was right. There was the small matter of my juices pumping out freely. But Mata Angelica bent down, very gainly, fished around in my innards and picked out a wet tube.

'Tubes,' she said, 'can be repaired. You know that as well as I, Mutant.'

The Mutant and the Eroticon were cruising for face-off, but I paid little attention as by then my nog was off flitting; a reverie on the strangeness of Void travel, the peculiarities of the new dimension I'd fallen in, the pneumatic bearing of Mata Angelica. You know, now I'm thinking back on it, the Eroticon probably saved me from Void, for my goolies – dead to the Harridan's poke – swelled up like a marrow as I fantasized on her flesh-gifts, so that when my dream swoon had passed, Drufus Scumscratch was ogling my loins.

'By golly! The Reject has spunk even if his tubes are all mangled.'

Mata Angelica raised an eyebrow. 'Well, that's that. I'll take him,' she said. 'I need a new project.'

The Mutant's jowls dangled preposterously low to the ground. 'Beg your pardon, Mata Angelica, but I found him first.'

'Ah, how sweetly proprietary,' she said, stroking Drufus's cheek with one digit. 'Nevertheless,' she continued (now wiping his cheek slime onto his jerkin), 'your special skill's rent-pimping not fixing and, let's be straightforward, this character's in need of integral repair.'

Drufus coloured beetroot to the tips of his head-tentacles and some of the WeirdFucks guffawed and made arse-rings and goolies in finger-sign, so that Drufus came proud-chested and said, 'There's no shame in my nog, not none. But if you want the Reject so bad as to slang me, Mata Angelica, you have 'im.'

With that he stuck his snout in the air, turned tail and beat a retreat. Only when he was small enough distant could I see his lower half was uniped, snail-wise, which counted for the mucus drench-up I suspect, but that was my last thought before crash-mode.

A Day at the Yews

The movement of the train makes Lionel sleepy and he watches the clouds with his cheek squashed against the window. Battalions of cumuli pursue an army of cirrus, which look like animal skeletons. If only he could be up there with them – chasing across the weightless expanse – not trapped in this carriage. He closes his eyes.

When Lilith's away, things always tilt into chaos, although he'd never admit it to her. On Monday there was more bad news about Buddha. The vet informed him that 'the treatment options have all been exhausted'. Ridiculous! That vet is cold as a stone. Then on Wednesday he sneaked Ludi past the security protocols on the game server, but halfway through upload the connection glitched and he had to abort the process. It took most of Thursday to reconfigure everything and reroute the sourcecode through a proxy in the Ukraine. Even now he's left a script running, verifying Ludi's status. Still, everything feels better now Lilith's back. He can't wait to see her, even though it means he has to see Judy.

At some point Lionel nods off. When the train stops at Sunnyvale ('Another carbon-neutral development'), he comes round with a start and makes it onto the platform by the seat of his pants. Groggy with sleep, he jumps up and down a few times to gee himself up.

'Come on. Wakey, wakey,' he shouts.

An old woman, seated near by, pulls her bags closer. The station assistants have drifted away and the woman seems agitated to be alone with him on the platform. He wants to reassure her he's harmless, but she's checking around for CCTV and fumbling with an old-fashioned phone. People often mistake his intentions. It's been happening more these last months. Only two weeks ago a new operative in his section complained to his supervisor that he kept staring at her and it was 'creeping her out'.

'When I'm tired,' he explained in the subsequent complaint assessment, 'my eyes rest on nothing.'

Pema, his supervisor, said she understood, but people could be sensitive and he should concentrate on the screen not the girls.

When he spluttered an objection Pema said, 'Joke, Lionel. Leave her to me.'

Crossed wires – they happen, especially when he's not sleeping properly and he's barely slept for weeks. The shifts at work followed by nights on the computer are taking their toll. If it weren't for the qat Saeed sells in his shop Lionel would have seized up with fatigue months ago.

Midway through the estate the first spots of rain begin to pattern the pavements. But instead of walking more briskly, Lionel dawdles the last half-kilometre, thinking about David's wrecked body and wondering how much more shrivelled a man can become.

Judy maintains the Alzheimer's had afflicted David for years, undiagnosed. She would have soldiered on alone, she insists, if it weren't for the violence. Lionel had witnessed a slap or two in those early days. Once, he saw David bite her – his teeth drew a dotted crescent of blood on her arm. Of course, the boys weren't around. Ben had gone up north with his young family. James had settled in America after a failed stab at Divinity (he never saw eye to eye with his supervising professor). The physical tasks, such as bathing, or coaxing David out of the shed (he would occasionally barricade himself in) fell to Lionel. Judy said David would be ashamed for anyone, apart from – and here she hesitated – *family*, to see him in extremis. Alzheimer's is so degrading, she said.

It was a Friday when Judy told Lionel his father had been taken into the Yews. 'Respite' she called it. A temporary arrangement. But David never returned to the bungalow. There was no discussion or fanfare. No fuss. It was done. That was Judy all over.

'It's nice. It's clean,' she'd said. 'They can deal with him better than I can.'

That his father has lost his marbles and will never retrieve them again is a fact Lionel's resigned to; it's the family visits he finds hard to endure.

Lilith's place is on the commuter estate of Sunnyvale – 'executive eco-build'. The house is double-fronted, mock-Georgian with a garage that's too full of junk to house her electric car (Lilith was 'green' long before the fuel restrictions began in earnest). The charger trails under the garage door and across the drive. Judy always complains about the state of the garden – 'it's such a mess' – but Lilith couldn't care less what people think. Sunnyvale is the kind of place Lilith hates to her core. She bought the house during the last recession so she could rent it out to 'all the salary slaves', but somehow she's ended up living here permanently and Lionel knows it galls her. After he graduated she put him up in the spare room for a while and she was forever swearing and breaking things or being rude to the neighbours. When he moved to the flat it was obvious that she preferred it to her house, despite the curry smell. Lilith still goes on about how *cool* Milk Street is, and her seal of approval makes Lionel feel quite puffed up.

Lilith is dressed, boho-casual, in a tiered gypsy skirt and loose blouse. She grimaces and touches his hair as he enters.

'You're wet.'

'It's beastly out there.'

'Beastly, eh?' She always mocks his outdated words. 'Shit, Lionel. You've let that old man massacre your hair again.'

'Well, I wouldn't say massa–'

'And you're getting so frickin skinny!'

'Am I? Sorry.'

'Don't apologize, just eat more,' she says. 'And grow your hair, for God's sake. I keep telling you. You look like that character in that old film, what's it called?' She screws up her face, thinking. '*Artificial Intelligence*, you know the one?'

'You think I look like Gigolo Joe?' He doesn't know whether to be pleased or offended.

'Just the hair, nothing else.'

'Right, yes, of course.'

'Anyway, step into the dragon's lair.' Lilith gestures towards the living room. 'I warn you, she's pretty pissed off that you're late.'

'Am I late?'

Judy is sitting on the high-backed Chesterfield repro, drinking tea from one of Lilith's proper teacups – the ones Lilith keeps in the living-room cabinet so they'd survived the smash-up. Last month, when Lilith hadn't been in touch for a week, Lionel called round. She didn't answer the door, so he let himself in and found all the cups and plates in smithereens on the kitchen floor. There were depressions in the cupboard doors and the walls where the crockery had been hurled with great force. Every surface was covered in plaster and splinters of glaze. Lilith was on the floor, holding her knees. Rings of mascara blackened her cheeks. He couldn't get anything out of her. When she's going through one of her bleak phases he finds it best to sit quietly and wait. Lilith always pulls herself together in the end. Now, if they refer to the incident, they call it 'the great smash-up', as if it was a natural disaster – not Lilith – that destroyed all the crockery.

Judy holds the cup and saucer in her prim, upright fashion, but with the suppressed fatigue he knows prefaces a visit to his father. His mother can never truly relax. Unusually, she is wearing a trouser suit and she has combed her hair back off her face. Apart from a shawl draped over one shoulder she looks rather masculine.

'Hello, Judy,' he says and brushes her forehead with his cheek.

'Lionel.'

Here he is, hands in pockets, standing in the middle of the room and rocking awkwardly, heel to toe. There's something stuck in his throat, a hair or a burr, and he can't clear it. Foolish, utterly foolish, this is how he feels in Judy's presence. Fortunately his mother doesn't require a conversation. Instead, she angles her body away from him and surveys the road through a gap in the blinds while he hammers his chest with his fist.

Eventually he shouts through to the kitchen. 'You've recovered from your ordeal then, Lil?'

Judy rearranges her shawl as if his voice has chilled her.

'It was a fucking nightmare. Eight hours from Plymouth to Birmingham. Bristol was horrendous. The trains were packed. We were like those poor migrant workers, jammed in like sausage meat. Can you believe it? I've been shattered ever since.' She calls something else that he doesn't quite hear.

'Lil, you know,' he says to Judy. 'When she was stuck down south . . . ahem.' The burr will not budge.

'Yes, well, it happens.' Judy sets her cup down.

'I phoned you, remember? It was that security scare. I told you about it.'

Lilith enters the room and puffs despondently. 'I'm totally crap – the ham's out of date and the bread's stale, so we'll have to buy sandwiches on the way.'

Judy massages her forehead with two fingers. 'I can't believe you still do this, Lionel.'

'What?' Lilith is aghast. 'Oh, fucking hell, Lionel, after everything I said you didn't call her.'

'I did call. She's forgotten that's all.' He rummages for his Google device. 'I can show you the call log. It was last Friday, right? Or the Friday before.'

'I *am* in the room.'

'Mum!' Lilith sighs. 'I was in Plymouth for work. Anyway, let's not talk about this now, for Christ's sake.'

He searches the log, but can't find the entry. 'Lil, I swear I called her.'

Judy is indignant. 'Lionel, really.'

'How else would she have known you weren't coming back that night?'

'Mum, Lionel . . . Are we going?' Lilith is drawing a line under the subject.

Judy stands. 'This is ridiculous. I've been waiting here for an hour already.'

Lilith is a crazy driver and it's an unspoken rule that Lionel drives when they're all together. He takes the back route to the Yews along country lanes, leaning to one side then the other as he goes round the bends. Electric cars are too quiet, too passive. He misses the kick of internal combustion and he can't resist making engine noises under his breath while Judy rattles on about the EcoHome scheme and the council's intention to build five hundred new properties adjacent to the village where she lives.

'It's the same up and down the country.' She's tense, talking quickly over his engine impressions. 'There are too many people and nowhere to put them.' His mother looks at his knees, not his face. 'Lionel, could you refrain from making those perfectly ridiculous noises?'

'Oh. Sorry.'

'Anyway, it's simple!' she continues. 'Close the doors. Stop letting them in.'

Lilith's ire is preceded by sarcasm. 'Yeah, simple.' She pokes her head in between them from the back seat. 'Let's turn the whole fucking country into a fortress, shall we? Then we can be sure the poor people will have no choice but to slave away on the energy farms while we slurp up the resources. We'll never have to lay eyes on their needy brown faces again.'

Migration. The old argument, which always results in furious silences, prompts Lionel to a well-practised strategy. 'So,' he says brightly. 'Any news of Ben or James?'

Judy pulls her shoulders back, reluctant to be sidetracked, but she can never resist talking about her boys.

'Ben has a new job.' She sniffs. 'An executive position.'

'Ah!' Lilith throws herself back in the seat. 'An executive position – how totally bloody thrilling.'

Judy ignores her. 'He has such responsibilities – it's very hard for him with the twins, and Susan. Agoraphobic! I'm sure I've told you that before. It's a modern plague.'

'I remember you saying.'

'And then, well, they've been campaigning against a *transit* centre up there, too. Imagine having one of those on your doorstep.'

'Racists,' mutters Lilith.

Judy chooses not to react, but continues with the terse certainty of a schoolmistress. 'The whole country's angry,' she says, smoothing the fabric of her trousers. 'You can feel it, everywhere you go. It's not racism, it's pragmatism.'

Lilith's reflection in the rearview mirror says it all. Teeth lacerating her bottom lip, eyes wide and dreadful. She's about to blow. The quicker they get to the Yews the better. Lionel slips the car into turbo and swings out to overtake a bus.

The tendons in Judy's neck stretch tight. 'Heavens, Lionel.'

He tries to sound jaunty when he speaks again. 'And James, how's the good old US of A treating the Reverend Byrd?'

Judy closes her eyes, finding some peace in sensory deprivation. 'What? Oh, well, he doesn't have much time to speak to me, but he sent me the link to his Spirit Domain online.' She over-enunciates 'Spirit Domain' as if she's speaking another language. 'He's putting on rallies. Thousands of people. Thousands. He fills football stadiums in cyberspace. Real churches are too small to hold everyone.'

'Our darlin' brother,' Lilith says in her Southern Belle accent, 'is an all-American fundamentalist these days. He's got a *megapresence* not just a domain. It's whizzy and shiny and crazeeee – 3D videos, interactive avatar areas, easy donation schemes.' She drops the accent and goes on in a sneer. 'Some pretty dodgy shit he's espousing, too. I listened to one of his sermons. Dear James, sorry,' she corrects herself, 'Reverend Father James has set up a spiritual franchise dontcha know. *Ker-ching.*'

'Can you slow down, Lionel, please?' Judy's knuckles have turned yellow.

'He's only doing fifty. This thing is speed restricted, for Christ's sake.'

'Lionel! Please.' The skin of Judy's neck is a florid patchwork of blotches.

'James was' – he takes his foot off the accelerator – 'always going to be the successful one.'

Lilith snorts. 'He's a selfish fuck with a tenuous grip on reality. They're both twisted, egocentric twats. I'm ashamed to call them brothers.'

Lionel coughs and the obstruction in his chest finally clears. 'Lilith!' he shouts, rather too loudly.

Judy holds her head. 'Dear God.'

'I blame the parents. Don't you?'

He catches a devilish look from Lilith in the rearview mirror. More and more she enjoys hurting their mother – the swearing, the blasphemy, the ferociousness. Judy's lip is quivering. Perhaps she'll cry. But it's unlikely.

'Does it always have to be like this?' Judy hardens her jaw. 'I don't understand you at all. Truly.'

The Yews is a country pile that became a private school after World War II, and was then acquired by the Full Health Group early in the new millennium. Like thousands of dilapidated stately homes and inner-city office blocks it was converted to a care home in an attempt to address the problem of a burgeoning geriatric population. The home has acres of grounds, ornamental ponds and a landscaped garden. The centrepiece is an avenue of ancient yews that features in all the promotional literature. But, like many establishments since the last recession, it's seen better days. The site no longer bears close scrutiny. Parts of the exterior are shabby and in disrepair: the yews need clipping and the grounds need attention. But still, it's an impressive façade.

'Welcome, welcome, welcome.' Short and corpulent, David's nurse, George, greets them over-enthusiastically. When Judy's not around he treats Lilith and Lionel with thinly veiled contempt, but when she's present he's a heap of smarm. 'Look, David, it's your loving family.'

George is from the Ivory Coast and has a grating voice that makes people unconsciously bare their teeth. David has been a good boy since their last visit, he tells them, and this pleases Judy so thoroughly she flashes everyone a rare smile. Even David appears to be listening to the nurse's report, although his head, lolling heavily on one shoulder, is at an odd angle to his neck.

'Heh heh. He's just playing with you.' George laughs as if he's learned laughter from a book. He pushes David's cheek to make him lift his head, but when he stops pushing David's chin falls forward again.

'David, hold up your head. Come on, be good boy for me now.'

'Darling.' Judy reaches to touch David's hand and everyone sees him shift away from her with a small, decisive movement.

'Yet another afternoon watching the old man dribble down his shirt,' says Lilith under her breath. And then, in a false, bright voice, 'We're going outside.'

'Ahem, yes.' Lionel twists the hem of his shirt round one finger. 'We're going for a quick smoke.'

'But it's raining.'

'And no smoking in the grounds,' George reminds them pointedly.

'I know, I know, for fuck's sake. We need some air anyway. Come on, Lionel.'

He's smiling, but the African's face radiates spite.

*

'Cheeky fuck, that nurse.' Lilith lights a cigarette the moment they're outside. 'Do you notice how he never shakes my hand? Some men have a thing about strong women. And how did he get so fucking fat? That's what I want to know. Eating all the inmates' rations I'll bet. I hate this place.'

He takes a light from her cigarette. 'They're patients, Lil, not inmates.'

'Inmates, patients.' She shrugs. 'Dad's going to die here, with that fat prick in the corner laughing his moronic laugh. "Heh heh heh",' she mocks, shoulders riding up and down. 'Anyway . . .' She turns her face to the rain and closes her eyes. 'Why should you care? He's not your real dad. He was useless where you were concerned. Epic failure!' Lilith looks back in through the window. 'And Mum, insane little *wifey* – "David darling, darling David",' she mimics. 'I swear she'll spontaneously combust when he finally turns his toes up. That's if she cares at all. Never can tell with our mother.'

'Come on, Lil, don't fret.'

'Fret? What kind of a word is that? Jesus, Lionel, you're so bloody stiff. I don't know why you defend them.'

'I don't defend them.' He exhales his smoke away from the door. 'I just don't like to see you upset.'

'I'm upset because' – Lilith stands in front of the window, puffing away in clear view of George and Judy – 'unlike you, dear brother of mine, I remember every millisecond of our *wonderful* childhood. Dad abandoned you. He left you for years with his mad old maid of a sister.'

'Aunt Rachel isn't mad.'

'Come on, Lionel, she's as mad as a wet hen.'

Aunt Rachel doesn't do email or NetPhone. She doesn't do electronic communication at all. And Lionel never gets round to calling her. A spinster back then, Aunt Rachel was a practical, earthy woman who didn't subscribe to her brother David's beliefs. In fact, she wasn't at all religious. 'God's a nice idea and all that,' she'd say to Lionel when he lived with her, 'but it's only a comfort, isn't it – for weak-minded people.' She'd occasionally call on the Almighty to add emphasis to her declamations or as a last resort invocation when she was in crisis, but she rarely got into a flap about anything. 'I'm your *illegal* guardian,' she'd say. 'We make a right funny pair.'

She had a benign frown that doubled as her crossword face and she would regard Lionel daily with this expression, so he came to believe that he, like the crossword, must be rather cryptic. There's no doubt she was eccentric. She wore plastic bags inside her shoes, even in summer, and never used the lavatory for 'piddles' – preferring to squat in the garden, rain or shine, beside the hydrangeas. But she cared for Lionel and took his part when it was necessary. After one particular conversation with David, the one where his father told him he couldn't come home that first Christmas, Lionel passed the phone to his aunt, who went scarlet and swore into the receiver. 'I'm ashamed of you, bloody hypocrite,' she said, and flung the handset across the carpet. It took Lionel the whole after-noon to fix it, but when he did Aunt Rachel smiled and riffled his frizz. 'You are rather brilliant and charming,' she told him. And she meant it.

Her house, in Shoeburyness, was the one he returned to during the holidays. She, not Judy, accompanied David on Lionel's first day at university. Food parcels and paper clippings and book tokens (and once an owl pellet with the bones of several small mammals inside) would arrive in the post every week.

Unexpectedly, when he was in his final year, Aunt Rachel married Mr Dawes, an Australian with a weather-beaten face and a penchant for boiled sweets. They had adjacent allotments and had been 'friends' for some years, but when Mr D (that's what she called him) announced his intention to move back home, Aunt Rachel said she'd like to go with him. It was all very expedient, but Lionel could tell she thought fondly of him.

'You do understand, don't you, Lionel?' she'd said, wringing her hands in an uncharacteristic display of guilt. 'Everyone deserves to land with their bum in the butter – just one time.'

Lionel held her hands loosely. 'You've been *my* butter,' he told her.

Her laughter was more like a sigh of relief. 'You could come with us,' she said, as if she'd just thought of it.

But he said he didn't like the thought of Australia. Besides, he had his studies, and he might try and reconnect with his family, at which Aunt Rachel frowned and reclaimed her hands.

'Well, that's up to you,' she said. 'But I wouldn't waste my time if I was you.'

Lionel knew his aunt didn't approve of his adoptive family, even though David was her own brother. But now she's so far away Lionel sometimes wonders if she ever existed at all. He makes a mental note to call her.

There's less heat in Lilith's voice when she continues. 'Some people say we should bury the past – you either can or you can't, I suppose.' She's doing one of her philosophical preambles. 'But I remember *her* satisfaction when Dad punished you.' Through the window, Judy is trying to coax a reaction – any senile reaction – from her husband. 'Her . . .' – Lilith searches for the word – 'contempt for you was worse than any punishment.'

'It must be hard to love a child who's not yours. Anyway, I'm sure they punished us all. I don't feel singled out.'

'Bollocks!' She flicks her ash into the wind. 'You know, you amaze me. Everything you've been through and you act as if it's nothing. Look at you. It must be that bloody accident that's made you so submissive. At least you had a bit of *oomph* before you landed on your head.'

Lionel tries to trace the timeline of his early life to find some evidence to defend himself. 'I'm not submissive,' he says weakly. 'I honestly don't think I am.'

'You are! You're too nice to even realize.'

Her voice has acquired a faraway sadness and he knows her anger has migrated with it. She lays her head on his shoulder and he kisses her hair.

'You're scared, Lil, that's all. David'll be okay.'

Lilith pulls away in disgust. 'I'm not scared. And he won't be okay. He's going to die, the sooner the better. Put the coward out of his misery.'

Lilith is prone to saying the wrong things, Lionel thinks, but she cares. Lilith is always angry when she cares.

@GameAddict (#23756745): 06:3:27

Choose a fabulous story – any story you like:
soldiers, warriors, gangsters, damsels or Realms
in distress. It can be anything. Ravishing women
will be desperate to court you (if that's what
you want). Willing characters will be happy to
serve (in any imaginable way). Everything exists
simply to enrich your experience. And once
you've chosen a Quest you'll have a purpose
beyond hedonism. A clear purpose. You know
what you're *for* on the Game Layer. And when
you succeed (and everyone loves you) you can
do it all over again.

Level 2: Historicals

For the benefit of newcomers it's worth nutshelling the dimension and if you access the archives you'll find files that explain the structure and chronology. I missed out on the detail – falloloping into the square as I did – and had to piece it all jigsaw while I was being repaired.

First the historicals. Long ago, when the Creators said 'Let there be wicked graphics' and so forth, the Realm had been lush-green and gorgeous. There were mosses and fern-fronds, great sparkling oceans and all manner of fabulous beasters. But the Realm came corrupted. The oceans dried up or came poison and one vast desert grew between four tribal regions. This desert was called Gog.

The four tribes skirmished a bit but mostly kept to their own: Thrars (toga-wearers, prone to excess), Vadarians (pagans who dwelt in the mountains), Krin-Balwrin (beefy bastards – half dog and half bear) and Darzirians (pious custodians of a place called the Core).

The tribal characters collected strange little slave-clones called Grinders. With enough Grinders a character could play on indefinitely. Say you were in battle and an enemy pulled all your tubes out – then you'd become Wisp – a ghost state, like Limbo. But if you had Grinders you could send them to the Core to earn your release. Then you could replay.

No one knew what tasks the Grinders performed in the Core (the place was a mysterious engine), but after their stint the Grinders were magicked away to a far-off Realm called 'Retirement'. The talk was of feets-up, oodles of scran and a long lazy time of do-nothing. Thus, every Grinder I met was eager to get to the Core.

There were other characters wafting about in the Realm – wizards, seers, Mutants and the like. Some played for themselves, others were agents for shady, unseen characters called Bosses. The Realm was in thrall to these powerful players.

Characters like me were called OtherWorlders – illegal migrants from distant dimensions. We played in fear of expulsion. It was OtherWorlders who had used up the Realm's energy in past times (so it was said) and sent the dimension into catastrophic decline. Unless we had special skills (like Mata Angelica), we were hunted and sent back to the Void. Anomalies, Rejects and Insurgents still took their chances. We arrived from other worlds, flushed through the Wormhole by fate or misfortune. Some came half-corrupted from dimensions so far off they never took full form. Not ever. Lucky ones crashed down, nogs gone loon for a while, but recovered.

I was such.

Poor Little Orphan Boy

Mordecai was Lionel's first cat. A rescued stray. No collar or chip. Lionel loved the cat so much Lilith was jealous. She admits she was secretly pleased when it first disappeared. But when she saw the extent of his misery Lilith soon jumped to it, helping him scour the gardens and lanes round the village. Between them they found all manner of roadkill and became expert at estimating the time of death by the rate at which things decomposed. But there was no sign of Lionel's beloved Mordecai. They put up posters, offered a reward, went door to door; every house and farm was canvassed.

'Definitely run over,' David said in the end, not without sympathy. 'You might never find him. I once saw a dog fly forty yards when it'd been hit.'

When Lionel's eyes moistened, his father regretted having been forthright and improvised a yarn. There was one cat, he remembered, that had hitched a ride in a van. It turned up miles away on the coast. 'Yes, come to think of it,' said David, 'that's the most likely explanation. Mordecai's not dead, he's visiting the seaside.'

The story didn't alter the fact that Lionel's cherished tabby was gone. Lilith says he must have known, deep down, that Mordecai was dead. One thing is certain: the knowledge burrowed its way into some previously unassailable chamber of his heart and, when every search had proved futile, he promised he would never own or love another cat again.

*

A year and a half ago, when his supervisor rested the cardboard box on the coffee table in Lilith's front room (he was still living there at the time), Lionel scratched his scalp nervously. It felt wrong for his supervisor to be there. She belonged to the world of team meetings, performance reviews and helpdesk enquiries. Out of context she made him uneasy.

'I'm sorry, Mrs Khalsa.'

'Call me Pema. We're not at work now.'

'Pema, yes.' He stopped scratching and felt his forehead. 'The problem is, I'm not in the market for a cat. I can't have one.'

Lionel wasn't sure how his supervisor had persuaded him to look at the kitten in the first place, but like Lilith she had a knack of getting him to do things he hadn't expected to do and here she was now, acting the boss, even though they weren't at Meddingley.

'If I can't place him,' his supervisor said, eyeing the box with pity, 'I'll have to consider the worst.'

'What do you mean?'

'You know.' She tilted her head to one side.

Rather death than a bad home, Lionel thought. It was absurd, but Pema, despite her position, was not renowned for the quality of her reasoning. That's why she came to Lionel whenever she was 'in a mess' at work. She would stand behind him biting her nails as he unpicked the mistakes she'd made in her workflow schematics, assuring him of her 'eternal gratitude' for his 'discreet assistance'.

A series of holes in the top of the box exuded a warm animal scent. Pema lifted the lid and light flooded in. A small tortoiseshell ball blinked at Lionel with green-black eyes. Its fur was on end, its tiny paws pulled into its body, shivering.

Lionel edged closer. 'He looks like a little Buddha,' he said.

'Yes! Buddha!' Pema clapped her hands. 'That's the perfect name.' She lifted the creature out of the box and proffered it to Lionel. 'Put your hands out, come on.'

He held the kitten warily at first – he could feel its heart beating, quick as a fledgling crow, and the sensation gave him a lump in his throat.

'See!' Pema took two steps backwards. 'He likes you already.'

'I can't take him.' He swallowed hard. 'This isn't my house, it's my sister's, and I think she might be allergic.'

'It's now or never.' Pema grimaced and drew a graphic line across her neck with her forefinger. 'He's been defleaed,' she went on, without looking at him, 'and microchipped and he's had all his jabs, so that's it. Here's some kitten food.' She brought a box out of her bag and shook it unnecessarily. 'It's all you need.'

The kitten looked up at him and emitted a touching meow and Lionel, knowing he had been pressed into pet-ownership, made the same noise back at the kitten. It settled its chin on the heel of his thumb and fell asleep.

Lionel promptly fell in love. Buddha was perfect; clambering up curtains, gambolling after the toys Lionel bought him, curling in his lap as he played *CoreQuest*, sleeping next to his pillow. But it was after he moved out of Lilith's and into Milk Street that the twitching started. It was imperceptible at first, but Lionel could feel an unnatural quiver in Buddha's paws, mostly at night when the rest of the world fell still. Initially he thought it was idiosyncratic, that Buddha had a powerful purr that caused some deep-seated, essential tremor to reverberate through his body. But soon the cat began to shake all the time and Lionel took him to a vet.

A scan revealed a tumour in Buddha's brain, the size of a quail's egg.

'Cancer. Malignant. There's no hope,' said the vet. 'Buddha will have to be put down.'

Lionel went to three different vets, but they all said the same thing. The quail's egg was inoperable and getting bigger every day. That was six months ago. Now the tumour has begun to encroach on Buddha's motor centre and it's making him pitiful. The cat veers sideways when he walks and must test each footstep before committing his weight in case his front legs give way. Sometimes his back legs collapse altogether and he has to drag the rest of his body along with his front paws. He drools and twitches constantly. Lionel loves him more than ever.

When the symptoms began he'd carry Buddha everywhere and feed him from a spoon – he couldn't bear to see him suffer. But this only hastened Buddha's decline and, since then, Lionel has implemented a hands-off strategy. The cat can still feed himself and get about the flat in his bizarre, crippled way and, to help him, Lionel has made sloping walkways onto the bed and the sofa. But Lionel discerns that Buddha understands what was, what is and what will be. The wise old puss knows all. He is going to die, there is no doubt, and Lionel cannot bear it. If it weren't for Lilith, Lionel would have to accept that everyone he loves abandons him.

A multicoloured heap of cat vomit in the shape of an internal organ has been expelled beside the sofa.

'Dry food,' explains Lionel, 'always comes out undigested, in weird shapes like that.'

'Nice,' says Lilith.

'I might have to put him back on kitten food if this carries on.'

'I'd have done it weeks ago.'

'Would you?'

'Hell, yeah. I suggested it, remember?'

'So you did.'

He appreciates how Lilith is always supportive when it comes to Buddha.

The Google terminal brightens one corner of the room and Lionel clears the cat sick while Lilith settles at his desk, her face pale and unworldly in the holographic glow.

'Mum looked old today,' she says, moving the frames on the display with quick flicks and taps.

'She's sixty this year.'

'Sixty! Is she really? I've never been good at remembering the numbers. So much younger than Dad.' She blinks at the screen. 'What's this?'

Lionel looks up. 'How did you log in without my password?'

'It was on.'

'I thought I'd logged out. Anyway, you've seen that. It's my Buddha Project, remember?'

'No, not that. This!'

In the kitchen he flicks the switch on the kettle and empties the cat sick into the bin without answering.

'You're not playing another one of those games, are you, Lionel?'

He braces himself for censure.

'Lionel, answer me.'

He tries to sound casual. 'Yes. It's a game.'

'Games, games, games.' Lilith is scornful. 'I can't believe you still play them.'

He keeps quiet.

'They stop you engaging with *real life*, remember?'

'The game *is* real to me,' he mutters.

'What's that?'

'I said,' he speaks up, 'it's only a game. It helps me relax.'

The kettle reaches a disgruntled boil.

'Didn't Mum and Dad delete that game you had when you were a kid, what was it called?' Lilith drums the desk.

'I don't remember.'

'*Dragon Quest.* That's it. You played it till your eyes went square. You lived for that game, but then they deleted it, or banned you from playing it. Ha! Except' – Lilith bounces in the chair with childish excitement – 'you dressed up as the knight. Made yourself a sword and everything. Carried on acting it out in real life.' She curls up laughing. 'They thought you were insane. It was hilarious.'

'I honestly don't remember.'

'Believe me, it was classic. Anyway, come on.' She isn't going to let him off the hook. 'How many hours a day do you play?'

Why does she have to make it sound like an addiction?

'Games occupy me when I'm alone.'

'I bet they do.' Lilith puts her tongue in her cheek and pretends she's a bloke, jerking off. 'I bet you're pursuing some cheesy warrior princess, fluffing her up so her approval rating hits the roof and you can take advantage of her well-drawn pixels.' She laughs coarsely. 'And in real life she's a dumpy sales rep from Wolverhampton, disappointed with the Ryan or Kevin she's found herself hitched to. Or a gender-confused teenager wanking in his bedroom on . . . Canvey Island' – she's warming to her theme – 'hoping his mum won't hear him moan when he comes. *Ah ah aaahhhh.*'

Lionel stares at his feet. He can't bear it when Lilith is so cruel and critical.

'You need to find someone – a *real* someone. When was the last time you had sex, and I don't mean pervy cybersex, I mean with a real woman?'

'Please don't be vulgar. I-I don't play the games to . . .' He splutters to a stop. Sex between avatars is part of the game. He couldn't bear Lilith to know about his forays through the tripleX portals; clip after clip of hard-faced humans mechanically pummelling away at one another's hairless bodies. Why does he flip the blind shut and watch? Shame makes him spit his words out. 'You don't understand, you've never understood about the games.'

'I think I do. You're a man. I forgive you. But you're looking for someone, Lionel, and you can't find her, can you?'

It's more than a year since Lilith dragged him up town to one of the dingy clubs off the strip. He noticed the blonde as soon as they walked in – drinking a cocktail, sitting alone in a booth. He'd hardly touched his beer when his sister pressed his arm.

'Don't look behind you, Mack,' she said in her Film Noir voice, 'but some broad's checking out your curriculum vitae.'

Lionel turned and caught the woman's eye. Immediately Lilith shoved his shoulder – so pushy – and he fell off the bar stool. When he tried to sit up Lilith moved his stool. He tripped over like an idiot. Knocked his drink everywhere. He didn't know where to look as he wiped beer off himself and the bar.

'Don't duel with destiny, Mack.' Lilith laughed. 'Go ahead. Speak to her. What've you got to lose?'

When he refused to budge she stopped laughing. 'Of all the gin joints, in all the towns . . . now I shall have to tell her you fancy her,' she said, and slipped off her seat without missing a beat.

Lilith never made empty threats and Lionel had to scramble to get to the woman before his sister embarrassed them all.

The blonde, Samantha, was drunk, but she managed to smile and say, 'Tricky things bar stools.' The minute he joined her she launched into a monologue about 'players' and 'cheaters' that went on for an age and made Lionel regret caving in to his sister. He slung a pleading look over his shoulder, but she'd already disappeared. Typical Lilith. Now he was stuck and, as Samantha blabbed on, he imagined an animal in a box clawing at the corners, but he wasn't sure if it was her or him who was trapped.

Samantha gave his hand a meaningful squeeze and said, 'You're lovely you are, Café Latte – such a good listener,' and asked him to walk her up town. Lionel heard himself saying 'Yeah . . . okay,' although it was the last thing he wanted to do. Still, he held her at the waist most of the way – her knees kept buckling. She told him he was a real gent, not like the bastards she usually hung around with.

'Funny how it takes a stranger to make a woman feel cared for,' she said, grazing his cheeks with her lips. Her breath smelled of spirits.

But then she made a joke, which he didn't get, about stranger danger and laughed so hard she had to cross her legs. 'Oh you're awful,' she said, giggling. 'Look, you've made me wet meself.'

Lionel tried not to gawp at the damp patch darkening her crotch.

Samantha's place was piled with boxes and bin bags, as if she was just moving in or out. Clothes, towels, papers and computer tablets were all mixed in with dirty cups and plates. He wanted to tidy up, but he thought she might feel insulted. Instead he pushed one or two things with his foot, checking the items flashing on her MediaReader. *Glamour* magazine articles. Nothing that interested him.

Samantha said, 'Sorry 'bout the mess,' and gave him a fleshy smile before going off to change her trousers.

Several swigs from a bottle of whiskey on the side table gave him an injection of courage, and he decided to slip away while he had the chance. But Samantha emerged from the bathroom before he could escape and came straight at him, obviously resolved in her course of action. She was naked except for a floaty silk affair that splayed open at the front. Everything on show. She kissed him with clumsy passion, even though he was rigid as a brick.

'Stay for a bit, go on, stay,' she said, in between snogs.

By then she smelled minty and bathroom-fresh.

Moments before his brief and unexpected climax Samantha called out a name, and he wondered, afterwards, if it had been his name or not. His mind had been focused elsewhere and he hadn't quite processed the word.

They lay in a tangle of sheets for some minutes before Samantha said, 'You could sleep here, if you like.'

She sounded indifferent. He paused before he answered, watching her acrylic-tipped fingers as they worried a thread from the mattress.

In the end he said he was sorry, but he couldn't stay – he had work in the morning. They were both relieved. But she put his number in her mobile device. She would call him. He said that would be fine. Lionel never heard from her again, but when he's in that part of town he still thinks about Samantha. She's the only woman he's ever had sex with.

Lilith is waiting for an answer. 'So! When did you last have sex?' she repeats.

'I can't remember.'

'There's a woman out there for you, Lionel.'

'Don't start this again.'

'Geeks are fashionable these days. If you say the right things they might think you're an entrepreneur – like that Zuckerman guy. Remember him from way back? Everyone wanted to sleep with him and he was a twat. My advice, though, when you talk to them about all your programming stuff? Don't crap on about *actual coding* for too long. It's boring and you tend to get bogged down in the details.'

'Lil!'

She makes a V with her fingers and points at her eyes. 'Your biggest problem is you never look them in the eyes,' she says. 'It's a turn-off – kind of psycho.' She shows her teeth and stabs the air with an invisible dagger.

'Lil.'

'You've got to make an effort to be normal. Ask them about their likes and dislikes. Tell them they've got nice eyes – don't mention their tits, though. It's simple really. Women are easily pleased. Eyes, mouth, teeth – even teeth – no, actually, teeth are weird; don't mention their teeth.'

'Lil!'

'There's someone for everyone.' She smiles uncertainly on one side of her face, mentally questioning her own statement.

He raises his hand. 'Lilith, stop pushing me, just stop. If you're so intent on everyone having a relationship or whatever, then why are *you* on your own? Eh?'

Lilith's uncertain smile falls away.

He wipes his forehead and stalks back to the kitchen where he presses his palms on the worktop, counting to ten. When he comes back with

Lilith's tea she's seething and turns away from him with her arms folded when he offers her the mug.

'Look, I'm sorry, but I'm happy the way I am. I like the single life.' He hears an echo of Mr Barber. *No woman to nag me, no pickney to worry about.*

'Fuck off, Lionel.'

'It's true though, Lil, I do. Anyway, I've never seen you with a man. Never.'

Lilith is out of the chair quick as a boxer after the bell. 'Don't you psychoanalyse me, Lionel Byrd, I swear I'll –' She knocks the tea out of his hand and it sprays across the laminate and up the wall next to the sofa, exactly where he's just cleared Buddha's sick.

He looks from the liquid running over the floor to Lilith. 'I'm sorry,' he says, and tries to touch her arm.

'Screw you.' She bats his hand away. 'You play those fucking games thinking it's real life, but it's fantasy. You're retarded, Lionel Byrd, fucking retarded.'

'That's not fair.'

'Yes, it is. You've always been the *retarded* little orphan boy. Are you going to spend your whole life in that weird code-filled, computer bubble of yours while the world falls apart around you? You've got to snap out of it. Retard. Do you hear?'

Retarded orphan boy. Was it him that echoed her words? Lilith's voice fades to a buzz and his mind fills with a story he's imagined so often it plays like a movie.

It starts with a blank screen – music building in the background, a plucky rhythm, backed up by the woody clonk of some African instrument. Then the voices come in – parallel octaves, alternating between a chorus and joyful call-and-response. The camera of his mind tracks across ramshackle rooftops to a wide, dusty street and a clean, whitewashed building. Cut to interior: Ngomie Orphanage. Music fades.

The temperature in the Ngomie Orphanage is hotter than usual the day that David comes to say his farewells. After twelve years in Africa – first in Liberia, and then in Kenya – David is returning to England and, with two growing boys to educate, he already feels he's left it too long to make the move home. The charity, he finally accepts, will operate just fine without him.

Out at sea, thunder drum-rolls distantly. Here, inland, the air is heavy and the babies in the nursery are unusually fractious as David casts his eyes over the cots and the baskets. This is the last time he'll trudge round in the swelter, peering in on the rejected mites that haunt his conscience. This is the last time he'll make a report on 'conditions' or the 'efficient use of charity funds'. The nurse in charge today is called Delia and, as he's leaving, almost as an afterthought, she shows him a strange little baby who's been left at the gates of the mission in Mombasa.

'This one is special,' she says. 'When he looks in your eyes it feels like he's reading your soul.'

The baby is not crying. He is preternaturally quiet and watches David with a mysterious, infant calm. Gangly, with a complexion that is at the same time pink and caramel, the boy has a wild growth of strawberry-brown frizz and wide, hazel eyes. He seems to know David will lift him from his cot and hold him at arm's length. He seems to expect David to say, to no one in particular, 'Extraordinary!'

Jump cut: A cloudless summer's day. Camera pans from a river, across a field of ripening barley, to alight on a typical English village. Birds sing. Cut to interior. Bedroom. A father sits on the edge of a child's bed, stroking the boy's hair. The father is white. The child is mixed-race with a curly caramel halo.

The father is telling the child his birth story for the hundredth time. He's saying he'd never seen a baby so lovely as the baby he rescued from Ngomie Orphanage.

'Yes,' affirms the father, 'you were a lucky find, Lionel. A very lucky find.'

Cue 'Jerusalem' sung by schoolchildren, quietly at first, then louder until the hymn reaches a rousing crescendo as the scene fades to credits. The end.

*

Lionel turns to Lilith. 'If I'm so retarded, then why do you bother to visit me all the time?'

Lilith watches the tea trickling round the feet of the sofa. 'Because I love you.'

Does she ever feel remorse for her overreactions? Lionel wonders.

But, look, here's her most earnest expression. 'And let's get it straight while we're at it,' she says. 'You need me. You lose the frigging plot when I'm away.'

'You're right.'

'Damn straight I'm right.'

'Yes.' He pauses. 'I can't even remember what we're arguing about.'

Lilith gives him one of her pathetic looks. 'We're not arguing, Lionel. You were being hurtful and obtuse.'

'Obtuse. Yes.'

Her tone softens. 'Actually, I suppose I should be proud of you, standing up for yourself for once. You should bite back more often.'

Bite back more often! Lilith, with her tongue lash and temper, would eat him alive. He's not equipped for the fight. Conciliatory must be his default mode, if he wants a quiet life. Perhaps Lilith, like him, is not good with the opposite sex, that's why she's never with anyone. He wonders what Lilith would say about the anime girl, her perfect oval face and laser-beam eyes and the exquisite moment of knowing her without speaking? It's on the tip of his tongue, his anime girl secret, but he stops. Lilith won't understand. He goes to fetch the mop before the tea spreads further across the laminate.

'Okay, my furry friend, let's have a look at you.' The vet lifts Buddha onto the counter and offers the cat the end of his pen. Buddha attempts to rub his scent on the tip, but misses, time and again.

'Hmm.' The vet pulls his it's-not-looking-good face.

He holds Buddha's head, a little too roughly in Lionel's opinion, and shines a light into the animal's eyes.

'He can't coordinate too well at all.' He turns to Lionel. 'Basically, it's the endgame. I'm surprised he's survived this long to be honest, and if he was my cat . . . well, you know my feelings.'

Lionel stares at the wooden counter. He certainly does know the vet's feelings. The vile man offers to euthanize Buddha at every opportunity. He wouldn't take Buddha to him at all if it weren't for the spectre of pain, but so far either Buddha feels none or is an uncomplaining martyr. He suspects the latter.

'Two months.' The vet passes judgement. 'Maximum.'

At the last check-up the vet had intoned, mock-sincerely, that Buddha, like his namesake, might be reincarnated – perhaps as a horse or a dog. The man obviously thought he was being clever.

'Why would someone say that?' Lionel ranted to Lilith later, feeling something close to rage. 'A cat would never want to come back as a dog. I mean, a dog!'

Lilith was grave. 'People are insensitive, Lionel. They're small-minded.'

'If he was going to be reincarnated,' Lionel said, shaping great conceptual globes in the air with his hands, 'Buddha would want to be, I don't know, something heroic, something fearsome.'

There was a moment's pause before Lilith's eyes lit up. 'Then *make* him heroic.'

'What?'

'You do all of that computer stuff. You can bring Buddha back.' She was excited. 'Give him a new life. A virtual life.'

Lilith was talking about 3D avatar programming as if it was the easiest thing in the world to do, as if a virtual Buddha could make up for the loss of the real one. But all Lionel said was, 'It takes months to programme something as complex as Buddha. Anyway, I thought you hated my games.'

'This is different. This is life and death.' The idea had her in its grip. 'This is the Reincarnation of Buddha.'

He scratched his head. 'The last avatar took a thousand hours.'

'So what are you waiting for? Chop chop. Action, Lionel. Action.'

Lilith was right. Three months on and the process of creating the virtual Buddha was well underway. First he created a series of 2D textures using digital photographs taken from every angle. Next, he made the 3D wireframes and animations, covering them with iterative renders based on the original photographs. *Colour and texture maintained.*

Guaranteed. Soon Buddha will be as authentic in 3D as he is in real life. He can practically see the code come alive as he writes it – the way a composer hears the music as he sets his dots and tails on the stave.

'So.' The vet purses his lips and puts his hands flat on the counter. 'Is it time, Mr Byrd?'

'Time for what?'

'The inevitable.' The vet has a vivisectionist's gleam in his eye.

Lionel scoops Buddha up in his arms. 'Never, you know I could never –' But he can't finish the sentence.

He sweeps out of the room, barely managing to refrain from swearing at the man.

The air outside the vet's surgery is sugary and sweet. A blackbird sings 'bravo' from the rooftop. Sunlight blesses the skin on Lionel's face.

'We'll have you chasing pigeons again, Buddha,' he whispers. 'I suppose I'll have to programme the pigeons too, eh? But I will. I promise I will.'

Buddha hears his name and tries to meow in response, but even his meow is breaking. Still, Lionel is certain that his cat feels a new, quiet hope.

@GameAddict (#23756745): 07:3:27

It takes time to acclimatize – work out your
new skills and functions. But on the Game Layer
you're superhuman. Your shots are on target.
Your lines are droll, super cool. You leap from
mountain to mountain.

Level 3: Wakey up

Mata Angelica had Grinders a-plenty. The clones did her bidding, stone-faced and obedient, tho I noticed a restive murmur or two. The Eroticon's house was in the Ghetto, north Thrar, where city-dwellers lived cheeky-jowl next to licensed OtherWorld migrants. Thrars (male and female) visited Mata Angelica often – I could hear them bump-humping day and night from my cell. In between clients the Grinders fed her on sweetmeats and spick-spanned her room for when the next Thrar came sniffing. By morning she'd be bandy and ragged. Mata Angelica was oppressed as much as those Grinders and she knew it, but at least she was mistress, not like the Sirens who spent their spans on their backs in the PimpHouses. But I'm running ahead, telling Mata Angelica's business.

The Eroticon rescued me from the square and her Grinders flushed out my tubes, replumbed them and patchworked me up good as new. I stayed in crash-mode for ten whole moon-transits and Mata Angelica said I slipped in and out of the Void all that time – tho my memory of that's quite corrupted. Only once I made conscious and there was Mata Angelica up zoom-close in my Visor, stroking my brow and saying, 'Don't give up, Ludi, we need you.' But my nog kept trotting back up the Wormhole and I'll never know what was truth or tableau.

When at last I recovered some function it was night and I was alone. I had no idea of the dimension's routines, but I knew from other worlds I'd been in (*Masquerade*, *Last Epoch*, *WarCraft* and the like) that at night I had to be hush. I could hear a clone snoring and see a Shem gecko suck-padding the wall, shifty-shifty. Far off a hound made plaintive howl-whoops in the night. Since my senses had come back full sharp I was minded to snoop round my host-house.

I struggled out of my cot – a wax-wood contraption with feather-filled mattress – but I could only take jelly steps and soon fell on all fours, wheezing and coughing up muck. I'd dragged a small table with bottles and potions down with me and the whole *crash-rattle-smash* of it brought Grinders running and Mata Angelica – 'What is it, what is it?' – into my cell.

The clones held jars full of stars (that I later discovered were insects whose bum-domes burned bright), and the buzzy light made the whole scene bewitching. There was Mata Angelica, ripe naked except for a gossamer cape, loosely worn, and all the graphics her Creator had given her proudly on show. No detail missing.

'You're back,' she said, crouching to help me.

The clones fettled round sweeping up shard-glass and I caught one give me a wink, tho it was doubtless a trick of the light.

'Thought I'd try out my pins,' I said, catching my breath.

Mata Angelica shooed off the Grinders and sat feeling my pulse as I lay in my cot. 'It's been touch and go, but I knew you'd pull through.'

'I thought I was stronger.'

She bit the edge of her lip. 'You're very strong,' she said. 'A real He-Man.'

Without checking my approval she pulled back my loincloth. On auto I snatched at her wrist.

She cried, 'Let go,' in surprise before coming all wounded and pouty.

'Forgive me.' I released her. 'It's a reflex.'

Hot hues burnished her cheeks. 'No, forgive me. Fluffing's a habit, that's all.' She folded her mitts in her lap. 'Fact is you're a real He-Man, and a He-Man's the thing I'm in need of.'

'That's why you repaired me?'

'One reason, yes.'

'What else?'

She hesitated (judging how much to let on, I wagered), but in a click she turned on the whimsy. 'I like you,' she said. 'I'm interested to hear all about you.'

My systems were janky. I couldn't access her approval meter and I had to rely on my wits. My wits said she was trying to gull me. 'You want to know if I've brought any contraband with me.' I pointed upwards. We both knew I meant swag from another dimension.

I'd clocked her dissembling and she had the good grace to study her nails. Cheats were what she was after. Smuggled in from outside, bootlegged weapons, Keys, currency or skills could turn a strumpet to a sorceress in three levels flat.

'I've searched your knapsack,' she said, now disdainful, 'and you've nothing to pay for your rescue. I'm hosting you at great risk. My Grinders have completed a costly repair.' She hard-eyed my Visor. 'I hoped you'd show some more gratitude.'

I said nothing.

'Well, this has been enlightening.' She stood up. 'I'm grinding right now and I've got a Thrar waiting.' She pushed her dugteats right out to prove it (and it's not worth comparison twixt the Eroticon and the Harridan back in the square. Sufficient to say Mata Angelica's flesh-gifts were bounteous). 'We'll chin-wag again when the sun's brimming. And no more crashing about, d'you hear?'

I gave an obedient nod and she swished out of my cell, huffish and gorgeous, tho my trust in Mata Angelica had not seeded at all.

Ask Yourself: 'Why Me?'

There's rarely a seat on the 7.05 and commuters are packed in tight in the aisles. A young office-type, with a razor-cut and a garish tie, is hanging from the overhead rail, adjusting his wraparound Spex. He hisses and elbows his neighbours, and they silently accommodate him as best they can. But there's nowhere to go, not even shuffle-room. He must be new to the 7.05, thinks Lionel. He still has the energy to defend his boundaries.

The old hands in the carriage are barely conscious or they're lost in whatever spectacle is playing in their Spex, but Lionel's mind is racing. The journey from Milk Street to Meddingley is a tortuous forty minutes of silent proximity. To survive, Lionel fixes on the view from the window, eyes constantly focusing and refocusing on the blurred near, the long and lazy far away; branches stippled with the green of spring, a breaker's yard, marshland, warehouse and depot, stacks of pallets, piles of rubble and pipes – all the obsolete, unwanted things that find their way onto the sidings. In *CoreQuest* he would be sure to rake over the rubbish for items he could use in the game. A Key. A clue. A connection.

Lionel can't imagine why, but his mind's eye momentarily conjures the back of her African head, the slope of her shoulder – his birth mother turning away, casting him off. He has David to thank for raking over the cast-offs and rescuing him.

On his last visit to the Yews Judy had left him alone with David. His father's hand, hard and skeletal, shot out to grip his wrist.

'Help me, son.' The old man was in anguish. 'I'm fading to nothing.' He held his other hand up and turned it round in the air as if watching his very substance dissolving. 'Where am I?' he begged. 'Where is *me*?'

David had proceeded to hit his own head with surprising ferocity, before George appeared and restrained him. Once everything was calm, the Ivorian gave Lionel an unctuous sneer that felt like an accusation of neglect.

The thought makes Lionel jump in his seat, as if he's waking from a falling dream, and he glances round the carriage to see if anyone has noticed. No. They're lost in their own worlds, heads buried in their MediaReaders and mobiles.

David had accused Judy of all manner of cruelty during his last weeks at Bethesda. He cursed her. Sometimes he snarled at her like an animal – eyes flinty with hatred. It was clear he'd lost his grip on reality. Still, it was shocking to hear such vitriol. Judy didn't defend herself – she'd always been the handmaid to her husband's robust patriarchy. Now David's a shell. And Judy's gone bitter. But perhaps bitterness, Lionel thinks, was always Judy's resting emotion.

The train crawls the last quarter-kilometre into the city's maw – through cuttings and past signal boxes, where the concrete is a graffiti-daubed canvas with barely a centimetre of clean surface visible below head height. Passengers squash together, touching yet unconnected, until they spill onto the platform, on through the screens and barriers, past men in peaked caps – checking the machines that check the charge codes and the chipped cards – past the flak-jacketed response teams, now a fixture on the concourses, *for your safety*, as cameras perching high on their gimbals scan the crowds like mechanical vultures with kino eyes. Lionel puts his head down, hides his face, a habit in the city.

A meeting-alert on his Google means that Lionel's prepared for the monthly team briefing. He's not keen on surprises at work. Pema, his supervisor, presides over the group while wall-mounted cameras record the proceedings (for any operatives who might be on leave).

'Vigilance,' asserts Pema, 'is your buzzword. A security breach begins with an unexpected association, a friend request on your social network, a follower on your cloudfeed. You are all potential targets. With every new partner, and every new friend, ask yourself the question . . .' Pema grasps her chest, as if she's protecting her dignity, and continues, 'why would *they* be interested in *me*?'

Meddingley HQ has been designed to engender a sense of futuristic gravitas. A dedicated train brings employees to the heart of the site, which covers forty hectares of former greenbelt to the west of the city. The perimeter is planted with tall trees to disguise the high wire-fencing. Near the complex, white, frosted walkways wend round man-made pools lit from below so that the water looks irradiated. The main building is ring-shaped with quartz-white outer walls and inner walls made of sheer glass. Solar panels are angled on the roofs and, in the centre of it all, is the Hub, shiny and black as a magpie's eye. All the offices in the ring are visible from the Hub, where the control desks and executive offices occupy a central sanctum, unobserved. News networks were quick to dub Meddingley 'The Eye' before it was complete, and the employees took to the name, as employees are inclined to do.

Lionel's office is on the second floor of the Eye, south side, where he works in a team of twenty operatives providing technical support for government system users across the country. The wireless headset he wears with its tiny microphone is standard issue. *Your query will be recorded for training purposes.* The service desk enquiries he answers about virtual data, information access and retrieval rarely challenge him. *This could be a network problem. I'm logging in.* But when he's working, time is reduced to a series of problem-solution intervals and he feels like part of a fantastic machine. His voice takes on the quality of the robotic auto-answerers that first categorize the calls. It is a comfort to know that, in this part of his life as in the games he plays, he has a straightforward, achievable purpose.

Pema's voice intones indistinctly in the background and Lionel ponders what Lilith would think of his machine-like processes. She'd blanch if she knew that sometimes, after a day trawling through code, his thoughts travel along lines like a circuit board, lighting up nodes. Electric. But then every brain has systems. Without systems, biology fails. But how would he know if he wasn't genuinely human? How could he tell?

With startling clarity, he remembers the game he once played with his brothers.

'You see,' he hears James say, 'Replicants don't know they're Replicants and that makes them hard to catch. But there are signs that Replicant hunters can look out for.'

'Yeah, that's right.' Ben nods vigorously.

'First of all.' James drags his forefinger along the skin of Lionel's forearm. 'Replicants are a different colour from normal humans. Not always, but most of the time. In fact, the typical Replicant colour is, well, your colour.'

Lionel watches his brother's nail make a pale pressure trail in his flesh.

'Then there's the *mother* question.' James leans close, focusing in on Lionel's eyes. He continues with scientific certainty. 'Your iris will give you away. It's an involuntary reaction in humans. If you say something emotional or *taboo* to a human, his pupils will dilate.' James grabs Lionel's chin and holds it fast. 'But if you talk about emotions to a Replicant' – the corners of James's mouth sag with clownish misery implying there is nothing he can do to prevent the inevitable exposé – 'then there's no iris reaction. Nothing.'

This is the game. This is how it begins.

'So, are you ready for the question, Lionel?'

Lionel attempts to nod, but James has a virile grip on his head.

Ben steps forward holding a large, long-handled magnifying glass, the one David uses for reading the small print in the concordance. He positions it over Lionel's right eye. His brothers' faces loom surreally in the dial.

'Tell me.' James's voice is impassive. 'Just the good things about your mother.'

'No, James.' Ben jumps in with a pedant's zeal. 'That's not the right words, it's "describe in single words . . ."'

'Shut up, Ben, leave this to me.'

'But it must be single words.'

James speaks through his teeth. 'Okay, for fuck's sake.' He takes a breath. 'Tell me, in *single words*, the good things about your mother.'

Lionel's eyes dart from Ben to James and back again. 'Who me?'

'Who' – James gives Lionel's face a shake – 'the fuck else are we examining?'

'Er . . .'

James releases Lionel with a disgusted shove. 'There, you see: Replicant.'

Lionel rubs his chin where James's fingers have been digging in. 'But I didn't say anything.'

'You didn't have to; your pupils gave you away. You don't have a mother; we all know that – so you're not even human. You're not worthy of love or justice.' The adolescent James is already beginning to demonstrate the logic of a fundamentalist. 'You're a robot, nothing more. A *skin job*.'

Lionel is on the point of tears. 'You can tell all that from my eyes?'

James nods gravely. 'Yep. So we have to decommission you. It's the law.'

Ben says, 'Let's give him a head start, though.' Ben enjoys a chase. He's a proper blade runner.

'Jesus, Ben, I was going to.' James turns to Lionel. 'You've got sixty seconds, *skin job*, and when we catch you, you're dead. Sixty, fifty-nine, fifty-eight . . .'

Lionel is unnerved by the intensity of this memory. It has edges and flat planes and voices and proper dialogue and he's excited by the prospect of remembering more. In fact, he's sure that Blade Runner was a regular game. Yes. He has the feeling that he and his brothers may have played Blade Runner more than once.

'So, to round up,' says Pema, 'the new archiving and surveillance system comes on stream at the end of the month.' She nods towards Lionel and another person at the far end of the room. 'If you've been identified as a feedback node please register your ID and start posting via the network as soon as possible. More importantly – circumspection, colleagues, in all your social relationships . . .' The supervisor raises her eyebrows, but doesn't finish the sentence, although her hands remain on her breasts in a heartfelt pose.

As the meeting disperses Pema approaches him. 'Lionel,' she says, with customary brusqueness. 'Can I see you in my office?'

Pema's office is small and would be claustrophobic if, as with all the managerial offices at Meddingley, it wasn't glass-fronted. Transparency is another of Meddingley's buzzwords and glass is the perfect medium to give the right impression. However, Lionel has noticed that even when something is designed for openness you can never eliminate the shadows. There are little places in the locker rooms and the toilets where the cameras' sightlines are impeded. One of the tables in the canteen is half shielded from the Hub by a temporary screen. Lionel has happened upon trysts, office romances, once even a drug deal here, at Meddingley. People will always find ways to assert their individuality.

Pema has a picture viewer on her desk – several images rotating in a slideshow: a clean-shaven Asian man whose eyes are slightly magnified by the lenses of his old-fashioned spectacles, a school portrait of two children in outmoded uniforms, and an old man, quite grey, but with a curious smile that makes him look impish.

Pema joins Lionel so their backs are to the glass. 'Thank you for your time, Lionel.'

He makes a gesture he's seen other people use, to imply it's not onerous at all for him to be there.

'Your family?' he asks, nodding towards the picture viewer.

'Er, yes. Look . . .' Pema makes a rigid shape with her hands to help her structure the next sentence more effectively. 'You know that *thing* you did for me the other week?' She's slightly sheepish, but continues without waiting for him to answer. 'Well, I need you to help me again, but this time, you see, I'm really struggling. I know I've been taking advantage of you a little bit and I will make it up to you come the next promotion recommendations –'

'It's okay, I don't mind.'

'Seriously, I couldn't be more grateful.' Her hands flop into her lap. 'It's the management you see, above me.' Her voice becomes a whisper. 'They're out to ruin me – the old guard. They're suspicious of minorities – can you believe it? In this day and age. They think we're not truly British if we've migrated. Think we can't be trusted. I know *you* understand.'

He shakes his head. 'What do you need me to do?' He can tell she's distressed.

Pema shifts in her seat. 'Remember the directory you set up, off the network, where I could put the projects I was having trouble with? I need to be able to access that directory remotely.'

'That's . . . difficult. And I wouldn't . . . I mean, I couldn't do anything as *me*, if you understand.'

Pema holds her hands up. 'No, no, of course, that's why I thought, well, maybe, you might have another idea of how that might . . .' She chews the side of her thumb and looks at him intently. 'I mean, we can't use your login and we can't use mine so . . .' She squints, thoughtfully, at the ceiling.

'I suppose we could use someone else's login, someone who doesn't work here any more, for example.'

'Brilliant, that's brilliant.' Pema claps her hands. 'You're a genius.'

'But what about prints?' Lionel holds his hands up and wiggles his fingers.

'Well,' she says, leaning even closer and speaking very softly. 'I have access to the bio-database of every employee at Meddingley.'

Lionel's eyes widen. 'Really? What for?'

'Security. So we can get into an employee's file system, locker, et cetera, without having to ring-fence that part of the network should they leave us, unexpectedly.'

'Why not reconfigure everything centrally?'

'Oh, I don't know.' She shakes her head as if he's asked her a particularly taxing question. 'But if I need information or fingerprints I have a tame bod in archiving who can get latex copies made, with clearance of course, but then I'm not a programming whizz kid like you.' Her laugh is quite girlish. 'You can get into any database you want, I'm sure.'

She's laying it on thick, but he likes to hear her extol his virtues.

'I'll get you everything I can, to assist,' she goes on without looking at him. 'A username, for instance, although you might have to work out the password yourself, but you'll have no trouble with that – and then if you could set up a little place where I can download things, you know, at home.'

'That's quite risky Mrs Khalsa.'

'Call me Pema – not out there, of course.' She tilts her head backwards to the glass. 'But in private I'm Pema, okay?'

'Okay.'

'If I'm going to get on top of this job, Lionel, then I've got to stop asking for your help, and that means putting some hours in at home.'

'I don't –'

Her voice cracks. 'My whole family, my career is at stake.'

He senses she's overdramatizing, but he says, 'I'll do what I can.'

'How can I ever thank you?'

'It's fine. Really.'

'Let me know what you need; no digital messages, just come see me. And remember you shouldn't set anything up from your own computer, just in case.'

'No.' He has no intention of doing so.

'And don't – of course I know you won't – but don't tell anyone about our arrangement.'

'Of course not.'

Pema blows air out through flaccid lips, as if to say, I'm floundering, truly floundering, and you alone are my salvation.

'You're wonderful, Lionel. You know that?'

A fierce flush rises to his cheeks; he's proud to be solving Pema's little problems.

'Oh, by the way,' she calls as he opens the door. 'How's my darling Buddha?'

Lionel shakes his head. 'Not so good, Mrs Khalsa.'

'I am sorry,' she says, and her eyes suggest she's not simply being courteous. 'What's wrong with him?'

'Cancer.' It's hard for him to say the word. 'A tumour. I thought I told you.'

'No, you didn't. He's still with us, isn't he?' Pema seems genuinely concerned.

'Yes, he's alive. But he's very sick.'

Pema reaches for her handbag and finds a card. 'You must take him to my vet. Here's his number. I'll help with the fee.'

'Really, I –'

'I insist. It's the least I can do.' She gives him a grave look. 'But, you know, every creature has a purpose, Lionel, however tragic their lives are.'

Lionel's not sure that she's right but he nods, once, and makes his way back to his desk, thinking of Buddha, thinking of Replicants and avatars and the way memories might be captured and stored and – if they can – then consciousness itself could be copied and downloaded. Now, that would be useful.

As Lionel eats his lunch he considers Pema's parting sentence. What is Buddha's purpose, or his for that matter? Everyone and everything is randomly conceived, cherished or abandoned until, eventually, they die. Perhaps Buddha's purpose is to bring him comfort. But that's selfish, distasteful. His purpose is to comfort Buddha. That's better.

Two men occupy the next table. One of them is in a wheelchair. His bulky torso and shrivelled legs make Lionel think of a tadpole. The man he's with keeps jolting the table and making cutlery rattle. It's Michael Unger, a co-worker from Lionel's section – new, six months, perhaps seven, but past his probationary period. He's American and his self-assured twang rings out above the other voices in the canteen. Lionel wishes he would shut up.

'Jesus Christ on a bike,' says Michael, 'you'd think we were working for the Feds or something.' He slaps the tabletop to make his point. '"Circumspection is our buzzword" – hell – where do these douchebags get off?'

Several people around him shift in their seats and hide their mouths as they speak. Lionel keeps his head down.

The man in the wheelchair laughs nervously. 'Shush, Mike.'

'What? I'm loud. So sack me. You Brits are so goddamn lame.'

Michael's friend stifles more laughter and, despite the American's bravado, they continue their conversation *sotto voce* until the wheelchair man finally rolls out of the canteen. 'Friday then,' he calls from the door.

'You got it, buddy,' shouts Michael.

Lionel has seen the man in the wheelchair a few times before and marvelled at his machine, which seems to be powered remotely. No buttons or wires. Or perhaps it's one of those new, thought-controlled chairs, where the software learns the user's brainwave beta commands transmitted from tiny receptors on the cerebral cortex direct to the machine's onboard computer.

'Join you?' asks Michael, standing above him, ruining his train of thought.

The question is redundant since the American begins shoving his legs under the table before he can answer. Lionel shrugs and carries on eating. He only eats properly at work. Buying and preparing food rarely occurs to him and the cupboards in his flat contain tea and coffee, perhaps a small loaf for toast, or a packet of biscuits. Little else.

The American's tray is stacked with food, each moulded compartment containing a biodegradable dish – soup, red-flecked pasta, fruit, salad, a cheese slice, water biscuit, coffee with creamer.

'Food's shit today, but you can't turn it down, right?' Michael smiles, adjusts his position in the chair. 'You know, I've been meaning to talk to you for weeks. You don't mind?'

Lionel is inexplicably irked by Michael's presumption of fellowship, but he says, 'Nope. Not at all.'

Three years – that's how long Lionel's been at Meddingley – and apart from the weekly briefings and the users who come through on his headset he doesn't speak to many people in the office. He exchanges pleasantries with co-workers; he's on reluctant nodding terms with several men in D-section, who make a point of acknowledging him, simply because they consider him to be one of them. Black. Pema is his touchstone. She's taken him under her wing and he's grateful. Men like Michael Unger; well, he steers clear.

Lionel avoids looking directly at Michael, snatching a stealthy glance here and there as he prods the food on his tray with a fork. Michael has wide-set, intelligent eyes, blue-green, with skin loosening over the lids to form sad little tucks at the outer corners. His nose, albeit too large, is proud, patrician, and he has some hard nobility around the mouth accentuated by a deep dimple in his chin. Close-up, stubble pokes through on his cheeks, and in one earlobe the suggestion of a piercing from long ago. Michael bears the furtive scrutiny good-naturedly and talks about the frustrations of booking annual leave, team targets and the logging system.

Finally, he stops speaking and, as if announcing the end of an informal prelude, bangs his hand down hard on the tabletop. He looks over towards the window of the canteen, to the Hub, then looks up, wrinkling his nose.

'I hate these fucking strip lights, don't you?' Michael's laugh is hollow. 'I saw you sitting on your own. I see you every day.'

Lionel puts his knife and fork down and scratches one eyebrow.

Solemn now, Michael presses on. 'I thought – it's Lionel, right? You know, you work with someone for ages and –'

'Yes.'

'Yes. Strange, isn't it? I mean, we're in the same section and I've spoken to you what, twice? Once in our team review and . . . now.'

'I don't remember.'

Michael is undaunted. 'Sometimes I wonder, you know, what all this surveillance bullshit is about. I mean, what the fuck is a *feedback node* anyway, for Jesus Christ's sake? What the fuck are we feeding back on? One another?' Michael stops again and scans the cafeteria, eyeing the camera above the self-service salad bar with special interest. 'Strange, isn't it? Everything we do is public and yet we do it all alone. Do you ever think about that?'

Lionel shakes his head, even though he's thought about it a lot. He's counted all the cameras on Milk Street, made a note of all the 'magic eyes' on the trains and the buses; every policeman, every security guard has a tiny device attached to their jacket or helmet. Three hundred and thirty-five times each day he is filmed or photographed. He's averaged this out: his face, his actions, arbitrarily passed over or pored over by hundreds, if not thousands, of anonymous people or recognition pro-grammes every week. Yet for most of those times he's alone. All alone.

Michael slaps the table again and Lionel recoils slightly. 'Shit, you must think I'm a freak.' Michael laughs again, but there isn't a gram of joy in it.

Perhaps Michael is mad, Lionel thinks. His food is untouched and his fork hovers equivocally above his pasta, occasionally advancing towards it then retreating.

'You don't owe me any explanations,' Michael goes on. 'You . . . *we*,' he corrects himself, 'don't owe anybody anything, right? None of us do.

We're just individual animals surviving in this fucked-up world. On our own.' Michael brandishes his fork in mid-air.

Lionel puts both hands in his lap. 'I'm sorry,' he says softly. 'Is this about my work?'

'What?'

'My work – is this some sort of test?'

Michael gives him a quizzical look. 'What?'

Lionel wishes he could disappear in a little puff of smoke. He keeps quiet and studies the floor.

'Jeez, chill out, buddy. You're the hardest-working dude in the whole building. I saw you were alone again, that's all.'

'Uh huh.'

'Hey, shit, you're not falling for all that "vigilance is your buzzword" bullshit, are you? Ha! The team peppy this morning didn't mean we weren't allowed to talk to each other, y'know. I've been security checked. We all have, right? They know what our farts smell like. I just thought you could use some company.'

'That's very kind of you.'

'No sweat.'

Michael appears to be wrestling with some internal conflict. It shows in his face as a small twitch at the edge of his mouth and in one eye. It takes a moment to plough through whatever crosscurrents have besieged this process, but after a few seconds his eyes sweep up to the clock.

'Heck, would you look at the time?'

Lionel suspects Michael has tired of their encounter. But when he stands the American's posture betrays a less robust man than his bluster suggests. His trousers are at least two sizes too large – cinched in at the waist with a thin belt – and his shoulders are hunched. Michael's stance is verging on defensive and it strikes Lionel that the American might be the one who's lonely, that although he gives the impression of being popular he rarely sits with the garrulous men who talk about sports with their mouths full. He's more often with people like the man in the wheelchair. The outcasts.

Michael says, 'Well, I'll stop rattling your cage. Didn't mean to interrupt you, dude.'

Rattling the cage. That's what Lilith says. Lionel examines Michael's defeated gait as he makes his way across the room. He looks at the empty seat for a second and back to Michael, who is placing his tray on the clearing trolley, the food still intact. He wants to shout, 'Hey, don't go. I'm useless at this. You're right, we should be friends,' but the words catch in his throat. The noise of cutlery and coffee machines and steam and mumbled conversations close over the path Michael has taken, like snow filling in footsteps.

How did I manage to do that? he thinks. There was a consideration in Michael's gesture of friendship that suggested days, or weeks, of planning. Not an off-the-cuff decision. *I saw you were alone again, that's all.* He feels uncommonly amenable towards Michael in that instant and decides that if he approaches him again he'll try to relax, be more civil. He'll ask if Michael plays *CoreQuest.* They could meet online. They could make a real connection.

@GameAddict (#23756745): 30:3:27

Identify your enemies. Plot their locations on your map if you can. By all means keep an eye on your comrades. On the Game Layer, as in the grey world, you can't always tell who your friends are. Try to access their meters. Approval, trust, attraction, loyalty – are all represented in their control panels. If they deny access to their data – mistrust them. If only the grey world was as simple.

Level 4: Drufus Comes Sniffing Around

Next morning I heard the Eroticon commanding her Grinders. 'No one must see him. No one! D'you hear?' With that she slammed out, hurry-up, late-wise. So I was surprised when a clone shuffled in and announced Drufus Scumscratch.

I was minded of some grey discharge as Drufus oozed through the door of my cell. The skin of his body was slimy and bump-blistered and his fizzog was wreathed with soft-drooping jowl-flaps. In his demeanour was a shade of hard-earned authority now ebbing and this diminishment came off pathetic. After slurping three bowls of DumGrog, Drufus got up a chin-wag, old-boy style.

'Well, Ludi my lad.' He'd learned my name. 'I've been meaning to call, but you know how it is – busy, busy.'

I said I'd been too weak for company. Repairing's a singular business.

'No matter,' said the snail. 'I'm more of a chin-wagger than listener, so we'll make a fine duo.' He laughed so expansive it jiggled his dewlap. 'So, what do you make of the Grinders?' he began. 'Fine little slaves, eh? And so willing.'

I said I was grateful for their attention, but sadly I couldn't tell them apart. Their face-features were too similar.

'They're clones every one, but if you look close you'll see they do hairstyles and feature paint. Ridiculous.'

I told him these superficials had escaped me.

'They're pre-programmed, you see. Or meant to be.' Drufus snorted. 'But in Br'mab, they say, there's a group of 'em gone AWOL. Think of that.'

'Is that a bad thing?'

'Yes, bad, and unnatural.'

'Why?'

'Can't have Grinders individualizing, flitting off-duty. Every character has a contribution to make.' He cleared some phlegm from his throat. 'Next thing you know they'll refuse to go to the Core.'

'The Core?'

'It's where all Grinders must go in the end. Keeps the Realm going round.' He lowered his voice. 'That's why OtherWorld characters, like you, are illegal. Don't worry – your secret's safe. You're all Viral, you see. You corrupt the dimension. Seditious elements get into the game and do nasty jiggery-pokery.'

'I don't understand.'

He leaned back, bump-blisters stacking into tight little rows. 'I thought you were too weary for chin-wagging and here you are grilling me, good 'n' proper.'

I apologized, but explained that I needed to grasp the dimension. There was so much to learn and I couldn't rely on Mata Angelica's goodwill for ever.

'Listen,' said Drufus, coming chummy and secret. 'It's actually Mata Angelica I want to divulge about.' He stopped for a click, commanded the Grinder to keep vigilant. 'Don't be buffooned by her charms. I know I'm a Creator's grim fiddling-trick. No! You don't have to pretend.' He indicated his blubber, tho I hadn't protested. 'But I know when there's business afoot.'

'Business?'

He laid a moist mitt on my thigh. 'You, dear boy, are no ordinary OtherWorld Reject.' He gave my thigh a soft pat. 'You're a rare one – believe me. And I have it on authority that, soon as you're hearty, Mata Angelica plans a trade-up. She's stoking a bid-war. Thrars and Vadarians are sizing you up for their own.'

'Why would they want an illegal like me?'

'Battle, dear boy.' He made the pretence of sword-swinging. 'A campaign for Grinders and Power Rings.'

'Perhaps if I prove myself in battle I might get licence to stay?'

'You're missing the point.' Drufus's frustration made him slobber. 'The piddling pursuits of the tribes are not yours. You're made for Quests; look at those biceps, that handsome He-Man physique. Anyone can see your true purpose.'

'Go on.'

His eyes sharpened as he leaned in close-wise. 'I have a powerful client with a top secret Quest. I can't give out details, but if it's licence to stay that you want, you will have it.'

The gastropod folded his mitts while I mulled it over. He was sure he had me.

Finally I said, 'I'm grateful, but my fate's with Mata Angelica.'

'That's a grave mistake.'

'Perhaps.'

Drufus extracted himself from the chair doing mutter words, but he stopped at the door and came fiendish. 'You'll be wanting this back, I suppose? It was in your knapsack. I took the liberty of safe-keeping it for you.'

He waved a gold Key in the air. I'd forgotten the Key. I must have picked it up in some other dimension.

'I'm obliged.' I held out a mitt.

Drufus laughed. 'Not so easy, Reject.' He dandled it glint-wise in front of my fizzog. 'I deserve a reward, wouldn't you say? For concealing your contraband. One whiff of this and the Big Boss'll have you. His agents'll boot you right back to the Void.'

Maybe I was too weak for a face-off, or maybe I'd lost patience, but I darkened my Visor and said, 'Do your worst.'

'I didn't take you for a fool, Ludi. You've fallen for an Eroticon – how quaint, how original.' (He said that bit with a snipe-tongue.) 'She's got a galore of sex-features, I'll grant you, but she's no match for my mistress, you'll see.'

The snail made a moody show of it when he left. He squashed the Grinder to the wall and fired parting verbals all through the house as he left, still holding my Key in his fist.

An Unexpected Visit from Judy

A nime girls fight dirty. They look like schoolgirls with their limpid eyes, plaid skirts, knock knees and toes touching – so cute. But beware, there's always a gun or a knife tucked in their knickers; they thrive on the raw excitement of hand-to-hand combat. They've mastered all the sly moves – ultra-athletic, flexi-jointed – and they're so lithe and mobile their clothes can't contain them. Their blouses bust open and their skirts fly up round their waists as they punch and kick ass, ninja-style. Everyone can see their peachy young breasts and nymphettes' buttocks, clad in white cotton panties. They look innocent, but they're deadly.

Lionel draws her again and again, but he's never satisfied with the result. The anime girl has not materialized since their connection in the rain – he's kept watch for her from his window. He's tried to capture her likeness, sketched her in detail on his graphics programme with her hair flowing free in the wind, a noble expression on her heart-shaped face, her eyes dewy with suppressed sadness and pride. But he hasn't been able to nail her.

Now, here she is, on the street, on her own. Lionel is stupidly over-excited. She's standing in the doorway opposite his flat, smoking a cigarette and examining the platforms she's wearing, twisting her heel out and looking down at her shoes. They make her feet look like hooves. Lionel jumps around at the window and waves his arms frantically.

'Look up,' he shouts and he knows she'll look up at him again, any minute. She would not, could not, forget the connection they had on that first day.

But she doesn't look up, and as she *clip clops* down to the junction, her gaze never strays higher then eye-level. She has blinkers on now and her hair doesn't flow free in the wind. She looks drained and vacant and, by the time Lionel's sprinted down to the junction to try and talk to her, she's been spirited away. The girls at the health centre are prostitutes. He knows that. But his anime girl is untouchable. Surely. There's a gun in her knickers – a big, fat, automatic revolver – and she'll use it too, if she has to. As he walks back along Milk Street he imagines she's a warrior, samurai tradition, and he begins to storyboard the gameplay and work out the levels she'll fight on. Yes, those anime girls fight dirty all right.

Since her first visit a year ago Judy hasn't been back to Lionel's flat. She says the walk from the railway station to Milk Street is too frightening and at her age she hasn't the stomach for it. The mired pavements, the boarded-up shops, the doorways full of rubbish and half-digested takeaways puked up in pink piles: it's disgusting. The women wearing hijabs and the addicts beside the parking machines asking for 'chits', hoping for pay tokens, and the North Africans and activists handing out memory disks about refugees and transit camps – they scare her. She says everyone she knows would feel the same. But still, here she is in Lionel's living room, unannounced, checking the mantelpiece for dust, glancing over his papers and in his waste bin, surveying the street below with suspicion and distaste. The years in Africa haven't prepared her for the colour on her doorstep.

Lionel pokes his head through the kitchen door. 'Did you say you wanted sugar?'

'No, thank you.'

He comes through with the tea. 'There. Take a seat.'

Judy remains standing. Her arrival has thrown Lionel into disarray. At least when Lilith is present there's a conversation, albeit one full of anger. But Lilith has been working away for more than a month now.

Buddha wobbles around Judy's feet attempting to transfer his scent onto her ankles, but he only manages to collapse onto her shoes, mewling painfully and dribbling.

Judy puts a hand to her chest. 'I was in the area.' She's trying not to gag.

'Yes.'

'Yes. There are a couple of things I need to go over with you.'

'You're lucky to catch me in.'

'I know, Lionel.'

'I work alternate weekends.'

'I know. You've told me many times.'

Judy is petite, fleshless, and he imagines her bones are as hollow as a bird's and he could lift her up – *whoopee* – in one easy movement, toss her high into the air.

'Would you like a biscuit? I've got a digestive somewhere. Chocolate.'

'No. No, thank you. This paper,' she says, reaching into her bag. 'It's nothing much, but with David in the state he's in . . .' She pauses to compose herself, touching the top of her nose. 'You just need to sign.'

The tap drips in the kitchen. The washer has broken and he must tell Saeed, his landlord, to come and fix it.

'Okay.'

He holds his hand out for the document, but Judy takes it to his desk where she smooths it flat. 'Here and here.' She points to two places where someone has drawn an asterisk, in pencil.

His signature is neat and precise and he underlines it firmly. 'More solicitor stuff?'

She nods, tight-lipped. 'It's been so quick, really, the Alzheimer's.' She folds the paper and puts it back in her bag. 'We should have got things sorted out earlier.'

They sit and sip tea. The dripping tap chops the silence into awkward little sections. The drips get louder. They echo round the room.

'Actually.' Judy clears her throat and moves to the edge of her chair. 'There's something else we need to discuss.'

'Fire away.'

'Have you heard from your Aunt Rachel recently?'

'No.' He's keenly aware of his failure of duty. 'I must write to her. I'm not so good at writing – with a pen,' he adds quickly. 'And she doesn't use email.'

'So she hasn't written to you here at all?' presses Judy.

'No.'

'Good. I mean okay. Well, the other thing I want to talk about is . . .' She takes a deep breath before continuing. 'When David has gone' – she says each word cautiously, as if she's testing their explosive qualities – 'you might not, I might – when David dies I'll probably move away. Leave the area completely. I never cared for it here really. It was David who loved it.'

His conversations with Lilith have prepared him for the prospect of his father's death, but he's surprised that Judy is taking his passing for granted.

'I thought you'd move,' he says. 'I thought you might go to America.'

Since Aunt Rachel went to Australia, Lionel has harboured the belief that women are wont to relocate to new continents in their autumn years.

'No, not America, whatever gave you that idea? I'll be going to Blyth – to be near Ben.'

'Ah! Lilith will be . . .' He is about to say sad, but it strikes him that Lilith won't mind at all if Judy goes. 'She'll be surprised.'

Judy closes her eyes. 'What can I say?'

Lionel shrugs. The drips come loud as cymbal crashes.

'Can you *do* something about that tap?'

If married people are supposed to have something in common, then Lionel can't imagine what attracted Judy and David to each other. The huge husk of his father is entirely at odds with the tight little coil of his mother. Once, when he'd been over to help Judy with David one night, Lionel asked why she'd married a man so much older than herself. His mother had been unusually candid.

'I was a surprise baby,' she'd said. 'The one who arrives when their parents are old and don't really want any more.' She'd had the conscience to bite her lip before going on. 'Still, they were devoted and my childhood was idyllic. But then it changed.' She added softly, 'Life often does.'

Judy had never talked to Lionel about his grandfather's death, but that day she'd stared out of the window and, gripped by a dreamy nostalgia, recalled it all. Her voice turned to cream when she talked of him. Lionel tried not to make a sound in case it broke the spell.

It was February, the twelfth to be precise, and still dark when her father had left the house – off to a conference in Harrogate – calling out goodbye to them all as he stepped into the wintry morning, opening the door again to wish her good luck in her maths test, apologizing for another blast of cold air.

Later, the headteacher came into the class right in the middle of the test and ranged over the children's faces until he found hers, then turned away quickly – too quickly – and spoke in a whisper to her teacher.

'A glance, that's all it was, but I can still see his pity.' Judy gave in to a shiver. 'Unbearable.'

Her father's car was one of several involved in a pile-up. A pile-up! What a neat word to describe the mangled metal she saw pictures of later. His death changed everything, of course. Judy was thirteen. Her eldest siblings had already left home. A remaining brother spent months in his bedroom until he fled to London the following year. If the children had all been younger her mother might have attempted some sort of recovery – but with only Judy to think of she had time to indulge her grief. She got a taste for misery. It sustained her. Even the joy she once took in her children ebbed away.

'A girl at school at that time told me life was a test.' Judy frowned. 'She was a Christian. I didn't really care for her, but I liked the idea that death was the beginning and I might see my father again, so I went along with her to the Assembly.' Judy's voice had regained some of its familiar hardness. 'Though I suppose I started going mainly to get out of the house.' She smiled briefly. 'Strange. The decisions we make.'

David had proposed after a gospel meeting when she was eighteen. She'd barely noticed him before. He was too old for her, but she knew she had to escape. She said 'yes' right away. David had recognized that Judy had the necessary traits to survive the privations of Africa. Stoic and practical. A tough little Christian. She was flattered.

'Now I realize he wanted me because I was young and malleable – not tough. I just wanted a father.'

They married two months later and three weeks after that she was gripping David's hand as the prop plane bounced down on a tiny airstrip in north-eastern Liberia. Her mother died of an aneurism the following winter and when Judy flew back for the funeral she learned that her siblings blamed her for their mother's death.

'They said I'd abandoned her.' She showed her teeth for a second. 'They abandoned me first.'

*

Lionel puts a sponge under the tap. He expects Judy to leave directly and he's unsettled when she starts questioning him about his work. It's unusual for her to show this much interest in his life. At one point she uses the bathroom and afterwards questions him, cagily. Has he seen Dr Rand? How often does he visit the barber? How's his health?

He says he follows his old tutor's cloudfeed, and she nods although he knows she doesn't really know what this means. He tells her he's growing his hair – it looks untidy right now, but this phase will pass.

'Anyway, I'm feeling great, never better,' he assures her.

They talk about Buddha and he tries to explain his avatar project as they sit side by side on the sofa. He pulls up all his photos on his Google device and she's enthralled as he scrolls through the shots – zooming into this image and that with deft pinches and flicks of his fingers. He explains how he used different textures or expressions to get the required effects in 3D and Judy says it's amazing, his skill with computers – just amazing – and she's so glad that, after everything, he has found his niche. She's baffled by modern technology.

There are some pictures and movies of Buddha, when he was a kitten, before the tumour, and Judy says, 'I'm not a cat person, you know that, but Buddha really was quite handsome before he got ill. Sickness, in the brain, really doesn't suit anyone – animal or human.'

Her voice is full of regret and Lionel thinks she's alluding to the breakdown she had after his accident, and he feels an affinity with her he's never felt before – or at least an affinity he can't remember feeling. Sitting this close, he can smell her maternal perfume and it sets off a muffled stampede of memories: Judy kissing him goodnight, Judy laughing as James and Ben chase her with their water pistols, Judy at the kitchen sink, wiggling her hips with her hands in the suds singing 'Hit Me Baby One More Time', saying, 'Shh – don't tell your dad we're doing pop songs, it's so worldly,' with mischief in her eyes. The images charge gently through his mind and it occurs to him that there was a time when Judy was happy, long ago, before the breakdown, before he caused her so much pain (although he doesn't know how he did), and he reaches to touch her hand, but she stiffens, rigid as a board now, and makes a petrified squeak that piques Buddha's interest. It's so mouse-like – so fearful – that Lionel edges away and makes space for her to stand. He wouldn't want her to have to endure anything unsavoury or painful.

'Well,' she says. Her voice has a high-pitched finality to it. 'It was very nice to see you, Lionel.'

'Yes.'

She brushes her skirt and walks to the door. 'I can see myself out.'

'Are you sure you'll be all right, you know, walking back to the station?'

'Perfectly. Perfectly fine.'

'Fucking typical,' says Lilith. 'That's it. I'm coming back. I can't believe she came by like that. It's because I'm away. She'd never pull a stunt like that if I was around.'

'Lilith!'

'Lionel, don't *Lilith* me. I'm fucked off with you, too. I mean, what were you thinking? Did you even check what that paper was? No. She just strolls in, waves something under your nose and you put your autograph on it without any thought or consideration.'

'I don't care. She was lovely actually. She was normal – kind of.'

There's a long silence and he knows Lilith is trying to control her anger. 'Listen to me,' she says eventually, a patronizing firmness reinforcing her delivery. 'That thing you signed, that was probably your birthright and you've signed it away.'

He clears his throat, preparing to object.

'No, shut up a minute. You gave it to her. You're a fool, Lionel Byrd – a damn fool. Just because you were adopted she wants to ring-fence everything for her precious sons and you're letting her. From now on I shall call you Esau.'

'Lil –'

'Yes, Esau.'

Lionel sighs. 'I've got everything I need. I've got a job, a flat, enough to live on. Let Judy worry about Ben and James. We're okay, you and I. We've got each other.'

Lilith never holds back when she screams and this time a rough screech explodes from the speaker. Lionel holds the device away from his ear.

'For God's sake, Lionel.' She continues in the same hysterical register. 'I'm not always going to be here. You can't rely on me. Fuck.' She pauses to take a breath. 'You need to sort things out for yourself. Action. Fucking hell. It starts with not letting our mother bully you into giving everything to our shitty, selfish, twat-faced arses of brothers.'

He sniffs. 'Can you have a twat-faced arse?'

'Oh shut up!'

Dear Lilith. Always so pushy. But she's right. He can't expect her to look out for him; she's got her own life. And when he comes to think of it, they spent all their teenage years apart, and even now she'll slip away for days or weeks without warning. Perhaps, one day, she won't come back at all. Think of that.

When he lived with her in Sunnyvale (a temporary arrangement that he quickly took for granted), Lilith marched into his room – the spare room – early one morning and told him to leave. She wasn't angry with him, at least she didn't seem angry, but she was absolutely clear that he should go right away. She'd been thinking about it for weeks, apparently. She was doing him a favour. Kicking him out would force him to be resourceful.

'You've been here more than three years. You have credit and you can fend for yourself.' Lilith's eyes had shone with vicarious excitement. 'Why hang out in this tedious village a minute longer when there's so much out there to discover?'

She'd decided that he must make his own way in the world; find some interesting, unorthodox friends (she stressed the word 'unorthodox'). Begin the adventure. If he stayed with her any longer he'd get into the habit of relying on her, and Lilith really wasn't the type to be relied on. Lilith was not the type to be argued with either.

Buddha, still a kitten, didn't protest when Lionel tucked him under his shirt. The cancer had already taken root, though no one knew. How could they have done?

'I'll come back for my stuff when I've found somewhere,' Lionel had said.

'Okay. Whenever.' Lilith was offhand. 'And, Lionel,' she added as he stepped over the threshold, 'this is entirely for your own good.'

It was different when they were little, so the story goes. Lilith remembers following *him* around, the way a duckling waddles after its mother.

David thought their devotion was amusing, but Judy did all she could to keep them apart; it was 'unnatural' for children to be so obsessive about one another. But when she separated them – Lilith in her playpen, Lionel in his room – Lilith was broken-hearted and cried the entire time until David threw his hands up and let them play together again in spite of Judy's qualms. Their father liked a quiet life.

Lilith says it was as if the world had ended when Lionel was sent away, but when she tries to work out the dates and why they had no contact through their adolescence, she gets confused.

'I must have been ten when you had the accident,' she says. Lilith has a startling memory, but she's always been muddled about numbers.

'You were nine and I was ten,' he says.

'Yes, of course. And then you went to Cranbrooks.'

'Correct.'

'But I didn't see you again, properly, until Norwich.'

'Yes, Norwich was the place.'

During the first terms at Cranbrooks Lionel had emailed Lilith every week, but at some point he must have stopped. Perhaps school became too prominent and family life faded; certainly his recall of the normal round of birthdays is interrupted. Lilith growing up, Lilith's first boyfriend, Lilith learning to drive or taking her exams – he can only imagine these things happening. But soon time had flown and Lionel was at university. When she'd burst into his room in Norwich, eager-eyed, smelling of springtime, exactly how he'd imagined her, she was a woman – *ta-da*. It was magic. That was five years ago and, although Lilith swears she will never lose touch with him again, he knows, with her temperament, that she can't be expected to keep that kind of promise.

'I've had enough of Mum's machinations. You'll have to call her, Lionel, and get that paper back.'

'I'm not calling her. I don't care about any of that stuff, Lil. Anyway, it's too late, I've signed it now – whatever it was.'

Lilith is growling on the end of the line. 'Fine. But I'm coming back at the weekend, and I'll get to the bottom of it. I swear you need something seismic to kick you up the arse.'

'Please don't interrupt what you're doing, sis. I'm cool. I'm getting on with the Buddha Project.'

'You're *cool*, are you?'

'Yes, I am. I'm cool.'

'As long as you're sure.'

'I'm sure.'

She's taking the piss. He doesn't mind. In fact, there's something about the conversation that makes him feel rather capable. He's not sure if it's because Lilith is away and he's had to deal with Judy on his own, but his meeting with their mother, although unexpected, had felt normal until the very end. Sitting together on the sofa, looking at photos, discussing the past and the future. It was wonderful. It was ordinary.

A friend request is awaiting his approval on his SocialNet. *Michael Unger. Connection: Colleague.* An animated headshot of Michael touching his forehead in an informal salute loops ad infinitum in the request header – very retro. *Ignore. Confirm.* Lionel's finger hovers.

He joined SocialNet on Lilith's account. 'We can use it to stay in touch when I'm away,' she'd said. But Lilith quickly tired of social networking. It was 'banal'. If she wanted to drown in meaningless verbiage she could visit their mother. Nevertheless, her account is still active – and even today her name shows up in his feed. She's become a fan of Evolution. Lionel follows the link to a nightclub uptown. It boasts a private VIP lounge and 'legal high' cocktails. Lionel is intrigued by Lilith's other life – the one she keeps separate from him.

There was a flurry of friend requests when Lionel first signed up to SocialNet – mostly colleagues he barely knew. But then there was Pablo, an overseas student he shared digs with in his second year at Norwich. Total geek. Pablo taught him his first hacking techniques. Now he's a security consultant for an international investment bank. After that there was Joseph Knox, an acquaintance from school, who contacted him from Sydney. Their friendship was predicated on being bullied by thugs in the year above. They'd found some solace in common misery for a term, but then Joseph began to swamp him and in the end Lionel had kept him at arm's length.

Joseph advertises the fact that he is now studying to be a psycho-therapist 'down under'. His personal details declare that he is married and fertile – two children – and more than five thousand images show the advancement of Joseph's life and career in high definition: barbies on the beach, 'surf's up', kiddies in fluorescent head-to-toe swimwear. Lionel enjoys following Joseph's life from a distance although sometimes it feels as if he's spying – but then why would Joseph upload all the videos and images if he didn't want people to see them? Lilith says that everyone's desperate for affirmation because status has become something people 'update' rather than earn. Lionel never knows what to say on SocialNet. His other connections are retail outlets he's used or recording artists whose music he's downloaded. There's a tripleX portal that keeps spamming him and an anti-slavery organization, which Lilith signed him up to, that sends event invitations each week. But it would cost him his job if he's seen to be partisan – so he never responds. And now here's Michael and his animated avatar, saluting in the header bar.

Ignore. Confirm. He confirms. Lionel Byrd and Michael Unger are friends.

@GameAddict (#23756745): 05:6:27

Love. There's a thing. You reach out in the grey
world but nobody reaches back. They're stuck,
like you, in their mediated bubbles – Spex on,
earplugs in. The Game Layer is the place for
romance. You're handsome, heroic and physi-
cally perfect. The women are uninhibited and
enter into the spirit of the chase, unafraid. It's
wonderful, carnal, all-encompassing. Risk free.

Level 5: Falling for Mata Angelica

Mata Angelica was created for FantasyV, a pleasure dimension, where every imagining and proclivity was catered for, even to the Last Taboos. FantasyV was deleted after Wonderlanders were discovered using Lovematch Messenger to communicate with minors in multi-dimensions. This was prohibited.

'Spoiled it for everyone,' sighed Mata Angelica. 'Now we're all refugees.'

The Eroticons, PornQueens and RentArthurs from FantasyV were mostly made Void. Their Creators should have been rapped for it, but they were living it big-style somewhere called Baltik. The ones that suffered were rank-and-file characters looking for love or using their flesh-gifts for credit. The Dot-tripleX bubble finally burst. But Mata Angelica's Creator salvaged her code and smuggled her to the Realm, where she carved a niche offering unusual extras. She did things that GrindSirens weren't programmed to do, so naturally she had licence to stay.

Mata Angelica gave me this back story as we lounged in her palanquin, borne through the streets by six Grinders. The palanquin – velvet-decked, curtained but with little grid-meshes for spying – had plump bolster cushions and dazzling bling-jewels worked into the frame. Exquisite. Mata Angelica called it her mobile boudoir and we rode with the curtains drawn into the citadel, peeking at routines and chin-wagging.

The rich men of Thrar wore wreaths round their nogs and skimpy white togas, while the women were done up in purple and jewels. There were soldiers on prancers, or in formation marching this way and that. Thrar's walls were rendered stone – all higgledy and old-some – and some parts were totally crumbly – any He-Man worth salt could have shouldered it down into rubble. But the place had ruined Roman appeal. There were arches, columns and wide-open plazas. There were fine-polished statues of patrician gods – athletic and sinewed – all perfectly wrought. I wanted to soft-finger them or lay my cheek on their marble-hewn bellies. Thrar, long ago, had masterful craftsmen.

'Look,' said Mata Angelica, voice smeared with contempt. 'Look at that moon-arsed matron. Thinks she's an empress, they all do.'

I marked a Thrar woman – squattish and dumpy, but with the nose-up haughtiness that afflicts leeches and loot junkies in every dimension. She was doing fancy steps through the market, pointing at items that her Grinders then nipped and retrieved. Her entourage snaked behind her, laden with goods, tho I couldn't see what they carried.

'What are they trading?'

'Power Rings for frippery. Wickedly wasteful.'

'Power Rings?'

'Energy supply. Slip a ring on and watch your meter nip up to 100.'

'Do I need them for my energy meter?'

Mata Angelica did a shoulder-shrug. 'Desire is always sold off as need.'

I peered at the street. Save for the soldiers most Thrar men were full-bellied and lung-puffy. They didn't go about on their pins, just tottered a bit and fell back on their palanquins with a 'walk on' or 'look lively' to the Grinders that carried them.

'Do you think it's right that the Grinders are slaves?'

The Eroticon lazy-stretched back on her cushions. 'We're all slaves, Ludi. Didn't you know? Just depends on the grade.'

I thought for a moment. 'I don't feel like a slave.'

'Well, that's dandy,' she said, tho I detected a sharp dash of scorn.

Next day Mata Angelica took me on a seeing-tour outside the citadel. She instructed the Grinders to remove the curtains so the palanquin came more like a litter, open to skyblue and breezes. As we progressed, an orchard of blossom trees rained petal confetti all round us. It caught in the Eroticon's lashes and hair. She was more natural beauty than sexy-bomb, I clocked on that day.

At a hostelry – a rough thatch and stables affair – she nodded to everyone as if she knew them and we swapped the palanquin for two nag-prancers. We left the Grinders with vitals and rode across a wide steppe that finished – full stop – on the edge of a plateau. I didn't know Thrar was elevated up and the vista was marvellous, panoramic. As we slid off our prancers and looked out on it all, the wind picked the last of the petals away.

'The Desert of Gog,' she said sadly, 'where the Wisps wander. And there' – she pointed eastways across the basin of desert – 'see those mountains, that's Vadar.'

In the distance, a snaggletooth mass spiked out of the wilderness.

'What's that place over there?' I pointed southways to where another citadel hankered for heaven – its spires so transparent and spindly it could have been from a dream.

'That's Darzir. The Core is deep in her catacombs. It's where the Grinders go to save their Masters from Wisp. The priesters who guard it want to come like Creators. See, they've built towers that stretch to the gods. They sit in the clouds and sing like the clappers to pure-up their souls. If you listen you'll hear 'em.'

We stood cupping our lug-holes for a click.

'I can't hear a thing.'

'No, me neither,' she said.

We laughed for a bit then fell silent, coming hypnotized by the vast sand-bound wilderness stretching off, east and west.

'It's a wasteland but beautiful,' I said. 'Is it dangerous down there with those Wisps?'

'Wisps can't hurt you. It's the Bosses and their agents you have to be scared of. They'll rip off your nog and kick you back to the Void if they find you.'

'Definitely safe then!'

I made her laugh twice times and her face-features shone, quite delightful. But she came sober in less than a click. 'Can I trust you, Reject?' she said, trying to make out my eyes through my Visor.

'It depends.' I paused for a beat. 'I'm not programmed for subterfuge. I don't want to deceive you.'

She frowned deeply, but still carried on. 'You. Me. We're here for a purp–'

Before she could finish a huge boulder came horizontal from east-field and landed with a terrifying thud to our left. The shock of it flattened us prostrate. Our prancers reared up whinny and fraidy before hoofing off into the distance. My Visor flashed *live* for the first time since re-nogging. Fight-mode. At last! I felt Ludi the warrior enliven my wireframe and I roared so loud the whole scene shook with the sound.

Evolution

L ionel has been spending too much time pretending to be a cat.
Perfecting Buddha's mannerisms requires total immersion. The
gait and the feline visage demand subtle coding and he must *feel* what
it's like to be Buddha: four-legged, low-slung and compact. He licks
his hands as if they're paws; he mews and purrs, stretches and makes
toothy yawns. No laughter, no language.

But now, whenever he catches his own reflection, he's confused. Here's
the familiar square chin, full lips, the African nose flecked with freckles
and the eyes of limed hazel. Yet he barely recognizes himself. Where are
his whiskers, the reflective layer behind the retinas to make spook-eyes
of his lenses, the little pink tongue testing the air? His jute-coloured skin
is lifeless compared to Buddha's luxurious mackerel fur – striped bold,
black and silver. At least the crude dreadlocks budding from Lionel's
scalp make him look more animated. Lilith will be impressed.

Since his sister's been away he's been sleeping badly, though that's
nothing unusual. He's up half the night, every night, programming
Buddha, chewing qat. Sometimes he doesn't sleep at all. Life loses its
shape when Lilith's not around. These days, if it weren't for his job, he
probably wouldn't leave the flat at all. He wonders if he'd even bother
to wash. The dreadlocks mean Mr Barber doesn't need to tend to his
hair as often, and Judy has cancelled their last three trips to the Yews.
David is too fragile for visitors, she says.

But the Buddha Project is almost finished. He's worked through the
avatar's physical interactions with buildings and objects, modified the

semantic cause-effect routines to refine Buddha's reactions to other characters in *CoreQuest*; a hundred and sixty, multi-layered response scenarios – fight, flight, hunt, clean, stretch, jump, run, purr – the list goes on. He has even given Buddha a clever, cattish grin, and posted the base code to the *CoreQuest* technical forum in a thread titled 'Digital Evolution' along with all his sketches. It's risky to boast since hacking the servers is an offence, but he cloaks his ID whenever he posts. Once the tests are finished and the file debugged he'll upload Buddha to the new dimension and the cat's reincarnation will be complete before schedule. But he needs to make sure he's alert before starting the upload – especially since Ludi's transfer to *CoreQuest* was so fraught and long-winded.

Sleep first, he thinks, rest my overworked brain – and he carries Buddha into the bedroom, whispering in his ear. 'You'll have another life,' he says, enjoying the cat's warm smell. 'A life so much better than this one, old boy.'

Once he's in bed Lionel still can't drop off. Jaw clenched, fists opening and closing, his brain's doing overtime. He's aware of each minute sensation – the rise and fall of his chest, his weight against the mattress, the brush of the sheet on his skin – and although his body is heavy, his mind flits and flies, crazy as a burning flea. Perhaps he's addicted to qat – he's thought about it several times recently, especially since Saeed often gives him more than he pays for. But then unsold leaves are good for nothing but compost.

'Take, take another,' the Yemeni says when Lionel hands him a note. 'Go on, take two bunch. This one is in with the rent.'

And he does 'take'. He'll get through a bunch without noticing, riding the buzz of it all through the night – cheeks packed with leaves like a greedy hamster.

Lionel pads back through to the living room and plays *CoreQuest*, unblinking, hoping the game will make him drowsy. But instead of fatigue he feels feverish. The room is alive. Things throb at the periphery of his vision. He blinks, trying to readjust his sightline as the walls pulsate.

'Got to get out of here,' he says. His voice is a loose bolt, rattling round his skull.

The room, the whole flat, contracts like a womb and delivers him onto the pavement as blood churns through the ventricles of his heart.

Nervously, he lights a cigarette and stands in his doorway on Milk Street studying the night sky, wondering if blood, like the ocean, is subject to the moon's gravitational pull.

Youths, crude with hormones, goad the street women with obscene banter. The women yawn theatrically, but – with an eye on future custom – they blow them worn-out kisses before sloping inside the all-night café for a warm drink. Lionel cranes forward to get a better view. Perhaps the anime girl is in the café sipping frothy coffee, eating fairy cake. He walks past the posturing youths and stops at the window.

A stocky Asian lad strolls up, thumbs in his belt-loops, and nudges Lionel with his shoulder. 'Checkin' out the goods eh, bruv?'

'No, I . . .' He steps back.

'No? What, you a homo or somefing?'

'I, I . . .'

'Ai, ai,' mocks the youth, making spastic gestures with his hands.

Lionel notices the stains on the youth's trousers, threadbare knees, half-moons of dirt under his fingernails. He's poor – this lad – poor and posing as something else, but for what? For him, for the cameras, for his mates?

The youth calls after Lionel as he retreats. 'Hey, come back, blood, we can get you a discount, innit.' The lads laugh as a pack, flick their wrists and snap their fingers – the way Mr Barber does when he makes a point, or wins at dominoes.

There's a footbridge that crosses the river to northtown and Lionel walks a kilometre, along streets lined with identical terraces, before coming to the commercial district where several nightclubs leak a *whumping* bass-beat on a back street off the main drag. It's seedy, badly lit, behind the fast food outlets and a late-night supermarket, where the odour of a dozen industrial bins mingles with the smell of fried onions, alcohol and piss.

Here it is. EVOLUTION: the name is spelled out in white letters above the door. This is the club Lilith advertised on SocialNet. After a cursory pat down, the bouncers let him through the barriers. Inside, the atmosphere has reached a point of drug-fuelled fluidity. People are pouring onto the dance floor, uninhibited, arms raised high. Lionel puts his hands in his pockets and makes for the bar wondering what the anime girl is doing right now. *Does she let anyone touch her? Does she have a choice?* He doesn't want to think about it, but he can't get her out of his mind.

There, across the room, right there, sitting at a table, deep in conversation, is Lilith. Lionel stops and dodges back and forth to get a direct view through the crowd. Yes, it's definitely Lilith, with her hair piled into a bun and metallic thread woven through it. On either side of her face sleek lengths of hair extend to her shoulders. The blue-violet sparkle of her sequinned dress competes with the dazzle of her earrings. A metallic bag is balanced on her knees. My God, he thinks, she's radiant. Glinting all over. He's never seen her so dressed up and glamorous.

He's brimming with excitement. 'Lilith. Hey, Lil.' Lilith is back. She must have decided to come back at the last minute – thank God. He can't wait to be near her. 'Lilith, hey sis, over here.'

Lionel pushes through the crowd towards her, both hands raised now, waving to attract her attention. Halfway across the dance floor a skinny blonde in a strapless top blocks his way. 'Woah, slow down,' says the woman, pushing her chin at him, hand on hip. 'You've got some balls coming back in here after last time.'

'Sorry?'

The woman is a rough, boozy type, but her reproach shifts seamlessly to allure.

'Still, I've always liked a man with balls.' She steps closer, reaching for a button on his shirt. 'Dance with me. Come on. No point pretending you're shy – not with me.' She gives him a brassy wink.

Balls. What? She's drunk. She's mistaken him for someone else.

'I-I'm just going over there.' He points to where Lilith is sitting, although he's lost sight of her for a moment. The place is packed.

'You're not going anywhere. I've got you cornered.'

The woman mirrors Lionel's movements each time he tries to go around her, so that she is perpetually in his way. Across the dance floor, Lilith laughs at something someone has said. She's so carefree and beautiful. Lionel is surprised how much his sister's happiness affects him.

'Lil,' he calls over the top of the woman's head.

'I won't take no for an answer,' insists the blonde. She minces closer, shaking her breasts. 'You didn't turn these down last time.'

Distracted by the woman's efforts, he takes his eyes off Lilith and when he looks for her again she's been swallowed in a pother of cardice and laserlight. But her bag is on the table and the group she was with is still there, huddled, chatting, so he capitulates and starts to dance with the blonde, who punches the air with a whoop before shimmying backwards, winking at him again and licking her lips.

'Drink,' he shouts, when the track eventually segues into another.

The woman does a twirl and yells, 'Vodka, Power Kick.' But as he edges away she wags her finger. 'Don't you disappear on me, my little coffee bean. I'll come and find you.'

Even though Lionel is shouting, trying to be heard above the din, the people at Lilith's table ignore him.

'The woman who was here, in the sequinned dress,' he explains. 'She's my sister.'

One man yawns and examines his fingernails while the other two sip their drinks and stare at the dancers.

'She was with you, at this table. Her bag was just here.' He makes the shape of the bag with his hands. 'Did you see where she went?'

The largest of the men (Lionel is suddenly aware they are all men) has an eye-patch and a shiny, shaved head with a thick roll of flesh at the base of his skull. The man mops his head with a tissue. He's mixed-race – Asian, with something else – and he's fat. A huge belly rests on his thighs. He expectorates and openly spits.

The music pitches up a register and Lionel raises his voice. 'It's just that she was here, right here.' He points at the floor. 'Like, a minute ago.'

The men stare right through him, but Lionel stays near their table and scans the club for Lilith. He has a mind to shake these rude characters. What kind of person ignores someone so roundly? The best-dressed of the men gets up slowly. He's short compared to Lionel, and impeccably groomed. Tapered trousers with a high, reflective shine, black shoes with pointed toes – capped with purplish snakeskin – and a velvet jacket, voluminous and dandyish. He appears to glide to the bar without walking. The two remaining men give Lionel the henchman's once-over.

The one with the eye-patch says, 'You best fuck off, cos H there' – he nods to the man at the bar – 'don't appreciate pasty groids like you hanging round on his night off. Get it?' His accent sits somewhere between Shanghai and South London.

Lionel pretends not to hear. He pings the location app on his mobile – Lilith's definitely here.

The one-eyed man stands suddenly. He's immense, and his voice cuts through the noise of the club, clean as a cheese wire. 'You not hear me, freaky groid boy?'

Lionel feels a hot prickle of fear and he nods quickly and moves away. There's something uncomfortably familiar about the well-dressed man and his chunky friend, although he can't put them in context. And he can't think why Lilith would want to hang out with them. Needing to piss, he casts a quick, backward glance at the men as he goes off in search of the toilet.

There's a deep colonic smell mixed with the hedonic spritz of recreational chemicals. A guy with a mohawk and digital monocle sways in front of the urinal. Lionel takes a cubicle. He watches the jet of his piss as it makes foam in the bowl and for some reason he giggles – perhaps there's something in the air. He throws his head back, laughs louder. The beautiful anime girl, the persistent blonde on the dance floor, the cyberpunk at the urinal, the threatening men at the table, even Lilith randomly appearing then disappearing – they're all faintly ridiculous, as if someone's made them all up, tonight, especially for him to interact with. And here he is in this cubicle, pissing, with the sound of a bass-beat bareknuckling his chest from inside. If he didn't know better he'd think someone was inside him, hammering to get out.

'Who? Who is it in there? Heh?' he asks as he zips his fly.

Shouldering out of the cubicle Lionel imagines he's the avatar in someone else's game and wonders what they'll do with him next.

Lionel is aware of the shape beside him, as a person is aware of all danger with hindsight. But he chooses to ignore it for the split second that the choice remains, until several men set upon him. He didn't hear them come in; they must have been waiting outside the stall, signalling to one another like soldiers on urban manoeuvres. They grab his shoulders and push his face to the wall, precisely where someone has drawn a graphic cock and big hairy balls, in marker pen. He closes his eyes and submits as the men call him names. They shout as they frisk him.

'Got any weapons eh, boy? Got any drugs?'

Their accents are unplaceable. One of them takes his Google device. They must be police, he thinks, and he manages to say, 'No, officer.'

'Oh *officer*,' says another, putting on a posh, camp voice.

Then he blurts that he's not a terrorist or a drug dealer, or anything, he's 'mixed-race, nothing more' and that he doesn't want to 'hurt a soul'. He's not sure if they've understood him; his mouth is contorted from the force of them squashing his face to the wall. But after he's said it he realizes that what he *is* and what he *wants* are probably irrelevant, although he still feels the urge to explain that he was adopted, raised by white people – a lay preacher and his wife.

Instead he says, 'It's okay, really, I'm the same as you.'

A mistake. The mood changes. At least one of the men is enraged and strikes him on the head, hard enough to make him realize the situation is getting out of hand.

'Stop! Please!'

He *is* the same as they are, isn't he? Isn't everyone the same underneath? But the men are pressing too hard between his shoulder blades and he can't breathe. One of them pushes his hand into Lionel's trousers. *Not police?* The hand feels huge and indiscriminate.

A man says, 'Hold him,' in a commanding voice, and he resists as best he can, but the hand edges further into the privacy of his underpants, snagging on his pubic hair, past his shrivelling penis until it finds his balls. *You've got some balls coming in here.* The hand becomes a warm, ball-filled fist.

He manages to say, 'No. Please,' before someone unbuckles his belt and pulls his clothes past his buttocks.

'Please.'

He's crying dry tears as his neck is pushed down and he's wrenched back at the hips, bent forwards, exposed.

'Keep. Fucking. Still.' This voice is more familiar – Hong Kong South London.

The hand at his genitals shifts and his buttocks are pulled apart. He can't stop them.

Someone laughs and says something in Chinese.

Another says, 'Look, man, he got a boner.'

How did that happen? Please.

'Go on, give it to him.'

No. Please.

There is a feeble eructation of laughter. 'Oh, man, put it away, don't be rank.'

He can't see what they're doing – he's not in on the joke – although he can feel the man directly behind him preparing for action.

'You're not. Seriously. Aw, man.'

This was not planned.

'Why the fuck not.'

This is ad hoc. This is unscripted.

Deliberate fingers twist the flesh of his buttocks; naked thrusts slam his face to the wall. It goes on for so long. Synchronized. An invasion. Into his territory. In time with the penetrating beat of the drum and the bass in the club – onetwothreefour-fivesixseveneight-onetwothreefour-fivesixseveneight – and again. Finally, an angry biting grunt, a moment's hiatus, until the anonymous hand envelops his genitals once more and twists his scrotum with such force that he imagines ripe fruit bursting open, spilling its slimy seeds. He screams. A reflex. He's ashamed by his own hysteria.

Please!

Someone sniggers, unsure. They're just naughty boys, aren't they? Aren't they? He's manhandled to the floor. Hands quickly tighten across his windpipe. Choking. Another man clasps his wrists. He can't break free, he can't do anything but endure the humiliation, until at the last moment there's a blow to the back of his head, his neck jars and with a final shove he can taste the bitterness in his blood.

A mouth moves very close to his ear and he shrinks from the warmth of the man's breath.

'You got some gall, you fucker. We don't want you in here,' says the man. 'D'you get it? Don't come back or you dead.'

He can't answer, but he nods and lies very still. They are whispering; they are in a hurry; they are tripping over one another as they exit the toilets and they're laughing. *It's only a game.*

Pain. A living thing, a rat or a parasite, is gnawing away, feeding on his prostate and his balls. He pulls his knees to his chest and whimpers. No one comes in. It's several minutes before he can get up, which he does in stages, hands and knees, then up on one knee holding the wall, then upright bending forward trying not to vomit. His trousers are soaked with piss from the floor, but he gathers them round his waist and buckles his belt, then flushes his face with cold water from the tap. He gags into the sink but nothing comes up. The Google device is on the floor of one of the cubicles and he remembers Lilith, but can't bring himself to call her. What if they come back? What if Lilith is in danger? The sound of his own gutless breathing drowns out the music as he re-enters the club.

Hard, mechanical strobes slow everything down to a series of malign snapshots and the dancers are caught wearing death masks with painted, rictus mouths. He clings to the wall, saying, 'C'mon, Lionel, get out of here.' *Please*. No longer hoping that Lilith will appear from the crowd, he berates himself for being spineless, but he hasn't seen the men's faces, he couldn't swear his attackers were the men he accosted at the table – but then, who else could they be? He makes his way to the exit and trips onto the street. People step away from him as if he's the pariah, corrupted, stinking of piss. He is the pariah.

There's a keen wind out sparring. It's coming from the north, harsh and pugnacious, as he limps towards the main drag. Pain, smart as a blade, is making his legs give way. One of the bouncers, bulldog of a man, has got the blonde against a lamppost. He's cupping one of her breasts in a detached way, and jawing something at her while she flops about, jointless as a ragdoll, and Lionel thinks, She's cornered now. The bouncer spots him and stretches his neck like a spectator at a hanging.

'Oi, screamer,' barks the man. 'You take care.'

Lionel hears the woman say, 'Hey, leave him alone, why don't you? That's Café Latte. He's a *proper* gent he is.'

The woman's name forms in his mind – Samantha. The wind sucker-punches him full in the face and he reels away into darkness. Nothing feels right. Nothing feels real.

It takes him an age to reach Milk Street, crawling part of the way along the unlit canal. He's covered in filth. Agony has mastered his body entirely. Stomach. Chest. Head. And somewhere deep – somewhere further in that he doesn't have a name for. He prowls the room in a pitch-black funk, kicking the furniture and beating the walls with his fists.

Later, when he's calm, he pours a neat whiskey and swallows it down. Pours another, and another. There's a lump on the back of his head big enough to fill the bowl of his hand. *Mixed-race, nothing more*. What a bullshit thing to say. *Please*. The room is in darkness except for a scuff of ambient light coming in from the street. But here's poor crippled Buddha, advancing towards him from the kitchen, surrounded by a fluorescent aura that crackles and fizzes at the end of his fur – as if the cat has been electrified in his absence. Lionel blinks fiercely.

'Don't bug me now, Buddha, not now.'

The cat lies at his feet – quietly sacrificial – and Lionel weeps.

Let the water assail you, until it runs cold, until your hands are pinked and wrinkled. Let the water blast the piss and the dirt from your skin. Let the darkness. What? Let the darkness . . . just let the darkness.

Later you lurk by the window, watchful but exhausted. The prostitutes are touting for tricks at the intersection and you look for the beautiful anime girl – you look for the connection. But she's not there. Is that her pimp in the shadows – yes, him – with the blue light from a Google device frisking his cheek with its ice-light? Perhaps she'll break into the flat while you're sleeping, whup your arse with her ninja moves, cut out your heart and eat it for tea. Blood turns black if it's left out too long in the air. Your mind's turning everything bad.

Your energy's sapped, used up on the journey from Evolution to Milk Street and you crawl to the sofa, ape-like, pre-human, and collapse in the cushions, sinking through folds and soft layers, until you reach a primeval end-point – in there, in your mind, where the darkness is palpable. Suddenly you're fighting, defending your throat. The darkness is really a man and the man has you – yes, he has you – and you're gasping and thrashing for air until, with great force, the blackness rips open. Scimitars are slashing through heavy, plush velvet, and blood sprays freely from above, and your mind is the dark and the stars in your mind are pinpricks of reason, turning crimson, one by one, until they are all winked out. Blank, black with spots of red. You're gone.

@GameAddict (#23756745): 09:6:27

In the grey world you'd rather die than hurt
anyone – let alone beat them to death. But you
get carried away on the Game Layer. You slash
your combatants to ribbons; disembowel them,
splat their melon heads and spill their brains
all over the floor. It's slapstick. Doesn't mean
anything. It feels good to take your rage out on
an avatar.

Level 6: Fight with a Cyclops

It's piss-dull scribing fight scenes. They're better off captured and played back on the digiline. But for the benefit of warrior geeks and juice-lusters I'll sketch it here swift-wise. Remember, I was new to the Realm – no weapons accrued – and I'd lost my scimitar as I came through the Wormhole.

My Visor blipped *red alert* after the boulder had floored us. Advancing our way, with thunderous *booms* making the earth quake with each footstep – a Cyclops. Bald, corpulent specimen with rolls of brown flab on his belly and neck, and using the thigh bone of some giant beast as a club.

I took two nervy steps back. 'That thing's enormous. Weapons or skills would be welcome.'

Mata Angelica fumbled about and found me a pulsar. 'Will that do?'

I didn't answer, but toggled my Visor to seek-and-destroy and measured its range by firing two beams off. One fell short, but the other scooped a raw chunk from the Cyclops's shoulder. His chest ran scarlet with gore. Rather than retreat he came more gutsy – tho I sensed this was simple belligerence. Nothing strategic. I leaped forward in one grunt-thrust and came down, battering his nog with the edge of my fist. But the Cyclops was tough. Grabbed my scruff with one meaty paw and launched me sky-wise. Landed flat on my back some distance away with a *thwump*.

Mata Angelica stepped up next, both eyes fixed on his bonce. But before she could attack he swung round with his club and she flew twenty-five paces into the dust. Without missing a beat he came straight for me (I was only just getting my wind back). He was bellowing – cold kamikaze – any ego he had now lost in the fray, but he'd not counted on Mata Angelica bouncing up, all nymph-gone-horrific and screaming with rage. She pulled a sword (from where I don't know, tho I suspected a Cheat) and took a slice off his neck just as he managed to frisk me.

When an enemy's innard-juice is on you – slicing your hair, trickling into your mouthparts – the metallic lick of it peps you up drug-wise and I was pumped and hungry for more. Fortunate for me, the Cyclops was beckoning, bashing the earth with his bony old club and ready to fight to the death.

'Attack him each side,' I called, zipping off to the left.

'I'm running on empty. Can you take him alone?'

I grinned. Enjoying the fight. Now it was just me against the Cyclops. Big fella was bald as a melon except for the horn that stuck out of his head and I wanted that growth for a trophy. I won't say the combat was easy. Big'uns like a Cyclops take some work – have to pick out their weak spot and smack it till it tires 'em. It was dusk by the time he eventually fell. The shock as he died gave his one bulbous eye a brief twinkle that dulled as he snouted the sand.

After he'd toppled, Mata Angelica limped over to join me and we sat on his rump and shared a good flask of Grog saying 'cheers' and 'your health' as if we were battle-scarred muckers from time.

'You fought bravely,' I said, wiping drink from my chin.

'You too, He-Man.' She grinned. 'Cyclops are notorious strong.' She patted the dead monster's hindquarters.

'It felt good to be fighting again.'

'Trouble is,' her voice came doom-laden, 'why would a Cyclops waste time on a low-level skirmish?'

'Low-level!' I feigned offence. 'I'm a fabled warrior.'

'You've proved it.' She smiled.

I kneeled down to inspect her injury – a small flesh wound on her thigh.

'Bastard caught me off guard,' she said, watching my ministrations astutely.

'Not deep, tho. You'll not be seeing the Void.'

She stroked my cheek as I kneeled there. 'Take off your Visor.' Brazen creature had instantly come the seductress. 'I want to look at you.'

'I can't take it off. It's integral.'

'I don't think so, Ludi.'

But tho she fumbled for a button or a catch she couldn't get my Visor to budge and she was sore disappointed.

We found the nag-prancers in the moonlight and rode back to the hostelry, taking our time. I could see the sky westward rendered black through to purple. A comet rocketed over us. Its tail made fizz-swishing swirls in the Realm's magnetism, reflecting paisley on Mata Angelica's skin. I told her she was beautiful and my praise gave her a fillip. She dug her heels in the flanks of her prancer and raced into the cosmic display at a gallop. I followed eagerly after.

At the hostelry the Grinders were already in sleep-mode. I bedded down in the stables and drifted on snooze till Mata Angelica joined me. Scrubbed up and fresh with her nut-coloured flesh-gifts wrapped in a woollen shawl I discerned she was wont to be calculating. Nevertheless, she spoke cosy words to me. Said she trusted me. Said it had taken this while to be sure. But now it was time for some truth.

Last moon-cycle a character wandered into the Ghetto. An OtherWorld Sylph, corrupted, not fully rendered. Gone mad in the nog.

'Scrambled on entry?'

'Perhaps, tho she couldn't speak or say where she'd come from. She spent her days crooning a soft *tra-la-la* about love. Off with the fairies.'

'How sad.'

'Yes. But I believe this character is very important.'

'Why do you say that?'

'Boss agents came searching for her. Ransacked the Ghetto. They don't do that for any old avatar. But she vanished, *pouff*, before they could find her.'

'Where did she go?'

'Don't know. But the Sylph must be an asset. A weapon or a Cheat.' Mata Angelica touched my knee. 'You're sure you didn't bring any such items with you?'

'I'm sure.'

'Not an amulet or a screed?'

'I told you. Nothing.'

She was crestfallen and I was tempted to mention the Key that Scumscratch'd filched from me, but in truth I was ashamed to have let him snaffle it so easily. 'What's the significance of these assets?'

The Eroticon soft-stroked her throat. 'Every dimension works on two levels. There's all of this.' She lassoed the air with a digit to signify the Realm and everything in it. 'And then there's the Quest.'

I felt a part of my programme kick in. 'A Quest?'

She studied her nails. 'Yes. A journey.'

'Where to? What's the aim?'

'To the Core. To find the Big Boss.'

I rubbed my mitts. 'How exciting. The Final Level, yes?'

Mata Angelica clocked I was thrilled and went on in whisper-words. 'Destroy the Big Boss and the Realm is restored. The oceans will fill. The forests will grow. The Bosses are our enemies. They ravaged this place and turned the land to a dust bowl. We must strike at the heart of evil. Set things right.' She listed more benefits on her digits. 'No more profligate characters, no more grinding or slave tribes. Default mode – everything equal.' Her eye-gems were vivid and I believed her.

'I thought only Grinders could enter the Core.'

'Yes. But a He-Man could do it if he has the right Keys.'

'What if you're wrong?'

'There's a chance,' she said, shrugging. 'But I'm not wrong. You mark me.'

Mata Angelica's animation sent the shawl *oops-slip*, exposing her ebony limbs. The marvellous creature was luring me. If she was right the Realm could become our dominion. The tribes with their armies of Grinders would reset to zero and immigrants, like us, could wrest all their power. On cue, the shawl fell right off and her abundant flesh-gifts lay bare. She was offering a bargain – her and a slice of the power in exchange for my sword arm.

One of the nag-prancers puff-snorted, turned in its stall and showed us its arse. Tension broke and we laughed. Our approval meters both hit 100 and soon we were kissing. Tender, long-lingering, juicy. Her arms canopied my nog as my lips traced routes along her clavicles and into her underarm fur pits. She sighed – musk 'n' muscle, damp in the lamplight.

But even as we made lust in the hay, I backtracked over her story. 'You didn't finish your telling about the Sylph.'

Breathing hot on my neck she said, 'The Sylph? Yes, she was rare, very rare.'

Her mouth besieged mine tho I managed to say, 'But why mention her?'

'She's a Key, Ludi. We must get her back.'

'How do you know she's a Key?'

Mata Angelica huffed and sat up. 'Because her *tra-la-la* went like this: *Ludi, Ludi my love, I'm your Key, oh Ludi my love.* You see, she knew your name and said she was a Key. Now, no more questions.'

The Eroticon's body flowed over mine – silky and keen – but tho I spoke no more on it, thoughts of the Sylph and her prior knowledge of me were an impediment to my bliss. I sensed I was part of a shady scheme, but the thought of a Quest was too tempting. I set my Visor to sense-mode and tried to give in to the delicious thrust of it all and presently the expert and patient Mata Angelica made me forget my misgivings.

A Walk in the Park

Vivaldi whirrs, annoying as bluebottle on a window. It's Lilith. She's trying to come through on his Google device, but he's not fully conscious and the ringtone brings him round slowly. Lionel's eyelids flicker, heavy, then lighter, until he's looking at the wall. Then lighter still. He's in the room. Yes. He's alive, in his flat. Vivaldi stops. Lilith is being transferred to voicemail. *The person you are trying to reach is unavailable.* Light bleaches the room. He's been asleep for hours. It's weeks since he slept so long.

In the kitchen he fixes coffee like a drone and connects to the service centre at Meddingley. After navigating a maze of nested options he finally accesses the automated Human Resource centre.

'Please state your employee number.'

'311457E,' he says blankly.

'What is the nature of your call?'

'I'm sick,' he says. Lionel has never been off sick from work before.

The computer-generated voice is female and faintly aggressive. 'Please supply your medical reference number. Without a medical reference number you can reconnect later or take annual leave. Please make your choice.'

He hesitates, winces with shame as he clenches his buttocks. 'Annual leave.'

'I'm sorry I didn't quite catch that.'

'Annual leave.' He enunciates the words clearly into the mouthpiece.

'That's annual leave. You have six days remaining. Your timesheet will be amended accordingly. Thank you.'

'What do you mean –' he begins, but the Resource has disconnected.

He hasn't taken any leave this year. How can there be only six days remaining? He raps the top of his skull with his knuckles and sits at his desk. Maybe he'll call back. At least when he was talking to the Resource he wasn't thinking. He wasn't being sucked back to the club, to the toilets, to the cold white tiles and the cock and big hairy balls on the wall, against the wall, so graphic. So terribly graphic.

Lilith. Dear Lilith. He looks at his mobile screen. *The person you are trying to reach is unavailable.* She has left a video message and he plays it back as he takes sour sips of coffee.

'It's me. I'm back,' she says and pokes her tongue out, acting kooky for the camera – for him. Then she pulls her serious face. 'Look, I'm worried about you. You pinged me last night, right? Anyway, call me back. We need to talk about Judy. *I* need to talk about Judy. Yeah, I know it's a drag.'

She doesn't sign off straight away; she touches her mouth lightly and sighs. Brave Lilith. Her hair is loose today, unkempt, not up in the bun like last night. She's always worn it long and now it falls over one shoulder, in silky coils, past her well-defined collarbone. The muscles stand proud in her forearms – the result of all the exercise she takes: tae kwon do, karate. There's always some martial art class she's attending. Her barefoot anarchy requires discipline. Lilith looks into the camera – not so much beautiful as intriguing. Unreadable.

'I've missed you,' she says and, being Lilith, she makes it sound as if it's him that's been remiss, rather than her that's been gallivanting. 'Anyway,' she sniffs. 'Call me, damn you. You're never there when I call.'

The screen goes blank.

For once, he's not certain if he cares whether Lilith is back – just the thought of her makes him slog back over the events of the previous night. The humiliation of it feels like a thing – a huge *thing* in his bowels. He checks the mirror to see if the event is evinced in his features. It must have altered him visually. But he looks the same, except for some dull marks on his neck and his cheek. The main, visible injury is around his left eye. He can't remember being hit there and the skin isn't broken, but a fat leech of a bruise has filled up on his eyelid. His balls ache, deep in his groin, and he discerns a more complex wound further up, close to his heart, but he turns his mind from it, even though the attack has opened a vent to some unformed memory. *It's only a game.* Don't think about it. Don't think about any of it, he tells himself.

Toast. Food. It makes him feel more present and his eyes sweep wearily over the room as he chews. Across from the desk, behind the sofa, he can see the tip of Buddha's tail. Judy gave him that sofa when he moved into Milk Street. She would never give him money – he'd had enough credit from David, she was clear on that. But the sofa was unexpected – big and homely, from a good store. Lionel was delighted. He discovered later that it had been bought for Ben, but his wife had hated it. And because it was a sale item Judy couldn't take it back and there was nowhere else for it to go. Still, he remains grateful for it.

'Buddha, hey Budds.' Lionel kisses the air noisily. With Buddha to hug he'll find some comfort.

But Buddha's tail doesn't move.

'Hey, big boy.'

Panic, a twinge of it, a missed heartbeat, and he's up on the sofa in a flash, hesitating for a second, then peering over the back, deflecting grim thoughts of the inevitable – Buddha. Dead. But, thank God, he's alive. He's stretched out with one paw extended towards a tiny bird. The bird is on its back with its head turned delicately to one side and its legs pointing upward – feet clawing the air.

Lionel cranes forward and inspects the creature more closely; its black beak is long and fluted, its plumage runs from green to cobalt. Its tail is an iridescent quill of violet and blue. At its throat a bib shimmers lapis. In profile, only its perfect round eye lacks lustre. Buddha tries to meow – victory and cunning coming together in his clouded old face.

'What have you got there, Budds? Did you do this?'

Lionel retrieves the bird. It is so light he can barely feel the sensation of it in his hands. It's not an indigenous bird, more like a bird of paradise in miniature. The tail feathers are twice the length of its body. He's never seen anything like it. Something about its livery makes him think of Lilith's glamorous outfit – her sequinned dress, the sheen of her metallic bag. The bird must have escaped from a zoo, or an aviary.

'Buddha, what have you done?'

Buddha exudes feline pride. There's not a mark on the bird, no roughing up of feathers, no tell-tale crimson spot. Lionel holds its wing-tips and pulls them apart to their full span, eight centimetres from tip to tip – the size of a hummingbird.

'You are spectacular,' he tells the bird, even though it's a lifeless specimen.

Lionel logs in, goes to Google search, and chooses natural history before typing the bird's description. There are fifty thousand results – images, videos, 3D flyrounds. None of the first hits are the same as the bird on his desk. He refines the search, placing emphasis on the unique tail feathers, scrolling through hummingbirds and birds of paradise, always refining the results with the advanced settings. Meanwhile, Buddha flops weakly at his ankles, purring in his broken way, begging for his prize. Finally Lionel finds it. It's a Sylph. A Violet-tailed Sylph. Amazing. It seems hardly possible that something so small and perfect could exist. Lionel sniffs the bird – it smells of heat and dust. Then, uncertain what he should do with it, he seals it in a plastic bag and puts it in the freezer compartment of the fridge.

Buddha isn't capable of catching birds; the cat has never left the flat. The bird must have flown in and died. That's it. It came in through the window, flew at the mirror thinking it was a way out, cracked its head and fell. All Buddha had to do was lay his paw on it – an accidental conqueror – in the right place at the right time. He's sure it must have happened this way, but when he checks the windows they're all closed. A mystery. Now the bird is stiffening in the ice compartment. Lionel imagines a drop of blood, crystallizing inside its fragile heart.

Colossal shadows, cast by low clouds, are moving along Milk Street, as if a malign legion is gathering overhead, but whenever Lionel looks up the sky is sheer and blue and he thinks the shadows must be birds or planes passing across the face of the sun. Eventually he returns Lilith's call.

'You sound awful,' she says.

'I'm not well.'

'Oh dear. Is that why you called?'

'You left me a message. Remember? You said you wanted to see me.'

'I'll meet you in the park if you like. I'm in town. Your place is too depressing. I don't know how you live in that fucking dump.'

'But you always say how much you like it.'

'Well, being away has made me realize how miserable it is.'

'Right.' He pauses. 'But I'm not well enough to come out.'

'You need fresh air, Lionel. Riverside café. One o'clock. I'll buy you lunch.'

'I don't know, I'm really not –'

'For fuck's sake, Lionel, stop whining. You're alive, aren't you?'

Prim borders, regimented beds and some tight-laced topiary constrain the park's wilful nature. Attempts to tame the river have been less successful, but some shoring up of the banks is underway near the gatehouse. The area is prone to flooding. The river is particularly sullen today, faithlessly reflecting the May sky and shuttling dead wood from shore to shore. Lionel arrives before Lilith and takes a table in the café overlooking the water.

The café's windows – designed to slide back onto a wooden platform that overhangs the river – are closed. Showers are intermittent and only the Canada geese circuit the decking, leaving daubs of shit behind them as they go. From where Lionel is sitting there's a clear view past the fountains and the war memorial to the ornamental gates that mark the entrance to the park. Cameras, *for your safety*, survey people as they swan in and out.

Here's Lilith. He spots her as soon as she comes through the gates. She's wearing an old jumper and a skirt that billows up with each stride. She slouches past a line of tall trees – tips dervishing above her – as she talks on her Google device. At the monument she stops and shouts at the screen, then slings the phone in her bag. She's livid. *Still in her bleak phase*. Lilith catches sight of him as she ascends the steps to the café and her brief smile still bears the stain of whatever has made her angry.

'I'm late,' she says, but she's unapologetic.

Hair gripped loosely by a silver clasp, varnish peeling off her nails – Lilith is a study in dishevelment. How can the shining princess in the club have become this mess overnight? She's in a bad way, he can tell.

Lilith sits, pulls her chair in sharply and gives him her full attention. 'You've been in a fight.'

'I was attacked.'

'When? Where? Let me see that. God, you look awful.' She holds his chin and turns his head to get a better view of his wounds.

'Last night. It was my fault. That hurts by the way.'

'Were you drunk?'

'No. I don't know. It doesn't matter. Careful, Lil, don't touch. Don't make a fuss.'

'Who was it? Who did this?'

He wants to say, your friends did this – the people you were larking about with – they came and defiled me in the toilets of your favourite club. But he can't say it; he can barely think it. 'It's nothing.'

She takes his hand in both of hers. 'It doesn't look like nothing. Why didn't you say on the phone? I'd've come to yours if you'd said.'

'I tried to say. Anyway, I'm fine.'

She strokes his fingers, slowly, thoughtfully, down to each slim, lozenge-shaped nail, inspecting the white half-moons rising at the cuticles. 'When I was little, I thought . . .' She stops, thinks better of speaking. 'No.'

'Go on, tell me. What did you think?'

'I thought you were . . .' She closes her eyes. 'So very brave. And you still are.'

Before he can say anything the waiter approaches, pencil poised. Lilith asks for coffee, black. Lionel plumps for a latte, but quickly changes his mind. Cappuccino. They will order food later, he tells the waiter, who looks confounded until Lilith shoos him off.

'Bloody service is awful in here,' she says. 'It's shit everywhere these days.'

'People do their best,' he says.

'You're too soft,' she says, examining her own hands now. 'It's not supposed to be this complex, is it?'

'What?'

'Life.' She looks up. 'God, Lionel, that shiner is fucking epic. Did you go to the police? Have you put anything on it?'

'No . . . and no.' He wants her to carry on thinking he's brave – her esteem shores him up. 'Please. You said you wanted to talk about Judy.'

A crack of thunder makes them look up. The rain begins. Lilith grimaces before delicately removing some grit from the corner of each eye with her ring finger. 'Ben and James don't return my calls. Why should they? I hate them and they hate me. But they don't call Judy either. Not since Dad went in the funny farm. I mean, I think they message her now and again but . . .' She sighs. 'And Dad, well, he's all finished. Argh – I need a cigarette.'

'David will be fine.'

'Stop it, Lionel. He's dying. God, you must see that.'

He bows his head.

The grit has made her eyes water and she dabs at her cheeks with a napkin. 'It's like . . . everything's finally coming to a head, you know?'

He nods. He has a sense of what she means.

'I was thinking about when we were kids.' She laughs mirthlessly. 'She was always so ashamed of you.'

'Who?'

'Mum, who else? It would have been better if you were black, you know, I mean *really* black. At least people would've realized you were adopted. But they thought you were hers. Two rinky white boys, a brown one in the middle, then me. Well, it looked bad, didn't it? It looked like she'd been playing dirty little games on the sly. Hah! People talked and she heard them. It's hilarious really, or it would be if her shame hadn't rubbed off on our dear brothers.' Lilith grits her teeth. 'I wish *she* was dying. At least Dad wasn't ashamed. But he could never stand up to her. Never.'

'I didn't know she was ashamed of me. I just thought she couldn't cope.'

Lilith breathes in through her teeth. 'Well, there it is; she's a coward, a nasty piece of work – and I don't want any responsibility for her, do you understand? I can't handle it.'

The waiter returns, serves their coffees and Lionel watches the weltering river. Powerful currents have swamped a colourful soda bottle and carried it off in the surge. It's being buffeted. Dragged under. But every time the river pulls it down, the soda bottle pops back up. There it is now, by the weir. Incredible how a bit of discarded plastic can defeat the strong brown god of the river.

'I can't bear it,' Lilith continues when the waiter has gone. 'When *he's* dead I don't want any of it. I'm finished with the whole family thing.'

Lionel turns to her, glad he has some good news. 'It's okay, Lil, Judy told me. She said she's going to move away if David dies. She's planning to move up north, to be nearer Ben.'

'It's bullshit, Lionel.' Lilith dismisses his news with a tight shake of her head. 'She's making it up. Ben doesn't talk to her if he can help it. James is a cock. I'll be the one she turns to.' She takes a deep breath. 'She won't bother you, though; she's made that bloody clear to everyone. What were they thinking, adopting you, taking you away from your country, your culture?'

He lowers his eyes.

Lilith reaches for his arm. 'I'm glad they did, though – for my sake. I don't have to say it, do I?'

'No, you don't have to say it.'

'But they didn't love you, and it was wrong.'

A group of people has gathered on the opposite river bank. They are pointing to a lump of wood as big as a tree trunk, that's got caught in the weeds a few metres from shore.

'We could go to Kenya together,' Lilith says. 'Find your parents.'

'I'm an orphan, remember.'

'I wouldn't believe a word they've told you. You're a prince.'

'Lil –'

'You are; I know it.' She looks to the ceiling, searching for threads to embroider her fantasy. 'You're the illegitimate son of an African princess, who slept with a dashing diplomat, or a spy.'

'Lilith, stop.'

'What? It could be true.'

The sound of a drone or a helicopter distracts them for a second before Lionel says, 'Lilith, listen to me, I need to ask you a question.'

'A question, that's not like *you*, brother dear.'

'Last night . . . I saw you, at least I thought it was you, in the club where this happened.' He points to his face. 'Evolution.'

She shakes her head. 'Not me. I was sparked out by eight.'

Lionel rubs his chin. 'It looked like you.'

'I've upset you,' she says, touching his hand.

'No.'

'You're always agitated when we talk about Kenya. You go all weird and paranoid.'

'No, I don't.'

'Yes, you do. You're afraid. You're afraid of everything; finding out who you are, or . . . or having real friends that aren't *me*.'

'I only asked if you were out last night. I could see you were there from the GPS app.'

Lilith bridles, leans away from him, pulls her hair with both hands. 'Jesus, admit it, Lionel. You spend so much energy running away from yourself – all the games and the fantasies, your obsession with me. I can't move without you wanting to know where I am, messaging every five minutes. Checking my location on your bloody *apps*! You'd even hack my fucking mail if you could. Do you? Do you hack my mail?'

He's annoyed with himself for not seeing the outburst coming. 'Don't be silly. I only asked about –'

'You're intolerable. I'm losing the will to exist.'

'Honestly, Lil, you're being unfair. Hysterical.'

Lilith isn't listening. 'Everyone would be happier if I disappeared anyway.'

'Now you're not making sense. First you can't move, now nobody cares.'

'Judy craps on all the time, *my* Ben, *my* James, when she's spoiled them to the point of wickedness. And they hate her for it, too. Stupid cunt of a woman.' Tears are welling up. 'And now you accuse me of being . . . I don't know what? Jesus, Lionel. Do you understand for a second what a responsibility you are?'

Lionel decides to sit quietly and wait. But Lilith has that unhinged look that presages a full-blown convulsion. Her voice is gaining power. A couple of customers are eyeing them nervously and the waiter is having a confabulation with the doorman. None of them know, of course, that Lilith will pull herself together – eventually. Lionel sips his cappuccino, but inside he's fuming. The pain he's in, the wounds she inflicts – he loves her insanely, but when she's in a bleak phase she can be so irrational. It's all he can do to hold back from shaking her.

The café fills up as the rain comes down. People blow in, shaking water off their coats and hair, some of them are laughing as if it's romantic or funny to get caught in a downpour. They all point at the crowd gathering on the opposite bank. Gradually Lilith quietens.

Long moments fall away until finally Lionel puts his head on one side. 'You okay?'

'Uh huh.' Lilith's contrition comes less easily than her anger.

'Was it that bad, our childhood? I mean, compared to other people.' He gestures towards a couple at another table.

'It was shit, Lionel. I think you don't remember because it was so bad. But then you always accepted it all. You were placid.' She can't look at him. 'You were lovely.'

He scratches his head, trawling the files in his mind, the snapshots and movies, the moments, the echoes. There's Lilith the child, walking through buttercups, sun bleaching the green of the meadow. And there, David preaching, shaking his hand heavenward, or shaking the hands of the congregation, or shaking the boughs of the Bramley to make it drop a cooker or two for the crumble. Light falling at an angle through the upper windows of the Assembly Hall, Judy peeling onions – silently crying – Ben smelling sharp as fresh nettles, showing him a secret place, where a decomposing cat, eyes eaten out, is a thing of dreadful wonder. Mordecai? Surely not.

'I remember things, but none of them are joined up. None of it seems so bad.'

Lilith lets the corners of her mouth hang down. 'You've always been in a world of your own, Lionel. Even before that bump on your head.'

The skin covering the depression in his skull is soft to the touch; he presses it gently.

The decomposing cat had a maggot wriggling from its nostril – a tufted shroud of fur was loosening on its bones. He thinks of Buddha and feels a wave of anguish break over his heart.

He says, 'I only want good things for both of us. I didn't mean to upset you. I don't know what we're arguing about.'

Lilith puts the salt and pepper shakers and the sugar bowl in a precise line. 'We're not arguing, Lionel. It's me. I'm being horrid this time.' She stands. 'You really must put something on that eye.'

'I will.'

'I've got to go.'

'We haven't ordered anything.'

'I'm not hungry.'

He sighs. 'No, neither am I.'

Lilith's retreating figure looks almost mythical in the leftover storm. When she reaches the war memorial she turns to wave. The wind whips her hair up and for an instant she's a mad Medusa, mouthing farewell. He holds one hand high. After she's gone he considers the river's murky depths. What's the proverb? Time is like a river – you can't touch the same water twice. If Lilith's right about Judy then, he wonders, what has become of her shame? Rinsed away? Or are some stains too deeply ingrained?

A police team has floated a boom onto the river and two divers are preparing to enter the water. A wide area on the opposite bank has been cordoned off and idle onlookers stand on Lionel's side of the river.

'It's definitely a body,' says one man. 'I saw it. All bloated it was.' The man shivers. 'Look, there.'

'It's such a shame,' says a woman. 'Must've fallen in somewhere upstream and got washed down here. You'd think people'd learn to stand back from the edge.'

The man makes a sceptical face. 'Could've been pushed.'

The divers manoeuvre the waterlogged body towards the far bank and a gasp rises from the crowd as a swollen hand breaks the surface of the water. The police struggle to pull a body bag over the corpse. Lionel turns away as he glimpses a deathly face with an eye-patch and a fat roll of neck flesh.

@GameAddict (#23756745): 12:6:27

Who are you playing? That's the question. It
could be the King of England. It could be a
road sweeper from Tokyo. It could be a little
old lady on a bus in the Andes, tapping away
on her Google. It could be your boss or your
minion. It's democracy, that's what it is. You
might have had sex with the President, no less,
or with someone you're sitting next to on the
train. You could have shared victories, despair or
intimate moments and there you are scanning
your e-readers, trying not to make eye contact,
unaware that your avatars could be in love – or
close combat.

Level 7: An Anomaly Sneaks through the Wormhole

The Eroticon and I set forth from the hostelry after our night of carousing. The plan: return to Mata Angelica's dwell-place, stock up on essential supplies, and set off to find Keys and glory. The morning sun gilded our bodies as we eked out our flesh-scene on the palanquin, quite shameless. Poor Grinders that carried us didn't know where to look. Drawing close to Thrar, the clones took a detour. They'd spied troops up ahead and thought it expedient to slip off the road till they'd passed.

We eagled the troops as they quick-marched alongside us. The ranks were made up of Grinders and a number of Krin-Balwrin (big bears of tribesmen). At the rearguard were high-ranking Generals – Thrars and Vadarians. (Mata Angelica had never known them campaign side by side.) As they drew level to our hidy-place, they slowed. A teensy sorceress hovered beside them. She carried a wand and wore a head-to-toe cloak that hid her face-features.

A Thrar – top-brass – sporting rows of chest-medals and oversized epaulettes said, 'Mistress, our scouts have found fifty clones, decapitated,' and he made a fluent gesture across his neck.

The sorceress spoke coolly. 'It's definitely the work of a MauMau. The end times are near. Even *my* power is not equal.'

The group groaned in unison and held up their mitts. 'We must find the beaster and kill it,' they said. 'Or we're doomed.'

'I've despatched the Cyclops to eliminate it. I have high hopes of success.'

'Yes,' the Generals agreed. 'The Cyclops is our best hope.'

With that the troops trudged off distant and we clambered out of our nook.

'Seems you were right about the Cyclops,' I said. 'Do you think we should've told 'em I despatched him to the Void?'

Mata Angelica was roundly unnerved. 'Say nothing to anyone. And stay away from that sorceress – a Boss agent if ever I saw one. It's the MauMau that should worry us now.'

'What is a MauMau?'

'An anomaly. Very rare.'

'But why were the soldiers so shaken?'

'Nothing can match its ferocity. Even that sorceress has no power against it. No,' she said, shaking her nog, 'if a MauMau has snuck through the Wormhole it means a Creator wants to wreak havoc and that could interfere with our Quest.'

'What can we do?'

Without one speck of optimism she said, 'Avoid the MauMau. Collect three Keys, find the Sylph and head for the Core.'

It was then I resolved to retrieve my Key from Drufus.

'Pox on your code, Reject – you dare come to my dwell-place fists up and thuggish? My Grinders'll flatten you lengthwise, like that.' Drufus Scumscratch tried a finger-snap but his attempt came off slimy and silent.

I'd overstepped boundaries threatening the snail on his turf, but I wanted that Key. His clones were aquiver and fraidy but it was admirable to see how they defended the ground. I could've laid waste to a host of 'em, especially since Mata Angelica had gifted me a long-sword as a token of trust.

Drufus piped up again. 'Are you ignoring me, Reject? D'you know who you're dealing with?'

'I'm dealing with a gobshite low-life, who'd be better off in the swamp he squelched out from.' I was pleased with my answer and knuckled my snout with a flourish.

'Well, you can't have the Key and that's that.'

I drew my sword and his Grinders instantly flanked me, dagger-blades drawn.

I warned Drufus not to push it or I'd be obliged to delete them, but a small twitch of his nog signalled they should attack. They lunged forward obediently, poor clones, and were both disembowelled with one pass of my steel. Oily innard-juice splattered the room. A greasy spurt of it slid down the gastropod's fizzog. The only sign of the Mutant's distaste was a smack of his lips, whereon twenty more Grinders appeared from the wings.

'I thought we could be chums,' said Drufus, wiping his cheek, 'but I was wrong. Prepare yourself, Reject. I've got hundreds of Grinders in there,' and he tipped his nog in a vague, backstage direction.

'I'll delete every one and you along with 'em.' I held out my mitt. 'Give me the Key.'

The Mutant was on the point of retort when a teensy figure emerged from the wings. 'The Key,' said the figure, 'is no longer the Mutant's to give. It's not even in this Realm any more.'

The character's voice, tho quietsome, had the deep wooden emptiness of a hollowed-out tree. Drufus, on cue, slid to the background while I turned to the character floating towards me. It was the sorceress from the previous day and tho she was pocket-sized there was something potent about her and my nog said, Hold off from attack, she's got nifty conflict skills hidden.

'Tell me, He-Man, why do you want Keys so badly?' She flew round me twice-times, getting the measure of my muscles, no doubt.

'I wanted *my* Key. I had it on entry and he' – I pointed to Drufus – 'stole it.'

'You gave it up freely,' retorted the snail.

The sorceress rose to the height of my Visor and pushed back her hood. For the first time I could study her face-features: exotic, softly cheeks, crack for a mouth, lightless eyes embellished with ink patterns. She regarded me, in turn, with an expression of defiant serenity. All this time Drufus lounged on a day bed, surrounded by Grinders who fed him with DumGrog and greens.

'Watch,' the sorceress commanded.

She held out one mitt and conjured miniature 3D footage into her palm. It was a horror flick starring a giant beaster – fur pelt and pring-claw with teeth flashing ivory-sharp. It pounced on a battalion of Grinders, slashed and gnashed and flicked them away as if they were toothpicks. The Grinders fought valiantly, tho their spears bounced off the beaster's flanks. The monster hooked clone after clone and tugged off their nogs with its mouthparts. Astonishing, vicious and cruel.

'That,' she said, 'is a MauMau. Kill it and I'll give you a better Key.'

'Why not send your own Champion? An enchantress of your stature must have one.'

I was angling to discover if she knew her Cyclops was deleted and, hey presto, her eyes came backlit with fire.

'My Champion,' she said, raising her chin, 'did not succeed.'

I wanted to say, 'Your Champion Cyclops was a wimp. I mashed his fat skull without breaking sweat.' But I was a warrior, Ludi the brave, a He-Man in every dimension. I had no desire to dishonour her. And there was something about the MauMau, as if I'd dreamed it, as if I knew it of old in my nog. It was errorsome to be double with Mata Angelica, but if I fought this fight for the sorceress I'd still be Key collecting, and if I despatched the MauMau it would please the Eroticon – since even she thought the beaster could scupper our plans.

'Lead me to the monster,' I said, and put my sword in its cingulum.

Drufus slid off his day bed, clapping his mitts and giving it, 'Bravo, Reject,' while dribbling green matter over his flab. 'Knew we'd persuade you, old boy.'

The sorceress managed a joyless nod.

The first noticeable thing about the sorceress's palanquin was the absence of Grinders to convey it. It floated, as she did, off the ground. It was austere – dull-metal studs and no cushions except, hanging down from one corner, a filigree cage where two passerines perched, tweeting full-throated. These tweeters were counterpoint to the drabness, their plumage vivid, their construction particular – with long-fluted tail feathers and bibs of bright blue.

'What beautiful birds,' I said, dreamy.

'My magical beauties.' She sighed. 'After the Cyclops went off, one escaped. But I'll find it.' She smiled. 'I always recover my assets.'

I let the passerines serenade me as I prepared my nog for battle, thinking only of Victory not Void.

A Party –
People Still Have Them

The loud Jamaican says, 'Disgustin', that's what it is. All a them on drugs. All a them. Showin' off them glamity down the street there – no see – then come back up the health shop with them John. Hot step. Y'know what I'm saying?'

The man, bald except for a semicircle of hair horseshoeing his head from behind, gives his fellow customers a prurient look via the mirror as Mr Barber goes at his scalp with the clippers. He's talking about the health centre, trying to come off superior and moral. But Lionel's seen him checking the cameras before sneaking down the alley at four a.m.

'And did you hear about that gangsta bwoy?' The Jamaican is determined to capitalize on being the centre of attention. 'Somebody slice him, y'know. Slice him and throw him in the river.' He mimes being slashed at the jugular. 'Kill him dead.'

Lionel's ears prick up.

'Me have a friend,' the man continues. 'In the force – admin man, y'understand, not filth – and them been trying to pin something on that bwoy for ever. Never ketch him till now.'

Mr Barber sneezes suddenly and the sound silences the man.

'Who was he?' asks Lionel.

'Does it matter?' The barber sighs, squeezing his eyes shut.

The loud Jamaican squints at Lionel's reflection. 'Him call Grippa,' he says. 'Him been runnin' some rude bwoy business for that Chinaman own dem nightclubs and ting.'

'Does he have an eye-patch?' Lionel covers one eye.

'That's right. Swatty man; half Chinese, half Nigerian. You know 'im?'

Lionel's suppresses his joy and shrugs carelessly. 'I've seen him.'

The Jamaican flares his nostrils in approval as the barber brushes him down and displays his handiwork in a small mirror.

'There, look!' The loud man swings round and points out of the window. 'There's one a them ho now. Broad daylight. Swear to sweet Jesus.'

The men on the sofa turn to watch the anime girl pass by. Blank-eyed, exhausted, she looks through the barber-shop window, through them and the room that they're sitting in, on through time, with the vacancy of an addict. Her hair is greasy and dull; her skin has lost its lustre. At the last moment, a miracle, she catches Lionel's eye and there, between them, is a brief jolt of recognition that animates her face before she disappears from view. Her face had lit up. They have a connection. They really do.

'Careful, son,' warns the Jamaican, standing now. 'It look like you already in trouble with that shine on your eye.'

Lionel has an urge to smack the man's head. Since the attack he's felt increasingly agitated, but he tries to rein in his emotions. 'I can look after myself, thank you,' he says, and takes his place in the chair.

The man laughs and motions to Lionel's beaten up face. 'So the ragamuffin that slap you up come off worse than you, uh huh, right?'

The men on the sofa laugh.

'Maybe he did,' says Lionel.

'You a big man now, eh?'

Mr Barber glares at the loud man. 'Ease up on the boy.'

The man mumbles something and puts a pay token on the counter. 'Redbone bwoy' – he means Lionel – 'always think they better than the rest, y'nah. Anyway him nah bwoy no more, *Barber*, him a man you no see?' And he leaves the shop with his nose in the air.

'Don't listen to him, Lionel. Him family from Yallahs and all a them lemon tongue. I know them from time.'

'It doesn't bother me, Mr Barber. Truly.'

As the old man fastens the gown at the back of his neck Lionel closes his eyes. Grippa's disembodied face floats somewhere in the distance of his imagination, sniggering. *Go on, give it to him.* Suddenly Grippa's face is right in front of him, in his mind's eye, moony and sallow, as if the dead man is inside him and Lionel's own eye is the gangster's spyhole onto the world. Lionel shudders. Keeps his eyes open.

Some people deserve to die and Grippa is one of them, he thinks. In braver moments, Lionel believes he has the stomach for reprisal. A few hours' work with a whetstone and he's sharpened the blade of his scimitar to a razor. He's been perfecting his samurai moves, pretending he has the nerve to fight, swinging the blade as if he was a warrior. And, for a few fugitive moments, he could be Ludi. A hero. If he blinks now he might see Ludi in the mirror staring back. Lionel makes a wish. *Blink. Blink.*

The old man is poking a comb in his hair. 'Tell me 'bout this *mess* here now.'

Lionel closes his eyes again. 'It needs twisting up, if you don't mind, Mr Barber. Maybe separate the strands out. Wax the ends.'

'Mi not the barber for dreadlocks, y'nah. Mi tellin' you flat, son.'

'They aren't real dreadlocks. It's just a style.'

'If them look like dreadlocks and feel like dreadlocks what else can them be?'

The diagnostic report is confusing. It appears Buddha's avatar has already uploaded to *CoreQuest*. The time-stamp in his cloaking programme shows the date and time of the attack in the club. Lionel can't remember initiating the upload and he tries to run through how it could have happened, but he can't think clearly. On top of that he appears to have miscalculated Buddha's ratios. Stupid. Novice mistake. The avatar is using an extraordinary amount of memory, slowing the whole system down. By his estimation Buddha is a hundred times larger than he should be. Frantically, he compares the original files with the previews. The dimensions appear to be correct, but the energy drain is incontrovertible. He scans the *CoreQuest* map for anomalies or abnormal combat signals, but finds nothing. Buddha is *in* the Realm somewhere but he can't locate him. Finally he navigates to where Ludi is ensconced in the citadel.

Here, too, there's a perplexing coincidence. The sorceress's caged songbirds are based on the same species as the one Buddha caught in the flat. Lionel presses his temples. The specimen he's retrieved from the freezer and the 3D images are almost exactly the same. He wants to find the programmer and quiz him. But there's no time to post to the forum – he'll be late for his train.

Tonight there's a hazy smudge around a fat yellow moon. Its face leers at the world like a dissolute judge and Lionel can make out the pits and scars on its cheesy skin. *Nightshift*. A card pass and fingerprint entry get him through security at Meddingley and he takes his seat with the other shift workers on the second floor. At midnight, when he logs off for coffee, Michael gets up from his workstation and follows a few paces behind.

'Hey, buddy. Wait up.'

He turns. Michael is grinning and he smiles a subliminal flash in return, smooths his hand over the back of his nubby dreads.

'That's some bruise.'

He touches his cheekbone. 'I forget it's still there.'

'You're okay, though?'

'I'm fine.'

'Your hair's grown. Crazy. Shows how long it's been since I've seen ya.'

'I booked time off. I've been back for three weeks.'

Michael winks. 'Hey, it's no sweat, dude. I'm not keeping tabs.'

'Our shifts haven't overlapped, that's all it is.'

'Whatever! Bleed the system, that's what I say.'

Lionel's not sure what prompts him to lurch forward as rashly as he does, but he takes Michael firmly by the shoulder and presses the soft flesh at the top of the American's arm. 'I haven't been myself,' he says, emphatically.

No longer flippant, Michael stiffens. A nip of fear dilates his pupils. 'I see it, buddy, okay.'

Lionel releases his grip, looks round to the Hub and the cameras.

There's a pause before Michael speaks. His voice taut with forced mirth. 'Ha ha, you crack me up you know, man. I thought you were going to paste me or something.' He punches a quick one-two in the air to relieve the tension.

Lionel steps back. 'I don't want to hit you. I don't want to hurt anyone.'

Even as he says it he knows it's a lie – the way he feels right now he could lay waste to an army.

'Sure you don't, big guy, sure you don't. Well, I'm gonna grab some coffee. Wanna join me – since we're SocialNet chums and all?' Michael's shaking as he drapes his arm across Lionel's shoulder. 'I want to know what you think about all the drama.'

'Drama?'

'Yeah, haven't you heard? The goons in the Hub have discovered a security breach. The official line is "server compromise", y'know, cyber-attack from outside. Terrorist threat and all of that bull crap. But I reckon someone's leaking data from inside.'

'What kind of data?'

Michael steers him towards the cafeteria. 'Search me, buddy. I'm keeping my head down. Don't wanna be in the firing line when the goon squad realize it's an inside job, y'know what I'm saying?'

Michael, like Lionel, knows where every camera is located in the corridors and his eyes range from one device to another as they walk. The cheap clink of cutlery echoes off the tiles and the stainless steel. There are several people eating: lone workers hunched over their food, staring at nothing. Lionel and Michael fill their mugs from the self-service machine and sit by the window. Inside the Hub shapes coalesce and break apart like visions forming in a crystal ball. Michael – who's been mechanically stirring his drink – stops and taps the mug three times with his spoon. When Lionel looks at him the American pins him with an unflinching gaze. Lionel feels as if he's being taken apart, but Michael toasts him with his coffee mug, apparently pleased he's regained the advantage.

'I have a good feeling about you, Lionel,' he asserts cheerily.

'I'm not gay.' He can't believe he's just said it. He hadn't meant to. He hadn't even thought about it before it came out.

Michael pulls a stupid face. 'It's okay, man, I'm not gay either.'

'I like gay people. I like everyone.'

Michael runs one finger round the rim of his mug. 'Course you do, buddy.'

They sit awkwardly for a minute until Michael says, 'Look, I know I'm like, mouthing off all the time and shit, but I need this job.' It sounds as if he's about to make a confession. 'I mean – I hate it, all right – but I need it. And to be totally honest I'm, well, I'm finding it hard to fit in here.'

'You?'

'Straight.' Michael shields his mouth with his hand. 'I don't feel the *same* as these people. Sometimes' – he pauses – 'sometimes I feel like we're the only real Homo sapiens in the place – no gay pun intended.' There's a sarcastic twitch in his lip when he laughs. 'Seriously, though, these guys are all freaking zombies, dontcha think?'

Lionel gives a small nod.

'Excellent. I knew it.' He sits back, knees wide, and goes on expansively. 'Look, I'm having a party on Saturday. Why don't you come?'

'A party?'

'People still have them.' Michael is amused. 'No pressure, there'll only be a few of us. Not a crowd or anything. I'll message you the address on SocialNet. It'll be a gas.' He winks. 'From eight.'

Michael is saying something else as Lionel considers the prospect of a party, but then the American stands and drinks back his coffee in gulps.

'Are you leaving already?'

'Super's breaking my balls about quotas. Don't wanna get on the wrong side of Khalsa with all this shit going down, right?'

Lionel shakes his head doubtfully. 'Right.'

When he's on the other side of the cafeteria, Michael calls, 'Saturday remember, after eight,' and he touches his wrist with one finger – although no one, except the likes of Mr Barber, wears a wristwatch these days.

Lionel has a suspicion that he and Michael have been speaking entirely at cross-purposes.

Early evening. The sky has turned grainy in the gathering dusk. Lionel takes the bus from the central terminus – through the business districts, the suburbs, the factories, the homogenous new-build estates. Through edgelands of endless construction covering the countryside, dip and mound, devouring the greenbelt – on and on. He imagines the city's history as a time-lapse movie. A slow expansion; settlement became hamlet, medieval village became Tudor market town – until the nineteenth century when the furnaces of industry pumped out progress with pyroclastic exuberance and the soft, green land became grey and hard for miles around.

David's voice comes to him from the past. A liquid sound at first, purling over pumice, rippling round the obstructions of memory. 'Restraint, boy,' it murmurs, 'you must show restraint, even if they bully you – convert your passion into piety and prayer.' The voice soaks away sublimely, down through the rock. But then a new voice takes over.

'We are inheriting the legacy of profligacy,' David bellows, thumping the lectern before him. He grips one lapel and sweeps his eyes over the petrified congregation. Magma burns in his eyes. When his gaze reaches Lionel he pauses and sighs. 'We are paying for the iniquities of the fathers.'

Michael lives in a bland town cowering twenty miles west of the city centre; its arse-end subsumed by the sprawl but necking its way out over swathes of waste ground sliced through with crumbling motorways. His house is at the very edge of the town, where an ancient flyover dominates the skyline. Its concrete stanchions look like the columns of a derelict temple supporting a road that disappears into the misty distance. Only occasional headlights suggest its true purpose.

Lionel remembers Lilith predicting that, far in the future, when the cars were all gone and the cantilevered intersections and tangles of junctions had become overgrown, no one would remember what roads had been for. Archaeologists would imagine them as massive artworks telling dreamtime stories. Or as walkways, perhaps, constructed by giants. Collective knowledge erodes quickly, she'd said.

The bus hisses to a stop and Lionel alights into the gloom. Behind him, a parliament of rooks derides the oncoming night, leaping and hee-hawing in the uppermost branches of a crop of poplars. They make Lionel feel wary. A party. *People still have them.* How many people will there be? What will he say to them? He consults the GPS on his Google device and turns back on himself. After fifty metres, he heads along a lane with no streetlights or pavements and walks along the middle, where he can take advantage of the ambient light. He can just make out a patch of unruly snapdragons clumping beneath the overhanging boughs of new-budding blackthorn. The dwellings are all bungalows, some unlit, others with the thin radiance of eco-bulbs glowing behind their curtains. Electric cars and bicycles are parked on the verges. He turns the torch on his Google to full and tries to read the house names on the gates and fence posts.

Ebenezer . . . Goose Cottage . . . Albion: this is it. A bungalow behind a wooden gate with a broken latch and a box hedge that encloses a front garden, dug out ready for planting. A narrow path lit with tealights leads along the left-hand side to a porch where the front door stands ajar and the smell of something heady, jasmine or myrrh, fingers the air. There's music playing somewhere – a guitar and a voice, and the sloppy thud of hand drums.

'Hello,' Lionel calls.

No one answers.

The bulb has gone in the corridor and he advances, feeling along the wall. Candles are guttering on a stone mantelpiece in a room to his right, sinister eddies chase over the chimney breast. Apart from smoke and shadows the room is empty. Further up is another room; an eco-lamp illuminates a pile of coats that looks like a slumbering bear. At the end of the corridor, behind the final closed door – the party. He can hear it now, a paragraph of voices, a woman's laugh punctuating with a 'ha', and a 'ha-ha', and someone saying, 'Michael. Darling. Have you got a light?'

He stands, immobile, gripping his bottle like a bludgeon. *The same as these people?* No, he can't stay here. There will be conversations and dancing. People will require him to smile, to interact. What if the men from the nightclub are here? What if this whole thing is a ruse to trap him, defile him again? He knows these thoughts are irrational. But then a lot of things seem irrational and they still happen. Some things are beyond anyone's control. He presses his forehead to the door, composing himself, and turns to leave. As he does he knocks something with his elbow, something that yelps and falls against the wall, something that says 'Fuck' rather vehemently. There are flashes of white in the darkness: eyes and teeth.

'Oh God, did I hit you?'

'Shit!'

'I really am terribly sorry.' He's mortified. 'Are you okay?'

'Uh huh.'

'I didn't see you.'

'Evidently.'

'Sorry.'

'If you're so sorry then help me up, will you?' The voice is reproachful, female.

As his vision adjusts he can distinguish the woman's outline. He finds her hand, cool and strong, and hauls her to her feet. There's a good weight to her, not like Lilith, who is light as air.

'I'm truly sorry.'

'Yes, you've said that.' There's the hint of an accent.

Lionel opens the door to the party and leads the woman inside.

Michael is wearing a white linen shirt, open at the neck, sleeves rolled up. He's casually wrecked and his head rolls drunkenly in their direction before his face stretches to a rakish grin.

'You came. Excellent!'

A path opens as he lurches forward, half stumbling, half dancing, holding his drink above the other guests' heads.

He grabs Lionel roughly. 'And you found the gorgeous Eve. Excellent!'

Lionel turns to the woman. Eve is a shave shorter than Michael, black, with her hair pulled clean off her face and a mass of sable curls tumbling from a grip at the back of her head. She raises her chin regally, but when her eyes catch Lionel's they suggest something less formal, something sexual. Lionel can't speak she's so beautiful.

Michael bends to kiss Eve's cheek, but stops. 'What's this?' He touches her clumsily above the ear and examines the smear of red on his fingers. 'You're bleeding.'

'Ouch! Careful! I banged my head out there. You need to get a light in that corridor. Go on, kiss me then.' She offers Michael her lips.

After a theatrical kiss, Michael says, 'Are you sure he didn't beat up on you?' He fires a glance at Lionel. 'He's got a shiner of his own, you know. I'll bet he wants to dish them out to everyone. Is that it, eh, buddy? Feeling alone with your bruises? Wanna take it out on the world, right?'

Eve scowls. 'I'm sure it was an accident.'

Michael ignores her. 'How d'you get your shiner then, buddy boy? C'mon, you can tell us. We're not at Meddingley now.'

'You're pissed,' Eve says firmly. 'Don't pick on him.' She places an admonitory hand on Michael's chest.

Lionel is surprised she's taking his side.

'I am. Never. Pissed.' Michael pretends to be offended.

'Go and do the bonfire.' She pats his arm. 'Look, Prospero needs you.'

Michael squints at the garden where the man in the wheelchair, from the cafeteria, is motioning for him to come outside. Scratching his face absently, he looks from Lionel to Eve. 'Perhaps I am a bit pissed. Sorry.' He kisses Eve once more. 'Excellent!' he says again, and dances his way across the room.

'Don't mind Michael,' she says when he's out of earshot. 'He's in his *excellent* phase. You have to learn how to distract him when he's like this. He'll drink himself sober by the end of the night.'

Lionel opens his mouth, but nothing comes out. Eve absolves his reticence with laughter. The sound is round and deep, and Lionel thinks that if her laugh were an object it would be a river pebble. Smooth. Perfect.

'Come on, I'll get you a drink.' She takes his hand.

As Eve makes cocktails he watches the graceful movement of her limbs, the way she holds her shoulders. The way she licks her protuberant lips before beginning each sentence. She reminds him of someone. Look at the conspiratorial glint in her eyes, half wicked, half coy, as if she knows him already.

'This one's my special recipe,' she says, adding the finishing touches from a row of bottles lined up on the table.

Sensual fingers brush the back of his hand as she passes his drink. Her skin is polished, dark as roast carob, no embellishments except for a sticky shine on her lips and a thick stripe of kohl underlining her eyes. The plumpness on her hips and belly makes him wonder if she could be pregnant, but Eve says, 'Bottoms up,' and gulps down most of her cocktail in one.

He looks in her eyes and says, 'Cheers,' but takes only a sip. He's trembling.

'So, Lionel – Michael's told me *all* about you.'

'Why would he tell you about me?'

'He thinks you're interesting.'

'I'm really not.'

She dismisses his modesty with a gesture. 'Michael says' – she pauses to pluck a cigarette from the hand of another guest as he walks by – 'that you have hidden depths.' After taking a deep drag on the cigarette she hands it back to its owner. 'I'm trying to give up,' she says, 'but I don't have the discipline.' She blows a column of smoke past his ear. 'So, do you?'

'Have discipline?'

Her gaze is instantly penetrating. 'No. Hidden depths.'

The room they are in is open-plan – a fin de siècle knock-through with sliding glass doors where the back wall used to be. In one corner an Arab-looking man is playing the guitar, flamenco-style, and singing a Moorish tune while a white woman – hair hidden by an African-print turban – beats an incompetent rhythm on a small djembe. A light flutter of applause follows each song. Lionel takes another sip of his drink. In the garden Michael and Prospero appear in deep conversation. The bonfire is spraying filaments of orange into the night and the two men stare into the conflagration as they talk. The woodsmoke smells primitive, comforting – and he feels lightheaded, suddenly, as if he could lie down and sleep. He puts his hand to his throat, feels his pulse against his fingertips.

Eve squeezes his arm. 'Are you okay?'

'Yep. Fine.'

'Let's get some air.'

In the garden Michael has vanished, but Prospero, who's speaking on a handheld device, nods to them as they come outside.

'You don't say much,' Eve says.

'I'm sorry.'

'Don't apologize.' Her smile is seductive. 'I like quiet men.'

'I'm . . . well . . .' He makes a face. 'I'm out of my depth, to be honest.'

She lowers her voice. 'You seem charming to me. You seem good.'

She says 'good' with a pointed sincerity that makes him look at the ground and hold his earlobe.

In the firelight, the skin of Eve's face shines as she tries to put him at ease. She talks about her job, her interests. It's rewarding being a doctor, she says, but it's the voluntary work she does with refugees in the city that she's most passionate about.

'They arrive here with nothing,' she says. 'They're sick and malnourished: young men, who used to be strong, treated like dogs. Women and children, abused.'

A bright yellow halterneck clings to her breasts and her hips, contrasting with the colour of her skin. Muscular arms and strong wrists taper to long delicate fingers; she makes sophisticated shapes with her hands as she speaks, holding one palm up in an attitude of explication as if she's showing him round a gallery – or like a magician's assistant, misdirecting attention.

'We try and help them, Michael and the rest of us.'

Her mouth is so mobile it could be a separate organism. He watches her lips open and close over her teeth. He's fascinated.

'Anyway, enough about me.' She licks her lips. 'Where are you from, Lionel? Lionel?'

'Oh er, I don't know. Originally from somewhere in Kenya. I'm adopted, you see, but I'm from here, the Midlands . . . it's where I grew up. Judy says it doesn't matter who my real parents were, but – there's some black and some white, wouldn't you say?' He grins, hoping he's made a joke.

'Judy?'

He clears his throat. 'My mother, you know. Adopted.'

Eve nods slowly. 'And you've never tried to find your real family in Africa?'

'My sister says I should have a DNA test, try and find my *people* but –'

'But what?'

'It's another country. I'm English now and I'm an orphan, so what's the point?'

Eve bites her tongue. It's improbably pink and glistening with moisture. Her nostrils flare when she speaks. 'To find out who you are, to discover your true identity.' Her tone is careful, yet critical. 'To know where you're really from.'

'I told you, I'm from the Midlands.'

Eve responds gravely. 'No, Lionel, I don't think so.'

There's a crash and a muttered expletive as Michael stumbles onto the patio. He dances round them for a minute, swigging straight from a bottle, before trying to nuzzle Eve's neck.

'You're ridiculous.' She leans away from the American, feigning indignation.

'Yeah, but I'm *the sex*, right? Come on, shake your booty with me, princess.'

'No. You are too bad.' She's scolding him, but smiling too and she soon submits.

As Michael leads her away Eve throws Lionel a commanding look that has some provocation in it, a call to action, and he salutes her with his glass and drinks down the rest of his cocktail. The live music from earlier has been replaced by dance beats and he watches Eve give herself up to the rhythm. They are a couple, Michael and Eve, he decides. He focuses on her graphic features as the two of them snake around one another. With her hips swaying like that she reminds him of Mata Angelica. An Eroticon made flesh. He laughs, shakes his head. It's a trick of the light, that's all.

'Hey, Lionel, come on, man,' shouts Michael. 'Stop hanging about on the sidelines. Throw yourself into it, for Jesus Christ's sake.'

He calls back, 'I'm fine. You go ahead.'

Eve makes sensual circles with one shoulder, biting her bottom lip, eyes half closed. Lionel stretches his lower back as a wave of desire rises through him. What systems we have, he thinks. Another wave follows swiftly on the first. This time it surges right up through his chest and crashes at the base of his brain. If he's not careful he'll be overwhelmed. Bowled right off his feet. Hold on, here's another. He's being deluged; in this garden, at this party, something is flooding him. It's uncontrollable. He makes it as far as the flowerbed before sinking to his knees.

@GameAddict (#23756745): 20:6:27

You're a puppeteer – but the strings you're pulling are coiled round the globe. Lift your sword
in London and someone bows to your blade in
Taiwan. It's magic. Ordinary people, like you,
in control of a Realm. You can hear players
talking from Timbuktu to Jerusalem – a babble
of voices. You can't see it, but the Game Layer
is everywhere.

Level 8: The MauMau

Picture this: a wide expanse of desert so dark it looks like the Void. But in night-vision mode, an infinite flock of white Fallion are roosting and flapping their wings in the sand. Now listen: a riotous chuckle and cluck. Fowl nesting, chicks begging, mating pairs making love-calls so the very darkness has a synaesthetic pulse.

'It's out there,' said the sorceress, sniffing the air. 'It's stalking the Fallion.'

'You're a magician,' I said. 'Why not zap it with a spell?'

Two sedan chairs, each borne by four Grinders, arrived before she could answer. From the chairs stepped two Generals: Thrar and Vadarian. Behind them a Krin-Balwrin loped along on all fours.

Before she floated to greet them the crone spoke under her breath. 'Magic won't work on a MauMau. But at least this useless triumvirate' – she jutted her chin towards the Generals – 'can find common ground in a crisis.'

As the bigwigs did politicking I sat on the edge of the palanquin, tightening my straps, checking the cutting edge of my sword with my thumb.

'Generals, this is Ludi, an OtherWorld Reject,' the sorceress announced. 'But we don't mind since he's our new Champion.' She did a smug nose-cough to finish.

The Brass clicked their heels and saluted, assessing my facets. The figure I cut was impressive: nog 'n' shoulders above them and broad as any Goliath with ripped pecs and abs and biceps like boulders. I wore leather wrist cuffs and a cingulum – slung over one shoulder – to hold all my weaponry. My loincloth was now overlaid with long leather lappets that hung to the thigh and showed off the muscular line of my pins. I stood, gave each soldier a stiff nod.

'Trick is,' said the Thrar, stepping forward, demonstrating his combat suggestions with hand gestures, 'to go for the jugular, hook the beast's arterial tube out. Once he's down we'll bomb over and finish him off. Huzzah!'

'They're attracted to irregular movements,' added the Vadarian, ignoring the Thrar's peculiar gung-ho. 'Try luring it first with your whip, before striking.'

The Generals now looked to the Krin.

'Whatever strategy takes you.' The bear shrugged, eyeing my scars. 'You look sufficient acquainted with combat to make your own game plan.'

The Krin was solid and wore his Balwriqin (the ceremonial girdle of his tribe) low on his pelvis to accommodate an oversized belly bulge. He moved rather sluggish and had battle-scars of his own cross his forepaws and chest. But tho he was gruff his demeanour was warm and my approval meter shot straight up to 60. Still there was some war-boredom in his bearing, as if years of conflict had wearied him down.

'Well,' said the sorceress. 'We wait for the MauMau to strike.' And with that she folded her arms and withdrew.

We didn't wait long. Almost at once squawks of alarm spread through the flock. At the far edge of the field a mad tumult of feathers developed.

The Generals peered through night-scopes and said, 'It's a killing machine.'

The witch rose to my eye-level. 'Are you ready, Ludi?'

As she spoke she laid a timely mitt on my shoulder and tho I was thirsty for the romp of close combat, I froze. The sorceress's touch sent a weird shiver right to my offal. I felt nauseous and tried to glance sideways, to catch more sense of her and measure her up. I could grasp the craven depths of someone like Drufus – a simple self-serving baddie, gratifying his greed meter – but this crone was different. Wicked, that's what she was. Her touch cast a pall on my heart.

I wanted to back off, say 'no' to the fight. But I nogged this character was an instrument of some deeper force and I discerned I must do some dissembling.

On instinct I commanded, 'You, Krin, be my wingman. It's worth it for glory.'

Rather than balk the Krin adjusted his girdle and stood to attention. 'Stay at the fringes,' I said, 'and hang back till my signal. Are you armed?'

'Locked and loaded.' He lifted a crossbow and grinned.

I gave no time for protest but charged forward, forming a plan on the hoof. I'd drive through the flock, avoiding the MauMau, and in the mêlée I'd scarper. Abandon the sorceress and her Generals to their fate (tho I was sad the Krin would be fodder).

The scene went like this: on one side of the field, the MauMau in its Fallion death cloud; on the other side, me, making an avian smokescreen. The result was a fabulous bird jamboree. But my plan had a flaw. I could see nothing past beaks and feathers and there was a chance I'd come face to face with the MauMau regardless. And I did. A lethal quiver of ivories came out of the mass so sudden there was no time to withdraw. On reflex I protected my nog with my shield, fumbling for weaponry, muttering oaths, bracing myself for the bite. But none came. When at last I peeked out the MauMau was at ease, chewing bird bits from its toes. It turned to me – a Bedlam smile distorting its chops – and emitted a strange mechanical chuffle. Amazing! It had instantly come all-domestic. From some artesian memory-hole a name sprang and, without more cogitating, I said the word *Buddha*, out loud. The chuffle grew to a deafening pitch and the MauMau rolled on its back, displaying a rug of soft belly-fur. Claws retracted, ears flattened back and, from its mouth, a pink tongue-tip protruded.

'Buddha.' I said it again and the beaster rolled over, mewling, quite cutesome. It was only as the Fallions settled back down around it that I clocked the Krin. He'd circled round, as commanded, and was lying in a midden of corpses. Crossbow raised, sniper-eye planing the shaft of the bow, bolt aimed directly twixt the MauMau's eyes. The Krin was a far better soldier than I'd bargained.

Judy, Prim as a Duchess

E ve's not speaking, but her lips are puckering, as if she's covering an invisible man in small kisses. Lionel has never seen such
enormous lips. *Kiss. Kiss. Kiss.* The sun anoints his bare skin. *So
comforting.* Salt seasons the air. He's on a lilo, adrift on the ocean,
peering down through deep water. Ha ha! There's Eve's mouth, way
down there, drifting towards the ocean floor. How did it detach from
her body? He dives after it, reaching through bracelets of light to
rescue it. *Kiss. Kiss. Kiss.* At last he draws near and sees a sinuous
crust in the shape of a shell round her mouth. Flashes of nacre reflect
light from above. What a surprise – Eve's mouth is a fat, wet mol-
lusc, plump as a young vulva. Grasping it tight with both hands he
studies its bright pink innards. He has the urge to devour it. Taste
the brine of it. Taste her.

Snap, snap, snap! Hold on. This mouth is nothing but a snappy little
clam. It has his tongue and it won't let go. Lionel gives it a powerful tug
and something ruptures. Pain discharges through his neck. Blood – his
blood – coils up through the blue. Frantic now, he begins his ascent.
Up, up. He's out of his depth all right. Air expands in his lungs; it will
rip them apart like paper bellows. Still he swims up. The clam on his
tongue and the pain in his chest go up. Up.

'Lionel, can you hear me? Lionel? Are you awake?' Eve looks down
at him. 'You fainted . . . passed out.'

'What? Where am I?'

She sweeps her arm up and around. 'Welcome to the spare room.'

There's a bitter taste in his mouth. 'Where is everyone?'

'Gone. The party's over.'

He groans. 'Michael?'

'Sleeping.'

'What happened?'

'Shh!' She puts a finger to her lips. 'So many questions.'

He's in a sparsely furnished room on a pull-out bed. Eve is beside him, wrapped in a sheet. She reclines on one elbow like a guest at a Roman feast, the spice of her sweat mixed in with something sweet – ambergris or musk. He rubs his eyes and tries to focus while Eve appraises him coolly.

'Go on.' He winces. 'I have to know, so you might as well tell me.'

'You vomited, then you went over, simple as that.'

'I had one drink.'

'I know. I think you're unwell.' Eve presses her palm to his brow. 'You felt very hot when we carried you in. But your temperature's fine now.'

He closes his eyes. 'Damn.'

'Don't be embarrassed. It happens to the best of us.'

'The best of us,' he repeats. 'Why aren't you with Michael? I thought you two were . . .' He opens his eyes and his gaze falls to where the sheet bunches at her breasts.

She laughs and clasps her chest. 'Me and Michael? God in heaven, no! Not my type. Too white.'

'I'm not a good colour for you then either,' Lionel says, and cringes. *Does it sound as if he wants to be her type?*

She overlooks his faux pas. 'My grandfather was light-skinned, like you. He had these.' Eve touches several freckles on his cheeks with the tip of one finger. 'Anyway, it's not about colour. I *am* bad to say things like that.' She smiles wickedly until a flash of realization widens her eyes. 'You don't think you *are* black.'

'I'm not black.'

'There's no need to shout.'

'But I'm not black. I am this.' He points at his face. 'I am this man, in here. Inside here.' But even as he says it he's not sure where 'here' is, or what 'man' exactly it is that he's talking about.

'Of course.' Her voice is clipped. 'That's fine.'

His outburst has alarmed them both and they're silent for a minute before he goes on more quietly, holding his throat. 'I was attacked recently. Some men attacked me.' He wants to justify his behaviour. 'My mouth is so dry.'

'Here.' She passes him a glass of water and holds the back of his head while he takes a sip. 'Do you know who attacked you?'

'No.' He sits up. 'Look, I'm sorry, but I've got to go home.'

'I'll drive you.'

'No, I –'

'I insist.' Eve stands; the sheet barely covers her nakedness. 'I'm a doctor. It's my duty to make sure you get home safely.'

Eve turns to dress, the sheet falls, and in an instant he has committed the curve of her back, the dimples in her buttocks, the swell of her breasts and her belly and the voluptuous mass of her hair to memory.

There's a late frost. Dawn is breaking and a smouldering layer of blood-red light seeps along the horizon in the east, although everything close-up remains ghostly and grey.

Eve describes efficient arcs with a scraper on the windscreen. 'Get in,' she says, shivering. 'Who'd think there'd be frost in June? The seasons have gone crazy.'

There's a box full of pamphlets on the back seat, a bottle of water in the footwell and a GPS licence tag fixed to the passenger side of the window. Lionel reads the parking pass below it. Daily permit: University Hospital.

'Where did you do your medical training?'

'Kenya. Where I grew up.'

'That's a coincidence.'

'African.' She grins. 'Like you.'

African, he *is* African. He touches his face. When he overhears the Ghanaians and Nigerians at the taxi rank – the quickfire accents, the somatic gestures and loud humour – they're not like him. They are *other*. They are mythical.

Eve starts the car, depresses the clutch and pumps the gas a few times. The engine emits a guttural *yirr*. The seats vibrate.

'It's a real engine!'

'It's a hybrid.' She hits the gas one more time before pulling away. 'Sounds authentic though, doesn't it?' She winks mischievously. 'Men always appreciate a bit of thrust.'

Shafts of dawn light glide over their faces as they drive and they pull their sun visors down to shield their eyes. Lionel's thoughts travel back to the night before.

'I'm not sure,' he starts, 'but my drink, back there, could've been spiked.'

Eve glances at him. 'What? Who'd do a thing like that? Anyway, I made your drink.' She sounds offended. 'I was with you the whole time.'

'It's unusual though, don't you think, to pass out for no reason?'

'Actually,' she says, adopting a sympathetic tone. 'And I can tell you don't want to talk about it, but it's probably post-traumatic shock. A reaction to that attack.'

'Does that happen?'

'I come across it all the time in my line of work.' She looks straight ahead as she speaks. 'If an incident is too much for the mind to process the brain shuts down. Closes off the pain.'

'I see.' He pauses, scratches his neck. 'But I wasn't thinking about the attack when I fainted. I was fine.'

'Well, don't underestimate your subconscious.'

Lionel turns away, wondering if his subconscious really could sabotage reality like that. Life could be a constant fugue of trauma and protective forgetting. The countryside slides by. There are large loop-tracks in the fields and surface water lies in elongated strips in the muddy depressions. Flocks of white birds have colonized the temporary pools and other, singular birds watch over them – a limp-crested heron, princely against a flaky, slate sky. A herring gull, stiff as a cardboard cut-out on a fence post. It could be a film set, he thinks. The whole of existence could be simply 'made up'.

'All the small farms are abandoned,' says Eve. 'It makes me feel sad. And now half of Africa is solar generation and half of East Europe is ploughed up to feed the West's greed and still governments won't let the displaced people in.'

He doesn't respond. She sounds like Lilith.

Eve tells him her parents were land-owning farmers before the redistribution. They believed in clean energy and were happy their land was earmarked for solar generation. The droughts had become too severe to cultivate anything. But the government gave their land to middle-ranking officials. It was theft. Blatant theft. And even though they fought for two years they were eventually forced to move to Nairobi.

'They joined an anti-government collective, but they were both killed the same year, in the energy riots.'

'I'm sorry.'

'Everyone will be sorry.' She says it as a prediction not a threat.

Eve's alone in the world. No siblings. She wants to change things. She wants to help people. Doctor, nurse, aid worker, it doesn't matter; she just wants to make a difference if she can.

'I met Michael at a political meeting.' She flicks him a sideways glance, but he makes a point of focusing on the road.

Lionel can't think how Michael came by his job at Meddingley. The Human Resources department checks potential employees zealously: history, social networks, browsing habits, leisure and political affiliations – all scrutinized. But perhaps Michael's sharp enough to conceal his interests.

Eve changes gear roughly. 'Hundreds of people, every week, every day – hiding in ships or trains – trying to get here, or America, trying to survive. But everywhere is hatred. Everywhere they say "no" to the displaced and the poor.' Her voice, for the first time, carries a little fervour in it. 'Too many good people are lost. Me and Michael and the others, we try and help them. Do you know what I'm talking about, Lionel?'

'I think so.'

'There are things we can do.'

'You mean illegal things?'

Eve weighs up the question. 'Moral things,' she says.

An electric refuse truck is making slow progress towards the intersection where Milk Street joins the High Street, stopping every ten metres to empty the communal bins. Its robotic loading arm reaches over with balletic ease to pick and swivel and dump the contents of several huge, blue containers. *Rubbish*.

'Just here.' He points to the door of his flat.

Eve pulls in at the kerb. 'You do understand what I'm saying, Lionel?'

'Action.' He nods. 'You need action.'

'Exactly!' Her enthusiasm alarms him. 'And you're just the kind of man I'm looking for.'

It suddenly feels stuffy inside the car. Eve's checking him from under her brows with one of those expressions Lilith wears when she wants him to stand and be counted.

'Well,' he says, rubbing his thighs. 'I should go and rest.'

'You'll be all right?'

'Of course.'

'Do you want me to come in?'

'It's okay. I feel tiptop now. Totally recovered – just tired.'

Eve touches his hand. 'What are you afraid of, Lionel?'

'I'm not afraid.'

'Then why are you shaking?'

He pulls his hand away. 'Cold, I'm cold,' he insists.

Once on the pavement, he leans back inside, one arm on the roof. 'When you said that thing about Michael earlier, what did you mean?'

'What thing?'

'About him being "too white". What exactly is wrong with being white?'

'Nothing at all, I only meant that white's not right for me. Call it historical prejudice.' Her eyes shine with impish assurance. 'I can forgive a white man his colonial past, but I could never . . .' She grimaces. 'You know, surrender myself. Besides, white men are generally charmless.'

'Generally charmless,' he echoes. 'That means I'm half charmless, doesn't it?'

She revs the engine. A raw shiver runs through him.

'It means you're half charming,' Eve shouts above the noise. 'Call me.'

Hands outstretched as she pulls away, he says, 'I don't have your number.'

But she's gone.

Something is wrong. He feels it as soon as he enters the flat. Buddha is asleep next to the sofa, curled into a sombre wreath, his breath coming in irregular wheezes. Nothing has been moved or disturbed. Still, it feels different. Someone's here. Sweat greases Lionel's palms as he listens. The blood quickens in his veins. Could the men from the club have found him? Could they have tracked him down to his flat?

A minute passes before he musters the courage to move. He checks the kitchen first. The solar-bulb slings a weak circle of light to the ceiling – as he left it. The kettle feels cold. He makes his way along the hallway, treading cautiously, the thump of life high in his chest. The muffled *tish* of a bottle breaking reaches him from the street. A dog barks in a faraway yard.

The air is old in this flat, he thinks, and he wonders how many times his lungs have recycled the stale particles of his life. But on the air comes a fresher smell that he recognizes, and his fear is quelled. He stops at the bedroom door and there's the mound of a person stirring in his bed. Lilith's face surfaces from beneath the duvet.

'Lionel,' she says with relief. 'Where have you been?'

'I've been to a party. What are you doing here?'

She tries to focus on her mobile device. 'What time is it?'

'Six, seven?'

'I let myself in. You don't mind, do you?'

'Of course not.'

'A party! You don't go to parties.'

'Lil, what's wrong?' He is using his 'big brother' voice – calm and firm.

As she props herself up on the pillows the sun penetrates the gap in the curtains and a slim wall of light partitions the room – Lilith on one side, him on the other. Dust swims randomly in the brightness between them.

'I was dreaming of that day.' She smiles. 'You remember that day? It was hot. The best day of the summer. We built that den by the river, in the meadow. You remember, don't you? Can I smoke?'

He nods.

'All those buttercups. Like a sea of gold. I was so little and they came up to here.' She holds her hand horizontal at her chin. 'That can't be right, can it? But, oh my God, they went on for ever. I was skipping right through them and spinning round in my dress. You remember the one, the red one? It had a circular skirt that *twizzled*.' Her smile falls away. 'That's when I heard them.'

She lights her cigarette, takes a drag and exhales. The smoke whorls in the light between them, obscuring her face.

'Who did you hear?'

'*Lionel, shit face!* No,' she corrects herself. '*Little brown shit*, that's it.' She nods emphatically. 'You were standing on the go-kart under that awful laburnum, with a rope round your neck and your hands tied in front, like this.' She demonstrates by pushing her wrists together to make a lotus flower with her hands. She takes another drag on her cigarette, still miming – a handcuffed convict now, smoking her last before the firing squad. 'What had they watched? Some movie. I forget. Ha! With a lynching in it.' She leans forward suddenly. 'Say you remember.'

He strokes his throat, but doesn't answer.

'I was out in the meadow skipping through the buttercups.' She cups her ear. '*Little brown shit – let's hang him*. They liked the sound of that. A fucking movie. Insane! Of course, when I saw you I screamed and screamed and screamed.' Lilith stretches her head back and continues in a slow, pained voice. 'I can still feel that scream here.' She thumps her chest forcefully.

'Lil, look, just –'

'It was James who kicked the go-kart away. I saw him. The creep. That smirk of his, then a sneaky flick with his foot and there you were, dangling and kicking.'

They sit in silence for a moment. A train travels past at speed, sounding its horn with a desolate Doppler shift, and they wait for the note to recede, as if the train has something mournful and important to add even as the sound decays.

'There was a helicopter flying overhead. That can't be right either.' She shakes her head, eyes shut tight now, trying to make two disparate memories fit together. 'Perhaps . . . no, I don't know. But I held you up. I thought that if I let you go, you would die. Do you remember?'

'No.'

'You *must* remember,' she commands. 'James and Ben ran away. "It was only a game," they said. For God's sake, Lionel! Remember?' Lilith's face pinches to ugliness.

'Stop it! Stop!'

There is a hint of insanity at the far border of her laughter. 'But the rope just tumbled down in a coil. They hadn't tied it properly, thank God. They just wound it round a couple of times and it unravelled with the weight of you. It was –'

'It *was* a game,' he interrupts. 'Just a stupid game, Lil. You're remembering it all too seriously.'

She shakes her head. 'We got the punishment. You got it worse; you always did – even though the rope burns were raw on your neck. It was him, he did it.'

Through the swim of smoke and light he can see she's crying. 'James you mean?'

'No. Fuck James.'

'I don't understand.'

'It doesn't matter. It doesn't matter because he's dead.'

'Good God. James is dead?'

'Oh, Lionel.' She's growling with frustration.

'Tell me. I don't know what you're saying.'

'It's Dad. David. He's dead.'

There's a triumphal angle to Lilith's head as she pronounces the death of her father. But her mouth, pulled down at the corners, gives away the strain and she looks as if the anticipation will kill her as she waits for him to respond. At first, what he feels is close to nothing; he holds his jaw, thinking about what he should say. But Lilith needs him to speak.

'Dead? I can't believe it,' he says at last. 'I mean, of course. He was sick. But I still can't believe it. What did he die of? Where's Judy?'

Lilith casts her eyes down. Did she want him to cheer?

'It was his heart in the end,' she says flatly.

He covers his own heart with his hand. 'His heart, is that right?'

'I drove Judy to the Yews last night. I left her there. I *abandoned* her.' She makes a guilty face. 'She's been messaging, over and over. I switched my mobile off in the end.'

There are five missed calls and two messages on Lionel's Google device. 'Look, she's been calling me too.'

'I can't deal with her on my own. I know you don't care. I don't expect you to care.'

He reaches out to touch his sister's forearm. 'Of course I care, Lilith. I care about you.'

At his touch Lilith falls to sobbing. 'Can we stay here together, Lionel, just for a little while longer?'

'For as long as you like.'

She holds the duvet back and he can see she's fully clothed under the covers.

'Get in with me. I need you to hold me. You make me feel safe.'

He travels through the thin wall of sunlight bisecting the room and climbs in beside her. Lilith curls into the nest of his arm and he kisses the top of her head. He can smell apples and meadow flowers mixed with the sharp, milky sap from inside a dandelion stalk. Everything about her is familiar and he strokes her hair as she takes shuddering breaths.

'I love you, Lionel.' She is full of sorrow. 'I love you so much.'

'I love you too, Lilith. More than you can ever know.'

As he enfolds her he forgives her everything; her bleak phase, her truculence, her rages and outbursts. A cloud passes over the sun and the wall of light vanishes.

The day has developed light and bright. Dry brush-strokes of cloud diffuse the sunlight so that the fields are painted in pastels. The earlier frost is a fairytale now the warmth of the day has taken hold. Now David is dead.

They're silent, each in the separate mystery of their thoughts. Lilith puffs away in the passenger seat, hair loose like in childhood, untamed. She wears scruffy jeans and one of his old T-shirts. The black fist motif on her chest demands 'Action Against Racism'. It's a T-shirt she gave him years ago, but he never wore it and she stole it back.

'My mind's running everywhere at once.' The sound of her voice makes him jump and she touches his thigh. 'Sorry. I can barely pin a thought down. Is this shock do you think? Is that what this is?'

'Yes. I think so.'

She takes an addict's last drag and flicks the butt from the window. 'And what's going on with Buddha? That did my fucking head in last night.'

'He's getting worse,' he says quietly. 'He won't last much longer.' The thought gives him a physical pain. Will he grieve more for the cat than his father? 'I read that the micro-ID chips can cause feline cancers, so I told Mr Mutterjee to remove the one he got as a kitten. But he says the chip has "migrated". He can't locate it.'

Mr Mutterjee is Buddha's new vet. Lionel gets a discount (as a friend of Pema's), but he suspects that this vet too has no genuine commitment to extending Buddha's life.

'Migrated?' Lilith scoffs. 'Where to – fucking Australia?'

'Exactly. I said if the chip's inside him the reader should pick up the signal.'

'What did he say?'

'He said I was better off forgetting about the chip. It'll cause more distress to remove it than leave it be.'

Lilith looks puzzled. 'It still doesn't explain how a cat, who can barely crawl, ended up on top of the wardrobe.'

'What?'

'That's what I was trying to tell you – when I let myself in last night he was crying, that baby sound cats make.' She pulls a face. 'So I looked for him everywhere and found him on top of the wardrobe.'

He frowns. 'You mean the wardrobe in the bedroom? Are you sure?'

The wardrobe is nearly two metres tall, with boxes and dusty computer parts stacked on top in perilous piles.

'I had to get a chair to get him down. He was all weird and floppy, like normal, but I was freaked. There's no way up there.'

'It's impossible.'

'That's what I thought.'

Judy sits prim as a duchess on a wooden bench outside the Yews. The bench is in an arched recess to the right of the main entrance, in a spot where Judy can look down the drive for approaching cars. Lionel waves, pointlessly, as they walk towards her; she looks through them both. Guilt quickens Lilith's pace and Lionel breaks into a jog to keep up with her. Judy holds a teacup in her lap. Stiff and contained, her disposition acknowledges bygone rituals of bereavement that involve suppression and formality. But there's something selfish in the martyr's look she slings them as they approach.

'Mum!' Lilith starts gushing. 'I'm *so* sorry I left you. I couldn't handle it all, sorry, sorry, sorry.'

Judy hands Lionel her teacup and stands. She's about to speak when George approaches, wearing punctiliousness like an ill-fitting coat, clasping his hands to his solar plexus in a posture that aspires to empathy – or possibly humility – but fails in both.

'I am so sorry for your loss,' recites the African with his head inclined, his eyes still managing to gather each of them in. He turns to Judy and goes on in an obsequious tone. 'There is just one more form to sign, Mrs Byrd.'

Lionel notices his mother's age. Her mouth, a flaccid, down-hanging crescent, impinges on the definition of her jaw. She looks haggard.

'I am so sorry to burden you, Mrs Byrd, but if you could just return to the office for a moment.' George unclasps his hands and guides her to the entrance where she disappears inside. 'And you,' he says, turning abruptly, abandoning the deference of a moment before. 'If you want, you can see his body.'

'It's still here?' Lilith is taken off guard.

Without missing a beat George replies, 'We have a chapel of rest and offer a complete funeral service.'

'Of course you do. How convenient. Well, we'll decide if we want your' – Lilith over-enunciates the words – 'complete funeral service.'

'Your mother has already signed the forms.' An idiotic smile creeps onto the side of the fat African's mouth. 'Your father is peaceful at last.'

Lilith turns to Lionel. 'I don't want to see him. Do you want to see him?'

He shakes his head. 'No, we don't want to see him.'

George laughs roundly, but quickly composes himself so that false rectitude, once again, is smarmed across his chops.

Lilith almost spits as she speaks. 'I think you're forgetting yourself, nurse.' If she had hackles they would be standing proud.

The African chooses to ignore the cautionary glance Lionel gifts him.

'Excuse me,' he says, pausing to remove something from his nostril. 'I have work to do.' He flicks his find into a bed of drooping fritillaries.

Things move very swiftly. Lilith barks something abusive and, springing up as unfeasibly as one of Lionel's avatars, she floors the man with one clean kick to his belly. George lands on the overstuffed cushion of his arse – both hands behind him in the dirt. The fritillaries bob their heads in unison and Lionel hears a flutter of appreciative, floral applause. George looks at Lionel with wary amusement as he picks himself up off the floor. But Lilith isn't done. She goes for him a second time and discharges a swift blow with her fist straight to the bridge of his nose. In an instant there is blood and a fine spray of vermillion peppers the fist on her 'Action Against Racism' T-shirt. George flattens back to the ground, hands at his face, making a sound like the dregs of a milkshake being sucked through a straw. The martial arts training has been a success.

Lilith regards her victim dispassionately. 'You'd better get Judy,' she says turning to Lionel, rubbing the knuckles of her punching hand. 'We're leaving.'

Lionel is never sure when to wade in. His hand, he notices, aches in sympathy and the cup and saucer Judy gave him to hold are in pieces on the path.

@GameAddict (#23756745): 10:7:27

When your avatar dies gamers say you're
'taking a dirt nap'. You see it in the grey world,
on gravestones – 'Here lies so-and-so. Only
Sleeping'. But you don't really need euphe-
misms to disguise mortality on the Game Layer.
Death is temporary. What joy it is to exist in
a world where nothing is final. There's always
the chance to 'Play Again'. There's no one to
mourn. Nothing to fear.

Level 9: In the Wilderness

The Desert of Gog faded to a supernatural nothingness – no beginning, no end. Only the twinklers indicated where heaven met land. In Past Times the desert was ocean and the sand was composed of a trillion dust-crumbling shells and dotted-about Gredlapods – lustrous as mother-of-pearl. In the far-off the ribcages of gargantuan Miina whales arced out of the sand like ruined cathedrals.

Earlier, on the battlefield, as the Krin dead-eyed the MauMau, something came to me crystal. The sorceress was arch but the MauMau, tho programmed to kill, could be tamed. I thanked the Creators that the Krin was an inveterate soldier, for when I ordered, 'Don't shoot!' he instantly put up his weapon. But in a few beats the witch had clocked my defection and targeted us with a blast of pure magic. It took the Krin clean off his feet, tho the MauMau and I remained unaffected. The Krin, spitting out feathers, cussed and ranted but he was unharmed.

I shouted, 'Retreat,' as death charges began to rain all around us.

The Krin, I could tell, was considering his course. But a bulb went *bing* in his nog – a light that said, 'Bugger it, let's have an adventure.' He got up and hastened towards open ground saying, 'Follow me.' Now he was commander and I his lieutenant and I copied his low-crouching zigzags as we headed away from the scene. We only eased up when the death blasts stopped singeing our heels. All the while, to our rear-guard, the MauMau leaped fun-wise, chasing my whip and meowing.

We'd travelled this way for two thousand clicks when a storm got going close by. The wind churned in the darkness and sloughed up the sand in mountainous sting-clouds so it felt like my skin might be flayed.

'We need shelter,' shouted the Krin, shielding his nog with his paws.

We braved the storm to a Miina hull, by which time the air was a torture of sand. When we finally squeezed through the whale's stiff baleen my skin bore raw grazes and my lug-holes were full up with grit. The whale carcass gave welcome protection and once we'd recovered our puff the Krin pointed out ashy fires and stale beast droppings where other travellers had made overnight camp. There were various items strewn about – cook-pots, a flagon of Grog, a blanket or two – half buried, as if the sand was sucking all static things into its barren collective. The gale skirmished around us and yowled, full-mournful, in the upper arcs of the carcass as if reviving the ghostly lament of the long-dead Miina on that night, just for us.

Krin-Balwrin, half dog, half bear, are hefty as Heeber bulls, and on the battlefield they'll broadside an opponent and tear them apart with their ivories. But now the General sat a small distance away, his huge nog bowed, sad-wise and pondersome. I felt a pang for the beast.

'Expert campfire,' I said, poking the flames with a stick.

The Krin made an unreadable noise.

I tried again. 'The MauMau's run off. Can't find it anywhere.'

'Riddance to it,' he gruffed.

'Quite right! Still, it's not the merciless fiend I expected.'

'In my tribe we call it Mafdet. Stuff of sprog nightmares.'

'Mafdet. Good name.' I stirred up the flames once again. 'Do you have a mate? Any sprogs of your own?'

The Krin looked up. 'A mate – moons ago – and a daughter. Both deleted.'

'I'm sorry.'

The bear shrugged. 'My fault – never collected the Grinders for replay.'

The strand was raw and I changed tack. 'What made you run from the sorceress?'

'Apart from her casting death spells?' He laughed emptily then made a low growl. 'Impulse, stupidity.'

'Why stupidity?'

'Prudent to stay close to power, good or ill.'

'The sorceress is powerful?'

He threw a stone in the flames and the fire danced blood-orange. 'She's connected.'

'Connected,' I echoed. 'Well, sometimes decisions rush up from the gut.'

'I've come too far in this game for gut-choices. Still, here I am, on the run with a Reject.' He slung me a glum side-glance.

We passed the flagon between us in silence, but in time the Grog loosened his mood and the Krin told me his back story. In Past Times his tribe farmed the Nur Delta – a paradise place slaked by the mighty Nur river. But the river dried to dust and the Krin-Balwrin became nomads. Only the toughest were chosen for military service.

'I'm Krinnin, first order. I've made sixteen levels.'

'You must be brave.'

'Not brave, just beefy.' He patted his belly with both paws.

I laughed. 'Still, I'd be happier if you were an ally, not foe.'

The Krin didn't laugh but regarded me solemnly, searching my fizzog, peering deep in my Visor. At last he said, 'You can call me Dan-Albwr-han.'

'Greetings to you then, Dan-Albwr-han,' I said. 'And I'm Ludi.'

The Krin held one paw to his chest. 'Greetings, Ludi.' After a bit he said, 'I'm not the player I was, but I'm witted enough to know there are strange things afoot.'

'You mean the MauMau?'

'Yes, the MauMau and other illegal characters shooting through the Wormhole – yourself included.'

'What harm does it do?'

'Destabilizes the dimension. Inferior characters keep rolling up Viral – or smuggling assets.' He realized he was firing off insults and added, 'No offence. I'm sure your code's clean. Still, illegal migration means more competition for Power Rings. They're already scarce.'

'Why's that?'

'Finite resource. Never enough. And with all these Quests to find Keys and rogue characters –'

'I have a Quest.' I'm not sure why it slid out so easy.

The Krin wrinkled his snout. 'What Quest?'

'To find a rogue character – a Sylph. She's illegal. Corrupted.'

'And what must you do with her when you find her?'

'I'm not sure. I suspect I'll try and repair her.'

'See what I mean – illegal characters popping up everywhere. More energy meters to service.' The Krin puffed horsily. 'But since we're comrades I'll give you this snippet – I've heard of a character, an alchemist in Br'mab, who can repair corrupt characters. Not sure if it's true, but there it is.'

I acknowledged the tip with a grateful nog-bob. 'What would happen,' I started cautious, 'if the Realm could be reset?'

'Huh? Dire notion! My whole span would be pointless. All my deeds, everyone's deeds – striving, fighting, acquiring skills – would be null.'

'But you'd know nothing of it. You'd be reborn after a fashion.'

The Krin massaged his temples. 'Replay. Rebirth. Why this fascination with doing things over and over again?'

'To get it right. To rectify our mistakes.'

'Pah!' He batted the air with a paw.

Tho I tried more chin-wagging, the Krin did several giant-size yawns and turned quiet and snoozy. Soon the wind went gentle too and the Miina hull creaked, ship-wise, in the leftover breeze like the rigging of a sea-borne galleon. The night sky peeped through raggedy holes where the Miina's hide had been wind-ripped. A pantheon of twinklers needled the canopy and the moon, at the apex, unravelled its bolts of light earth-wise like lengths of buttery silk. A Reve owl hooted somewhere on high. I drifted, soporific, nurturing thoughts of Mata Angelica; her long-luscious pins, her hip girdle, the subtle curve of her belly-dip, the bloom on her Eroticon skin. I let the memory suffuse me. Would she think I'd betrayed her? Would she look for me in the desert? Why did she think I could gather up Keys when the sorceress, it seemed, was mistress of all?

My thoughts turned to the Sylph. What had become of her? I felt drawn to the lovelorn character as if destiny called me.

The Krin curled to a wool-mound. 'Well, Reject,' he said, 'our paths overlap for the present.'

And with that his nog nodded daft-wise and one long, bovine expiration signalled he was in sleep-mode.

Crystal's Room

On quiet nights the buildings on Milk Street amplify the street sounds as clearly as an amphitheatre. Tonight a bright slit of moon puts a hard edge on everything and stray-bullet voices ricochet in through Lionel's window. Two women, feisty and shrill, have collared a couple of piss-heads out prospecting together.

One man says, 'Thirty credits? Do me a favour! It's half that in there.'

'Well, I'd check my dick if I'd been in that shithole,' a woman replies. 'I'd check my wallet 'n' all.'

Lionel's only half-listening; he's going over the scene at the Yews. His dead father, his miserable mother and Lilith – violent and churlish. After attacking the African, Lilith upped and vanished until the drama was over, left Lionel gawping as George rolled his awkward bulk to one side, trying to stand. Several staff came running and there was talk of the police being called, but George staunched the blood and said, 'No,' in a nasal but heroic monosyllable. Blood spotted his tunic and made a crimson mandala on his chest that looked like a rosette or a medal. He came off almost valiant.

On the journey back, Judy kept repeating, 'Why did you have to hit him? What has he ever done to hurt you? Isn't there enough pain?'

Lilith on the back seat, forehead against the glass, eyes on the blur of the road.

Is this shock do you think? Is that what this is?

At the bungalow he tried to support Judy's elbow as she walked from the car to the door, but she unhitched herself from him with a bristling roll of her shoulder.

'I'm fine from here, Lionel. I'd rather be alone.'

'Are you sure?'

'Perfectly.'

Since then neither Judy nor Lilith has returned his calls.

None of the forum threads he's posted have yielded any results, but he's determined to discover the programmer who designed the sorceress's passerines. He's about to post 3D flyrounds of the specimen to the *CoreQuest* technical blog when he notices that the voices on the street have changed key. There's a scream, not of fear but of fury. Lionel reaches the window in time to see the beautiful anime girl pitch into the road, manic with temper, cussing in English although he's convinced she's Japanese. She leaps high and lands, stamping her foot. Bizarre. It looks as if she's trying to fly.

'Fucking bastard. Fucking pimp,' she yells. 'My cousin will come and he will fuck *you* in the arse. Fucking *fuck*.'

An older woman comes out of the alleyway, trying to soothe her. She's dressed plainly and speaks in urgent, pacifying tones. She catches the beautiful girl's sleeve and attempts to drag her into the alley, but the anime girl writhes free. She's not scared. She can't be held.

'I fucking hate the fucking mens.' She bounces the flat of her hand off her forehead. 'I hate them.'

A small, foppishly dressed man emerges from the alley. His cursory glance up and down the road gives Lionel a view of his face in profile. Lionel ducks below the windowsill. It's the man from the club – the man Grippa was attending the night of the attack. Lionel watches from a gap at the bottom of the blind. His heart is pounding. *Good Lord.* The man's long, velvet jacket hangs in tailored pleats from a central button between his shoulder blades. With each purposeful stride it swishes round his knees like a woman's swing-coat. A red gemstone in the knot of his tie winks opulently in the streetlight. The anime girl continues to shout as he approaches, but she's unsettled and takes a few steps backwards, eyes alert, before the man stops in front of her. He puts a finger to his lips, encouraging silence.

Mouth tight now, arms folded, she stares back defiantly. Lionel grips the windowsill. Time slows. A light breeze moves the pavement litter around her feet. It blows a loose strand of hair across her face. It lifts the hem of her pleated skirt and reveals her bare thigh, a glimpse of cotton underwear. Was that the flash of steel he just saw? Whatever it was, she's invincible. He's aching for her to kick out and show off her ninja prowess. She's sure to have all the warrior moves. She'll kill the foppish man in a flash. *Woo-ya.* He digs his nails into the sill; remembers his scimitar in the box under the bed. Perhaps he should go down there. Back her up. It's what Ludi would do.

It's the slightest droop of her shoulders that signals her weakness. Her jaw remains hard, but her whole body shrinks and Lionel can see how thin she is – her emaciated wrists, her withered thighs. He wants to call out to her, tell her not to give in; a ninja like her can easily defeat an evil character like that – he's seen it in all the manga games. Where's your gun, anime girl? Where are your weapons? God!

The man raises his fist and on reflex the girl cringes. But his hand stops in mid-air, his brutish smile caught in the light from the streetlamp. Domination. It amuses the foppish man for a second before he gives himself up to a full-blown laugh. He swipes suddenly – grunting as his fist makes contact. It's a heartless blow delivered to her head, and the girl crumples against the wall, undignified, holding the side of her face until her legs fold away completely. The older woman backs into the doorway, in shadow now, except for her feet. The man says something to her, takes a long drag on his cigarette, gives a one-fingered salute to the observation camera that surveys Milk Street twenty-four-seven and strides away, down the alley.

Raise the blind, throw open the sash; Lionel summons a shout but it sticks in his windpipe. *Coward.* The night air is cool, but he's burning as he paces the room. He has witnessed acts of violence from his window before. He's watched deadbeat youths slug one another to pulp. *Who cares?* He saw a taxi driver slam a man with a turban against the café window, a knife at his jugular, while a couple inside looked on, faintly bored. *They'll sort it out.* Another man, on another night, twisted a girl's arm behind her back and took a chunk off her ear with his teeth as she begged *for pity's sake* and the blood made cherry-red jags on her cheek. There was no excuse for not getting involved. None. But close the blinds anyway. Go back to the game. What else could he do? How could he change anything? But tonight he feels different.

When he's down on the street he feels the rumble of a distant freight train. The high-pitched *more-tea* of a robin whistles close by. There's no sign of the anime girl. He jogs down past Mr Barber's then doubles back towards the junction. Near the railway station, staggering towards the oncoming traffic, he spots her. The older woman has abandoned her and he runs across the road to intercept her.

'Hey! Hey you!'

His shout sends her off-balance and she collapses, gracelessly, onto the kerb. He stops a few metres away, holding his hands above his head to show he's harmless.

'Are you okay?'

The anime girl gazes through him.

'You know me, right,' he says soothingly. 'I'm the man from the flat, the man from the barber's, down there.' He points in the general direction of the barber's shop.

A line of blood runs from her hairline to her chin. Her pupils swim, dark as onyx.

'I saw what happened back there.' He points the other way, back down the road. 'I can get a taxi, take you to the hospital.'

Head circling like a drunkard, she fumbles for cigarettes in her jacket pocket, picks one from the box and lights it.

'You need medical attention. A doctor. There's no doubt.' He's trying to pronounce all his words softly yet clearly, so she understands.

The girl takes several sucks on her cigarette. 'Twenty credit, blowjob – tsirty credit, do what you like.' Her voice is surprisingly balanced, reeling off learned patter. Brazen.

'No. I, I don't want . . . I don't want anything like that. I only . . . You know me, right? You remember me from the window, in the rain? From the –'

'Yes,' she interrupts with a sneer that makes him question his empathy. 'I know you!' Rearing up, coltish, lurching towards him, mouth twisting into an unattractive bow. 'You look, lookey me, like all the mens. I seen you.'

He wipes his nose with the back of his hand. 'I don't look at you like that.'

Her mouth relaxes and she bites her bottom lip and fingers the hem of his shirt, trying to make eye contact, pulling on his hem now, drawing him towards her. The blood on the side of her face is already drying, and this close he can see her pupils are dilated and her lips are cracked. She brings her thigh gently to his crotch, pressing her pelvis into his, and he shifts back, embarrassed.

'Ha! See!' She upbraids him, pushing him away. 'All the mens same.'

The anime girl struts off, leggy, unstable, and he follows behind, hands pushed in the pockets of his jeans.

'Why are you going back?' he asks. 'Don't go back there.'

She doesn't answer, but at the top of the alley she turns to him, altered suddenly, and says, 'You come in with me, yes?'

When he doesn't respond she takes his hand in both of hers and walks backwards, leading him down the alley. She reminds him of a foal, wobbly on newborn limbs, the line of blood accentuating the length and gauntness of her face.

'I can't. I can't come in. That man who hit you . . .'

'You scare of Huo?' She tuts at him, for shame. 'He gone now, is okay. Come.'

The blue neon sign from the taxi office barely penetrates the darkness. A *drip*, *drip* in the dampness echoes like a cave and he notices a smear of cool light reflecting off the slime creeping up the bricks on the furthest wall. How can he explain that her tormentor is his own? The urge to flee almost sends him, pell-mell, back down the alley. But there's something about her he can't resist.

'Come. Is safe.' She pouts.

Something moves in a corner, half-hidden by the doorway. Lionel freezes, stomach churning; but it's the older woman from earlier. She says something to the beautiful girl in another language and emerges from the shadows to fix her charge with a fishy eye.

'What do you think?' the anime girl snaps back in English, the natural hardness returning to her voice.

The older woman redirects her attention to Lionel. 'I know you?'

Sweat beads on his brow, he's trembling at the thought of the foppish man appearing. There's a camera above the doorway and Lionel lowers his face as he shakes his head.

If he's watching, the foppish man will recognize him in an instant. Who knows what he might do to him in the private fiefdom of the health centre. The scimitar remains in the box under his bed, but he could fight the man, couldn't he? Rip the red gem from his tie and tighten the material around his neck. He imagines the man choking, his face distorting and swelling, but he keeps his own face turned to the shadows.

The woman's scrutiny is unbearable. 'You are not regular?'

'I've n-never been,' he stammers.

The headlights of a taxi pulling up send stripes of slanted light along the alley, making all of them shield their eyes. But before they're bathed in darkness again the girl yanks him across the threshold.

'How can you come back when these people are hurting you?'

'Shh!'

They are in a short passageway papered in peeling, red-patterned flock. At the far end a single eco-bulb lights the top of a stairway, leading downwards. From behind a door he can hear men and women – bland encouragements, groans, a sniffle. The girl knocks on another door and waits, pressing her ear to the wood. When she's sure the room is empty she signals for him to follow her in.

A double bed, covered by a flimsy throw, dominates the room. A red-bulbed lamp casts striated patterns onto the walls. Somehow the room appears lopsided. Perfumed smoke coils up from an incense burner, masking other, thicker odours. There's a window in one wall, boarded and painted black. And there, propped in the corner, is the missing sign from the Caribbean bakery. A fat cartoon sun with a cheeky smile winks at him. *Bring a Lickle Taste of Sunshine in your Life*, says the legend.

The girl is already removing her clothes, stopping every now and then to pick her cigarette from the ashtray. There are tissues and baby wipes in a rattan box next to the bed. Mouthwash. Condoms. A selection of dildos.

Lionel keeps his clothes on. His head's buzzing louder than a faulty fuse. His mouth is dry and he turns away from her, biting his nails. There's a picture of an old woman on top of a cabinet, in a simple, stand-up frame. The woman is wearing a headscarf and her big-knuckled hands grip the top of a stick as she perches on the veranda of a rustic house. A chicken pecks by her feet. The woman looks out over a never-ending field of ripening corn that stretches away to an indigo sky.

'Hey, mans.'

The anime girl is anime no longer. She's a ghost with death-camp skin and spiritless eyes. Her flesh is too pale, contrasting the gloomy room, contrasting him. But her vulnerability is sexual. Her defencelessness an invitation to defile.

She reclines on the bed with well-rehearsed elegance. 'What is your name?' she says. Etiolated limbs move with the grace of an underwater plant.

'Ludi,' he replies without thinking.

She pushes the end of her cigarette into the ashtray. 'Ludi is nice name. Come,' and she offers herself to him; subtly shifting her shoulders to make her breasts more prominent, one thigh sliding off the other to show a way to her naked crack. She has no pubic hair. She is shining white porcelain, luminous.

When he doesn't move she says, 'Come, I make you very happy.' She sounds bored.

Lionel turns his lips inwards and looks at his feet.

'Perhaps you like fight. Eh? Your face. You look like you fight.' She holds her fists up like a boxer. 'You want fight with me?'

The wedge of flesh on his eye has ripened to purple and brown, but his fingers trace the outline of the old injury as he sits on the edge of the bed. 'I don't want to fight. I've never liked fighting.'

'I seen you. The mens all want fight.' She snaps puppy teeth at him.

Without thinking he leans towards her and kisses her, pins her mouth with his for a few seconds, then pulls away.

'What's your name?' he asks.

Her hand slides to his crotch. 'Call me Crystal.'

'Crystal.'

He encloses her hand with his and holds it, as if he's rescuing a bird. But she pulls it free and mutters something in her language.

'Come on, mans,' she says, impatiently.

'I don't . . . I don't want it, really, I don't,' he says and hangs his head.

'You're beautiful and I've wanted to talk to you for a long time. Since I saw you on the street, out there. But someone died today, you see. No yesterday,' he corrects. 'Or the day before or . . .' He stands, realizing he's lost track of time.

Her eyes flash fearfully to the door. 'You must pay. You cannot go without pay.'

'Of course I'll pay. Don't worry about that.'

Relieved, the girl gets onto her knees and covers her breasts with the throw. 'Who died?' she whispers. 'You tell me.'

Lionel sits down again. 'My father.'

'So sorry.'

'But not my father.'

She looks quizzical. 'No father.'

'He raised me, but he wasn't my real father.'

'Oh. He is good mans to raise you.'

'Yes. He was.'

'Where is the *blood* father?' She struggles to pronounce the word blood.

He gestures towards the photo on the cabinet. 'Is that your mother?'

'Beatrise grandmother, not mine mother.'

She gets off the bed and walks to the cabinet, turns the picture to the wall. Her skin reflects light as if she's a magical creature. She's a nymph or a fairy, not human at all.

'Beatrise works here?' He points to the floor, trying not to stare at her body.

'Yes.' She lights another cigarette. 'Where is *blood* father? You tell me.'

'I don't know.' Why is she questioning him like this? 'I don't know my mother or my father.' Now he wants to provoke her. 'Where's *your* father?'

She closes her eyes, turns away.

'Everyone wants me to find my *real* family,' he continues, 'but there's nothing real about the past. Nothing vaguely important or meaningful. This is reality. Here. Now.'

But even as he says it he knows this isn't real. It's too oppressive. If he could get some light in, yes, pull down the boarding from the window and break down the partition wall. Punch a wide hole in this roof and let the brightness flood in. If he could do these things then it might be more real – not this strange, crooked world where the sun's a Caribbean cartoon. Where ghost children offer themselves to grown men. Where baddies like Huo lurk in the shadows.

With some light in here the old woman in the photo would come to life and peer across from her side of the photo, and they'd all laugh and the chicken at her feet would laugh the hardest. When the greetings were over she'd charge across the divide, stick held high, followed by a great, righteous tribe – fathers and brothers and uncles – carrying pitchforks and scythes, ready to punish Huo and his despicable henchmen. The girl's family would save her. Her family *should* save her. Where are they? Where are all the families of people like her, and like him? Why is everyone so discarded and alone?

'Ludi?'

'Yes.'

'I sink you go now.'

'How old are you?' he says quickly.

She looks away again. 'Perhaps I have twenty year.'

'No, tell me. How old?'

She takes another drag and blows a delicate smokescreen between them. She will not answer.

'Why do you stay?' His tone is accusatory. 'That man, all the men . . .' He doesn't know what else to say.

'I must pay Huo plenty money. I borrow from the mans in China and he buy my . . .' She searches for the word, '. . . borrow.'

'Huo owns your debt.'

'He own me.' She stabs her chest with her finger.

'How much?'

'Tsirty thousand credit.'

'Crikey.'

Crystal shrugs. 'One day I pay.' She looks defeated, but her face quickly hardens. 'Maybe I same like you, too – no *blood* father – nowhere to run. That's why I stay. Where to go?'

'Come with me. I'll help you.'

He means it. He wants to scoop her up and carry her off.

Gratitude and pride are both disclosed in Crystal's face. She lifts her chin. 'You get passport for me, ID?'

'Well, I . . . I can try.'

'Money?'

'I have some credit, a little credit, yes. You can have it all.'

'You have gun?'

'Er, no.'

'Gang, you have gang?'

'Me? A gang?'

'Yes, tough mans, bad mans who fight.' The girl wipes her nose with her fist.

'No. I don't have a gang.'

'How you help me, mister, uh? Scare mans like you. How you fight Huo?'

The question floats between them for an age. Lionel is ashamed. The anime girl, once a vision, is raw and naked. He holds her gaze for a few more seconds before standing.

'I only want to help.' He can't look at her any more.

As he leaves he turns the picture of the old woman back round to face the girl and places several pay tokens beside it.

'Goodbye,' he whispers, and opens the door.

'Wait!' She is kneeling on the bed, clasping the throw at her throat. 'You really want help me?'

'If I can.'

'Come see me again.'

'Get some sleep now.' He touches his head where she was struck. 'You could have concussion.'

The girl presses the side of her face and winces. He can barely hear what she says next. His head is filled with a deafening susurrus – as if a quantity of glass is smashing close by. The anime girl is disintegrating. Crystal.

Lionel shields his face from the cameras in the corridor. Wireless devices can be disguised as houseflies, but the pictures they return are in broadcast definition. If he were Huo he'd have one hidden in every room. He makes a mental map – the staircase, an unlit corridor below with two doors leading off it. He should go down. Burst into the basement rooms and despatch the evil slavers – *boff, kerpow, splat.*

How you help me, mister? Scare mans like you.

A door opens and he runs out through the alley without looking back.

@GameAddict (#23756745): 14:7:27

Make allegiances. Even if you're a loner geek you'll need allies if you want to crack the Final Levels. Bosses are powerful bastards and you can only kill them if you band together with like-minded characters. With enough allies you can attempt a raid. Make a good ally and they'll look out for you to the end.

Level 10: Passerines Sing at the Oasis of Kilhm

The Miina hull produced a trove of supplies. Apart from the DumGrog there was a cache of Fallion feathers (magical, tradeable) and three Power Rings. Me and the Krin both slipped one on and soon we were roaring, making fists, as the energy did stiff-surges through us. In three clicks our meters hit 100. Totally druggish.

The decision to join forces in search of Keys and the Sylph came easy once the rushes eased off and we soon set off whistling as if we were veteran brothers-in-arms. Dan-Albwr-han knew a path across Gog and he led the way at a clip. We travelled through arid sea-valleys, up rugged cliffs, along wild and wonderful plateaus. The whole place would have been underwater in Past Times and I imagined great fishes sharking the canyons and Gredlapods skulling the spangly green shallows. On the journey we fought a few nasty characters – looted them for armour and skills. We saw plenty of Wisps mooning about waiting for replay, but the MauMau had vanished. It was as if the beast had been snaffled by sand.

Finally we arrived at the Oasis of Kilhm, traded Fallion feathers for hostelry and holed up, replenishing our health meters. Kilhm was a way-station of low-roofed dwell-places fashioned from straw and ripe Heeber dung. It smelled of manure and fresh water and we both marked that it had a nice hum. The lodgings were built round a series of deep-gurgling boreholes and these, in turn, were ranged about a circular pool that bubbled right out of the sand. We splashed about in it, as the women did scrubbing and pot-walloping, and washed off the crust of our travel.

The Krin, while we bathed, interrogated the women, softly-softly. We learned of a Vadarian circus troupe that had come through not three moon-transits previous. The troupe traded showtimes for vitals and the station was bereft when they left.

'I know that troupe,' said the Krin (tho he didn't). 'Did they perchance have the Sylph with them?'

'Oh yes,' said the dhobi-women – cow-eyed and plaintive as they scribed the child's *tra-la-la*. 'She made us all weep, specially since she was not long for this Realm. Quite corrupted.'

Dan-Albwr-han gave me a sleuth's wink. 'What song did she sing?' he asked, turning back to them.

'The one 'bout Love,' they replied in a chorus.

The women did swoon-faces as they recalled it and soon they were bawling and fanning one another with hankies.

'There, there.' The Krin tried to soothe them. 'Did she speak at all?'

'She did not. She only did *tra-la-la*.'

The women thought she must be a goddess, but when they brought her offerings (miniature Heeber shaped from dung), the Sylph only sighed and refused them.

'We hoped our worship would build her up. Her opacity was down 30/70.'

The Krin nodded in sympathy then said, 'Where were they headed?'

'Directly to Vadar, of course.'

'Ah yes, of course.'

The circus troupe sounded more like Gladiators than theatrical-types (the dhobi-women said there were Mutants and WeirdFucks among them), so we knew we were in for a scrap. But we were stoked to have ferreted the Sylph's trail so quickly and we celebrated our last evening in Kilhm with a Grog-fest out by the pool.

The night was balmy. The twinkling bowl of the heaven arced over us. Perfume-flowers hung in great bulbous bracts from the wellheads and soffits and gave off a fragrance so heady it altered the mind. Woozy-headed, heavy-eyed, we sang manly songs from our memories. Dan-Albwr-han's song was of a wide-hipped Krin maid with lash-batting lids and powerful thighs that she wrapped round her sire's flanks as they tumbled. My song was a deep-dirge about a carpenter whose father-Creator sent him to die in a tree. It was tiresome serious and the Krin turned his back, disgusted, and sang on about bawdy carousing till the night was near done.

It was just before sunrise when I dreamed the sound of the tweeters. Their song weaved in-out of the Krin's saucy shanty making a rousing refrain of it. But it wasn't a dream. The passerines were perched by the pool, their breast-bibs shimmering blue in the moonlight. I had to bash the Krin's rump several times before he stopped his rude racket.

'Look!' I whispered. 'Over there.'

'They must have escaped,' mused the Krin.

'Or the sorceress is close by and these are sent spy-watching.'

We sat up swift-wise, fear cooling our levity. But the birds flew down, one, two, and landed dainty and tame on our shoulders, still warbling.

The Krin hiccoughed and scowled. 'I've got a bad feeling 'bout this.'

When the sun brimmed we set off once more across the desert and the passerines followed us at every step. Shrill and insistent.

Home Truth

It shouldn't surprise him that Crystal's tormentor is his own. Everything's connected, after all. But to see Huo drifting about on Milk Street was as if a malevolent character from the Game Layer had come to life. Lionel's been trapped in the flat ever since, terrified of bumping into him. The scimitar sleeps with him under the duvet. It's next to his desk when he's zipping round *CoreQuest*. He's learning some nifty moves too – scything, swinging, jousting and stabbing. Skills – that's what he needs.

The fear is one thing, but Lionel's up to his neck in the long-forgotten. David's death has opened the sluice gates. There's the crow with the broken wing that he kept in the shed. Weeks of bread soaked in warm milk and worms dug from the garden couldn't save it. David carried it off eventually in gentle-giant hands with a grim look over his shoulder and said, 'Don't follow me, boy.' But Lionel did and watched from behind the water butt as David smashed the crow's skull with the flat of an axe. It sounded like an egg being cracked. David, pale and perspiring, wiped his brow when the deed was done. Solemn. Guilty.

There's the day David arrived at Aunt Rachel's, arms full of bright boxes – Christmas or birthday – and he kneeled with his father on the thick wool-twist carpet and David said, 'This one's from James and this one's from Ben and this one's from me and . . .' But all the gift tags were written in David's stark capitals.

There's a series of snapshots from Norwich: the cathedral, the low, stone-built conversion he rented, Pablo, his roommate, his tutor. David quizzing him seriously about his plans for the future. Father to son. Man to man. Shaking his hand, tears in his eyes.

Lionel adds all this up and concludes something strange and surprising. That David, distantly, cumbrously, loved him. And with this knowledge comes loss.

Another memory. Lionel is a child, hiding under the duvet, when a hand heaves him from his bed. Trousers and underpants come down unceremoniously and a cane meets his arse with monotonous strikes. *Thwack, thwack, thwack, thwack.* He grits his teeth but the tears come hot, involuntarily. It's David's duty to create God-fearing boys and it's a job well done, so far. Now he's set out on the back step to ruminate on his sins, to miss supper, to focus on the welts branding his buttocks, to draft and rehearse a script of repentance – when a sound from the dark end of the garden lures him away.

'Lilith, is that you?'

Perhaps it's an owl, or the wind in the trees. *It's only a game.* Perhaps it's a rat or a snake in the grass. He walks towards the sound, wiping snot on his sleeve, peering into the night.

'Lil?'

Is that a hand brushing his face?

'Who's there?'

Woo-hoo, an owl answers.

That's it; he's spooked and he's off, sprinting out through the gate. There's nothing to see but the faint contours of lollop-topped poplars, jack-knifing at clouds. The wind is a gale around him, commanding leaves to assault him and he counters the attack with blind, hysterical swipes and runs and runs, for miles it feels, until he buckles. Hands on his knees, he dry-heaves for minutes before he recovers. The wind drops. The pain of his punishment finally ebbs. Straightening, he searches for a point of reference and sees the light from a cottage further off. The light is coming from the back of the house where a window oozes a marmalade glow.

Through the window a mother and father and three rosy children are all sitting at table. A fat tabby prowls the chair legs. Their cat hasn't run away. The children, whose faces all share traits of their parents, have the bloom of unconditional love on them. They help themselves to food from huge earthenware dishes. They're happy.

When the meal's over, the father carries sleep-eyed children to bed. The mother, washing dishes, faces the night through the window, surrounded by light, wrapped up in snug thoughts of her family. Until the husband comes softly behind her, puts his hands on her hips as she scours a pan, and whispers a charm in her ear. She moves her mouth towards his, slit-eyed, like the cat, and after they kiss they both look at Lionel together, directly at him. Their faces are beacons of love, but he knows that they are lost in their own cosy reflection. Nothing is connected to him. No one loves him the way this family loves their own. The love in the Byrd family is closed up and wiry, meted out piecemeal to this one and not that, or most often it's simply withheld, folded away with the tea towels, or pushed into the pages of the Bible like the sketch of a sermon, left there, cold as doctrine.

If I could slide through hard surfaces, become as spirit or gas, he thinks . . . I would slip from this world into another. I will. I know I will one day.

Back on the lane, light-blind for a minute, he tries to work out where he is until an ambient glow some way off finally gives him his bearings and he sets out towards it, scrambling first over a farm gate and then trudging on through the fields not worrying about mud or cowpats or the sharp smell of silage accosting his nostrils. A rumble of thunder is closing in, although he can't work out which direction it's coming from. He hunches over – ready for rain.

He hears the motorway before he sees it, not the normal *hweesh hwoosh* of cars sweeping through the night, but an irritable grind of engines lowing like a corralled and dispirited herd. There's the *throck throck* of a helicopter and the whine of a camera-drone at lark's altitude. He follows the cattle path down to the embankment and finds the bridge, further along, that leads over the carriageways. It's where he and Lilith sit when they're sad; heads over the traffic, lost in the flow of other lives passing beneath them. Wishing they were inside the vehicles zooming north or south. Away from here.

The vast sweep of the road is backed up with cars and in the distance, where the motorway curves round a hill, he can see the helicopter projecting a cone of white light onto the road, coming towards him. There's been an accident.

In the centre of the bridge, where some previous bottleneck of cows has resulted in a few metal struts being hoofed away, he sits and dangles his legs off the edge. It's where they normally sit. Him and Lilith. *Careful, Lionel.* There are hundreds of cars, brake lights and headlights, oncoming and receding, and in each one a person or a family. The game is to try and imagine their faces, their lives and the sins they've committed. The hundreds upon thousands of souls, each as unimportant as his, stuck on the motorway, destined for the everlasting. The lights beneath him blur to plaits of crimson and halogen-blue and he rolls his head and sings a line or two from a hymn, but his throat is tight and he coughs the last line out.

The rain falls suddenly and he gives his face to the downpour and laughs. As it soaks him, a branch of lightning discharges above him with a simultaneous explosion of thunder – as if God has something to say about laughter. He jumps with fright, and he slips. He slips. He tries to hold on. But curtains of rain fall all at once, and he's laughing again, but still slipping. The helicopter is directly above him, now shining its beam on his face, and way below him, in between stationary cars, there's a girl looking up, in the helicopter's spotlight. She's soaking. Hair stuck to her face, she looks at him. She's looking directly and precisely at Lionel. Only him. The girl's gaze is so fixed and so intimate that Lionel doesn't recognize her at first; he wants to remain, endlessly locked in this moment, for the girl's gaze is freighted with love.

Lilith? What's she doing down there? Why have David and Judy not noticed she's missing? Why don't they come and find her? But he can't think about it, because at that moment he slips right down and gives in to the fall. And he falls and he falls and he continues to fall. There's no choice.

Despite cosmetic attempts to emphasize the contrary, Judy's face shows the ravages of sleeplessness and age. She's expecting him, but when she opens the door she presses one hand to the top of her chest as if she's surprised to see him.

'Oh, it's you, Lionel,' she says. 'Go straight through.'

She directs him out of the dining room – so neat, so clean – through the french windows and onto the sunny patio. The warmth of the day is disarming. A garden table is set with tea things, Judy's second best, and shaded by a large parasol.

'I have lemonade if you want it. It's homemade.'

'Tea's fine.'

'You never liked lemonade, is that right?' For a moment she seems concerned, but it's a polite detail she's checking.

'That's right, I never liked it.'

This bungalow is not the rambling house he grew up in. Not the isolated, post-African sanctuary David had longed for. This is the sick house; forced domicile after David's diagnosis when he could no longer drive, when he began to have trouble with the stairs. 'He needs something more manageable,' the consultants had said.

The grounds at Bethesda – its kitchen garden, its adjacent meadow and orchard – had become overgrown and it upset David to see the weeds encroaching. So many things upset him, but leaving the garden – the home he adored – was the biggest wrench.

The garden at the bungalow is a mere patch in comparison and at first glance Judy has made a praiseworthy job of it. The grass is edged, the beds are weeded, the patio free from moss. But further down, dandelions are brandishing their serrated leaves, threatening the lawn. David would have had those out in a trice.

Judy has overlooked a certain amount of reckless growth away from the house, and Lionel's gaze is drawn to an area, towards the back fence, that has turned wild. The greenhouse at the furthest end has become overrun by tall grass, and there are clutches of honesty, broken at angles, and last year's onions gone to seed, their extravagant pom-poms on dry stalks now relaxing into lilac decay.

'I don't have the energy or the inclination for it,' Judy says, reading his mind. 'Besides, *he* did the outside, I did the inside.'

'There's no need to feel guilty. No one can do everything.'

She looks at him askance, stung by his casual dispensation. 'I simply can't manage it. A man from the church does bits and pieces.' She nods to the raised beds. 'David hated to see it untidy.'

When will Judy stop talking as if he hadn't witnessed the decline?

*

It was three years ago, late summer and the apples already ripe, when it started in earnest. David took to holding his head in a constant, thoughtful pose. At first Judy thought it was one of his 'episodes'; he'd had them before, where hours turned to days of contemplation. She should have guessed it was Alzheimer's years before the diagnosis – but spiritual men can exhibit such unusual habits. It's hard to tell piety and sickness apart. David would stare into his lap as if the creases in his trousers, or perhaps his genitals beneath, were the cause of some profound anxiety.

The first time she phoned he sensed his mother was subjugating a sense of betrayal for the greater good. 'He's asking for *you*, Lionel,' she said, although it took a while for her to spit it out.

When he got to the bungalow the evening light was slanting through the back window and a precise shadow cut across his father's face. David was gripping the arms of the Parker Knoll, as if he expected the thing to take off. He'd rolled his trousers up above his knees and there were scabs and bruises on his dried-out skin. His head was bowed, but when he realized Lionel was there, he looked up, tears brimming, and said, 'Thank God you've come, son. Thank God.'

A few weeks later and David was watching his wife with tortured suspicion, following her movements, always mistrustful. He had become convinced of her murderous intentions. He bridled, nostrils flared, when Judy tried to change his shirt or coax him to bed. He kicked out, slapped her hands away.

'Watch her, she's a tricky one,' David warned, when the church elders came to call, fending her off with his fists.

Judy was unbalanced by it all and held onto things – furniture, banisters – as she went around the house, as if the very act of walking through the house was a slippery and exhausting business.

Photographs showed that David had been muscular in his youth. Sturdy, sandy-haired, with freckles on his cheeks and the backs of his hands, he had the face of a scholar: a penetrating, green-eyed gaze and grooves in his forehead gouged out by years of concentration. But he had the body of a pugilist – thick-necked, barrel-chested, with hands that could twist an apple into halves. Shoulders that stretched the seams of his shirts. At the end it was David's arms that alarmed Lionel most – the drapes of creamy flesh where his biceps had been. Skin and bone. To witness a strong man wither – to spectate on his increasing decrepitude – felt shameful and fascinating.

'I wanted to talk to you before the funeral.' Judy smooths her skirt then looks up, an ambiguous curl to her lip. 'I want to get some things out in the open. But first I want to talk about George.'

'George?'

'David's nurse.'

'Ah!' He shifts on his seat. 'He was rude to Lilith, very rude.'

Judy looks at the sky and takes a deep breath. 'Well, he maintains it was you, Lionel. You attacked him for no reason.'

Lionel considers for a second. If George is being chivalrous enough to protect Lilith by pointing the finger at him then he should play along.

'Okay.'

'So you admit it was you?'

'Yes.'

Judy clasps her hands and looks heavenward once more, as if God has somehow changed destiny and she's grateful for His intervention.

'If you write a letter of apology, the management won't press charges, and since we're using *all* their services, for the . . . funeral.' It fatigues her to say the word.

'I'll send an email.'

'I suppose that will do.' She's almost placated. 'Promise me.'

'I promise.'

They sit for a minute and watch the starlings hunt ground beetles on the lawn until Judy begins purposefully. 'Now, I won't beat round the bush. We never promised you anything. We made it quite clear you wouldn't have the same as the others when we're gone.'

'No,' he agrees. 'I thought we'd talked about this.'

'Er, I don't think so. There'll only be a small provision, you see, but it should be enough.'

'You don't have to explain. I'm not expecting anything. I'm grateful for everything you've done. Anyway, *you're* not gone, you're still here. Everything should be yours, shouldn't it?'

She takes a delicate sip of her tea. 'You're right. I am still here. But I want to make sure you moderate your expectations, Lionel. I don't want you to be disappointed further down the line.'

Disappointed. This is the word he's been searching for since David died. Not grief, not frustration or anger – but disappointment. He wonders if it even counts as a real emotion.

The largest starling has spied an insect but rears up in dismay as a smaller male beats him to the prize. The bird lifts off the ground, beak parted as if it will attack and there's a fury of squawking and flapping of wings. The small bird flattens to the grass, but although its stance is submissive it doesn't give in. Instead it screeches and snipes at its aggressor.

Judy raises her voice above the dispute on the lawn. 'It's Rachel, you see. She's misunderstood everything.'

'You mean Aunt Rachel?'

'Yes. Yes. She's adamant.'

'Adamant?'

'Oh, Lionel, please don't do that . . . repeating thing you do. I know she's written to you. She's told me.'

Lionel scratches his growing beard. 'But I haven't heard from her. I wouldn't lie.'

'You haven't spoken?'

'Not since . . .' He tries to work it out. 'I don't know, Christmas, I suppose.'

Judy searches Lionel's face. 'Right. Well. Then there's nothing to talk about. That's it.'

For no obvious reason, the starlings' quarrel resolves and the birds hunt on together in peace. It was posturing, that was all.

'But why are you cross?'

'I'm not cross.'

'You said you were cross with Aunt Rachel.'

'Yes, but if Rachel hasn't been in contact then it doesn't matter.'

'But what if she *does* write? What if there's a letter waiting at the flat?'

Judy plucks a dandelion seed from the sleeve of her cardigan. 'You've had so many troubles, Lionel.' She pauses, watches the seed as it's carried off in the breeze. 'Your accident was very damaging in so many ways.'

She stops suddenly and hangs her head, gripping on to the teak arm of the chair with her hand. 'Oh God, I can't do this.'

With more interest than concern Lionel watches his mother's shoulders heave. 'What about Lilith?' he says. 'If you can't talk to me, maybe you could explain it to her.'

'For heaven's sake, Lionel, please don't bring Lilith into this.' Judy sounds as if she might choke, but eventually she succeeds in manufacturing a tight little smile. 'Goodness, I don't know what came over me,' she says, fanning her face.

Her transformation from distress to polity unsettles him. 'Your husband's just died. Surely that's it.'

Judy holds the smile. She could be advertising washing powder, he thinks. She stands and points towards the patio doors with an open hand.

'You want me to leave?'

'You can stay if you like.' The smile is becoming more unconvincing.

'I thought there were things I could do to help. I'll do anything you need. I want to be useful. I could have a go at the garden.'

'That's very nice of you, Lionel, but really, it's not your concern.'

'No?' *Not his concern. His father is dead and it's not his concern.* He stands abruptly. 'Then I suppose I should go, yes, I should.'

As he manoeuvres out of his chair he trips on the base of the parasol and shunts the table sideways. An accident. Judy's second-best jug, the one with the hand-painted roses, pitches over. The starlings take flight. It is milk, mainly, that spills everywhere. It looks like the aftermath of a pathetic rebellion – the porcelain jug lying awkwardly on its side, milk pooling over the teak.

'I'm so clumsy. I've always been clumsy, haven't I?' He pulls a meek face. 'It must have been awful for you when I was a child – me being so clumsy. It's not broken, though.'

Judy, whose smile has faded a fraction, goes to fetch a cloth while he watches the milk trickle onto the paving slabs. It's a shame she doesn't have a cat, he thinks. Before he was sick, Buddha would have been at the milk in a flash, his tongue going ten to the dozen. Lionel curses his big feet. Clumsy oaf. Always unnatural and uncomfortable when Judy's around. The starlings have retreated to the Juneberry tree and he stretches round to watch them devour the bright berries and catches a glimpse of the far window – the spare room – just as the curtain flicks closed.

He has already picked the jug from its puddle when Judy comes back with a cloth and a towel.

'I'll take that,' she says, holding out her hand.

'It's okay. I'll hold it.'

'No, give it to me. I'll take it to the kitchen.' Her smile has vanished.

'I won't drop it. You've got your hands full. I can take it through.'

'N-no. Wait then. Hold onto it there.'

The space between mother and son inflates with Judy's anguish and Lionel makes room for it, stepping off to one side while Judy cleans up – the manic thrust of her fist as she wipes; the harsh flicks of the tea towel as she dries. When she's finished she holds out her hand again, and he's not sure why, but instead of passing the jug he loops the handle over his little finger and lets it dangle there. It looks precarious, but it's not. He's in control.

'It is a very pretty jug,' he says earnestly.

'Be careful, Lionel.'

'I'm being careful.'

'That was my father's. He loved it. Please.'

'My grandfather's then.'

'No . . . I mean yes, in a way, I suppose.'

A vein throbs at her neck. Her hand shakes as she begs.

'Is someone here?' he says.

Her hand drops to her side. 'Here?'

'I saw them at the window just now.'

Judy's eyes darken. 'Yes,' she admits guiltily. 'Ben's here. He came last night.'

'He didn't want to see me then.'

'He's tired. He's staying until after the funeral. There'll be plenty of time for reunions.'

'Yes. Plenty of time.' He places the jug on the table and adjusts it to get a better view of the hand-painted roses. 'There,' he says.

An invisible weight continues to impinge on Judy's self-possession. Shoulders sagging, she looks forlornly from Lionel to the jug. The starlings have returned to the lawn, but there are fifteen of them now, or twenty, and they attack the grass as an industrious tribe, green flashes on their heads and their wings, each yellow-tipped feather shimmering in the summer sun – common, yet kingly.

'Well, that's that. I'll be going then.'

'Yes.'

He hesitates. 'I know this is a bad time, but I'd like my documents if you don't mind.'

'What documents?'

'You know, birth certificate, adoption certificate, that kind of thing. I've tried to find them online but I can't . . . from Kenya, you know. They don't keep the same digital record as here.'

'There, I knew it. She has written to you.'

'Who? Aunt Rachel?'

'Of course Aunt Rachel.'

'No, honestly, I just want them. Now David's gone I might –'

'Might what?'

'I might want to, I don't know, find people.'

Judy abandons all attempts at restraint. 'Your mother's dead,' she cries. 'Dead and buried. Anyway, you're twenty-nine years old. What possible good will scratching in the past do you?'

'Twenty-eight.'

'What?'

'I'm twenty-eight. Twenty-nine next birthday.'

'I know exactly how old you are.' She snatches the jug from the table and clutches it to her breast. 'You have no idea.'

'I don't understand. I don't see how this can upset you so much.'

'Oh please.'

A bit of her saliva lands on his face. He recoils, but doesn't wipe it off.

Byrd men all bear the trademarks of a particular brand of masculinity and Ben is still solid despite being leaner than when Lionel last saw him. His resemblance to his father is uncanny – the light hair, rough jaw and thick neck. But there's a weary slope to his shoulders, as if he's been ill. Perhaps his *executive position* is proving too much for him. But his voice has lost none of its clarity.

'Can't you see she's in no state?' Ben bellows, stepping onto the patio and encircling his mother with a protective arm.

'Ben!' Lionel straightens.

'Go and lie down, Mum,' he says, patronizing her. 'I'll deal with this.' He escorts Judy, still holding the jug close to her heart, into the house.

Ben returns and says to him crisply, 'So?'

'She asked me to come.'

'Jesus, Lionel.'

Sweat pricks in his armpits. 'Hello, Ben, it's good to see you too.'

Ben shakes his head. 'I know you're supposed to be *vulnerable* and everything' – his brother pulls a dumb face to illustrate his point – 'but just stop punishing her for your poor, sad childhood. She's old and defenceless, and bloody grief-stricken. Can't you see?' Ben motions angrily towards the house. 'She's suffered enough. We all have.'

He wants to remonstrate with Ben, tell him he's not vulnerable. He doesn't want to punish anyone. If he did have a 'poor, sad childhood' he doesn't remember it. And while they're on the subject – how, precisely, has Ben suffered? But his brother is puffing and working his jaw and Lionel decides it might be better to pipe down.

Eventually Ben takes a pack of cigarettes from his pocket and, although his stubby fingers have hair sprouting above the knuckles, he manages a deft elegance as he goes through the rituals of addiction – running the cigarette through thumb and forefinger, bouncing the tip on the pack, placing the filter between his lips, on the right side – then *click* – the lighter's orange flame thawing some iciness. He calms further as he smokes until only the residue of his indignation remains.

'Want one?' Ben says, offering the pack. 'Dad was mortified when he found out we all smoked.' He laughs unexpectedly. 'You *do* still smoke, don't you?'

Ben is in his thirties, still with something of the boy about him. But he's lost some of the old swagger – that nose-thumbing certitude that characterized him and their older brother when they were young.

'It's been what, three years?' says Ben.

'More like seven.'

'God, really? You look the same, except for the hair thing. Are those *dreadlocks*?'

'Yes. Thought I'd try and, you know . . .' Embarrassed, Lionel flattens his dreads to his head.

'They suit you.'

'Thanks.'

'Work okay?'

'Fine. Really good.'

Ben adjusts his stance and Lionel suspects it's the end of their small talk.

'Ironic.' Ben stares at the hot tip of his cigarette. 'You're the adopted son and you saw more of Dad than any of us.'

'I wouldn't say that, Lil –'

'Of course, I'm up north and Jim's thousands of miles away, but it's weird, isn't it, considering everything?'

'I don't know. I barely saw them for years. I lived with Aunt Rachel, remember.'

'Yes, thing is, Lionel,' Ben says, talking over him, and Lionel wonders if he's witnessing his brother's executive persona. 'You need to hear some home truths.' Ben pauses to recover a hair from his tongue, which he examines briefly before flicking it off his fingers. 'You see, Mum and Dad had to . . . bend the truth a tad, when they adopted you.'

Ben gives Lionel room to respond, but he remains silent.

'Basically they lied, in Africa. They lied to get you a visa. But now Aunt Rachel – who's *doolally* herself' – he makes circles at his temple with one finger – 'has got the whole *thing* mixed up in her head. Do you understand?'

'No.'

Ben sniffs his fist, thinking, and begins again, choosing words carefully. 'Aunt Rachel is under the impression that you're not from Kenya. I've only just heard all this myself, so I don't have all the facts.'

Lionel sits down. 'Why would Aunt Rachel think that?'

'Well, when David found you in the orphanage he knew they wouldn't be able to adopt you legally, well not quickly anyway – and there was a time factor.'

'Time factor?'

'Like I said, I don't know the facts.'

'Facts.'

Ben is unable to meet his eye. 'Yes, facts, but anyway, they paid the right people, official people, to make sure you had papers. It's very simple, Lionel.'

'Very simple – I see. And Judy asked me here, so she could explain this?'

'Yes.'

'But none of it's true?'

'I know it's confusing –'

'I understand. No one knows who my real parents were and David and Judy adopted me illegally.'

Ben raises one eyebrow. 'I think that's the gist.'

Lionel massages in between his eyes with one finger. 'Why didn't they tell me before?'

Ben puts his head back and groans. 'Heavens. I don't know, Lionel.'

'I don't know either. It appears I don't know anything. You know everything about yourself – your parents, your nationality. I don't know any of that.'

Ben shifts his weight from one foot to another. 'I understand how you must feel.'

'No you don't. You have no idea.'

Ben bites his lip.

'I want my documents.'

Ben nods curtly. 'I'll make sure you get them.'

'Thanks.' He closes his eyes. 'So are there any more *home truths*?'

'I don't think so.' Ben wipes his forehead. 'You signed all the papers and Judy's told you about your inheritance et cetera, so that's everything.'

Home truths. Home lies. He's not sure if Ben has told him anything new or germane, and yet Judy seemed so hysterical when she said his mother was dead that Lionel wonders if there are other things she's neglected to disclose. He's read somewhere that if people tell a lie for long enough they begin to believe it themselves.

The starlings have flown the garden and joined a large flock, creating distant shadows in the sky. A synchronous shape – coming closer. The brothers watch from the patio as the afternoon light turns gauzy and the sun dips to kiss a line of trees that mark the boundary of the garden. The birds bloom and scatter and restructure to bloom again, closer and closer until they are displaying directly above their heads.

Ben stares skyward, blowing out smoke and shielding his eyes. 'Crazy! Didn't they used to flock in the autumn?'

'Yeah. The migratory patterns have all changed. It's to do with the magnetic poles changing position,' Lionel explains. 'I saw a documentary.'

Ben shivers. 'The whole world's gone topsy turvy.'

'Yes, it has,' he agrees.

'Look,' says Ben. 'I'm sorry about all this business. And I'm – well – I'm sorry if I was a shit to you when we were young. I was a kid. I –'

'I don't remember much before the accident. I'm sure we all drove each other mad – anyway, Lil's the one who gets upset about the family stuff.'

Ben squeezes his eyes shut and shakes his head.

'I'm sorry your dad's dead.'

'Pah!' Ben says, batting the air with his hand. 'We barely spoke for the last few years.'

'Well, I'm sorry he's dead. And I didn't mean to upset her, you know.' He nods towards the house. 'I only want to help.'

'You can't help her, Lionel. You know what she's like.' Ben takes his shoulder and guides him back inside towards the front door. 'We'll get together – you, James and me – for old times' sake. And I'll call about the arrangements, okay?'

'Arrangements?'

'Dad's funeral.'

'Of course.'

The bus takes an hour from Judy's to the city centre. From the back seat he watches the starlings' convulsive display, rippling and mushrooming in a peach and pewter sky. But where they were spectacular they have become frenzied – sooty fireworks at a festival of death – and as the last remnant of a cloud-beleaguered sun slips behind the beech trees and the bungalows Lionel turns in his seat and fixes his attention on the road, towards the city. Home. Truth.

@GameAddict (#23756745): 20:7:27

Do you think your mother plays? Or your brothers, or the man who sells 'recycled' memory chips by the station? You find yourself looking out for people you recognize. You can't help it. Smart types disguise their identities of course. That's the point. You want to be someone other than the pointless insurance broker, or the unappreciated tax clerk or the put-upon housewife that you are. Don't you?

Level 11: To Vadar

As we chased off to Vadar the passerines followed, abusing our lug-holes with their incessant chirrups and tweets.

'Do you think they're trying to tell us something?' I said.

'Insane-making racket's driving me to distraction,' answered the Krin, holding the sides of his nog with his paws. 'I'd squish the damn things if you'd let me.'

The birds seemed to savvy Dan-Albwr-han's threats and hid in my locks quick as spit. Once they were snug they cooed softly and I fed them on Jigga bugs snatched from the air.

We hid surplus supplies and hung back a while in the foothills, making strategy maps in the sand. There would be snipers and armies of Grinders impeding free passage to Vadar. Dan-Albwr-han took stock of our arsenal. Sword, shield, pulsar, whip and nine ninja discs made up my weaponry. The Krin boasted a crossbow and countless pierce-bolts. His breastplate and Balwriqin, both ceremonial, would afford little protection when the onslaught came, but he slapped his flank and quipped, 'Hide's thicker than Miina skin and almost as old.' Confident. Gladiatorial.

With my Visor on stealth we advanced up the mountain. A thousand clicks later (still no sign of a fight), we heard thunder far-distant and scanned the sky for the oncoming storm. But after the *boom boom* came a drawn-out rumble and the whole mountain did juddering earthshifts.

The Krin fell on all fours shouting, 'It's not a storm, it's a quake,' and we looked round for splits in the crust.

After the main tremor we carried on cautious-wise as substratal aftershocks rocked us time and again. Finally, after scrambling up scree, the city of Vadar came half into view. The citadel – stupas, domes and dwell-houses – all nestled cheeky-jowl in the bowl of an extinct lava-gusher. But as we crested the ridge and got a long-view, further eastwards, we tilted our nogs, disbelieving.

One whole side of the mountain had fallen away. The city had been cleave-split in two. We goggled for ages, too stunned to speak. The quake had turned half of Vadar into a billowing dust-blur. Voices, all seized by distress, echoed round in the crater while characters ran rescue missions, digging through rubble. We watched them until the sun set livid – yellow, purple and carmine. Bruised as the land.

'Unfathomable.' The Krin was choked. 'As if the dimension's collapsing.'

'The Realm isn't prone to this?'

'No. I've heard tales of Bosses punishing tribes – but not like this.'

'What do they punish them for?'

'Harbouring rogue characters.' The Krin turned to me, an anxious grimace wrinkling his snout. 'Perhaps we're not the only ones hunting this Sylph.'

I couldn't lie to the beast any longer. 'We're not. Before I crash-landed Boss agents ransacked the Ghetto in search of the character we seek.'

'Why didn't you tell me?'

'I didn't think it was important.'

'Not important, aargh!' He pushed the heel of one paw into his eye. After a long hush the old bear spoke wearily. 'So, what now?'

'Creep in, take advantage of the chaos and find the Sylph.'

Reluctantly, the Krin agreed to my tactics and we made manoeuvres forward. The whole place was undefended. Only battalions of Rihn vultures kept proprietary watch from the trees in case we competed for carrion. The passerines made woebegone clicks as we traversed the sombrous streets. Doors were open, houses abandoned, half-finished meals left on tables, uneaten.

'They've deserted the city,' whispered the Krin.

Right after he said it a loud conch-call – *wallooo* – came from close by. We exchanged a quick glance and nipped, shifty-shifty, towards it. Round the very next corner was a plaza. On its west side, a temple, typical of mountainous regions: carved, black wood – lintel and frame – with steps to a terrace, lined with wood columns. The terrace was strung with jars full of stars and the scene shone ghostly, peculiar. In the plaza the whole population of Vadar – what remained – stood facing the temple, some venerating, others pleading. A group of women slapped their nogs, ululating, for at the front of the crowd were bodies not yet Wisp, but limbs missing and with tubes hanging out. Abattoir grim.

'It's carnage,' moaned the Krin.

The temple doors heaved open and a man wearing flow-robes and mitre came out. A priester. He pacified the crowd with some hieratic semaphore and lifted his nog towards heaven.

'Vadarians,' he shouted, tho his voice was cracked. 'Our deliverance is nigh.'

'What's that he's saying?'

'Priest-talk,' I said. 'When there's disaster they say it's all part of the Creators' plans. The speech is common to every dimension I've been in. But look.'

An acolyte, stage-left, chimed on a prayer bowl – the signal for ten or so characters to spew from the temple. It was the circus troupe whose trail we'd followed from Kilhm. They were mostly Vadarians and Mutants, but there were one or two mercenary OtherWorld characters with them.

A He-Man (with abnormally muscular pins) and a Harlequin set off a *known player* alert in my Visor, but tho I scrolled through my database there wasn't a match to lock on to. I flipped back to zoom when the bowl chimed again. This time a childsome character stepped from the sanctum. The Sylph. Again my Visor alert went haywire. The crowd didn't clock her at first (her opacity was around 30/70), but when the light caught her she came like a dream and spun round three hundred and sixty degrees, holding the hem of her poppy-red dress. Each Vadarian was hush as she twirled full circle and then came to a stop – nog bowed, barefoot and wan.

Hiatus for a click before the Vadarians exploded with joy. They whooped and hoopla-ed and did little jig-steps, linking arms with their neighbours.

'Citizens!' The priester's voice rang above the clamour. 'We will suffer no more.' He gestured towards the Sylph. 'Behold, the character our oppressor seeks.'

The crowd erupted again saying, 'The half-Wisp will appease his wrath.'

Dan-Albwr-han stiffened. 'I think they mean the Big Boss.'

I adjusted my Visor and zoomed in on the Sylph's fizzog. Tho her wireframe was filmy her eyes were brilliant with terror. Her vulnerable beauty bewitched me.

'We must rescue her,' I said, quite determined.

'Of course. Simplicity itself.' The Krin used a mock-voice and indicated the circus troupe with a snort.

'Trust me,' I assured him, holding my heart. 'This character's linked to me. I can feel a connection.'

The Krin slumped against the wall, unconvinced. But as I watched her the Sylph lifted her chin. There was nothing haphazard about it, no searching around, no random glance at one fizzog then another. She looked directly at me. Only me. Beautiful character with a doll-face of ideal dimensions: slender oval, wide at the forehead, delicate at the chin – with pellucid eye-gems that sent blue beams of energy, from her to me, bridging the grief and the filth of that day.

Black Madonna

The night has drawn in sultrily for the time of year, but it's still early – dead time between rush hour and evening trade. Lionel fumbles with the keys to the communal door. The lock's been getting stiff and he has to jiggle the key to make the internal mechanism click into place. Several boxes block the hallway and he shunts them to one side before taking the stairs. Saeed must have let out the other flat, and he's glad he won't be the only tenant in the building for another month. But when he reaches the landing his door is ajar. Did he leave it on the latch again? He remembers locking it with the deadlock before going to see Judy, but this could be a false memory from the day before.

It can be a tricky thing, remembering. He wakes up sometimes, unable to recall what he was doing the previous night or when he went to sleep. Memories should be time-stamped like blog posts or files. *Door last opened: today 14.12 p.m.* But then he thinks, Lilith – she's let herself in again, left the door on the latch by mistake, and he's overjoyed that she's decided to face the world again.

'Sis,' he calls. 'Is that you?'

He pushes the door firmly and it swings wide to reveal the riffled desk, the half-emptied bookcase, the muddled cushions on the sofa and the floor. The window is open, there's a mug beside his Google desk unit, the picture of the Golden Temple has been tilted to the right, the cushion covers on the sofa have been removed and laid neatly on the back of the armchair. The drawers are open – the contents ploughed over – and all his disks have been moved from the shelves and stacked into piles on the floor. A burglary – but there's no sign of vandalism. Whoever did this was a tidy and systematic operator.

Buddha, welcoming his arrival with a plaintive croak, gives Lionel the nerve to enter, although his heart's beating full tilt.

'Hey, Budds,' he whispers, and then calls 'hello' in a forced, jaunty tone.

An announcement floats up from the railway platform just as the fridge shivers to life. With Buddha under one arm, Lionel makes a search of the rooms; whipping back the shower curtain, peering under the bed, poking in the bulkhead cupboard with a broom handle.

'Did you see them, Budds? Who was it, eh?'

Was this the work of Huo and his men? Please God it was only a common thief. But nothing of value has been stolen as far as he can see. There's nothing to steal except his three-sixty screen and his external drives – hardware and memory – are all still in place.

The people on Milk Street look unremarkable as Lionel leans out of the window, scanning them for clues. Could he identify an intruder by their demeanour? In the corridor he hangs over the banister and checks the stairwell, listening for sounds from the new tenant, upstairs. The building returns a hissing silence. He briefly considers calling the police, but since nothing's been stolen it seems foolish to bother them. Besides, he doesn't want to draw attention to himself.

The mug on his desk is cold. He sniffs the contents – tea. It occurs to him that his ID is the only thing in the flat that has any real value. Identity theft is always in the news – bank accounts plundered, bio-data appropriated for nefarious activities. Recently, Lionel heard about a man who'd got three years for fraud and drug trafficking, but was released when immigration officers found he was still committing crimes despite being locked in a cell. ID theft. They released him, but the poor man's life had been turned upside down.

Lionel taps his lip. It would take more than an opportunistic trespasser to get at his data – he has developed all his own security software. It's best to be safe. He logs on. Iris scan – check. Password – check. Fingerprint access – check. Straight away he looks for recent activity on his login. The access log fills the screen. *Oh my*. Someone has tried to access his domain. Adrenalin zips through his system like a virus. There have been 423,742 attempts to determine his password by circumventing the encryption protocols on his login. A back-end hack using some off-the-shelf 'break-in' software no doubt, but fortunately unsuccessful – obstructed by a sentry bot he's particularly proud of.

Lionel makes a celebratory fist – 'Yes!' – his defences have fought off the digital gatecrasher. But the celebration is brief. At the last minute there appears to have been a positive ID. A fingerprint and iris scan have been approved, and in the log there is evidence of an incursion – a brief foray into data files covering a three-week period ending less than a month ago. His fingers fly across the SensePad. The thought of someone, or even something, accessing his files – skimming his private messages, speed-reading his code – is unpalatable, but to do it using his own bio-data is unconscionable.

He searches for the files that have been accessed or downloaded. The list fills the screen. But there's nothing of any consequence – a few work schedules and his diary, the rest are game logs for *CoreQuest*, nothing more. A Buddha preview clip and several movie files have been accessed, but again, they're only recorded *CoreQuest* scenarios. There's no evidence of a breach in his finance accounts. The hack is the equivalent of someone breaking into a bank to steal the brochures. But he's uneasy. If someone has his ID they could use it again. Lionel sits for a minute, studying his fingertips.

'Camera,' he says at last. 'And e-DNA.'

The bio-ID software opens on voice command and an image of his face fills the screen. He zooms in on his left eye until it is magnified a hundred times. The pupil – black as deepspace – and the surrounding iris is like a mysterious flower set in aspic. Is this who I am? he thinks. This jelly. This tissue. Pema's revelation that employee bio-data is ripe for exploitation comes to mind. Iris and fingerprints are simply keys that can be copied. He feels quite sick.

With a feeling verging on panic, he checks the external superdrives and discovers that there, too, his defences have been violated. Buddha. Pictures of Buddha, 3D renders, preliminary semantic code, previews and development files. The intruder was looking for something specific that couldn't be hacked remotely. Something on his disks or drives. Why not steal the drives? They're right there on the shelf in full view. Perhaps the thief was interrupted. Perhaps Saeed arrived with the new tenant and scared them away before they could take anything. But why would they want his Buddha Project? How would they even know about it? He is about to check through the piles of disks when a noise makes him turn from the screen. He stands – too quickly – and the head rush makes him feel weak. The intruder is still in the flat, about to attack. But, as his eyes refocus, an outline of Eve develops in the doorway, her cotton blouse too bright at first, almost fluorescent.

'Hey you,' she says.

'Hi.' His voice is stupid and feeble. He holds onto the chair for balance.

'I thought I'd stop by. The door was open downstairs, so I came up.'

He has a surfeit of saliva. 'I'm, well, in a mess.' He swallows, considering whether to say he's been burgled, but reluctant to come across as a serial victim. 'I've been sorting some things out.'

'I saw the boxes in the hall.' She raises her eyebrows. 'Are you going to invite me in?'

'God, sorry – come in.'

There's an uncomfortable pause as he straightens the picture of the Golden Temple and picks the cushions from the floor. All the while Eve remains in the middle of the room, fiddling with a curl at the back of her neck. Watching him.

'There, have a seat,' he says.

'Why thank you.'

A vehicle passes under the window, lazy bass-beats pumping out; Eve nods her head in time, lounging back into the cushions, extending her legs in front of her. She's wearing leather pumps and lets one drop so her foot is bare. Shiny varnish reddens her nails. A silver ring encircles her middle toe.

'I've left messages.' She's apologetic. 'I know it's naughty to pursue someone, but I thought . . .'

'No, it's fine.'

'I was worried you might not want to see me again. But I've been thinking about you. You meet a guy, he passes out on you, you drive him home, he doesn't call.' She's being funny, pulling a cute face as she speaks.

'I do want to see you. It's . . .' He thinks before going on. 'It's my dad, he died.' He makes scatty circles in the air. 'I've been all over the place, basically.'

'I didn't know. I'm truly sorry.'

He should say something to save her from embarrassment, but his brain won't transmit words to his mouth. Eve approaches him smoothly. The slow shake of her head, the deep brown sincerity of her equine eyes, the consoling warmth of her breath as she kisses his wrist, his knuckles, his palm and the tips of his fingers, one by one – all of this makes his blood slide, with relief, through his veins.

'My poor baby,' she whispers. 'First the attack, and now this.'

Not sweet, her perfume, but comforting; he moves closer, to breathe it in.

'I want to look after you,' she says, plucking at the front of her blouse. 'I want to make you feel safe.'

A button pings off to the corner of the room and he turns to follow its trajectory, but she takes his face with both hands, quite firmly, and forces him to witness her blouse disgorging its soft, dark contents. He's paralysed for a second, unsure of what's required of him.

'Lionel, here.' She guides a solid brown nipple into his mouth.

A strange asexual scene begins to play as Lionel gums woozily, losing himself entirely in the generosity of her flesh.

She strokes his hair. 'There, there, dear Lionel.'

And for a moment he thinks he might fall asleep, simply drift off in the Void – and he sails back to his dream of the lilo. Sun warm on his back.

'Oh my God, what's that?' Eve unlatches his mouth and tugs her blouse back over her bosom.

'What?' He doesn't want to look round. He wants to luxuriate in maternal warmth and imagine himself tiny, and nourished. 'Where?'

She waggles her finger. 'There, on the floor, there!'

He turns. 'That? That's my cat.'

'It's having a fit.'

'No, not really, not a fit.' Reluctantly, Lionel kneels and strokes Buddha, who's stopped for a breather. 'He's got a tumour. It's pressing on the motor centre, inside his brain. It makes him twitch, that's all.'

Eve can't disguise her revulsion. 'How long has he been like that?'

'Six months. Maybe seven.'

Buddha tries to stand but falls forward – back legs motoring uselessly – as his body goes into brief, but total spasm.

'Is that normal?'

'He's bad today.'

'Wouldn't it be kinder? I mean, surely, there's quality of life to consider?'

'What are you saying?'

'Have him put down, Lionel.'

'You wouldn't say that if he was human.'

'I think I would.'

'But you're a doctor. There's an oath, isn't there, about preserving life?'

Eve hangs her head, ill at ease with her own hypocrisy, while Lionel reverently kisses Buddha's forepaws – 'It's all right, Budds, it's okay' – making it clear he'll not allow one whisker to be harmed.

'I'll take him to the bedroom. He won't offend you in there.'

'I didn't mean to upset you,' she calls. 'I'm sorry.'

Except for the errant button, Eve has refastened her blouse when he returns. 'You're grieving,' she says. 'It's not the right time for you. For us. And I apologize for what I said about your cat. Forgive me?'

Lionel can't look at her. They might have curled up dozily together. There's no doubt he wants to forget about everything. But her disgust is a blemish.

Lionel taps his lip. 'Okay,' he says. 'But –'

'Shh,' she says. 'You don't have to explain.'

@GameAddict (#23756745): 30:7:27

If you think you can recognize characters from
the grey world on the Game Layer the chances
are you're going crazy, right? But you know – it's
an easy mistake to make because you do know
them. Those princesses, elves and warlocks are
familiar because they're your family. You spend
more time with them than anyone on earth.

Level 12: The Corrupted Sylph

In no time we'd sketched out a strategy. The plan: break into the temple, turn all who stood in our way into Wisps and smuggle the Sylph down the mountain.

'If we're defeated,' said the Krin come oddly stiff, 'I want you to know.' He paused, cleared his throat. 'You've been a fine character to Quest with.'

I landed a play-punch on his chest. Those circus freaks were no match for our skills I assured him. But he remained sober and I nogged he was ploughing through question marks – survival rates, outcomes and motives. Presently he mumbled something about sprogs – if he'd had a son he'd want him to be just like me. Made me quite proud, if I'm honest.

The soldiers who guarded the temple were distracted when they should've been lookout and lively. They played cards 'n' dice on the sly and I heard them discussing the Sylph. Would her capture appease the Big Boss and make the earthshifts desist? Rumbling aftershocks still had the place by the scruff. We sneaked past, did a quick recce and discovered a window high up at the back of the shrine. The Krin laddered me onto his shoulders and I heaved up and used my whip to haul Dan-Albwr-han after. It took a few clicks to squeeze his belly-bulge in through the frame and I prayed his fat pins wouldn't be spotted kicking out at the night.

Inside, flame-torches lit a long corridor, illuminating frescoes depicting strange OtherWorld scenes. There were men (and some women) quite roughly drawn in drab costumes. Some had rimless goggles perched on their snouts that we guessed were retro-style Visors. Each separate pic was titled 'Lead Designer' or 'Project Co-ordinator' followed by OtherWorld names and the names of other dimensions I'd been in. It took a few moments to twig.

'These are Creators,' I whispered. 'Portraits of those that made us.'

The Krin's jaw dropped. 'Are you sure?'

'Look here, this one's called Steve. It says he did character design, had a hand in *WarriorClones III* – I've been there.' I turned to the Krin. 'I reached Level 9.'

I dislodged a torch and went along checking each portrait. None of the Creators had any warrior gifts to speak of. In fact, they were dreadfully puny.

'I thought Creators would be fantastical,' said the Krin. 'But they all look so feeble.'

'Perhaps Creators make us the way they'd *like* to be.'

We came preoccupied, ratcheting through the meaning of everything, reading the legends beneath each portrait, reverently touching their badly drawn fizzogs. I didn't clock the alert in my Visor or hear the softly-steps of characters doing ambush tactics till a Mutant, so close I could smell him, let out a yodelling cry. We spun on our heels as a creature snapped at us brandishing giant pink pincers. I unsheathed my sword as the Krin fell on all fours and did snarl-features.

The fight scene began.

I made short work of the lobster – sliced both his claws off with two arcs of my blade. The Krin ripped into the fray and I followed despatching several WeirdFucks who came at me dumb-fodder. I found my stride (I'd earned an enhanced skill pack on reaching the new level) and, despite my bulk, I turned exultant, slaughterhouse pirouettes. The Creator portraits were soon pebbledashed with enemy gore-bits.

The Krin and I exchanged hubristic high fives but our pride was previous. In waded the Harlequin we'd seen on the steps of the shrine. He was followed on by a Diva and a He-Man. Now these were the battle-worn pros – tougher close-up than they'd looked from a distance – and they sported some hardcore weaponry.

In a blink the Krin took a hit near the shoulder and fell to his knees with a *thwump*. It was the Diva's trident that got him – its prongs sent out sparks strong as snakebites that clung on while he crackled and spasmed.

The Harlequin stepped up to finish him off. 'You're on the wrong side, Reject,' he shouted as I tried a defence twixt him and the Krin.

I was too slow. The Krin took a whack square on the nog and, tho not instantly fatal, I knew we were doomed. Dan-Albwr-han's fizzog turned slowly towards me and he gave me a forlorn smile. Too accepting. Too brave.

'Hang in there,' I shouted. 'We can take them.'

The Harlequin grinned. 'You can't save him, buddy boy.'

I could've escaped, should've scarpered – my Visor command line was flashing *retreat*, but I couldn't abandon the Krin. In a trice the Diva had pinned my neck with her prongs and I took three successive hits from the He-Man – cheek, belly, thigh. Indescribable agony. But the only thing that slouched through my nog was the waste of it all. The Krin would be Wisp and for what? The Quest would be nothing. No Sylph. No rebirth or replay. No point to the whole damn shebang. Curiously, as I slipped towards crash-mode, clip-footage of my time in *CoreQuest* played in trebletime in the left frame of my Visor; Drufus Scumscratch, the sorceress, the corrupted gaze of the Sylph, the bold Krin, Mata Angelica (especially our lusty roll in the hay) and even the minor characters and Grinders had edited best-bits. It was Game Over. I'd been here before.

The Funeral

Why doesn't she answer? Lionel listens to Lilith's answerphone message again. It sounds vacant, computer-generated – even though it's Lilith's voice. 'Guess what? I'm not here. So try later.' No opportunity to leave a voicemail. She's disabled her location app since the night of the attack, so he posts a video to her roaming ID. He tries to appear relaxed, smiling, looking directly into the camera.

'Hey, Lil, it's me.' He points to his chest, as if she needs reminding she has a brother. 'I was wondering where you were. What you were up to.' He babbles on for a minute; says he's seen Ben, but doesn't mention the break-in or Eve.

There's more he wants to say, but he hesitates and the next words misfire. 'I. Shall. Where.' He sighs and gives up. 'Call me. Please.'

Lilith won't get in touch, he thinks, because in real life I am a *retard*.

Minutes later Ben texts him: *Funeral tomorrow 3 p.m. Assembly Hall.*

Tomorrow is so soon. He's never been to a funeral. He hasn't been to the Assembly Hall in years. He sends a text back: *I'll b there. Hope Judy's okay. Have u heard from Lil? James there yet?* No reply. Someone dies – the hub of a fragile network – and all the lines of connection withdraw to their isolated nodes. It makes him think of snails' eyes retracting on their stalks and he shudders, thinking of Drufus Scumscratch.

Mr Barber snaps the dust from a towel and the sound is loud enough to split the air. For once, Lionel is the only customer in the shop and he's glad there's no audience.

Mr Barber sucks his teeth disapprovingly. 'This style look scruffy, you no see? Mi think you need a young man barber now.'

Lionel pats the growth on his head. 'I don't want a young man's barber. I'm happy with you.' He smiles. 'A little wax is all it needs, I've seen a clip online,' he says, twisting the end of one dreadlock to demonstrate.

'Maybe you should spend less time on that computer and more time livin'.' The old man waxes the end of a rough-looking strand. 'Res' up,' he says, noticing Lionel's frown. 'A computer life is not natural, that's all I'm sayin'.'

Lionel relaxes back in the chair. 'It keeps me occupied.'

The barber raises one eyebrow and gets on with his work.

'David died. My father.' Lionel inserts the news matter-of-factly. 'Do you remember him?'

Mr Barber looks at Lionel's reflection obliquely, examining his expression for signs of grief. 'Of course mi remember him. I am very sorry,' he says. 'Him a fine man.'

'I think he probably was.'

'Probably? Why you sayin' *probably*?'

'I didn't really have chance to know him. Not deeply.'

The barber closes his eyes, as if he's offering a silent prayer. After a moment he straightens his tunic and says, 'I never know my own father *deeply* neither. The best fathers have a lickle mystery, a lickle distance – dread even. It give them authority.' The old man concludes with an emphatic grunt.

Lionel laughs. 'Like God, you mean?'

Mr Barber laughs too. 'Him not call God the Father for nuttin, y'nah.' But then he becomes serious and says, 'I would like to come to the funeral – if that is all right – to pay my respects.'

Lionel, overcome with unexpected gratitude, has to gulp back emotion before saying, 'I'd be very pleased if you could come, Mr Barber. Thank you. Thank you. But it's tomorrow. There's no time for you to organize things.'

'Tomorrow will be no problem at all. I'll put a sign in the window.'

For several minutes a lump in his throat stops Lionel from speaking. Mr Barber doesn't trouble him for more conversation; instead he hums an old hymn as he waxes Lionel's dreadlocks. But when he's finished the barber asks him if he'd like to come upstairs.

'I'd best be getting home. I don't want to disturb your routine.'

'You need a dark suit for the funeral, y'know?'

'Should I wear one?'

'Yes, mon.'

'I don't have one.'

'You can borrow one a mine if you like.' The old man washes his hands in the sink. 'Up to you.'

At the back of the shop, hidden behind a heavy velvet curtain, is a narrow staircase. Mr Barber leads the way to the top where a door, with an array of locks and bolts, bars the way. Before the break-in Lionel would have thought such muscular measures unnecessary, but now he makes a note of the brand names.

Mr Barber marks his interest. 'Better safe than sorry, that's right. You never know who might want to get in.'

The apartment is clean and spare. The furniture in the living room – a sideboard, an armchair, and a Formica-topped table– is unfussy, from another era, like the patterns on the curtains. The old man potters in the kitchen making tea, leaving him to try on several suits. The retro-style garments are pristine – box-cut, single-buttoned jackets with silk linings. Trousers, snug at the waist, with legs tapering to neat turn-ups.

Mr Barber calls, 'Tek your pick. You must wear the best I have for your father's send-off. Don't feel no way about it, neither.'

Lionel takes in the room as he dresses. On the sideboard, an antique computer that looks as if it hasn't been switched on in years. A bookcase full of paperbacks sits in the recess to one side of a blocked-in fireplace where a couple of family snapshots decorate the mantel. One of the photos is of a young black girl, posing for the camera, smiling broadly into the lens. She's wearing jeans and a slummy T-shirt that declares she is Destiny's Child. The other photo is of a neat couple on the deck of a huge ship. They are holding onto the railing as the whole world lists alarmingly to starboard – the woman's face is an expression of old-fashioned stoicism; the man's is gaunt and bilious.

'That is my family,' Mr Barber says, his face registering a time far in the past as he enters the room. 'Mom and Pop on the boat, comin' over.'

'They look like good people.'

Mr Barber sighs. 'All a dem dead.'

'Even the girl?'

'Even the girl,' he says.

'I'm sorry.'

'Not your fault, Lionel, jos the way the Creator wanted it to be. Tek them to a better place – yes mon – uh huh.' Mr Barber blows across the rim of his mug. 'You find a suit that fit then?'

Lionel stands with his arms akimbo, showing off the outfit. 'This one?'

'You longer in the leg than me by a *h*inch.' Mr Barber twists one corner of his mouth. 'But it'll do.'

The suit, despite being tight across the shoulders and a shave too short in the arms and legs, looks well on him. They set off for the funeral in the heat of the following day. It's early afternoon by the time they reach the city terminus to catch the connecting bus. The journey takes an hour, during which the barber reminisces about 'the old days' and Milk Street in the last century.

Lionel's heard it all before, sitting in the old man's shop. But later, as they approach their destination, Mr Barber's nostalgia turns inward.

'Y'know, I remember the first time your father bring you to the shop there.'

'Really? When was that? What year?'

'Your hair,' continues Mr Barber, ignoring the questions, 'was like a wild bwoy when you first come. Then I guess your white mama there got no idea 'bout coloured pickney hair. So mi jos lop it off, y'nah, kep it low.'

'How old was I?'

Mr Barber glances up to the ceiling of the bus. 'Oh, four, five year old praps.' He waves a hand dismissively above his head. 'You were a handsome lickle ting, ha! But quiet, always quiet.' Mr Barber turns to him thoughtfully before continuing. 'What I like about your father was him always respectful. Him listen politely, to the talk. Not high an' mighty, not at all. Not like some people.'

Not high an' mighty, not at all. Mr Barber's description of David – the way he listened, the way he tried to be fair – yes, this was accurate enough. And here's David, in his mind's eye, sitting in the sunny living room at Bethesda with a concordance open on the armrest of the big leather chair and a bible in his lap. The angles of his father's legs in stark definition, his trousers creased at the knees, his powerful arms and torso hidden beneath a starched shirt and buttoned waistcoat, thick-rimmed reading glasses halfway down the bridge of his nose, an eye-line with the severity of steel slicing over the frames, fixing a wriggling child – him – to his chair with the ruthlessness of an entomologist's pin. And yet this memory is full of warmth and sentiment, suffused with a sense of safety and gratitude, the quiet fellowship of father and son.

Accessing the precise geography of the village he grew up in is harder and when he catches sight of the canal bridge through the trees he stands abruptly in the aisle and buzzes for the driver to pull over. But when he and Mr Barber alight he realizes they are quite a way off from the village. Perhaps there was another bridge just like this but closer in. They walk the final kilometre or so along the lane, allowing their gaze to follow the route of the canal as it slackens away across the fields. At first he worries that Mr Barber might be too frail for the exercise, but the old man removes his jacket and pulls the brim of his hat low to shade his eyes – and there's something youthful and sophisticated about the slim Jamaican in his well-cut suit, sauntering down the country lane, jacket hooked over his shoulder. Together, they cut quite a pair.

It's not the weather for grief. A lemon-yellow sun shines at a benign angle, its chalky aura dissolving in a peerless blue. A breeze, soft as breath, caresses the cow parsley and makes the hawthorn branches dip and sigh. The lane takes them past a white cottage with a well-stocked garden where walls of hollyhocks hold back foaming drifts of lavender.

Here's old Jackson's farm past the bend in the lane, deserted now except for a loft of pigeons standing in military rows on the broken roof tiles. In the yard, a tomcat crouches inside an abandoned filing cabinet, following their approach with slant-eyed suspicion. He could be one of Mordecai's descendants.

'I used to play here,' Lionel says, looking back along their route. 'I used to know every centimetre of this lane, and all the fields around.

This was a working farm back then. Before the monocultures and everything.'

'I hate to see a place like this, all mash up.' Mr Barber sniffs, holding his hat to his chest. 'I hate to see everyting gone bad. I seen all these lickle farms from the bus, like they're out a business, rack and ruin, like the shops in town.'

'Stuff's mostly grown abroad now, agribusiness. Ukraine, Brazil, places like that where they can pollenate plants, like they're in factories.'

'It not natural. Mark me. It not right.'

They stroll on further and Bethesda comes into view, the house where he spent his early childhood. The last time he was here was just before his parents moved to the bungalow. Back then, David still had rare moments of lucidity. He'd begged Lionel to persuade Judy to change her mind about moving, but she wouldn't budge.

'Why don't *we* live here, just you and me, boy?' his father had pleaded. But it was too late. David was all but lost. Bethesda was already sold.

Lionel holds his breath until the frontage fills his vision, and then he stops. Mr Barber stops with him.

'It's very nice,' says the old man. 'Good solid house, this one.'

The new owners have erected a fence at the side, partitioning the property from the walled garden that used to lead onto the meadow, down to the river. On the other side of the wall a man on a tall step-ladder is examining the topmost branches of a dead laburnum. The lethal racemes would normally be dangling thick and sulphurous at this time of year, yellowing the air. But the tree is a leafless skeleton. Could it have given up the ghost in a year? Stories of children found dead beneath blond boughs used to haunt him as a child and he recalls a forgotten nightmare: Lilith asleep under the tree, poisonous petals straying into her mouth.

Lilith's account of the failed lynching pastes itself onto the scene – the rope, the go-kart, his brothers' brutal curiosity – but these images are chased off by the noise of a chainsaw spluttering to life. The man on the ladder has donned a pair of goggles. He lifts the saw and buzzes through the laburnum's dead wood with ease.

Lionel raises his voice above the strangled whine of the motor. 'I hated that tree. They should've chopped it down when we were small.'

238

Mr Barber shouts, 'Ah right! So this is your house from way back.'

'It was never mine. They just let me live here for a while.'

For the first time Lionel feels something close to resentment.

Mourners wait for the coffin outside the Assembly Hall. Several behatted old women have gathered in the shade of an adjacent building. Men in dour suits, bibles in hand, stand patiently on the pavement. The Assembly building was once a Methodist church, but over the years it has been modified in line with the Assembly's doctrine. Places of worship must be unadorned, workaday. 'Let the Roman Catholics explain their vainglorious idolatry on the Day of Reckoning,' his father would say.

The stubby spire has been taken down; an arched front door and porch have been removed and a bland entrance installed to the side of the building, out of sight. Modesty is paramount. A whitewashed extension has been added where a car park once was. And yet something about the extension's size, the way it protrudes from the main building, speaks of blunt self-importance. Altogether the Assembly Hall looks neither humble nor sacred; what remains is a blockish modernity, more in keeping with civic buildings.

A horse chestnut tree on the opposite side of the road provides shelter from the sun while they wait. Lionel peers up through its branches. 'This has grown three times its size since I last stood here,' he says. He gives the trunk a sturdy slap, as one would pat the flank of a beloved horse, and tries to imagine what the tree has witnessed in its lifetime. 'Nothing ever stops changing.'

'Nope, can't turn nuttin back neither. Not ever,' says Mr Barber. Lionel suspects the old man is alluding to disappointments in his own life.

Across the street several more mourners join the small group. Leaning against the chestnut, Lionel tries to work out who they are, thinking he won't be able to remember. But, surprisingly, he does. There's John Roland – a rival of David's for Judy's hand (so the story goes), who never married; Mrs Jenkins, the organist (only on Sunday evenings); and Mr Leckie, Assembly leader in all but name – always so certain and upright – now bent to a question mark with age. Lionel recognizes features in other faces that he hopes will prompt more memories when they're coupled with voices and gestures – but their identities stay muddied, shrouded. Time has made new, saggy versions of them.

Lionel turns to Mr Barber. 'Do you remember when I stopped coming to the shop – when I was a boy I mean?'

The old man squints into the leopard light filtering down through the leaves. 'Of course I remember. Your father him come in to tell me, very polite, 'bout that bad business on the bridge.' Mr Barber appraises him. 'Didn't see you for a good few years after that.'

'Was David upset about the accident when he spoke to you?'

'Hard to say – Mr Byrd was very *proper*, y'know, but him always look 'pon you gentle. You'd play console games, waiting for your haircut. Thumbs going mad on the lickle keys there.' Mr Barber attempts the actions. 'And he'd have his arm round you. Always give you lollipop to suck in the chair.'

Lionel squeezes his eyes shut, trying to feel David's arm on his shoulders. 'What did he say about the accident?'

Mr Barber strokes his chin. 'Him say you mek trouble with your bredrin on a regular. Kept disappearing off and all a that jivation. I remember thinking, How come that quiet pickney want lash out, slip him collar? Swear to God you never said 'boo' in the shop.' Mr Barber remembers something and raises his finger. 'There was one time you was vexed. That's right. You didn't want your hair off! You say it mek you look like . . . ah, what was that word you use? Robot or some such.' Mr Barber shows the upturned pink of his palms. 'Anyway, you cry *murder*. *H*eventually me say, "S'all right, Mr Byrd – the boys dem, they don't want haircut sometimes. Leave it till the next week." But you stamp foot – "I'm not a boy, I'm a warrior" – and your father drag you from the shop, apologizing, while you kick out.' The old man shrugs. 'You come back the next time sweet as sugar: "I'm very sorry, Mr Barber." That was the only time you get facety or rude.'

'Replicant.'

'What's that?'

Lionel shakes his head. 'It was a game my brothers played.'

The brim of his trilby hides the old man's eyes. 'Me always think you were like cuckoo – nappy-head cuckoo in with all a them white birds.'

'Cuckoo, eh?'

'But listen, most important ting – what I witness for meself – your father, him care for you, y'know.'

'Thank you.'

They share a cigarette and watch the mourners tug at their collars and fan themselves with paper.

'By God, it a warm one,' marks Mr Barber.

'Beautiful.'

The hearse is immaculate, old-fashioned. It appears from the opposite direction followed by a single limousine and, behind that, half a dozen men on foot, heads bowed.

'Him come now.' Mr Barber nods, slips his jacket on and steps into the sun.

The hearse draws up with silent gravitas and the footmen break formation and walk to its rear. Lionel's heart quickens when he realizes the two lead pall-bearers are his brothers. He always thought James was taller with darker hair, but here they are, sandy-haired clones, standing shoulder to shoulder. There's something unsettling about James in particular; it makes Lionel anxious to look at him.

Judy stares out from inside the limousine – Lilith's not with her, or with the rest of the mourners. The pall-bearers line up with their load on the forecourt and the driver opens the door for Judy, who climbs out, looking baffled.

Mr Barber touches Lionel lightly between the shoulders. 'Come,' he says.

The air in the hall smells old. The Assembly has become a victim of its own piety. The young people have jumped ship and now the congregation consists of a meek sorority of ladies and some once-stern men. Chairs have been arranged in a semicircle around the central space where David's coffin is elevated on a stand. Lionel sits with Mr Barber, towards the back.

There's no official order of service – this is the way of the Assembly – but after a few minutes the funeral begins and various men stand and hold forth about David's life and work. Judy cries soundlessly throughout; no one else sheds a tear. Eventually James stands, casts a righteous glance around the hall and begins the eulogy.

'My father, David Isaac Byrd, was born in the old century. He was a man of charity and understood that the greatest gift man has is God's word. Now my father's mortal body goes back to the earth. But' – he pauses, one finger raised – 'the body is merely a vessel. Right now, right this minute, David Byrd is sitting at the right hand of God.' James now points directly to heaven.

A few murmurs of 'Amen' warp the air. Lionel is obliged to hold his temples as James drones on. The light in the hall pulses gently and the coffin grows a thick black outline, as if the whole scene has been posterized. He closes his eyes.

'This life,' James continues, 'is not a rehearsal, or a staging post. Not an elastic continuum, or a parallel universe. Laws of physics do not govern it. No. It's a one-time-only moral exam. No resits. No if-at-first-you-don't-succeeds. No extenuating circumstances. No *replay*. This is it. Sudden death. God is the Creator. We are His creatures and we must conform to His rules.'

Is he hearing this right? He opens his eyes. The room is at an angle. The coffin has gained an otherworldly patina. The rest of the mourners appear unconcerned. Even Mr Barber, who turns to proffer a sympathetic smile, hasn't noticed the glitch in James's speech. *No replay. God is the Creator.* Lionel feels his brow: burning hot. James is very far away, a hologram disappearing into the distance, holding a filial palm towards Judy.

'My mother met my father in this very hall. Their marriage . . .'

A loud swooshing fills Lionel's head and, for a while, he can't hear anything except random words piercing James's muffled bombination.

'Three children . . . countless orphans in East Africa . . . salvation and education . . . sacrifice . . . personal tragedy. We pray, of course, for deliverance.'

Why has Lilith stayed away? The moment he thinks of her the door cracks open and she scuttles to a seat at the back of the hall. Her hair is unkempt; she's thrown on an ugly brown dress. Look at her! She's shabby, losing colour, rough around the edges. Is that some kind of sack she's wearing? His ears pop and James's voice comes through loud and clear.

'Before my parents returned to England they adopted one of the orphans I mention. They brought him to live with them. They gave him a life he could never have dreamed of and, er . . .'

One or two of the congregation squirm, perhaps because James hesitates, or maybe it's because Mr Barber has taken Lionel firmly by the shoulders and is giving him a serious shake. Several people twist round in their seats to frown at the 'orphan'. When Lionel turns to Lilith she's glaring at James, her face hard with hatred.

'My father became ill some time ago,' says James, rallying. 'And more recently he had to move from his beloved Bethesda into the bungalow. But he spent the final months of his life at the Yews, a nursing home, and my mother has asked me to mention the particular gratitude she has for the care my father received there.'

James adjusts his stance, an acrobat on a beam preparing to dismount. Both hands are gripping his lapels now, chin raised high, the perfect angle for full-throated rhetoric before the finale.

'We will miss our father,' he says, then pauses and moderates his delivery. 'We will miss his unequalled knowledge of the scriptures. We will miss the strength of his faith and the sharpness of his intellect. But we won't miss David Byrd for long. We will be joining him in the Promised Land. The Lord's covenant, brothers and sisters, will be manifest in our lifetime and we, that are saved, will be heirs to paradise.'

James finishes but remains standing, allowing the full effect of his perfect landing to garner the assenting Amens. He receives them with one hand held high, as if eschewing an unexpected ovation. Eventually he sits. Ben puts an arm around him and whispers something in his ear.

'Short and sweet,' says Mr Barber leaning close, echoing the camaraderie of the siblings at the front. 'But why you start choking so?'

Lionel shakes his head. Choking, he wasn't choking.

After the last hymn the pall-bearers rise and hoist the coffin to their shoulders. Lionel thinks of his father, alone in the darkness – in the Void. A woman he doesn't recognize squeezes his arm as she passes. 'So much tragedy,' she simpers.

James won't look at him, although Ben gives him an apologetic grimace. Judy, her face an awkward knot of emotions, closes her eyes as she passes. David's death is the end of Lionel's association with his family. He understands this with a shock. Existence is an act of faith. A tacit contract that all parties must buy into. Gods are perpetuated this way, and demons. But existence can be denied when faith is broken. His family are denying him – they are rubbing him out.

When the rest of the mourners have left the hall Lilith comes to his side. She is strangely tranquil. 'I'm not going to the graveside,' she says.

'No?'

'I might *do* something I'll regret.' She smiles unnaturally.

'Should I go to the grave, do you think?'

'Can't you see they don't want you, Lionel? They don't want either of us.'

Mr Barber clears his throat. 'You must go if you need to, but your family – it hurt me to say – them treat you very harsh.'

'They have more right to grieve than me.'

'What?' Mr Barber sucks his teeth. 'Why you say that?'

'He was their father, not mine.'

The old man stretches to his full height. 'If man a man treat you like a son then him a father, for true.'

'Well, what do you think, Lionel?' says Lilith. Contempt compounds her misery. 'Did David treat you like a son?'

@GameAddict (#23756745): 01:8:27

It's easy to become obsessed. It starts with half
an hour. You call it 'an escape' or 'down time'.
Before you know it, it's three hours, then four.
Evenings, whole nights disappear while your
Healthy Choice Chop Suey congeals in its microwave tray. And why not? What else is there
to do? Time leaches away in the grey world.
But the Game Layer unfolds – a never-ending
phantasmagoria of possibilities.

Level 13: Buried

A googly. A left-field strand. Instead of the Void, I escaped. I've fetched up the footage and had a scrub through and it seems that exactly as the He-Man went in for the kill another earthshift sent the whole lot of us mud-sliding down. Catastrophic. Everything plopped off the mountain – stupas, temples, citizens, dwell-places – and avalanched into oblivion. All buried. One giant mass grave.

I must've conked out for a bit, but when I renogged there was a great weight pon me. Earth in my mouth, claying my tongue. Deep in my lug-holes, dense against my Visor. Each limb encased in thick muck. Ages went by thus entombed, I bade farewell to it all and waited for Void. But again, by some miracle, the earth parted and I was suddenly free – *ta da* – and there was the night sky prickling with twinklers.

The MauMau, who'd followed our trail from the desert, had been stalking Rihn vultures when he snagged one and tortured it right on the spot I was buried. The predation ploughed up the earth and I was exposed, and I reared up all *Dawn of the Dead*, spitting and yacking to clear out my pipes. I fair crushed the MauMau once I could breathe, took its nog in my mitts and scratched under its chin saying, 'Buddha, my saviour,' before remembering the Krin.

There followed a breathless excavation of sod. I found the Krin's ceremonial Balwriqin – come clean off in the rough roly-poly – then I came pon his sword, but no paw at the end of it. I drilled down further and uncovered the Harlequin. Void. I saw the He-Man then, making off in the gloom, and I made half-hearted chase.

Leggy bastard turned and harangued me. 'You'll never catch me with these babies, you idiot,' he said, slapping his thighs.

I couldn't speak but threw lumps of clay at his back as he sprinted away.

When he was gone I slumped in a heap – overcome – never felt any-thing like it before. I scrolled through the data coming through in my

Visor: Health: 85. Approval: N/A. Energy: 45. Skills accrued: 761. The quake must've damaged my code as nothing explained why I was reeling. I even started to ask loony questions: Who was I? Why was I here? What a joke jumping from dimension to dimension and slogging through levels – for what? All these muscles and combat skills – yet I was alone. The Krin had made me feel something new and important. He'd wished I was his son. Imagine! I wept for him. Ridiculous. Great shuddering howls. Me, a He-Man – self-pitying – bemoaning the loss of a character I barely knew.

Later, when the sun brimmed, I got the full-impact death scene. Apocalypse-grim. A stinky miasma licked over the ground and from it a host of new Wisps came *woo-hooing*. And there, in amid all the chaos, the Sylph. I couldn't believe it. True, she was fully corrupted. Kept buzzing on and off like a janky connection. Her speech centre was blown (she could only respond with whimpery songs and hand gestures). But I had her. I had her. And, tho grief-stricken at the loss of the Krin, I was weirdly elated.

It was then that a plan took shape in my nog. First I must travel to Br'mab and connect with the alchemist Dan-Albwr-han spoke of in Level 9. If rumours were true he could repair the Sylph. I was sure now that she was my Key. Afterwards, get to the Core and destroy the Big Boss. I eased the Sylph onto my shoulders – she weighed nothing at all – and yomped down the mountain. I found my supplies, used my last Power Ring to crank up my energy and set off across Gog at a clip. The MauMau kept pace behind me – the passerines stuck like opulent pegs on the end of his tail.

Roses

It smells like cut grass. No, not quite grass but it has the same clean, green quality. There are floral head notes too, camomile or daffodil, light and fresh. He's been trying to work out the smell since Lilith moved in – *only a temporary arrangement* – but he can't place it. No matter; he's never been so happy, that's what really counts. Lilith has emerged from her bleak phase. David's death, his cruel brothers, Judy's grief, politics, finding his *real* family – all forgotten. Lilith is, at last, calm.

And this aroma she's brought with her is transporting. She must float round the flat when he's at work, wafting scent through all the rooms – a train of daisies flowing from her hair. Tender green shoots growing in her footsteps. The bodily incarnation of spring. He plans to go through her toiletries when she's out, discover the fragrance that's finally chased off the smell of stale curry. But Lilith hasn't left Milk Street since she arrived. It's been a week now, maybe more.

She phoned the day after the funeral. 'I need you,' she said, weeping. 'I can't be alone.'

When he brought her to Milk Street she curled up on the sofa. It looked as if she'd shrunk. The smoking lines had deepened around her lips. Broken capillaries reddened the sides of her septum. A streak of grey had appeared in her hair.

'I'm letting myself go,' she said.

There was no regret. It was as if she'd been her own jailer and now she was granting herself a pardon. Eventually she slept and he covered her with a blanket where she lay. This is what families are for, he thought, to bear one another up in a crisis.

Now Lilith looks healthier. If she had an energy meter it would be showing close to one hundred. They've fallen into a comfortable routine, brother and sister. He'd expected her to harry him, but she's self-contained, installed in the bedroom where she works and sleeps. The sofa is proving a comfortable alternative to his bed and he's set a clothes rail against the wall nearest the kitchen. The living room is noisy at night, but he doesn't mind. The youths declaring their territory, the coos and calls of the street girls and the late-night railway announcements coat the hard surfaces of Milk Street and lull him to sleep.

When he's not on shift he keeps watch for Crystal. The health centre girls don't work at the junction, but he's seen her stamping along with her head down. Despite her plea he hasn't been back to see her. Instead he's made several complaints about the centre to the council and the police. Emails – sent anonymously and signed 'Concerned Citizen' – should have reached the right people by now, but so far nothing has happened. Men still sneak down the alley – day and night.

It makes Lionel sick to see Huo, bold as brass, straightening the lace on his cuffs, adjusting the ruby in his cravat, as he flounces about. It's outrageous. If immigration officers haven't raided the health centre by Friday, Lionel plans to rescue Crystal himself. He'll wear a disguise. Flash his scimitar around (to be on the safe side). Put her over his shoulder and carry her off to a secret hideout. You have to fight fire with fire when it comes to characters as loathsome as Huo, he decides.

Tonight Lilith slopes off to bed early. Not wanting to disturb her, he plays *CoreQuest* wearing his Visor and nods off with the game running.

When he wakes he's in bed, Lilith is at his side.

'Darling,' she whispers. 'You were sobbing.'

Her hand feels warm through the covers.

'I was dreaming.'

She kisses his forehead and drifts away.

A data retrieval officer at Meddingley, from B section, has been arrested. Security personnel implemented a lockdown in record time. All exits from HQ were blocked by rows of special officers wearing full-face helmets and body armour. Everyone was forced to remain at their stations until the culprit, Larissa Greenough, was led into the Hub in plastic wrist-cuffs. Lionel wasn't there when it happened, but he's overheard the gossip in the toilets and the cafeteria. There's a growing sense of siege at Meddingley. The system servers have been under twenty-four-hour cyber-attack. It's been all hands on deck to defend the network. People with placards have been demonstrating around the perimeter. Thousands of confidential files have ended up in the public domain. It's a calamity.

Still, the consensus is that the special officers are too heavy-handed. A junior technician got 'roughed up' in the toilets after passing something to a colleague that turned out to be a tablet of gum. Another woman was kept in solitary for two days before a simple HR error was shown to have caused 'abnormal activity' on her login. Meddingley's insistence that Larissa Greenough has been selling material to unauthorized parties is being widely questioned. How could she have done it? Memory devices are banned on site. There are five secure tiers to the network and anything moving beyond it requires a Level One signature. The only way data can 'leak' is for someone with clearance to license a transfer.

An employee with a photographic memory could, conceivably, snapshot data over time and transcribe it outside the workplace – but it's unlikely. Nevertheless, a skilled programmer could create a data wormhole: seamlessly puncture a network artery and siphon off secrets. Information could pass into the cloud and no one would know. Lionel's certain this could happen because it's exactly the set-up he created for Pema Khalsa when she was struggling with her workload, months previously. But Larissa Greenough wouldn't be capable of that. They were on the same systems analysis course. Larissa, a matronly woman with wide cheekbones and friendly eyes, struggled with the simplest tasks – data visualization, automation praxis, workflow ciphers. She had to retake them all.

'Lionel, my man!' Michael shouts with prodigal exuberance – as if their acquaintance consists of more than one failed social encounter and a friendship confirmation on SocialNet.

The American barrels towards him through the men's room with his usual overblown bonhomie. So irritating. Nevertheless, Lionel's done some digging in the HR files and Michael's got an impressive CV. The son of a diplomat and an online security whizz – majored in simulated intelligence. He's just the person to ask how easy it is to forge a bio-ID. Still, there's something about him that makes Lionel uneasy.

He lowers his eyes. 'Hello, Michael.'

Michael mistakes Lionel's reticence for grief, and his face slumps to hangdog sympathy. 'Hey, I heard about all your shit, y'know, your pa and everything. Jeez, I'm sorry, yeah.'

Lionel shrugs.

'But hey.' Michael brightens inappropriately. 'A little bird told me you got it on with Eve.'

He attempts a modest smile. 'Well, not exac–'

Michael slaps his back. 'You wolf! I'm impressed. She's hot, buddy boy, I mean *really* hot. Hey, let's talk in the corridor. This place has turned into the freakin' house of rumours since that chick in Retrieval got bust. Did you know her?' Michael holds the door for him. 'After you, dude. They see us snuggling up in the men's room and *bam*, they've got the latex gloves on, fishing shit outta your ass, you know what I'm saying?'

Lionel nods, but he has no idea what Michael's talking about.

In the corridor Michael leans against the glass so his profile is exposed to the Hub. 'Yeah! Audacious, right? I heard she was selling secrets to every dodgy regime on the pla–'

'I'm late for my shift actually, Michael, but I do need to talk you about –'

'Oh yeah, I mean no, man. Of course, you chip out if you have to.' Michael takes a couple of steps backwards. 'Hey, what're you doing this weekend? I'm having some of the guys over. We're gonna drink some beers, listen to some tunes, have a smoke' – Michael winks – 'play some games, shit like that. There's this crazy new shooter game, you gotta try it, beats the crap outta *CoreQuest*. You play *CoreQuest*, right? Anyway, the graphics are awesome. Prospero'll be there, remember him?'

'Yes. Yes I do. But –'

'C'mon! You need to escape, Lionel. You need something to take you out of yourself, apart from' – he makes bosomy shapes with his hands – 'the voluptuous Eve.'

Lionel flushes. 'Things are complicated at the moment.'

'Sure. No pressure, man. Think about it.' Michael's a few metres away and he raises his hand – half reprieve, half valediction.

'Okay. I will. But I need to talk to you urgently about' – Lionel remembers where he is and lowers his voice – 'bio-IDs.'

'What's that, buddy?' Michael cups his ear.

'It's okay, it's nothing.'

'Message me.'

Midday. Sweltering hot. He clips on his three-sixty Visor, strokes the SensePad and rips free of reality. The Krin's death was a blow. Lionel had become attached to the character and now he's strangely rattled. Dan-Albwr-han's player was accessing *CoreQuest* via a local node. How mad is that? He might have passed him on the street or sat next to him on the train. The Sylph's a mystery, too. It blew his mind to see the avatar he'd begun months before – shades of Lilith (the inspiration for all his female avatars) mixed in with features stolen from Crystal. The code's corrupted, of course – the avatar was only a preview, but now she's part of the Quest.

From a precipice he surveys his virtual domain and, on a whim, pushes off, swallow dives into nothingness. Invincible – golden locks swept back by the air rushing past him – his body makes a graceful, gravity-defying arc. *Wooohooo.*

A delicious smell reaches him from the kitchen. Lilith is cooking something up. He's been refining his sister's basic avatar files, capturing a version of Lilith that's happy and strong. She struck stupid poses for the preliminary sketches, but when he asked her to model for the photos she wore a mock-serious face, standing in her underwear, as he snapped away all around her like a paparazzo.

The door opens a fraction. 'Hey, geek boy.' Lilith grins. 'Want a pancake?'

'Yeah.' He pauses the game.

They sit with plates on their knees, inspecting an animated Lilith, projected onto his desk in 3D.

'It's good. It's spooky, though. It's me but not me.'

'There are some final touches, you know.'

'Just think,' she says. 'As soon as you've finished we can run away and live together in digital paradise for ever.'

'I thought you hated my games.'

'I do.' She pauses, corrects herself. 'I did. But now I imagine . . . I imagine a glorious afterlife. I want shimmering waterfalls and birds with bright feathers and flowers and I want to fly. I've always wanted to fly.'

He pretends to make a list. 'Anything else, madam?'

'Contentment. Did I mention everlasting contentment?'

He laughs. 'It sounds heavenly.'

'Maybe Dad was right. Maybe there's something like heaven after *this* life. But I reckon heaven needs updating. Heaven 2.0.'

'Like a game?'

'Exactly! And you, dear brother, can make it all happen. You can immortalize us.' She puffs her chest out.

He smiles. 'I shall.'

She puts her plate aside and stands behind him, draping her arms round his neck, resting her lips on his ear. 'You're my saviour,' she whispers.

Lovely warm Lilith. He feels quite lightheaded, but she grips him suddenly and blows on his neck and he lets out a playful cry. He's her saviour. Not a mistake that an anonymous African woman made. Not a Freak or a Reject or a *Replicant*. Lilith holds him, tickles him, growls like a child, bites his shoulder and laughs. It's a forgotten sensation that reawakens the rough and tumble of childhood. He turns, grabs her, *it's only a game*, and wrestles her to the floor so that she's on her back writhing beneath him. She protests as he holds her arms above her head, her body vital and alive.

'Stop it. No, Lionel, stop,' she squeals.

Look at the elegant curve of her neck. Look at the perfect shape of her clavicles and, here, the shallow wells of her armpits. Adorable. He blows loudly into one hollow then the other. She smells of long ago. Yes, that's the smell, the meadow beyond the garden at Bethesda. Or was it always, simply, Lilith's smell?

'No, Lionel, stop, you bastard.' She's wriggling, the minx, shrieking with laughter.

Abandon – a flight – a swallow dive into the Void – a leap of consciousness. Something light and bloated rises from his loins towards his throat and lodges in his chest. This girl he's loved all his life. The only love he's ever known. Her laughter turns into quick, intent breathing and they stare into one another's eyes, caught in a shattered moment, petrified by it, until she parts her lips to speak.

'We're not really brother and sister,' she says softly. 'Not really.'

There are diamonds in her eyes, but he's turning to liquid. He will wash clean away if he moves. She stretches up, hesitates, then stretches further, to kiss him. Not a playful sibling's peck, but a sweet and lingering invitation to love her. His life's essence distils to a singular point. He's atomic. The power of the entire universe is contained in him, waiting to explode. But he stays in the same position, exerting the same pressure on her wrists, knees either side of her hips.

Slowly she breaks their lips' connection.

After the burglary, he installed a new buzzer entry system. When its harsh note assaults the silence they both jump.

'It's the door,' he says, but he doesn't move.

'Well, are you going to answer it?'

When he eventually releases her hands she stays on her back, panting softly. He can hear the air passing in and out of her body.

He wishes he was air.

The monitor shows the top of Eve's head and a view down her cleavage. She waits patiently on the street, but her eyes track to the camera and flick away.

'It's a friend.'

'So let them in,' says Lilith, getting up off the floor and straightening her vest top. 'I'll put some proper clothes on.'

Eve runs her hand along the clothes rail. 'You never told me you had a sister.'

'I thought I did.'

Eve's skirt comes to mid-thigh. She curls one leg beneath her and reclines into the corner of the sofa, the other leg outstretched – smooth and bare. The straps of her sandals criss-cross round her calves to her knee. From the waist down she reminds him of a gladiator or a centurion; from the waist up she looks like a predatory goddess. Now he thinks of it, Eve's allure is brash and overdone in contrast to Lilith's.

'She's staying with me for a few weeks.' He lowers his voice. Lionel thinks of Lilith dressing in his bedroom. 'She needs to be with people since our dad died, you know.'

'It's understandable.'

'I'm back at work, so she's here on her own.'

'What does she do – for a living, I mean?'

'It's boring really.'

Eve stretches her arms across the back of the sofa. 'I'm not easily bored.'

'Do you know, I don't know what Lilith does' – it's hard to look at Eve she's so dominating – 'but I know it's boring. That's what she says anyway.'

Eve frowns. 'Lilith. It's a nice name.'

He can't think of anything to say. Why doesn't Lilith come out and sit with them? She could tell them everything about her boring job, whatever it is. But then, he thinks, she must be embarrassed. She regrets what happened on the floor and can't face a polite social encounter.

'She's probably gone to sleep or something. I'll go and check.'

'No.' Eve leans towards him. 'Let's not disturb her. Let's go out.'

He looks towards Lilith's room. 'I don't know.'

'Please.' Eve clasps her hands together. 'We keep getting off on the wrong foot. One last try. Please. Friends. Just as friends.'

At the edge of town, where the landscape slips between urban waste and rural disuse, Eve accelerates. Velocity forces his skull into the headrest and the countryside whips past in triple time, kaleidoscoping through shades of pink, blue and umber. Eve shoots him a smile, presses forcefully on the gas. She's dynamic, exciting. But if she turns too quickly Lionel wonders if he'll be able to see the edges of her. A cardboard Eve; 2D. Only Lilith, he realizes, is totally and completely real.

'What are you thinking?'

He bites his lip. 'All of this . . .'

'What?'

'Sometimes. Often. Nothing seems real.'

Before Lionel can register what's happening Eve takes his hand and pushes it between her legs. Her skin is burning hot. She shuffles down in her seat to make room between feverish thighs, inching her legs open until he can feel the downy corona of her pubic hair. A moist touch on his finger.

She makes a noise that sounds like relief. 'Does that feel real?' she says.

The car moves faster than light. Eve's easy ecstasy, the whine of the engine, the heel of her hand rigid on the wheel, the other guiding his fingers further towards the core of her heat – it's too much. It's all too much.

'I have to go back.' He recovers his hand with some effort.

'Why? What is it?'

'Nothing. I feel . . . argh!' He must keep his mouth shut.

'Tell me.'

'I feel . . . no, I can't explain. You won't understand.'

Eve is exasperated. 'Try, for God's sake. You owe me that.'

'I think you're beautiful, I mean utterly, unbelievably gorgeous. And that's the thing. You're unbelievable.'

Eve puts her foot down and the car retaliates with a wilful surge. 'I feel the same about you.'

'No.' He shakes his head. 'It doesn't add up. I'm not in your league. You're playing with me. I'm just part of your game, whatever that is.'

There, he's said it.

'What are you talking about? What game?'

'I don't know.' He puts his hands to his face and he can smell her on his fingers – vaguely salty, vaguely ripe. 'I'm confused.'

Without warning Eve steps on the brakes and the car slides dramatically as she yanks the wheel one way then another, steering into the skid. Reaching for the dashboard, more to touch something solid than anything else, he steadies himself. He's not scared; in fact, he has time to look at her: the plump of her belly, her mighty man-arms going like a machine, her face inscrutable. Finally she brings the car to a stop – no hint of anxiety or remorse – and unlocks the passenger door from the control panel. It opens with a clunk.

It's an act, he thinks. All her movements are so carefully scripted. Perhaps *she's* a Replicant. Not him, it's never been him. It's like Lilith says – they're all robots. The whole world's probably overrun with *skin jobs*. All this time he's been obsessed with his own rigid processes and the Replicants have been taking over.

'Go on,' says Eve. 'Get out. I think I've tried hard enough.'

Yes, this drama is a fabrication. Her face gives nothing away. The decision to test her comes to him in a moment. He grabs her hand, holds it tight and manoeuvres quickly until he's straddling her. With his free hand he reaches for the lever and reclines the driver's seat – flat. He looks down at her. Eve, speechless with surprise, is trying to assess the situation. Is that a smile on her impossible lips? Does she think this is a sexual advance? Echoes of the episode with Lilith prompt him to swear and the gleam in her eyes is instantly banished.

'Tell me,' he whispers, his face too close to hers. 'Tell me only the good things about your mother.'

'You're insane.'

He grabs both her wrists and holds them above her head. She gasps and struggles. He can feel the steering wheel against his buttocks.

'I said, tell me only the good things about your mother and you can only use single words. No phrases.'

She writhes fruitlessly. 'Fuck off.'

Easily locking both her wrists in one hand, he fishes in his pocket for his Google, sets it to zoom, homes in on one of her liquid brown eyes. She's putting up an energetic fight now, twisting around, attempting to knee him.

'Let me go, you total fucking freak.' She bares her teeth and screams.

'Single words, c'mon,' he barks, intent on her magnified eye.

An urgent wave ripples along the length of her body, the well of her pupil dilates and the iris is forced to a mere rim of brown. Unadulterated fear. Human. Not robot.

'Oh God.' He releases her hands. 'I'm so sorry, I'm so sorry.'

'You fuck.' She's crying.

He tries to shield his face as she batters him.

'Forgive me, I'm so confused, please.'

The blows are still flying as he falls out of the car.

The seat flips up and she stares at him, eye-whites flashing. 'You, you . . .' She spits to one side.

'I know I'm *mad*.' His hands are held out in entreaty.

She rests her forehead on the wheel. 'Goddammit, Lionel.'

'I'm so sorry. Really I am.'

'Get in. I'll drive you back.'

He stays where he is. 'I'm good. I want to walk. I need to walk.'

'Get back in, for God's sake.'

A fat, unappetizing silence pads the spaces between them as Eve drives him back into town. When she draws in at the junction she touches his wrist lightly, thinks better of it and withdraws.

'Eve,' he says. 'I really don't know what –'

'No!' She holds her hand up. 'I mean it. No need. Let's just call it a day.'

Now he's brimming with thoughts of Lilith, picturing her face, rehearsing a speech as he jogs to the flat. She'll be waiting for him in the living room, wondering where he's been. There's so much to explain; *I'm going mad, Lil. I can't believe I did that to a woman.* She'll make light of it, no doubt. She'll say it's Eve's fault for pursuing him. That's Lilith. She'll have an opinion about what went on between them on the living-room floor, too. She'll say, 'Fuck it, we're not siblings – you're from a whole other gene pool,' or something like that, and she'll take his face and kiss him again. They'll pick up where they left off – they won't be able to control themselves. They'll devour one another, totally devour one another – forgetting all their coy terror from earlier.

The speech he's rehearsing isn't quite right. Should he begin with, 'I love you,' or leave that for the end?

Truth is, Lil, that I love you. I always have.

His shirt feels uncomfortably tight and he's started to sweat. At the door he drops his keys, swears, fumbles – fingers and thumbs – but then he's in the building, taking the stairs to the first floor in giant strides. On the landing he stops, heart bashing like billy-o. *Boom boom boom.* Only a door divides them. He takes a deep breath, flings it open. Lilith will be waiting for him – right there. *Not brother and sister.*

Lilith should be there, but she's not.

In a blink he's at her door, shaking his locks the way Ludi does. 'Lil, it's me.'

Excitement courses through him, fluent and sexual.

'Lil,' he shouts again and raps on the door. Should he barge in? Take his sister in his arms, hold her face in his hands and kiss her and tell her how utterly desperate he is. As the door opens his whole being yearns for her.

'Lil.' Her name sounds like a secret when he says it like that.

Lilith has taken great care in straightening the bedcovers. The room is clean and orderly and his belongings are lined up on the tabletop and along the mantelpiece – as he'd left them, weeks before. There are none of Lilith's things. The bottles, creams, shoes and clothes he's imagined have all gone; the fragrance of springtime – gone. Lilith. Gone. She's left nothing of herself, not one pin. It takes a while to sink in, but when it does he falls onto the bed.

Capricious, that's what she is: damaged and capricious and cruel. How could she abandon him now – again – when he needs her most? There's nothing to do but bury his face in the bedclothes and sob. But here, deep in the pillow, there's a residual shade of her and he breathes it in deeper; yes, it's her perfume deteriorating on the linen. She's left something, after all.

Roses. Of course! The smell is of roses. Why didn't he recognize it?

@GameAddict (#23756745): 12:8:27

Every one of your senses is engaged on the
Game Layer. It's technological alchemy – per-
ceptual manipulation, that's all. Touch and smell
were the last senses they nailed. Now they
can prompt you to sense things from memory
– make you believe you're kissing a mermaid
with the vague stink of fish in your nostrils – all
by using a few lines of code. Of course, they
can't make you smell what you've never smelled
before. It relies on memory, as I've said. But
they can get several sensory inputs and mash
them together to make a new experience.
Imagination and shit-hot graphics do the rest.

Level 14: The Alchemist of Br'mab

A forest of Br'mab trees – as far as my Visor could focus in zoom-mode – extended across Gog like a wall, their huge trunks ebony-smooth till up high, where a knot of branches made a thickly weaved canopy. In the forest, teensy peek-holes let ribbons of sunlight coil into the gloom. Otherwise it was blacker than Void, but I footed my way through the wildwood, determined.

I pined for the Krin in that shrouded place. The Sylph, a silent presence, faded fast on my shoulders and even the MauMau was subdued. As we pressed on I came convinced the alchemist must be a myth. Time itself grovels in darkness. But after an age a voice hailed me, 'Halloooo', through the forest – as if I was expected. I followed the voice to a lopsided hovel and ducked under the lintel, quite cautious. The hovel felt familiar and homely. All manner of books were stacked in great piles. Jars full of taxidermic creatures made up a curiosity of specimens muddled on sideboards and shelves. Flickery torches burned by the door and candles went *spit-spit* on a table where a game of Vingla, midway through, and piles of parchment scribbled over in cuneiform vied for space.

The character entered, stage-right. 'Well, well. I was wondering when you might get here.'

White locks and goggles gave the alchemist a prof-type authority and, despite being oldsome, his charisma said 'strong' even 'fatherly'. I felt instantly safe, tho a sacking and ashes get-up made him look as if he was doing some kind of penance. He made space for the Sylph – now almost transparent – on a day bed.

'The Sylph and a MauMau,' said the alchemist, voice like a charm. 'You've chosen some interesting baggage to carry.' He touched the bridge of his goggles – to stop them from slipping – and regarded me fondly.

'Yes, sir,' I said. 'I suppose I have.'

'It's understandable. But why bring them to me, son?'

I was awkward. The alchemist's gaze had a glitch that made me feel I'd already done this whole scene before. 'I heard you repaired corrupt characters.' I nodded towards the Sylph.

The alchemist turned away and riffled through parchments – he seemed to be wiping some brine from his eye-gems.

Impatient, I pushed him. 'Well. Can you?'

He turned back to me, assumed priester posture, mitts in a prayer-pose. 'I can't, son. I can't repair what's not there.'

I was confused. 'I've brought payment.'

The alchemist looked to the Sylph – a vague pixel outline was all that was left – and the old man's fizzog was grave. 'You've got to accept that she's gone.'

I shook my nog, hard-jawed. 'No. I can't. She's part of my Quest.'

The alchemist adjusted his goggles and sighed. 'Listen. If you bring her back again it will never –'

'I need her.' I interrupted. 'I can't reach the Final Level without her. Please. Please repair her.'

Tragic shadows clouded his eyes. He was weary. 'It'll take some nifty alchemy.' He sighed. 'And it won't last, mark me. It's not a repair. I can't guarantee more than three moon-transits till she's Wisp. Then that's it. You understand?'

Night, black as oblivion – except for a slab of sepulchral light reflecting back off the ground from a window. The nearest trees came jaundiced and strange in the glow. The old man was performing his magic in the hovel while the MauMau and I waited outside, tense and watchful.

'I hate this forest, Buddha,' I said. 'It's a dead place.'

Suddenly, from nowhere, a rush of air whipped past my fizzog at speed, shaved my cheek, ruffled my locks and set the passerines tweeting in earnest. The MauMau, spooked, ran off. But then, from the turbulence, a voice came *tra-la-la*-ing.

'Ludi,' it sang, breathy and sweet. 'Please save me.'

My heart fair battered my wireframe, but in the very same click a great whoop signalled the alchemist's task was complete.

'Come in now,' he said, tho his voice was frail. 'I've fixed your Sylph.'

The table showed proof of his magic – glass bulbs, flame burners, a crucible of hot molten metal. And, in one corner, the Sylph – her opacity up 50/50 I'd say, but shivering and with eye-gems empty as sink-holes.

'If she wasn't so precious to you, I'd say lay her to rest. She's not stable, not stable at all. Look there – teensy wormholes opening up in her aura. Can you see?' The alchemist directed my view and twiddled a widget at the side of my Visor.

'I can't see anything,' I said, tho the Sylph smelled delicious.

'Take my word. Of course, her destiny's always been connected to yours.'

'I knew it.' I wrapped the Sylph in a shawl and offered her Grog, but she refused it. 'Do you think she's a Key?'

The alchemist laid his mitt on my shoulder. 'Yes, son, she's a Key. Just as those passerines in your locks are both Keys. Violet-tailed Sylphs, if I'm not mistaken.'

'What a coincidence.' I scratched my nog. 'They're called the same thing.'

An old-fashioned grin creased the skin around his eyes. 'I've never believed in coincidence.'

We chin-wagged for a bit about Keys and finding the Big Boss in the Core. I showed him some of the footage I'd archived: the sorceress, taming the MauMau, the destruction of Vadar and the like.

'Killing a Boss isn't easy. But the Big Boss . . .' The old man looked doubtful.

'It's my Quest.'

'I know.'

The alchemist was in the doorway, waving us off from afar. But as the forest absorbed us – ta-da – he was there, six paces in front. He came up, softly-softly, laid his nog on my six-pack and breathed, very tender.

'Take care, son,' he said. 'You're no Reject. You're a He-Man and I'm proud.'

Before I could reply, pouff, he was gone again and when I looked back to his hovel he was shambling inside – decrepit suddenly, and cripplingly sad.

Another Daring Rescue

R ight this minute, he thinks, Lilith is in a room, or on a train, or walking through a field of black-eyed poppies skimming their papery petals with her hands. Or flying, yes. She's always wanted to fly.

As a child he hid in the willow and spied on her. An overture of birdsong accompanied her progress along the riverbank. She stopped a little way off near the bulrushes and held out her hand so the dragonflies could drink salted moisture from her palm. Lionel kept very quiet. It was amazing – people simply carried on when he wasn't there. There were men and women in space, no less. Ben, James and his mother were back at the house doing private things. His father would be reading or praying. Across the world human beings were engaged in secret, unknowable acts. But Lilith was different. Theirs was a deep connection.

On the bank, Lilith unpacked the brown head of a bulrush and scattered its seeds on the water – as expected. She scolded an imaginary minion and marched to the willow with her arms folded. He was bursting to laugh when her gaze swept up and rested where he was hiding. But she looked away again, narrowed her eyes and began to whisk her arms in the air. Lionel was unnerved. He hadn't anticipated this wild flailing and he thought – he truly thought – she might take off. Lilith, like everyone else, was entirely separate from him, after all. He sprang from the branches, shouting, determined to stop her. If she really could fly it would prove he was alone.

Lilith grinned when she saw him. 'I knew you were watching me,' she said, putting both hands over her heart. 'I could *feel* you.'

As he shouts through her letterbox at Sunnyvale he remembers it all – the green willow whips, the excitement of watching without being seen, the anxiety that Lilith might have a life that excluded him. This memory has been secreted away for years and today it chooses to surface. Where are all his old memories stored? They're piled up somewhere, files upon files, in his brain's mysterious repository.

The electric car is not on the drive and the curtains are closed, but he's sure Lilith is inside. He stands on the front lawn for several minutes throwing peas of gravel at the upstairs window until a neighbour, next door but one, spots him and makes conspicuous journeys up and down her driveway, talking on a Google device.

'It's okay,' he calls, tapping his chest. 'I'm Lilith's brother.'

But the woman won't meet his eye and he realizes his claim sounds preposterous. Lilith's brother. He's so tall and brown and Lilith is pale and petite. *We're not really brother and sister*.

Turning back to the door he puts his mouth to the letterbox. 'I've finished your avatar.' He stops to listen. 'It's brilliant. Totally lifelike. Come on, come and see it.'

A ratty dog yips at him through the fence to his left, one of those fervid little terriers with straggly hair and a ferret face.

'Lilith.' He's in misery. 'Please let me in.'

The house returns nothing.

Two fat wood pigeons regard him from the branches of a copper beech. The male sidesteps left and right, repeating a monotonous lament – *woohoo hoo, woohoo hoo*. The morose pigeon and the manic terrier are too much for Lionel and he sets off to the station, past the nosy neighbour, now clipping her hedge with long-handled shears, who's clearly relieved to see him go.

Milk Street is alive with activity. There's a police raid in progress and the health centre has a logjam of squad cars parked at angles at the front of the building, blue flares flashing. A man in overalls is boarding up the street-level windows. The neon sign continues to advertise ADULT HEALTH MASSAGE but the pink element has broken and the words flash only in blue. It's almost as if there's a sinister connection between the police cars and the health centre.

An ambulance pulls up. An unmarked van with tinted windows already has its rear doors open onto the alley and officers wearing visors are busy loading boxes from the premises into the back. Other officers wearing headsets that sport tiny cameras are questioning passers-by.

A young policeman steps into his path with the pretence of friendliness, as Lionel heads to his flat. 'Resident?' he asks.

Lionel nods, but looks down the street to where an NTV van has arrived on the scene.

'Noticed anything suspicious going on around here?' The officer makes a circular movement with his head, but ends up pointing towards the health centre with his chin.

Lionel shakes his head.

'Strange. No one's noticed *anything*. No girls going in and out of the building there? No one visiting the premises at unsocial times?'

Lionel shakes his head again – a longer, slower shake this time with his lower lip extended to imply that he's thinking about the question, mulling it over in a considered way.

'You speak English, right?'

He nods.

'You'd think locals would want to help with enquiries when sex slaves are being bought and sold right under their noses.'

He fixes his eyes on the policeman's boots.

The officer's voice becomes sad. 'You'd think people would want to take some responsibility.' He tones his voice down to a half-whisper. 'Come on, you seem like a decent kind of a bloke. Where d'you live? This one here?'

The officer uses his chin once more. Lionel glances at the door. Police annoy him. As soon as they don their uniforms they behave like robots. Every one of Mr Barber's customers has complained countless times about the health centre, but the police have never shown up. Recklessly he eyeballs the young officer, but keeps his lip buttoned. The policeman's chin is his most prominent feature and the reason – no doubt – he uses it as a pointer. His sideburns have been shaved to shark's teeth and the precision of his fascist's moustache is sickening. A smear of shaving cream under his jaw mitigates the cold-bloodedness a little, but apart from this oversight the man is intent on looking malicious.

'All right. ID.' The policeman's irritation gets the better of him.

The officer runs Lionel's bio-card through a portable scanner, momentarily hypnotized as he concentrates on his MonoSpex – a clear disc that sits invisibly across his left eye. Data scrolls past his retina.

'Lionel Bryde,' he reads.

'It's Byrd, Lionel Byrd.'

'Is it now?' The policeman is about to say something else when he pulls up abruptly and hands Lionel his card. 'Er, that's fine,' he says. 'That's all in order. The software failed to pick you up on face recognition. My apologies.'

He slips his card back in his wallet. 'Can I go?'

'Yes, sir.'

Being a government employee has some advantages.

Lionel has witnessed dozens of raids. He doesn't take much notice of them any more. Immigration officials are always sniffing around the fleapits along the High Street – Chinese, Libyans, Afghanis hauled out of bed in dawn raids, bleary-eyed. Taken to the out-of-town transit centres. Processed. Deported. But this raid is different because Crystal is in there.

Condensation has misted the inside of the window and he clears a circle to watch the events unfold. A group of community officers fan out along Milk Street, collaring pedestrians. A television camera is trained on the alley and a flabby reporter stands to the left of it, adjusting the waistband of his trousers, shouting directions at his crew. Two female officers emerge, trailing a line of women behind them. Lionel uses the zoom on his Google to home in on them, but most have blankets draped over their heads. The reporter straightens and speaks to camera, gesturing towards the action. Crystal's not there. Even with her head covered he'd know her. The women are driven away and three men are led out in plastic cuffs.

Huo, it seems, has evaded capture.

After the commotion has died down the health centre appears curiously festive – festooned with reflective tape criss-crossing the mouth of the alley. The blue neon sign winks on and off and two officers stand guard beside it. They're laughing at something on a mobile device. Laughing policemen. It could be the aftermath of a fancy dress party, not a raid. He ventures onto Milk Street and pops into Saeed's Grocery.

Feet up on the counter, smoking and talking on his mobile, Saeed greets Lionel with a quick nod of his head.

'Evening,' mouths Lionel.

Saeed brings his phone conversation to a close with a throaty 'ma'a as-salaama', then touches his forehead. 'Hello, my friend. You want qat?'

'Not today.'

The Yemeni is perplexed. 'But I have fresh.'

'No. I don't want any today.' He looks around him. 'Business is good, though?'

Saeed makes a non-committal gesture with one shoulder and blows smoke from the corner of his mouth. One or two shelves have something on display but, except for the crates of qat by the counter, there's not much produce to speak of.

'You've rented the flat upstairs. It's nice to have a neighbour.'

Saeed shakes his head. 'No neighbour.'

'The other day, there were boxes in the hall, I thought –'

'No, flat is empty.'

'No one's been upstairs?'

'Maybe my nephew, he is storing things.'

'Ah.' Lionel scratches his chin. 'But no neighbour.'

'No.'

'The lock jammed on my door.' He's not sure why he's lying. 'I had to change it.'

'I must have new key.'

'I'll bring one later.' Lionel gestures towards the window. 'What happened out there?'

'One girl she is hurt. Very bad. They take her.'

His heart sinks. 'Which girl was it, do you know?'

'Young girl.'

'Was she about this tall?' He holds his hand at Crystal's height.

Saeed curls his lip. 'I dunno. I don't see them girl. I have wife.'

'No, I don't see them either but . . .' He looks around again. 'Give me a pack of those.' He points to the cigarettes behind Saeed's chair. The

Yemeni reaches behind and slides a pack across the counter. 'So, you don't know which girl?'

'I don't see them girl, I tell you. Never.' The Yemeni is offended.

'Of course not. Forgive me.'

He thinks he might be suffering some kind of apoplexy because he's trying to move – to leave the shop – but he can't shift his limbs. The wounded girl must be Crystal. It's obvious. He should have made her come home with him; he should have fought Huo. He imagines his hands at the foppish man's throat. Hooded eyes bulging, tongue turning black.

Saeed stubs out his cigarette in a small brass ashtray. 'You okay, my friend?'

Outside the shop someone shouts, 'Fuckin' fascist pigs, *brraapp*, hear me now,' and Lionel is finally released from his paralysis. Dusk has fallen and when he looks to the window it returns a reflection of him and his landlord – a Yemeni and a black man in a near-empty shop. They could be in another country.

'Sorry. My head's somewhere else.' He adjusts his collar, heads for the door.

'Wait, my friend. I forget this. Special delivery from yesterday.' Saeed reaches under the counter and hands him a padded envelope. 'Now bring me key.'

A key, of course; he has a key for Lilith's house. He could have let himself in earlier, instead of standing on the drive like a fool. Why didn't he think of that?

The iCode reference is London and the iCode reader on his Google device shows the package is from a firm of solicitors on the Walworth Road. He props the envelope on the mantelpiece. Buddha, limbs in gentle spasm, is stretched along the length of his thigh. Lionel can feel the cat's bones through his fur as he pets him.

'Don't die, Buddha,' he whispers. 'Don't leave me. Not yet.'

Buddha closes his eyes but his front legs twitch and strings of saliva drain from his mouth. His lungs make complex clicks as he breathes.

You don't have to open the package, says Buddha. *Ignorance is bliss.*

'I know, old boy,' says Lionel, gratefully. 'But it's time for the truth.'

*

A covering letter explains that digital versions of the enclosed documents can be downloaded from the solicitors' domain. A username and password are provided to access a 'secure area'. The firm is acting on behalf of Judith Byrd and has been instructed to forward certain documents pertaining to his parentage and adoption. The solicitor goes on to explain that along with these documents there is a balance sheet detailing various monies due to him. He also draws his attention to the fact that the lease on the Sunnyvale house will terminate at the end of the current agreement: on the thirtieth of September.

What has Lilith's house got to do with anything? Lionel wonders. He reads on. The sums on the balance sheet, if accepted, will be considered full and final payment in respect of the estate of the late Mr David Isaac Byrd. It's signed, 'sincerely'. He folds the covering letter and puts it back in the envelope.

The balance sheet shows a large sum, much more than the 'small provision' Judy had led him to expect. Unmoved by the legacy, Lionel is gripped only by the prospect of disclosure. A pinball of excitement zips erratically in his chest. Nauseous, shaking, he spreads the documents in front of him.

Home truth. Here is his birth certificate, brown at the edges and bearing signs of neglect, even crumpling – as if it has been crushed into a tight ball and smoothed back out again. As he flattens it on the desk, Lionel notices that it is issued by the British High Commission in Mombasa. Legally, as Ben explained, he's British by birth, not by adoption. David and Judy must have known the right people, been able to swing British citizenship. His given name is Paul Lionel Johnson – he never knew that. And here is his 'legal' mother's name – Delia Rose Johnson. He says the name out loud. The woman's name in his mouth is an unexpected delight. Her nationality – British. Profession – nurse. He lifts his chin and says her name again slowly, allowing every syllable to ring out. But this isn't his real mother; this is the home truth, bent to fit his parents' devices, which Ben warned him of.

Here it is: Delia's death certificate. It's not a surprise. According to the document she passed away three days after he was born in the Ngomani Memorial Hospital, Mombasa. She was twenty-seven years old.

'Delia Johnson,' he repeats, forlornly this time.

She was a real person. She could have been his mother, but she's gone.

The cause of death is cited as 'acute post-partum infection'. Here is a letter from the director of Good News International to the department of immigration explaining that Delia Johnson, a paediatric nurse, who had been working for the charity for two years, had died. The letter is accompanied by an application for an exit visa for her son – Lionel Johnson, now aged three months. He notes how the 'Paul' has already been dropped in favour of 'Lionel'. It's extraordinary to see the signatures and rubber stamps that sealed his destiny, shaping his whole life.

Here's another letter, this one from Southwark Adoption Services, dated three months later, outlining the criteria for transfer of guardianship from one Harry Paul Johnson (Delia's brother or father perhaps) to Mr and Mrs David Byrd. There's an address, but no more papers. No more revelations.

Delia Johnson, his legal mother, if she ever was pregnant, was most likely a good Christian girl who succumbed to . . . to what? The heat? Africa? He imagines her having an illicit affair with a local man, her shame on discovering she was carrying a child, the parsimony of his mother and father when she confessed her secret to them, her untimely yet expedient death, which allowed his parents to transfer her child's identity to him. But if she was genuinely pregnant, and died, what happened to *her* child?

Lionel constructs another story, one where Delia Johnson is his real mother and she's holding his infant body to her breast; he can feel her flesh against his cheek. She counts his toes, kisses his curls and cries warmly onto his vernixed head. She knows they must part and can't bear to abandon him. Lionel folds the papers once more. It's a fantasy. He understands that the woman's tragic story is not his – his birth, her death are unconnected.

Delia Rose Johnson.

Immediately he wants to talk it through with his sister and he calls Lilith, rehearsing his news.

'I'm definitely British, well not *actually* British but, well, can you believe it? My legal mother, the mother on my birth certificate, not Judy, no definitely not Judy, hah, was a nurse, Delia Rose Johnson. David and Judy must have known her. They must have known who she was.'

The cruelty of it hits him. For the whole of his childhood, his youth and the years of his adulthood Judy and David have lied. Lilith has disabled her voicemail and he stares at the status bars as her number rings. The secrets, the disappointments and the resentments are growing day by day.

The door buzzer drags him away from his thoughts. The camera shows how Mr Barber is thinning on top – his scalp is visible through slick ripples of pomaded hair.

The old man puts his mouth too close to the speaker. 'It is me, Mr Barber. I need to speak wid you.'

'Come up, I'm on the first floor.' He buzzes him in.

Mr Barber holds his hat and sizes up the room. 'What in God name is that pathetic creature?' He points to Buddha, who is making his way across the carpet.

'This is Buddha. He's rather sick.'

'I never seen no cripple cat like that before.' The old man gets down and scratches the animal's ears. 'He could do with some wheels under him there, mek him more free and easy.' Mr Barber stands. 'I seen a dog like it in Kingston, no back legs, jos a lickle board with an axle and wheels. Very clever.'

'I wish it was that simple. It's in his head, you see. His legs are fine.'

'Ah!' The barber nods slowly as if everything is now clear. 'The brain is a powerful ting, y'know. It all come from there.' He runs his hand over his head, taking the opportunity to check the set of his hair.

'What can I help you with, Mr Barber?'

'Mi call to say you must come back a yard if you wouldn't mind.'

'To your place? Now?'

'That would be very helpful.'

'Is something wrong?'

Mr Barber puts a finger to his lips. 'I need some furniture shifting is all. Be sure and come.'

The Jamaican replaces his hat at the door. 'God in heaven, I ain't never seen a cat like that in all a my days. Nuh uh.'

Mr Barber ushers Lionel through the front of the shop without switching on the light.

'This is very mysterious.'

Mr Barber says, 'Hmm,' and pulls the shutters down behind them. The smell of cooking – something spicy and meaty – takes over from the smell of hairdressing as they climb the stairs.

'So, where's this furniture?'

Mr Barber eyes him sharply. 'There ain't no furniture. Me don't know what you been gettin' up to but me have a stray pickney in the flat and she say she want to see you. She callin' you Ludi or some name like that. But me sure it's you she want.'

'What?'

Mr Barber betrays nothing more. 'Come.'

The old man directs Lionel into the living room and slips into an adjoining room before coming out a minute later, trailing the anime girl by the hand.

Lionel's heart stops. 'Crystal!'

The beautiful girl appears grubby and frightened.

He moves towards her. 'You're okay?'

She takes a small step back. 'I sink you live here. I see you in the shop, so I come here.'

'I don't live here. I live opposite the centre, down there.' He waves his arm vaguely. 'You saw me at the window that time, remember?' He touches the outer corners of his eyes with his index fingers. 'When we had the connection.'

'I sink,' she says, nodding towards Mr Barber, 'he your father.'

Mr Barber smiles wearily and explains that Crystal crept in as he was shutting up shop.

'At least you're safe now,' says Lionel. 'Here, take the weight off your feet. You look awful.'

Crystal looks at the chair, but she doesn't sit. She says she's not safe. Not safe at all. She paces the room, stopping to cover her mouth occasionally as if speaking is an impulse she must control. But she tells them how Huo was warned there might be a raid and he made the necessary calls. The police were in his pocket. They told him an anonymous troublemaker had been sending messages, demanding action. They would have to be seen to take appropriate measures and they agreed a date. Huo was convinced one of the girls had persuaded a client to let them use their mobile device and when he overheard Beatrise persuading the other girls to run away he assumed it was her. Stupid – she'd always been the quiet one. But Huo made an example of her. Beat her senseless.

'It's Beatrise who's injured?' Lionel asks.

'Her face all smash up, her eye . . .' She shakes her head. 'He break her fingers, *snip*, *snap*, every one.'

Crystal cries quietly for a minute before explaining that she was in the yard when the raid began. It was not the day that Huo and his police contacts had arranged. Sirens blared. Chaos. But instead of obeying when Huo called her inside she'd climbed into the alley that led to the High Street. She hid in one of the industrial bins near the car park. Now she doesn't know where to go. She's heard terrible things about the transit centres.

Crystal peels laddered tights away from a scab encrusting one knee. 'I watch for long time in the garbage. I am frighten.'

She can't speculate why the police came when they did. But she's glad they did.

Lionel remembers Crystal's room, the picture of Beatrise's grandmother, the rattan box and the air freshener. He imagines a young girl, like Crystal, brusied and beaten by Huo. He never envisaged his actions would cause this suffering.

Crystal says, 'You help me? You say you want help me.'

'Of course. I'm so glad it's not you that's hurt.'

'Why? What is different if it me or Beatrise, what is different?' She's suddenly livid, spraying saliva along with her words.

'But I don't know Beatrise. I only know you,' he says defensively.

'I know Beatrise.' She beats her chest. 'Me. I know her. She is *my* friend.'

'What do you want me to do? Tell me. I'll do anything.'

Crystal falls into a chair and shakes her head. 'I am fifteen year old.' She looks at him with too-worldly fatigue. 'I am used up all mine strength. I owe Huo many credits.' She sighs. 'Is good the police have him.'

He crouches beside her, touches the back of her hand. He doesn't have the heart to tell her Huo wasn't apprehended.

Mr Barber's eyes are moist.

The canvas cover is heavy with dust and Mr Barber has to heave it back with an awkward up-and-over movement.

'There she is.'

With their hands on their hips they regard the machine with manly approval.

'She hasn't been out for five years, but she's tiptop.' Mr Barber pats the tank a couple of times. 'Me turn her over every month just to listen to the engine. It like sweet music.'

The motorbike is black, with rust-mottled chrome accenting the design. There is a sidecar with a stud-fastened cover. It has the air of something loved and reluctantly put aside.

'Them say no more petrol for the likes of us. Me understand all a that. Tings change. But me couldn't break her in pieces. It would feel like me killin' her, you know what I'm sayin'?'

'I can't ride.'

The old man scratches his chin. 'I will ride.'

'No, I'll do it. You're too old for trouble. Anyway, I've done a simulation. A game. And I can pull up a tutorial on my Google.'

Mr Barber lets out a sceptical snort. 'A game, eh? Google?' He sucks his teeth.

'We don't have petrol.'

'Me have some a that replacement fuel.' Mr Barber dislodges a can from under some boxes and its liquid contents slosh around inside. 'Not as good as petrol, but it will get you out of here.'

The old man explains the rudiments of riding – gears, brakes and accelerator. The sidecar, he says, makes it more difficult to fall off, but not impossible. Lionel mustn't get carried away. All they have to do is wheel the bike out to the deserted industrial estate and start her up. The cameras out there are all vandalized. It's a clear run out of town from there, although the magic eyes along the main routes might be a problem. He should stick to the back roads and hope the traffic drones are busy elsewhere.

Mr Barber's expression is gloomy. 'Now me know the pickney story me wish I could help her more.'

'You are helping,' Lionel assures him.

Crystal can't travel by taxi – it's too risky. She needs a charge code to get on the bus and she has no ID. Unless they walk to Sunnyvale, fourteen kilometres over open country, the motorbike is their only choice.

*

At first the engine won't start, but on the third try it coughs into life. Mr Barber says, 'Yes, Lord,' and gestures to heaven. Crystal is installed in the sidecar wrapped in a tartan blanket, but she's still shivering. Lionel thinks of the way she's been abused, remembers the kiss he planted on her scummy lips, turns his mind from the memory of her pubescent nakedness to the matter in hand.

The deep, rhythmic *gopff gopff gopff* of the engine in its explosive bass register will draw attention if they're not quick. Mr Barber checks up and down. Lionel squeezes the clutch, flicks the machine into first with his foot and lurches off.

'Easy on the clutch out,' shouts Mr Barber. 'Nice and steady now.'

The engine screams as he pulls back on the gas. Ease off. Second gear. *Get in*. It's stiff. No – he's forgotten the clutch. Second, there it is. Mr Barber shouts something a little way behind him, but he can't hear what it is. He makes third with no problem but hits the kerb and oversteers so that that the sidecar lifts off the ground before thumping back down with a jolt.

'Stop looking down, feel with your foot,' he says, annoyed with himself.

Fourth, he's getting it; he's back on course. He eases the throttle back and the machine whips forward, instantly energized. For a moment, hands gripping the handlebars, he imagines what it feels like to hold a bull by the horns.

'Ha ha.'

A wild seed is germinating in his brain. He looks over his shoulder to find that distance has swallowed up the old man, so he grins at Crystal instead, but all she can manage is a vacant smile.

The machine, he intuits, has more to give. It bucks and roars as he accelerates, itching to devour the asphalt. The wind sweeps the locks from his face and he holds his chin high, breasting the night air like a god. He's somebody. He's the legal son of Delia Rose Johnson – a nurse. She could be his real mother. Ben could be telling lies within lies. From now on he decides to let each moment steer him. With the town's lights behind them, he focuses on the road ahead, twists the throttle as far as it will go and lets out an ecstatic *harooo*.

@GameAddict (#23756745): 13:8:27

It's edgy when you're deep in a game. Violence.
Cruelty. Sadism. Some characters are so sinister
you can't bear to discover the despicable things
that they've done. But it's okay. You're there to
set it right and wield the sword of justice.

Level 15: Search for the Core

A body of static pulsed over Darzir and injected the citadel with a thousand electrical zip-zaps. We didn't rest till we reached the plateau. By then the storm had moved off and midday mugginess had taken its place. Before us a proliferation of minarets soared from the citadel's heart, the shafts of the towers lost in the clouds.

We left the MauMau in sleep-mode and approached Darzir's West Gate. I was expecting a fight, but the guards were indifferent and waved us through without blinking. The streets were full: Krin, Thrars and Vadarians clogged the thoroughfares. There were tribes represented from Magog to Nur. Long-necked Darzirian women winked at me as I passed – not what I expected from a faith-hungry tribe. But when we turned into narrower alleys that criss-crossed the heart of the city we found the pious-types Mata Angelica had promised. Priesters sang out from the tall minarets – each one producing an ethereal note in tune with his neighbour. The chorus caressed the streets from above and I came hypnotized by its snoozy, mellifluous beauty. I could hardly move for tranquillity.

The Sylph tugged at my loincloth – eyes grave and fraidy – and I bashed on my nog to stay focused. The place, the priesters' chants and the solemn-eyed Sylph had all made a weird stew in my nog and I'd come tottery on my pins, so the Sylph had to grasp my mitt and lead me on.

After a while we emerged in a wide-open space that didn't appear to be part of the city at all. I could hear the chorus way off, but we were in a large park with rolling hillocks and pretty, squat trees and all manner of flowers and tweeters. A hugesome bridge stood in the heart of it all. As we came to it I saw it was suspended over a canyon so deep and unnerving my nog came even more swimmy.

The Sylph grimaced and pointed into the abyss.

'The Core?' I whispered.

She nodded.

'How do we get down there?'

She stretched forward, arms as wings, and turned to me – pathetically sorrowful.

'You want us to fly?'

She nodded once more.

In scribing this crevice I don't want to come off too hyperbolic – you can access a 2D still-image by clicking the Visicode in the appendix. It's only a gist but you'll see it went to the root of the Realm. From the deep came such purgatory noises – a wrenching, industrial crunch that put me in mind of a beast chewing metal. Made me question the purpose of the Core. Surely this place should be avoided, not dived into. What if the Sylph's programme was janky? What if *her* Quest was to lead me to the Void for her own ends? But she dragged me to the cusp of the bridge and we stood there, toeing the edge, looking into the chasm. I felt helpless.

Then Drufus Scumscratch appeared – *ping* – at the far end of the bridge, with an army of Grinders. I've slogged through enough gameplay to know something like this was destined to happen. A character doesn't reach the penultimate level without a brawl or two before the main fight. But Drufus's cohort was a goodly wallop – armed, armoured and yap-snarling like terriers. Quite imposing. Before he spoke the gastropod calmed his troops to a murmur of growls.

'Reject,' he said. 'We meet again. But, ha, you appear to have your hands full.'

The Sylph was still struggling to pull us both into the rift.

I attempted a nonchalant stance but, without more warning, Drufus let loose his Grinders and they surged towards us like rats escaping a flood. Within three clicks a few of their daggers were spiking my hide. I despatched several of them, but mostly swung wide and ham-fisted. The Sylph was engaging my sword arm and I couldn't let go or she'd fall to oblivion.

After the first charge Drufus called off his boys so he could come close and deliver some gloat-words. 'It's time to give up, Reject,' he said, fizzog right up in my Visor. 'The sorceress will be delighted you've found the Sylph she's been seeking.'

I spat on the ground and lifted my chin. 'Just you try and take her.'

Drufus chuckled. 'Cheeky. Defiant. It's what I'd expect. But, you see, I can't lose. I have a never-ending supply of clones and if I should Wisp they'll bring me back in a click. Replay.' He held out his oily palms. 'You're doomed.'

I held the Sylph's wrist, but kept my beam fixed on Drufus.

The snail oozed hubris as he beckoned the Sylph. 'Coocachoo, come to Drufus. We don't want you falling down there.'

The Sylph gnawed at my digits, trying to get free. We were surrounded. NoHopers – 90/10. The air stank of uniped bile and I was ready to Void in a glorious spurt of gastropod innard-juice. But, before I could lunge, the passerines darted from under my locks (I'd almost forgot they were there) and dive-bombed the snail. Teensy things were tenacious, got a clawhold on his jowls and pinched for dear life. The snail came all hysterical – 'Get 'em off, get 'em off' – as they went for his eyes, *peck peck peck*. And quick as a flash his jelly-balls were rolling around on the floor. The Grinders stood, wide-mouthed, as Drufus screamed gurgling curse-words: 'Fucking slice them, you thickos, delete them.'

The Grinders followed orders and went for them in a frenzy. But the tweeters were nifty and did quicksilver zips in and out of the daggers. By the time the Grinders had finished they'd flown off to safety. Poor Drufus, however, was a minced, gelatinous heap. The irony! His own cohort had done for him. One Grinder stepped up cautious-wise and prodded his master's raw blubber. The snail managed a last gut-wrenching moan before his Wisp started peeling away.

The Grinders fell back in a half-moon around me, leaderless. Lost.

'Go on, off with you,' I said, too worn out to glory, or pity.

Drufus's Wisp whizzed into the crevice and some of the Grinders made to follow it. Their work in the Core was about to begin. But one Grinder stepped up and stopped his comrades from jumping. A radical light danced over his fizzog.

'Is it true what they say,' he said, 'that some Grinders are free?'

'Drufus told me himself.'

Mutter-words went round the cohort.

'Who feeds them?' he asked.

'They feed themselves I suppose, same as the rest of us.'

The Grinder addressed the crowd – argued that if they went to the Core Scumscratch would come back and torment more innocent clones. Going AWOL was a risk but, surely, worth it for freedom. It took some persuading but most of the clones fell in with him. One or two chose to go over. Said retirement was waiting down there, and we all clocked their freefall into the crack – me watching with interest to see if they copped it, but, even in zoom-mode, I couldn't make out if they splatted.

The Grinder pressed my arm. 'Thanks,' he said, 'and good Questing.' Then he led his chums back off the bridge. And that was that.

Crash. Wallop. The storm returned and the sky was boiling up, brutal. There was only one route left on my Quest. Down there. Into the Core.

Michael Reveals His Hand

'It is cold in here.' Crystal allows Lionel to remove her shoes as she perches on the edge of the spare bed. 'This your house?'

'My sister's house.'

'She is not here?'

'She's away.'

A hint of mould, unsuccessfully masked by some bleach-based product, has given Lilith's place a chilly, institutional air. It was obvious the house was empty when they arrived, but still his pulse raced as he poked his head in each room and whispered Lilith's name in the dark.

A tin of peaches he found in the kitchen cupboard didn't tempt Crystal, but she agreed to a cup of green tea, which he's placed on the bedside table. He doubts she'll drink it. The fight has gone out of her. It's pathetic the way her head keeps nodding. There's an awkward tension in her shoulders; she's trying to be alert even though she's exhausted.

'Come on, put your head down.' He plumps the pillow. 'You'll feel better when you've had some sleep. But don't open the blinds when you wake up, okay. I don't want the neighbours to know we're here.'

'I very good for hiding.' She covers her head with the duvet. 'I hide all the way from China in box full with jins.'

'Gin?'

'Jins . . . jins for wearing.' She reaches blindly for his thigh, pats him twice near the knee.

'Ah, jeans.'

'Yes, jins.'

Lionel smiles even though she can't see him. 'I have to go out for a while. Will you be okay?'

'I sleep for long time. Maybe never wake up.'

He flicks off the lamp. 'Rest now.'

'Don't tek her to no police, you hear?' That's what Mr Barber had cautioned. At best, the authorities would send Crystal to the nearest transit hub. At worst, corrupt officials would pass her back to Huo as soon as he surfaced. If not him, then a rival gang. Whichever way, she would fall victim to the traffickers again. She needed to get hold of some credit. She needed to be a *legal* adult. She needed fake ID. Mr Barber knew a lot about illegals once he got going; he even knew a place further north, with friends of his, where Crystal would be safe if she had the right cards.

Lilith is always going on about illegals, but Lionel tries to avoid thinking about the refugees in their mucky camps, begging for residency. His sister's high-minded pronouncements tend to wash over him. He thinks she's trying to make a point about his origins; that, being African by birth and orphaned by fate, he should feel some affinity with the unwanted waifs on the news. But he's never felt anything. And now here's Crystal – not African, but illegal – and along with her beautiful face he can see a procession of other faces in his mind: voiceless women, frightened children, dead-eyed men – all remembered from news reports or movies, perhaps. Or maybe they are faces from Milk Street. Yes, that's Saeed for heaven's sake and Mr Barber and poor, beaten-up Beatrise with haunted eyes. Dear God, even his own face is among them, brown and bearded. He could be a refugee. How would anyone know he's the legal son of Delia Johnson if they found him in a transit camp without ID?

Crystal must become a real person. Perhaps Michael can help, or Eve. At least they'll know what he should do.

First light and the sky above the waste ground is a dense, gunmetal grey. There's no break in the cloud and the air is close and spiked with something sharp. It reminds him of the smell in David's greenhouse years ago – the tang of compost and ripening tomatoes pricking the warm air. Michael's road looks different. The snapdragons have gone from the verges, but dead fronds indicate where they once rioted in summer. The poplars have yellowed and the blackthorns are past their verdant prime. Michael's front garden has changed from a square of mud to a picture of autumn fecundity. Pea sticks have been erected along the left-hand fence where coils of green intertwine with dried pods and dead heads. There are two lines of brassicas, ready to be harvested, a row of brussel sprouts and wintergreens. Michael's an unlikely gardener, but then everyone's growing vegetables these days.

Lionel checks his Google. It's only six-thirty – an unusual time to make a social call – so he slips round the back, intending to wait for the house to stir before presenting himself. There's no light in the kitchen. The dining-room curtains are drawn. Everything's quiet and he sits on the kitchen step with his eyes shut, going back over the last weeks and months. Now he puts everything in a row in his mind the year has been a catalogue of confusion and calamity: moving to Milk Street, the attack in the nightclub, David's death, Eve's unusual advances, Lilith and her issues, Buddha's decline and now Crystal turning up at Mr B's in desperation. It's hard to make sense of it all. Now here he is in Michael's back garden come to ask for help when he doesn't really like Michael at all.

The back garden is part-shaded by an enormous cherry tree. A surfeit of overripe fruit has bombarded the patio with juicy splats, random bursts of purple that look visceral in the fragile light. The front garden is a display of green-fingered abundance, but the back garden is unkempt with only a wilting tea-rose climbing the brickwork next to the sliding doors, and a vigorous covering of nettles. It's all front this house, he realizes.

The bonfire has been cleared but a charred circle remains in the over-grown grass. David would have strimmed all these weeds back ages ago – he would have nurtured the ground. That was his father's way. As the light strengthens he notices a dilapidated shed and some broken chairs where the fence delineates the garden from waste ground. The flyover looms in the distance, but there's no traffic crawling along it, no drones overhead. No one is awake. There's not a breath of wind. The world has come to a gluey standstill. Only the birdsong, piercing the expanse of silence as keenly as light, convinces him the gameplay of his life has not frozen. Lionel looks at his hands, turns them over. If only he could restart, go back to default mode. Perhaps that's what death really is: a nip into the Void for a spell before the Creator sets your avatar down in a new dimension to be reincarnated again and again. For eternity. And somewhere out there is a real Lionel, playing a game – and that Lionel is looking at these hands with augmented vision, right this second. Working this poor, gangly puppet.

Lionel starts suddenly.

From inside the house a voice exclaims urgently, 'Come, look at this. Shit, he's getting totally destroyed. This is bad. This is really bad.'

He peers into the kitchen. He can see a computer tablet glowing on the table, but whoever was talking has left the room. He creeps along the wall to the dining room. The sliding doors are closed, but the curtains have been opened while he's been daydreaming.

Prospero, in his wheelchair, is wearing a Visor and a microphone – a regular gameplaying set-up. A 3D multi-display processes data in one frame and runs *CoreQuest* in another. A third frame represents Prospero's brain activity as a cataract of symbols running down the screen. On the table: mugs, empty beer bottles, a half-full bottle of whiskey and a couple of overflowing ashtrays. It's been an all-night session. A glistening line of spittle runs from Prospero's mouth to his chin. His hands twitch rhythmically.

Michael walks into view, one hand on his head. He looks tense and grizzled. Whiskers are poking through on his chin in a bokeh of white and black. There's something of the ageing libertine about him, something reckless: the open-necked shirt billowing over the waistband of his jeans, the retro denims with rips across the thighs. Intrigued, Lionel gets on his haunches behind the water butt to spy.

The other man instructs the computer using voice-commands as Michael looks at the screen, inert with indecision. The cataract of symbols is drying to a trickle and the man turns to Michael.

'What now?' he says hopelessly.

Michael shakes his head.

'Shit, fucking shit.'

Suddenly Prospero goes rigid and both men galvanize, detaching the Visor, ripping the electrodes from his head.

'Hold him,' shouts Michael and they grip his body as it goes into violent convulsion.

When the seizure abates Michael wipes Prospero's face with a cloth and sits beside him, squeezing his hand, talking gently.

'Well, well. Look who's here.'

Lionel swings round, almost topples. It's Eve. She's wearing a raincoat and headscarf, hands on her hips like a battleaxe – washed out and dowdy.

'I'm . . .' He gets to his feet. 'I've come to see Michael.'

'I didn't think you'd come to find *me* after last time.' Eve glances to the sliding glass doors. 'Hmm,' she says. 'What have you seen, I wonder?'

'I just got here.'

'You were peeking,' Eve scolds. 'I saw you.'

'I didn't mean to –'

'No, you never mean to do anything.' She gives him a wide berth as she circles to the window, removing her scarf. 'But for such an unassuming man, Lionel, you manage to be in the wrong place at the wrong time far too often.'

Lionel nods disconsolately. He's interested to see how Eve has transformed from temptress to frump in a fortnight. Clothes crumpled, hair a dry frizz on her shoulders. Her complexion has lost its polished shine.

'Anyway, look!' She's checking inside. 'They're just playing a game.'

Lionel hesitates, but then says, 'I think something just went wrong.'

'Oh?'

'Prospero had a fit.'

Eve regards him slyly. 'I see. Well, you'd better come in.'

When she slides the door back Michael and the other man turn abruptly.

'Jesus Christ on a fucking bike.' Michael jumps up and blocks Lionel's view of Prospero. 'What's he doing here?'

Eve rolls her eyes. 'Too late, Superman, he's already seen everything.' She throws her raincoat on a chair and goes into the kitchen. 'You forgot to draw the bloody curtains,' she calls behind her.

'I only opened them' – Michael's gaze travels to the sliding doors and the fields beyond – 'a few minutes ago.' His shoulders slump, comprehending what Lionel must have seen in those minutes.

'You'll have to tell him,' shouts Eve.

An electric kettle comes to life.

'Why's he here? That's what I wanna know.' Michael decides attack is the best form of defence. He presses a yellow-stained finger into Lionel's chest. 'Eh, buddy? Why are you sneaking around in my yard?'

Nicotine and alcohol have soured Michael's breath. He's wearing some oily perfume that was once voluptuous but now smells stale.

'Stop it, Michael.' Eve stands at the door. 'We've done all the checks and he's harmless. You know that. Just tell him the truth.'

Lionel waits while Michael and the other man carry Prospero to the spare room where a subdued conference ensues, out of earshot. Eventually Michael and Eve join Lionel at the kitchen table. Eve speaks first but she's distracted, checking her Google device, stopping to listen for sounds from outside as if she's expecting someone. She explains that they belong to a political movement. It has supporters worldwide. Philanthropists, a few charities and some concerned 'high profile' individuals donate to the cause but it's very hush hush. Their organization is illegal.

'You told me you worked with refugees.'

'What? Did you think we were running a soup kitchen?'

'No! I don't know.' Lionel feels his throat constrict. 'You're not terrorists are you?'

'No!' Eve is adamant. 'Far from it.'

'I've seen things on the news, that's all. Riots and bombs.'

'In any movement there are individuals who get frustrated. Change can't come quickly enough when lives are at stake.'

'Who? What lives?'

'We help trafficked people escape exploitation. Our friends across the world maintain a series of safe houses where ex-slaves can stay while we get them new identities.'

'Like the Underground Railroad in America?'

She smiles and concentrates on his face. 'Yeah, exactly like that. Still, today hundreds of thousands of people are displaced and sold into slavery each year.'

'Why don't governments stop it, like ours does?'

Eve gives a cynical snort. 'First, it's in their interest for it to continue. Most economies would fail without cheap labour. Second, *your* government's no better.' She's beginning to bristle with rage. 'Politicians close their eyes to the human cost and focus on the bottom line. Cheap clothes, cheap food, cheap energy.'

Lionel is not surprised by Eve's burgeoning anger. She's been open about her political allegiances from the start. It's the reason he's here, after all: to get safe transit for Crystal.

'Michael's particular role . . .' Eve falters, looks at Michael before she continues, 'is to infiltrate government departments and recruit sympathetic people to our cause.'

'You mean Meddingley? You mean me?'

She nods.

'Why didn't you just ask me to help you?'

Michael speaks for the first time. 'You sit on your own every day. You never talk to anyone unless you have to. Do you know how many times I tried to get your attention? Then hooray.' He rolls his eyes theatrically. 'A miracle. Something finally shifts. You came in with a fat shiner and, well, you'd changed.'

Lionel is about to explain about the attack when Eve cuts in. 'Prospero was a gift: a long-term employee; disabled veteran from the Middle Eastern campaigns, increasingly politicized. It's a wonder he wasn't under surveillance, to be honest – beyond the usual, you know. But he signed up.' She snaps her fingers. 'In a second. But the real gift was you. You were perfect. An exploited geek with top-flight skills and trusted-user access. We couldn't have asked for more. That's why we had to –'

'We had to hook you, buddy.'

'Not hook him, Michael.' Eve fixes on the American. 'Persuade him gently.'

Michael smirks. 'Persuade. Okay. After we drugged him.'

'You drugged me?'

'Thank you, Michael.' Eve makes a prim face. 'The thing is, Lionel, we discovered a little problem. It appeared you were already working for someone else. We had to know the truth, so we gave you a relaxant. Nothing harmful, a little dose of something to loosen your tongue.'

'At the party! It's why I was sick?'

Eve scratches a line in the tabletop. 'Uh huh.'

Lionel pulls his collar away from his neck. 'I'm not working for anyone except my employer.'

'What you did was in good faith – we know that. But think about it, Lionel; you haven't stuck to the rules, have you?'

'I don't understand what's happening here. Or in there.' He jerks his head towards the living room where the other man is speaking heatedly on his mobile. 'My whole life has turned upside down. I didn't want any of this.' He straightens his back. 'In fact, I don't want to know anything else about your organization.' He stands, cradles his head.

'Sit down, Lionel. It's too late. You're in it up to here.' Eve holds her hand horizontally above her head.

'I'm not *in* anything. I'm nothing to do with anybody. Anything you think I've done, I haven't done. I'm innocent. I want. I just. I . . .' He stops, scratches his eyebrow and remembers what he came for. 'I need a fake ID.' This last sentence is delivered in a timid whisper.

Michael stalks round him, mocking and contemptuous. 'Fucking freak, buddy, that's what you are. *I'm innocent I'm innocent –*'

'Michael.' Eve raises her voice. 'You're not helping.'

'I'm not trying to help, goddammit. We're telling this nut some sensitive shit about our operation and he doesn't know his asshole from his dick. That's why we dumped him after he attacked you in your car, remember? He's a liability.'

Eve takes a deep breath. 'Lionel, listen to me.' She encourages him to sit, pulls her chair so she's sitting directly in front of him. 'Pema Khalsa has been stealing secrets from Meddingley. It took a while to work out how she was doing it, but now we know.' Eve draws an invisible diagram on the tabletop. 'Remember the hidden server spaces – the little leaks in the system you set up for her? Well, they were siphoning data from the network.'

Lionel can't move. He's not sure he can breathe. He did set up Pema's system; it's incontrovertible.

'We think she's on the payroll of an international crime gang – maybe more than one.' She puffs, incredulous. 'I know, it sounds like a film, right? But we've discovered payments, deposits into a secret offshore account. Sometimes the credits come from Hong Kong, sometimes the Philippines or Thailand – it depends.' Eve searches his face. 'These gangs are protected in some countries. Traffickers. They provide cheap labour to industry. Companies, in turn, pay governments to turn a blind eye. The practice is widespread, worth billions of credits. Victims can end up anywhere – as sex workers or domestics, here or in the US. Anywhere.'

Lionel finds his voice. 'I was helping Pema with her work.' He looks frantically from Michael to Eve. 'She said she couldn't cope. She'd lose her job.'

'I know. But she was using you to cover her tracks. Larissa Greenough got arrested because it was her login and bio-ID Pema gave you to set it all up.'

'She said it was an ex-worker's . . .' He stops. The connections between what he has done and what Eve is telling him begin to join up. 'What I set up couldn't . . . no, no, no.' He grips his head. 'It couldn't leak data, not in that way. It's impossible. It could only send authorized work files.'

'Authorized, Lionel, are you sure?'

'Well, not authorized exactly, but not sensitive.'

'Authorized, sensitive, it makes no difference. You're implicated. But Mrs Khalsa is quite the criminal mastermind.' Eve taps her temple three times. 'She's been very clever in getting the data across borders and she's set it up so no shit sticks to her. It's so elegant I almost admire her.'

'What? How's she doing it?'

Eve watches his expression intently. 'The game. She's been using the game to sneak information to agents around the globe.'

Lionel swallows. '*CoreQuest*?'

'Precisely. She found herself an expert programmer, one who could hack the servers and do the donkey work for her. He didn't even know he was doing it.'

'Me.' Lionel touches his chest.

Michael is leaning back in his chair with his arms folded. 'Send you some *assets*, did she? Interesting weapons or cheats you could use on your Quest.'

'One or two.'

'Data,' says Eve. 'A steady stream. But the main file was uploaded before your Ludi avatar even arrived in *CoreQuest*. You sneaked it onto the game servers and it fell into the wrong hands on entry.'

'I did upload things but –'

'Me and Prospero managed to salvage the most recent data file.' Michael talks over him, leaning in. 'But then you went and stole it back again and killed me in the process.'

'You're in the game? What character?'

'Harlequin. Deceased.'

Lionel turns to Eve. 'And you?'

'Seriously, do you need to ask?'

Lionel covers his mouth and whimpers.

'Listen, buddy, before you have a sci-fi moment and cream your pants, let's get something clear. There's a secret file containing the identities of thousands of vulnerable people buried in the side of a mountain – in a fucking game.' Michael has him locked in his sights. 'Prospero's been playing twenty-four-seven, trying to get hold of it before those shysters do. But he's just been deleted, okay! He had a fit in the process. Now they're going to find the file and . . . you know what?' Michael throws up his hands. 'I've had enough. I'm gonna go check on the dude.' He scrapes back his chair and leaves the room.

'He's in shock,' Eve says. 'We're all very distressed.'

'Please explain it to me,' Lionel says, trying to stop his hands from shaking. 'What is the data? I mean, how is it represented in the game?'

Eve arches one eyebrow. 'Can't you guess? It's the Sylph.'

It feels as if blood is draining from his brain. 'She was a test avatar, incomplete. She wasn't even meant to go up. I didn't upload her.' Lionel feels sick.

'Michael traced the hack to your cloaked ID.'

'But I didn't upload her.'

Eve considers him for a moment. 'I believe you,' she says. 'We did some research and there are other cases like this. Often there's a transmitter interacting with the host machine.'

'There's something communicating remotely with my domain?'

'That's what we thought, but we'd have found it when we swept your flat.'

'You? The burglary.'

'Yes, sorry.' She's unremorseful.

Michael comes in holding the whiskey bottle. 'The fact remains,' he begins, as if he's been eavesdropping, 'you've been a total asshole.

Bio-data is either hidden in that Sylph's code or she's a conduit for something interacting from outside. Either way she's fucking history, *capiche*?'

Eve throws Michael an acidic look. 'We stumbled on this, remember; we weren't looking for it. We were just trying to recruit people to help us legitimize IDs centrally . . .' She stops, squeezes the top of her nose. 'I'm sorry, I'm tired.'

Lionel was convinced he'd been in a qat-addled fugue when the Sylph and Buddha mysteriously uploaded. Now he's trawling through alternate possibilities: Pema tampering remotely with his domain, some device transmitting her sneaky agenda past his firewalls. But where could it be?

He smacks his forehead. 'Argh! Why don't you tell the authorities all this?'

Michael's laughter is quick and cynical. 'Listen to me.' He pours himself a whiskey and swills it aggressively round his glass. 'I don't know what planet you're on, but on *my* planet we don't tell the authorities anything.' He takes a healthy gulp and exhales potent fumes, showing his teeth. 'When Eve talks about governments having less or more integrity, we're already on predator level, you get it? We're all prey to them, nothing more. Besides, if we told the *authorities*' – Michael makes speech marks with his free hand – 'about our secret society here, d'you think they'd believe you were innocent?'

'You worked it out.'

'You saw what they did to Larissa Greenough and she's *entirely* innocent; I mean squeaky. We checked her out so thoroughly we know what her frikkin shit smells like. But she's been in solitary confinement for weeks.' Michael drains his glass and pours another. 'And if she can't convince them she's innocent – and she's a regular person – do you think they'd believe a freak like you?'

'What Michael is trying to say' – Eve takes Lionel's hands – 'is that we have to stop the information falling to the wrong people. We have to find the Sylph and destroy her. Then we can go back to our primary objective – helping to rebuild ruined lives. I know it sounds idealistic but at least we're doing something.' She squeezes his hands hopefully. 'And no one is going to tell the authorities anything, are they, Lionel?'

Lionel sits silently aggregating all the new knowledge, translating it into a plan. The memory of Crystal crying for Beatrise comes to him – *What is different if it me or Beatrise, what is different?* – and his mind finds another gear. Everything makes sense.

'I need an ID,' he says firmly. 'I need it quickly.'

Eve smiles. 'We'll organize it for you.'

'I need safe transit for a young woman, somewhere north.'

Eve counts off on her fingers. 'You'll have to supply us with prints, iris scan, a picture and a swab, okay? We'll do everything else.' Eve holds her hand up and raises her voice to divert Michael's rising objection. '*On the condition* . . . on the condition that you help us. You're in there, you see. You're in the game.'

'Eve!' Michael slaps his hand flat on the table. 'This is mad.'

Eve ignores him. 'Lionel. Please?'

@GameAddict (#23756745): 14:8:27

Once in a while the game is more difficult than the grey world. The storyline takes a twist you weren't expecting. Comrades reveal themselves to be false. Enemies show themselves to be friends. It's confusing. Unnecessarily dense. Bosses are exposed as more vicious and beastly than any tyrant in history. You want to switch off, take a walk and play a new game. But you must reach the Final Level. Then it's done. It's over and the euphoria of achievement will buoy you up for days, even weeks.

Level 16: Dimension's Deceit

Down, down, like Alice, through geological time; topsoil, silt, stony layers and so on, roots and fossils exposed. Past the prehistoricals to where myths lived. Where Wisps were called before replay. I expected to splatter on rock, or worse, land in some fiery lake. But tho we zoomed down we suddenly slowed, came buoyant, as if helium-filled, and floated the last few clicks bobbing about a bit and landing right on our feet. Not even a stumble. The passerines kept pace with us, on the wing.

We were in a dismal labyrinth. Hollow-eyed Wisps were jammed from here to there but they didn't trouble us. Replay alone was fixed in their nogs. There were Thrar Wisps and a glut of new Wisped Vadarians, fresh from the mudslide on the mountain. I found myself eagling for Dan-Albwr-han among the Krin, desperately scanning their face-features. But the Sylph urged me on and the crush came thicker as we edged towards some significant hub. Finally we emerged in a cavern but high up, peeping over a gallery. First thing that hit me was a burning, electrical smell. Below us were wall-to-wall Grinders, but they weren't Grinding. Not at all.

There was a giant lie underpinning the Realm. The lie was that after the Grinders had worked in the Core for their masters' replay they would get 'retirement' to make up for a whole span of servitude. Payback. But this wasn't the case. I sank to my knees as I clocked them all, herded in stalls. The monsters that corralled them were mechanical beasters with glass eyes and mitts like drill-bits or pincers. The Grinders were picked out, one by one, and deleted. Not switched off or *zap, zap and you're gone* and so on, but tortuous demolition scenes like none I'd come pon in any dimension. Now, if you're prone to squeamishness, or suffer offence in the nog, then skip the next section. But if you don't mind snuff footage – read on.

Rewiring, casement removal, circuit dismantling, drive crushing, node smashing. Grinders – not stunned first, but tortured while booted and conscious. And prior to the agony, witnessing the torment their comrades endured, knowing they were up next and done for. Utterly cruel. The monsters were searching for one teensy thing in each Grinder. They did quick scans using some kind of laser and went in with their pincers, quite unmoved by the smoke and the wails of alarm. Once they found what they searched for – about the size of a marble, tho I couldn't quite clock what it was – the Grinders were finally zapped and dumped in a tub marked 'Retirement'; great mounds of corpses, wires hanging out. Criminal.

When the Sylph dragged me off I was whimpering and tho she pulled me far away from the scene I couldn't recover my wits. I switched off the visuals in my Visor – the deceit of the Core too heavy in my nog to risk seeing more. I cursed the Creators. Not one character in this Realm was truly free. I was ready to give up. Game Over. Think of it. A He-Man turned to slush by a lie. A noise in the distance made me stop and I called for the Sylph, who must've gone on ahead, but she didn't reply. My Visor fired up, blipped *red alert* and out of the shadows came Mata Angelica – tooled-up and ready to fight.

Imagine this: pins bound in red leather past the knee-joint with stiletto-lifts that made her extraordinarily leggy. Leotard – this time in black rubber; high on the hip-girdle, flush to the mons, plunging and strapless – with nips poking through in crisp detail. Ultra-dominatrix, she strutted towards me, cracking her whip as she came. I gripped the hilt of my sword, not sure if I wanted to woo her or fight her.

'You made it! I knew you would.' She came close, dropped her whip, slid a warm digit right down my breastbone and sniffed me. 'I forgive you for running off with the sorceress. I've followed your Quest and I'm here to help with the raid.'

Before I could utter, she kissed me. Approval: (hers) 100 (mine) 85.

'This place,' I said, pulling away. 'It's gruesome. My nog's up the spout.'

She grimaced. 'You saw the Ring Room?'

'I saw snuff-scenes and wiring, if that's what you mean. What *are* those things they extract from the Grinders?'

'Power Rings, Ludi.' She folded her arms and appraised me.

'No!'

'The Realm's nasty secret. There's no retirement. Grinders are simply refurbished so characters like us can keep crawling up levels.'

'Oh God.' My own actions had contributed to this horror.

'We *can* exist without Power Rings, you know. We just have to put in some elbow grease. Make sacrifices.'

I realized I'd never seen Mata Angelica use one. Every character needed energy to play, but in other dimensions it took work to replenish your meter. In this Realm the characters had come overstuffed, overprivileged. Power Rings gave them a quick fix. No one cared where the energy came from.

The Eroticon sharpened her eye-gems. 'Where's the Sylph?'

I looked around. 'She was right with me. She must be up there.' I pointed vaguely ahead.

'Let's not hang about. We must find her if we're to put this world to rights.' She winked and trotted off swift-wise.

I set off grudgingly, stopping now and then to study strange pics that appeared on the walls as I passed. There was one of a dwell-place, very homely, and four childsome characters sketched in the foreground. Further along were two characters holding a rope slung over the branch of a tree. At the end of the rope, with a loop round its neck, dangled a teensy MauMau. Felt queasy when I clocked it. Another pic showed the scene on the bridge – the Sylph diving headfirst into the chasm. Bizarre.

Mata Angelica came to my shoulder. 'The Core is an archive – shows each individual character's gameplay.'

'But the gameplay in these pics isn't mine.'

'You must be in third-person view.'

I checked my PoV control. 'No, I'm in Player One, first person –'

'Look,' Mata Angelica interrupted. 'I see her. This is it, Ludi.'

The Eroticon wounded the Sylph before I could stop her. Went for the child with a knife and gouged a fair chunk from her belly. It took a few clicks to drag her off and by then the Sylph was stunned and quite pale. I stood on the Eroticon's chest, growling like a Krin. Incensed.

'What are you doing?' Mata Angelica thrashed about. Threads of saliva escaped from her mouth. 'This is the Quest. We have to destroy her.'

'But she's . . .' I was confused in the nog. 'Saving her is *my* Quest.'

'We agreed, remember. In the kitchen, at Michael's.'

'What?'

'Lionel. Look at me. In the kitchen – at Michael's house. Remember!'

Mordecai is a Thing
of Dreadful Wonder

L ionel warms the contents of a tin of chilli con carne. Its meaty
smell licks round the walls, turning the scene from monochrome to
Technicolor. It makes the place feel more alive. Lilith's house has three
rooms downstairs; a study that overlooks the garden, a living room and
an open-plan kitchen diner. An internal door leads to the garage where
Lionel has found some supplies.

Lilith always has a store of 'survival rations'. She's been preparing for
Armageddon, in a haphazard way, for years – stashing tins, water and gas
bottles. A couple of winters back she went on a course and learned how
to make rope and start a fire without a light. She'd toyed with the idea
of procuring a gun 'should the worst case scenario happen'. So Lionel
was surprised that Lilith's supplies were so meagre. But there were a
few tins of peaches, frankfurters, beans, chickpeas, chilli con carne and
so on, thrown randomly into storage tubs. But no gun.

'I've uploaded your scans to the secure site and Michael says a day,
maybe two, to infiltrate the system.' He carries the food to the table.
'Once you have your new ID we'll get you to Mr Barber's friends – careful, it's hot – and they can take it from there.'

Crystal looks scared. 'You come with me?'

'You'll be in the best hands with Michael. You mustn't worry. I'll make
sure you get there. I'll make sure you're safe.'

'And then?'

'Then you'll find a job. Make a new life. You'll be a new person.' He smiles woefully. 'No more Crystal.'

Crystal talks with her mouth full. 'What is new name?'

'Your new name?' He sucks his teeth. 'Whatever Michael comes up with – there won't be a choice. It'll be the name of, well' – he grimaces – 'someone who's died probably.'

'Maybe I be . . .' She pauses to think. 'Nǎocán, hah, somesing like that, yes?'

'Nǎo . . . cán?' He can't quite copy her pronunciation.

She raps her head with her knuckles. 'It mean *thick brain.*'

'Ah! Let's hope Michael finds something nicer than that.'

'I must have thick brain to believe mens in Shanghai, yes? You can be shop girl, or even model they say. I believe.' Crystal fills her mouth again.

'You came all the way from China to be a shop girl?'

'In Hubei everysing gone. Under water.'

'The sea level rose?'

'No sea in Hubei.' She laughs, unconcerned she's showing a mouth full of mince. 'Dams, giant dams. Half of China under water so the other half can have energy.'

'I heard about this.'

Crystal shrugs. His hearing about it means nothing. The outcome for her remains the same. She eats her food, nodding and smiling with each mouthful, until she says, 'When did sister move out?'

Lionel frowns. 'Er, she hasn't moved out. She's away that's all.'

Crystal is confused. 'But is nothing here. Everysing empty.'

She lays down her fork and motions for him to come upstairs. At the entrance to Lilith's bedroom she gestures inside.

'Empty,' she says.

The bed has been stripped and the wardrobe, its doors yawning wide, is bare. She goes into the bathroom and stands with her arms apart.

'Bathroom is same. Nobody live here.'

The bathroom is the source of the bleach-tinged dankness. There is half a toilet roll and a disc of dried soap in the dish next to the sink.

'Sister leave long time, yes?' Crystal goes down the stairs, talking over her shoulder. 'She take everysing but furnitch.' In the living room she picks up a cushion and hugs it to her chest. 'See?'

The room comes into focus. Crystal is right. Where are the personal items, the feminine things that Lilith would leave on the sideboard, or in the bathroom? Where are her clothes? He stands with both hands on his hips trying to take it all in.

'This is sad house.' Crystal touches his wrist. 'You very sad, no?'

After the life Crystal has endured it troubles him that she can still pronounce Lilith's home 'sad'. His eyes rest on the tub chair and the repro Chesterfield, both cast-offs from Bethesda – from when David and Judy moved and their furniture wouldn't fit into the new bungalow. Now he considers it, much of the old furniture from Bethesda has found its way here. Even the curtains and the cushions. Why hasn't he noticed this before? He goes through to the kitchen and opens the drawers and the cupboards.

'Hey, she's left the kitchen stuff,' he calls. 'She must be coming back.'

Crystal watches him from the doorway as he inspects the sauce-pan set, the casserole dish, the tea towels – all from Bethesda. He's confused. The cutlery is from Bethesda, the crockery that survived the smash-up – Bethesda. He finds four new mugs and side plates that he's sure he's seen, at Judy's bungalow. All these transactions between Lilith and their parents have been taking place without his knowledge. Things given and received, a flow of parental gifts he knew nothing about. How can Lilith be angry when she's had so much from them? And here, look, on the fridge, a note to Lilith in Judy's handwriting. No, wait, not to Lilith – to a woman called Jean. It says:

Jean. I've tidied upstairs & bleached the toilet but the kitchen could do with a thorough clean. Call me and let me know your hours.
Judy

Judy comes here to clean! She's even organized a stand-in cleaner in case she can't make it. Extraordinary. Lionel peels the note off the fridge. Something isn't right. If he could just think clearly for a minute without any distractions he might be able to work it out, but Crystal is staring at him with those huge, sympathetic eyes and he can't concentrate.

'What?'

'You very sad?'

'No. No I'm not.'

But Lionel knows now that he must go back and discuss things thoroughly with Judy, and the realization fills him with dread. If Lilith were here she'd sort it all out. Why can't he be fearless and pragmatic like his sister? Then he realizes Lilith would be proud of him for helping Crystal, Michael and Eve. In exchange for Crystal's safe transit he's agreed to modify Ludi's quest and alter the game. Tomorrow he'll return to Milk Street – collect Buddha, retrieve the original avatar files stored on his superdrives (for some reason his Google device isn't syncing with them remotely) and re-enter *CoreQuest* using an alternate login that Michael has generated. Only then – when Crystal is safe – will he talk to Judy. There's so much to do. *Action, Lionel. Action.*

'You are sure?' Crystal touches his elbow.

'What? Yes, yes I am. I'm fine.'

The panic begins early. Lionel's asleep on the sofa, dreaming of the Sylph, when Crystal shakes him awake, her eyes glowing in the dim light, and for a moment he's not sure if the Sylph is Crystal or vice versa.

'Mens come,' she whispers. Her teeth are chattering.

Lionel is instantly alert. A vehicle's doors slam. Male voices pass outside the window. There's a moment's hiatus when Lionel and Crystal remain utterly still until a key slides into the front-door lock. They scramble through to the kitchen, keeping low on instinct, and crawl under the breakfast bar. His heart is thumping so hard he's sure the sound of it will give them away.

'Smells rank in here,' the first man says, sniffing as he enters. 'Where shall we start?'

'Let's have a coffee first, my synapses need a kick.'

A tower of light falls across the floor beside them. Crystal gasps and Lionel squeezes her hand.

'Did she say all the furniture, everything.'

'Yep, the lot.'

The voices belong to Ben and James. There's nothing to worry about. They are his brothers, not burglars. Not traffickers come to steal Crystal away. So why doesn't he crawl from his hiding place and greet them?

'It'll take three trips at least.'

'I can't believe I've flown across the pond to be a fucking removal man.'

'Let's be fair, Jim, it was Dad's funeral that brought you, not this.'

James makes a bullish noise. 'He could never have *brought* me here. You know how I felt about Dad. He was a damn fool.'

'Yeah, well, let's not go there again.'

'Go where? God, you're touchy.'

'Maybe we're both touchy. Look, I can't face talking about everything any more. It's too early, or too late, I'm not sure which. Sorry.' Ben is back-pedalling. 'Let's get this done. It won't take long. Mum's nailed most of it already.'

James ignores his brother's apology. 'Check this shit out, look at it.' There is the sound of splintering wood. 'Jesus.'

'Careful with that – Mum wants to sell it.'

'Okay, take it easy. When did you say he moved out?'

'A year ago, perhaps more, I can't keep up. Mum says he still pops back and scares the neighbours sometimes.'

'Hah! What a freak. Nothing changes.'

'He's had a tough time, you know. I felt sorry for him at the funeral.'

James snorts. 'You can't have felt that bad. I didn't notice you reaching out to our *brother from another mother*.'

'Shut up! Will you?'

'Don't be an arse, Ben. You always were too sensitive. Hurry up and put the kettle on, I'm gasping.'

Ben doesn't move. 'I'm not an arse . . . God . . . don't you think sometimes, you know, what we did might have contributed to –? Argh! What the hell.'

'What are you talking about now?' James sounds bored.

'You can't have forgotten how we terrorized him. It eats me up when I think about it. I dream about it.'

'Oh, for God's sake, not this again. It was only a bit of fun.'

'What – locking him up, beating him, trying to hang him?'

James adopts a sarcastic tone. 'Poor Ben! Has your heart started bleeding Christian mercy in your old age?'

'Don't take the piss. You know what I'm saying. It was mad. Him . . .
Lily . . . everything.' Ben's voice becomes very quiet and childlike. 'You
killed his cat.'

James bridles. 'That cat was dying anyway. I put it out of its misery.'

'I have nightmares about that cat. Jesus, Jim, you strung it up by the
neck.'

'Shit, what do you want me to say? I mean, ask anyone – anyone in
the history of fucking childhood. Everyone played rough when they
were kids.' He continues almost under his breath. 'Terrorized him. Jesus
Christ alive – what utter garbage.'

'You know, Jim, sometimes you don't sound Christian at all.'

'I keep telling you – I'm not Christian, I'm in the faith industry. There's
a difference.'

'Fine.'

'Those spirit domains makes twelve thousand a month – every month.'

'You told me. It's amazing.' But Ben doesn't sound amazed.

'People need to feel they're doing something proactive to save their
sorry souls. Paying hard cash, well – in this day and age – it's all they
know.'

'I get it.'

'I offer them peace of mind in exchange for a premium.'

'Except they'll never know if the insurance pays out.'

'Brilliant, isn't it?'

'Indulgence.'

'What?'

'Indulgences. Priests used to sell indulgences as an insurance against
hell.'

'Precisely. They had it all figured out in the dark ages. The God business
went downhill after that – until now.' James does one of those clever
laughs he perfected when he was a child.

There's a long pause before Ben says, 'He's weird but he's harmless,
you know.'

James groans. 'Sweet Jesus! We're back to Lionel, are we? He's a nut-
ter. You heard him, choking and spluttering at the funeral when I was
trying to do the eulogy. And try convincing Mum he's harmless next
time she's sobbing about *everything*. Or ask that nurse at the Yews if

he's harmless, or that bloke at the gym. Remember him? Or Lil –' James lowers his voice suddenly. 'Did you hear something?'

'No.'

'I thought I heard . . . Shh.'

Silence can be deathly. Lionel and Crystal sit rigid as statues, preparing to be discovered. Her hand is a tourniquet on his arm. In his mind's eye he sees his brothers creeping through the doorway and into the kitchen. Lionel's breath comes quick and hard. They are stalking across the lino, a gleeful angle to their heads. Mouths slavering. He almost cries out. The torture of anticipation is too much to bear until four sharp raps on the front door interrupt his agony.

'Told you I heard something,' James says smugly.

Lionel peeps over the breakfast bar as his brothers go through to the hall. He grinds his teeth as he watches them – James pushing his weight back onto his heels, holding the door open as if it's his house, not Lilith's. And Ben, his head cocked on one side, rather like a spaniel's, still in thrall to his brother, if his body language is anything to go by, despite confronting him just now.

James killed Mordecai, his beloved cat. Murdered. A memory inhabits him suddenly.

Ben, remorseful, walking him down to the thicket.

'What is it? Where are we going?'

'I can't tell you. I can't say it out loud.'

Pulling back sprays of brambles, as if they were curtains across a miniature proscenium. As if Lionel should say 'ooh' or 'aah' in boyish wonder at some theatrical spectacle. A squadron of bluebottles flying out from a grim space where Mordecai is the main act, the only act – fur missing from his hindquarters and each chalky vertebra visible from tail tip to neck. His body degraded, discarded. Ben holding a hand over his nose and mouth for the smell and saying, 'I didn't do it. I found him like this.' Guilt giving his brother away as he cries, wiping his nose on the back of his hand, the slimy glint of mucus from knuckle to wrist. Grief encompassing him. The fur on Mordecai's front legs and his face making him want to take the cat in his arms and hold him. And weep. The lovely markings on the top of his soppy old head. But his eyes gone and his soul gone and his nose crusted and dry and, as if simple torture wasn't enough, a fat white maggot, plump with carrion, plopping out from his nostril.

A torrent of anger surges through Lionel. He'll kill James, that's what he'll do. He'll kill him for Mordecai and for Buddha. He thinks about what Lilith told him the night his father died, that James and Ben had hanged him too. His hand goes to his throat but something, someone, tugs the hem of his shirt. Pulls him back to here and now. He mustn't forget Crystal. Here she is beside him. Vulnerable. Petrified.

'It's okay,' he whispers and puts his finger to his lips.

His priority, Lionel reasons, must be this girl. He'll kill James later. He'll fly to America if he has to and kill him there. In Times Square. No, in the Grand Canyon, with a gun. No, with his bare hands or a sword. Yes, he'll use his scimitar. *Action, Lionel. Action*. He peeps back over the breakfast bar. Two men are standing in the porch and, by their tone and demeanour, Lionel senses that they're officials – plain-clothes police perhaps, or immigration officers.

James is saying, 'Of course, come in, come in.'

It takes a huge effort of will to sneak across the no-man's-land of lino to the garage door, but he guides Crystal out of the kitchen, closing the door after them with a soft click as the men enter the living room.

It's dark in the garage and he holds Crystal's hand to his chest.

'You know them?' Her voice is a fierce whisper.

'They're nothing to me.'

He rests his ear on the door and considers trying to get the key from the other side so he can lock it. But it's too late now. Ben is already in the kitchen.

'No,' Ben says. 'Neither of us has seen him since our father's funeral.'

Another man speaks at length, but Lionel can't hear what he's saying.

'You're joking,' Ben says eventually. 'Are you sure you've got the right person?'

What on earth are they talking about?

One of the official men says something else.

Ben speaks quickly. 'Yes I know, allegedly; still, here you are . . . I assume you've been to his flat.'

The man must have moved closer because now Lionel hears his voice clearly.

'We have this as his official address.'

'No, no – this house belongs to my parents, well to my mum now. He moved into the flat ages ago.'

'We'll need that address.'

'I don't know it off the top of my head. I'll have to call my mother.'

'Is there anywhere else he visits regularly – friends, associates, places he likes to go to get away from it all?'

'Erm, I'm not certain. I'll be honest, I never actually see him. We're not close. I live up north. My brother . . . he's here from the States for a fortnight. None of us is close to him, if you know what I mean. I'm not sure he has any friends. He's a bit of a loner, really.'

James's voice, when it comes, is mere centimetres from Lionel. He must be standing directly on the other side of the garage door.

'Still think he's harmless, eh, Ben?'

The up-and-over garage door opens silently and he pushes the motorbike onto the drive. It takes some effort to manoeuvre the machine past the van but he soon has it on the road where an unmarked silver hybrid is parked against the kerb. Lionel has a notion to steal the hybrid, but the car will be GPS tagged; it'll have a remote restriction device too. Besides, he feels like Ludi when he's on the motorbike, heroic. He and his anime sidekick will fare better with the wind in their hair, thundering along the country roads with a real engine beneath them. His muscles tighten. He's determined and intrepid – not afraid at all.

A hundred metres from the house Lionel risks turning the engine over with the foot-starter. The action achieves nothing but a grind and a pop. He tries again. The same. He checks over his shoulder and sees the blinds at Lilith's window yanked to one side.

'Shit.'

There's a shout as the front door flies open and all four men come out – officials in the lead at a loping trot – incredulity unfolding on their faces. One of the men speaks urgently into a receiver at his wrist. His brothers hang back on the front lawn, hands in their pockets. They are spectators, although Ben is peering at the ground, kicking a tuft of grass with the toe of his boot. Look away, Ben – it's what you always did, Lionel thinks.

Lionel turns the engine over again. Nothing.

'Come on,' Crystal screams, fists at her sides.

He kicks again and again.

'Push it,' she shouts and points to the clutch. 'Pull up handle and push.'

Squeezing the clutch, he summons all his strength to push the bike down the road, but one of the men is already in striking distance. Crystal boots him on the upper thigh and he falls backwards, reaching for something inside his jacket as he does. A weapon? Shit. The bike explodes into life.

'Get in,' he shouts, but the bike runs away from him. Only the very tips of his fingers snagging the ridges of the handlegrips keep the machine in his possession.

Crystal breaks into a surprisingly athletic sprint. 'Go, go.'

With his nails he nudges the throttle forward, enough to stop the bike from bucking away, and she jumps into the sidecar as he straddles the machine and accelerates.

Behind them, the men return to the hybrid and make chase along the old road that bypasses the village. It's a risk but Lionel turns onto the bridleway – a shortcut to the ring road. It's muddy, disused and strewn with fallen branches. Tree cover darkens the way, but he weaves round the obstacles that loom up in the headlight as if it's a game. But mud quickly thickens the tyres and the hybrid, rallying up dirt, gains ground and Lionel curses the bike's inferior traction. He pulls back harder on the throttle until the engine responds with a pleasing and resonant salvo. But his satisfaction is brief. In that instant, as if mechanical jaws have taken a bite from the top of his ear, he's wounded. He cries out, perceiving the dull whirr of a bullet as it shaves past his eyebrow and overtakes him at speed.

'Oh, dear Lord.'

To his left he catches sight of Crystal, ripping the leather covers from their stud fasteners around the top of the sidecar. She has a piece about a metre square, flapping about in the turbulence. She turns in her seat and gets onto her knees, facing backwards. His chest is flat to the tank.

'Get down, for heaven's sake, they're firing,' he yells.

But she stays upright, eyes level, weighing up the precise moment – the split second plus trajectory – that will make the biggest difference. She holds the cover aloft and it snaps round in her hands. He guesses her intention, but it's impossible. Even as he thinks it the cover is snatched from her grasp, flapping back and out of sight like a giant, upholstered crow, and as it takes flight Crystal folds into the sidecar as abruptly as a puppet with its strings cut. There's a crash and a high-pitched *zing* and when he looks back the hybrid is lodged between two trees, the leather crow half covering the windscreen, steam escaping from around the wheels.

He can't believe it. 'Fucking brilliant!' he shouts.

Ten kilometres off the ring road the bike sputters to a stop. The fuel tank is empty but Lionel is unconcerned. It's time to get off the road. In a field he camouflages the bike with dry bracken and attempts to clean himself up. His ear, split by the bullet, has bled dramatically onto one shoulder. Crystal, too, is injured.

'A scratch,' she says, dismissing his solicitude.

He checks the sky for drones, but knows he'll never see one with a naked eye – too high, too sophisticated. Instead, his gaze follows a boulevard of clouds that leads towards an early autumn sun, calving free from the horizon so that light pours into the field, slowly, like spilled honey, revealing the shapes of things in its amber progress – the hedges, abandoned farm machinery, two oak trees stately in the glow. He smiles, takes Crystal's hand and they set off at a steady clip across country.

Harmless, he thinks. James will soon know if he's harmless. Lilith is the one who battered George, not him, but still, he was rooting for her. If he could live life again he'd have joined in, given George the proper slap he deserved. But how did James know about the man in the gym? No one knows about that except Lilith.

Last year she bullied him into joining. He looked puny and needed to beef up, she said. He told her it felt unnatural to puff and sweat with people he didn't know, all of them with their ears plugged and their Spex on so they didn't have to see or listen to anyone else's exertion. But his sister would brook no protest. The gym, however, turned out to be relaxing. The pool was often empty and Lionel would do a few lengths and lie in the sauna for a while. He liked it best when he could feel the atmosphere pressing down on him. Lilith said this was a body memory of being in Africa, that he was remembering the heat on the day David 'found' him.

An old man came one time and took the bench below Lionel. The man's skin was soft on his bones, ruched like silk at the waistband of his trunks. Lionel had been holding his breath since the man came in and now he was dizzy. He wanted to reach down and touch the pin-pearls of sweat glistening in the creases of the man's skin. What would happen if he broke the fragile rules of contact?

Lionel hadn't meant to touch him, but his hand began to move as if it was disembodied. It stopped in mid-air, swaying like a cobra before alighting on the old man's thigh. The cobra gave the man a little pinch. The man opened his eyes. He was uncommonly strong for a pensioner and dragged Lionel out of the sauna, past the pool and into the foyer, both of them near-naked and dripping with sweat. The manager wasn't interested in Lionel's explanation or apology. Two previous complaints had already been overlooked and this was the last straw. Lionel was banned.

Panting, Lionel jogs along the alleyway that borders the industrial estate. He's dragging Crystal by the wrist and she's soaked. A fine rain is falling. They've been running for an hour and she can't keep it up for much longer.

'Quick,' he says. 'In here.'

They take refuge in a disused railway arch; express train powering overhead as Lionel scans the sky. Crystal squats against the damp brickwork, trying to catch her breath. She's very pale.

'Right.' Rolling stock screeches distantly. 'Let's go,' he says.

She implores him to wait, but he says, 'Quickly, come on,' and is about to set off again when Crystal doubles over.

'What's wrong?'

'I stay here. You come back.'

'I don't know.' He checks the alley, searches the sky again. 'It could be all right, I suppose. I think it's me they want, not you.'

'I hide, yes.' She nods towards the back of the railway arch.

A patch of red on her jacket catches his eye. 'Is that blood?'

'Is nothing.' She folds her arms across her stomach.

'You're hurt!'

'No, is the branch tree, hit me.'

Lionel gets on his knees. Crystal's skin is waxy and feverish and her eyes have gone glassy.

She touches his forearm. 'You nice mans. Thank you.'

'Don't say that. I'll come back.'

Lionel drapes a torn rubble sack across Crystal's shoulders to double as camouflage and protection from the rain. 'If I'm not back once it's dark,' he says, 'find Mr Barber. He'll look after you.'

He kisses the top of her head and tells her he'll be as quick as he can.

Lionel scales several wire fences, hurdles a wall and leaps over a barrier until, finally, he's moving swiftly along the alley behind Milk Street. There's no doubt he's a new man now. He scans himself for signs of the old Lionel and finds none. It's the power of adrenalin that's transforming me, he thinks. He stops at a gate and peers in. Except for a few crates and a brazier, Saeed's courtyard is empty. Lionel is on the brickwork in seconds and he tightropes along the top of the buttress that runs perpendicular to the back of the flats and follows the wall up a series of steps until he's high off the ground. His window is within touching distance and he stretches for the sill. But his foot slips and his arms helicopter as he tries to throw his weight backwards. The stone flags of Saeed's courtyard seem to fly towards him and he flails violently while a vision of a body splayed out in the rain – an imperfect tetraskelion – flashes in his mind. He regains his balance.

'Oh Lord,' he murmurs, heart dancing briskly.

It takes ten minutes to backtrack and scale the wall on the other side of the courtyard, where he clambers onto the air-conditioning unit, heaves himself onto the one above that, then onto the condenser a metre above that, until at last he can climb through the window of the flat above his.

The room he crawls into is exactly the same layout as his bedroom except there are boxes and industrial tubs of ghee stacked against the walls. The coast is clear on the landing and he creeps down the stairs.

Inside his flat there's a pungent whiff of ammonia. Buddha hasn't managed to reach the litter tray, but then he's been away for two nights. Poor thing. The blinds are drawn – did he do that?

Check the street. Don't switch on the light. If the officers in the hybrid have passed on this address to their colleagues they'll be here any time soon. This won't take long. He's only here for two things – his files and his cat.

'Hey, Buddha, where are you?' he calls in a stage whisper. He fires up his Google desk unit and logs in. 'Budds,' he calls again softly.

It takes less than five minutes to transfer everything from his superdrives to his handheld device. Once the transfer is complete he initiates a memory format. Drive one.

'Come on.'

While he's waiting for the data on the external memory to be deleted Lionel looks round. Buddha has had a reasonable go at his food; a few biscuits are spread round the bowl. He must be sleeping, curled on the bed. Lionel finds the letters about his birth – a life he might have had – in a pile on his desk. The sheaf takes a while to catch. A solitary flame licks round the waste bin until the paper ignites with a *woomph*. His certificates, his history, are consumed. After a minute nothing but powder remains. *Returned to dust.*

Lionel stops and kisses the air several times. The noise never fails to wake Buddha. He'll wobble in here any second, croaking a greeting, jerking round Lionel's feet, full of loyalty and love. Lionel frowns and looks along the passageway.

'Buddha?'

Panic turns the passage from the living room to the bedroom into a long, breathless corridor. He's panting hard when he reaches the doorway, and at first glance nothing's amiss. 'Buddha, where are you, big boy?' He shunts the chest of drawers away from the recess to see if he's got himself stuck. He's not there. Only dust billows up as he feels on top of the wardrobe. Lionel falls to his knees, checks under the bed. *No, no, no.*

Here's his beloved Buddha. His soft body lodged between the wall and the bed, his head at a distressing angle; scratch marks – where he must have tried to stop himself from slipping – gouged in the wallpaper.

'Budds.' Lionel strokes Buddha's nose with his fingertips. *Be gentle. Please.* The cat's eyes are shut tight but his pink tongue is still poking out, testing the air. A bright blue feather, tiny as a reptile scale, hangs from his mouth. When Lionel clasps Buddha to his chest he's no longer warm.

@GameAddict (#23756745): 10:9:27

If you're a bad person then you'll be bad
wherever you are. At work, at home, up on the
Game Layer. You'll play out your anxieties, your
shortcomings and wickedness even when you
have the chance to reinvent yourself entirely.

Level 17: The Boss

'It's a game. It's only a game.' I thumped her, quite unrestrained.

'All for nothing,' she screamed, nymph-gone-hysterical, smashing my nog with her fist.

I used a nifty back-kick to trip her and, once on the floor, I gave her one or two jabs in the kidney. 'You're making everything. Too. Serious.'

Her wireframe went limp.

'What's wrong? Come on, fight.'

'What's the use? I give up.'

When I was convinced she was calm I released her. But Mata Angelica bounced up instantly and sprinted away. She'd spotted the Sylph.

'Please don't –'

'Calm down, I won't hurt her,' she called over her shoulder.

During our fight the wounded Sylph had crawled off to hide. But as she scrambled away she'd come across the Lock quite by accident. Now we all stood and stared, trying to make sense of its mechanicals – knowing that once we unlocked it the Final Level awaited. The whole thing was inlaid in the floor and had three separate devices – as Mata Angelica had predicted. There were carvings and curlicues round each device and pretty engravings in copperplate script.

Mata Angelica read what was there, trembling with the prospect of altering the game. 'It says the Keys are all Sylphs.' She held up three digits. 'Three Sylphs?'

The passerines throated a warble, zipped down and perched on my shoulders.

At first the Eroticon tried to shoo them away, but then she turned to me and said, 'Are they relevant?'

'Violet-tailed Sylphs.' I smiled. 'So the alchemist told me.'

'Ah.' She tapped her snout, quick comprehending. 'I suppose the airy one makes three.' She looked to the Sylph, who was digging around in her belly wound.

At that point a kerfuffle erupted, stage-right, and the MauMau scampered onto the scene. In his mouthparts, the passerine the sorceress had lost back in Level 3. The beast placed the teensy inanimate thing at my feet, softly-softly.

'Good pussycat.' Mata Angelica examined the MauMau's offering. 'Another Sylph,' she said. 'But it's dead. Frozen solid.'

We exchanged useless gestures, but gathered our wits and placed the cold passerine in the Lock. Without prompting the other two tweeters took their places. Instantly there was a rumbling, industrial whirr, as if the dimension was wrenching apart, and one whole side of the labyrinth rolled back. A cavernous space lit with flame-torches was revealed and, in the middle, a circular stage. The battleground. The final raid was about to begin.

Family Matters

L ionel throws open the window and roars. The sound is more wolf than human – a deep, painful howl. People on Milk Street look up. Some stop and point and confer with one another as he rips the blinds from their fittings.

'What are you looking at – pathetic fucking lemmings?' he bellows. 'I'm a man. This is what men look like.' And he beats his chest with his fists.

At least they have their blinkers off, he thinks, and he stands there nodding at them, feeling quite proud that he's interrupted the tedious rhythm of their lives.

The North African man in the white djellaba takes a photograph of him – or perhaps it's a video – but the camera's eye is trained on him for some time as he shows his best side. And there, across the road, is Crystal, clutching her stomach, slinging a worried glance his way, before slipping under the reflective police tape and darting down the alley next to the health centre. He shouts her name, thumps the windowsill, but she's gone. She should have stayed under the railway arch and waited for him. What's she thinking, exposing herself to danger like that?

The knapsack is squashed between a defunct desk unit and his box of gaming paraphernalia, and his eyes fall on the scimitar, the Visor, the stash of ninja discs. He wraps Buddha in a towel and places his stiffening body in the knapsack. *Gentle now.*

'You comfortable, Budds?' he says. 'We're going on a trip – you and me.'

*

The Visor is made from reflective plastic and covers his eyes from forehead to cheekbones. It has a moulded nose strip that stops it from slipping and an elastic strap hidden under his dreadlocks. He pushes the bud-shaped receivers deep in his ears and syncs the Visor with his Google device to access the augmented reality functions. There's satellite mapping, face recognition and zoom. There's a light-sensor that auto-switches the view function to night vision. A jagged mane of brown dreadlocks falls over his face at an angle and thick, knotted strands graze the tops of his shoulders. The gleaming scimitar and ninja discs are stuck randomly into his belt and he stands in front of the mirror swinging his weapon, enhancing each swing with an intense, throaty hum. His skin is blacker, he looks handsome, taller, more developed across the chest and arms, and he struggles to fit the knapsack over his shoulders.

Five huge leaps down the stairs and he's on the ground floor, bursting onto Milk Street as if he's a superhero. Who cares if anyone sees him? Who cares? He has them in *his* sights and he zooms in on the CCTV cameras fixed high on the buildings, takes aim with two fingers and pulls an imaginary trigger. *Bang*. Who fucking cares? *They* should be wary of him.

. The women in saris with push-along trolleys stand aside for him. They hold their toddlers firmly and move away once they see a clear path. Commuters watch him, some scowling, some filming. They're prepared to miss their connections for a spectacle as good as this. The video will be on their cloudfeeds before he can say 'meme'. Even Saeed leans in the doorway of his shop, cheek bulging with qat. He nods when Lionel hails him and then ambles inside, speaking on his mobile device.

At the head of the alley Lionel slashes through the reflective tape and jogs into the darkness, his Visor toggles to night vision, compensating for the decrease in light. The earth feels springy and his anger builds with each footfall so that when he shoulders the door it flies open with a splintering crunch.

There's a sweet tang in the corridor, like fruit and fish rotting. A tiny camera, mounted in the crease where the wall meets the ceiling, follows his movements until he hooks it from its housing with his scimitar and crunches it under his heel. He journeys up and down the ground-floor corridor smashing down doors as he goes.

The rooms are all empty, but at the head of the stairs that lead down to the basement he stops, turns the amplification on his receivers to full and listens. The sound of scuffling comes from below, along with terse commands in Chinese. The first door he comes to gives way with no effort. Behind it is an office with two desks that have shapes in the dust where items once stood. Carried off in the raid? The next door is the same. He stops and listens again. The voices in his earphones have been replaced by quick, erratic breathing.

'Crystal, it's me,' he shouts. 'Where are you?'

A smothered cry reaches him – somewhere to his left. He moves along slowly, knocking, until dense brick gives way to plaster and lathe. Using his scimitar he starts to hack through. Dust and fibres get in his mouth as he works and there are shouts – a warning perhaps, to stand back – but he's deaf to them. Once the stud frame is revealed he shoulders into it, bellowing, and rips at the internal struts once a hole has been made. At last he climbs through.

Here he is. Huo – his attacker – in his hidy-hole, where he's been waiting for the heat to cool since the raid. There's a microwave oven and boxes of food, a chemical toilet and a bunch of computer tablets and other handheld devices. And Crystal.

A silver revolver is pressed to her cheek. Huo is holding her firmly from behind and talking non-stop in Chinese. He's clearly frightened. But Crystal is calm, looking directly at Lionel, smiling. Blue beams of energy connect them.

Lionel puts his hands on his hips. 'Let her go.'

Huo laughs briefly. Then, emphasizing the fact that he has the upper hand, he pushes the gun forcefully into Crystal's ear. 'You fucking insane or what?' he screams. 'What you want from me, eh?'

Lionel's costume is having an interesting effect.

'I want the girl.'

'You come to my club, attack me in front of my people. I teach you lesson. Don't fuck with me. Eh? But here you are again.'

What is this rot? It was Huo and his henchmen that attacked him. Months later, the memory of the toilet, the stench of piss on his clothes, the theft of his dignity still send him into private paroxysms of shame.

'I just want the girl.'

'Please, Ludi.' This is Crystal. 'I don't care if I die. Kill him. Kill him good.'

Huo cuffs her with the butt of the gun. 'You murder my man.' He waves the revolver in Lionel's direction. 'You murder him in cold blood.'

'I didn't murder anyone.'

Huo wipes his eyes with the hand holding the gun. He's been cooped up in this rat hole for two days wondering how his empire could collapse so effortlessly. The police – once in his pocket – raiding him like that. His best sidekick ending up in the river with his tubes slashed. One of his slaves escaping and turning the tables on him. It's enough to make a man lose his marbles.

'You come in my club . . .' But Huo doesn't bother trying to talk any more.

Sudden comprehension lights his face and he aims at Lionel, realizing belatedly that he can shoot his nemesis freely and then shoot the girl. Three shots in quick succession. *Pop, pop, pop.*

Instinctively Lionel raises his scimitar and it's as if he can see the bullets advancing. An inverted triangle, a heat shimmer lining their passage as they boil up the air. Two whizz either side of his Visor, but the final one strikes his raised scimitar and flies back towards Huo as a posy of sparks erupts in the air. The bullet lodges in his cheek and, even though it's a ricochet, it throws the foppish man backwards.

Lionel gasps. 'Goddamn, did you see that?' He looks at Crystal. 'Did you? That was like, awesome.'

'He not dead. Kill him.'

Lionel leaps forward, one knee to Huo's chest. A barely governable urge to smash his head with his bare hands ambushes his free will in waves. But he overcomes the temptation and relieves the man of his gun as his blood soaks the carpet. Flesh has been blasted away to expose Huo's jaw and back teeth. He looks like death itself with his skeleton on show like that.

'Will he die?' Crystal is standing behind him.

He finds a cloth to staunch the blood. 'No. He'll live.' Lionel gives Crystal the gun and directs her to guard the stunned man – barrel aimed at his head – while he finds some rope or cable to tie him. But as soon as he climbs back through the hole in the wall, two more shots sound.

Crystal stands over Huo with the gun to his head. The Chinese man is screaming and blood gloops freely from a wound in his stomach and another on his upper thigh.

'I aim for his dick,' she says coldly, 'but I miss.'

Then she squeezes the trigger again.

It's a beautiful autumn day. Lionel feels breezy. Alive. A yellow and russet quilt covers the ground and Lionel can't resist kicking the leaves up as he walks the last half-kilometre to Judy's bungalow. Look at these conkers – their pithy shells strewn in wide circles around the horse chestnuts on the lane. He breaks one open. It's a deep, unapologetic brown and he runs his thumb over its shiny surface, marvelling at the wood grain markings that show the history of how the seed has swollen and ripened to become this perfect specimen. He puts it in his pocket wondering if everyone feels this elated and at one with nature when they're about to commit murder.

A removal van is pulling away from Judy's bungalow. One of the men in the cab notices him and gives a nervous wave as they pass. The man says something to the driver from the corner of his mouth. Lionel must cut a worrying figure in his Visor, his scimitar swinging from his belt, pirate-style. Dried blood from the gunshot wound to his ear has made a sinister pattern on his shirt. Huo's blood is on his hands, his arms, his face.

After Crystal killed Huo, it was Mr Barber who whisked them off. The old man was waiting at the top of the alley in a borrowed car, engine running, and he commanded them to get in as sirens whined in the distance. The drones would have recorded it all – the Jamaican pulling up, their suspects bundling onto the back seat. But the old man told them to keep their heads down and drove like a pro. When Lionel pleaded with him to turn back – an old man like him shouldn't be risking his life – Mr Barber fired him a look in the rearview mirror.

'What?' he said. 'You think mi always been a barber?' A rogue's twinkle brightened his eye. 'Besides, you have that piece there. I'll tell dem this was a hijack.'

As they drove, Crystal explained that she'd returned to the health centre to retrieve some belongings – Beatrise's photos, a jade charm strung on red cotton, some credit notes she'd hidden under a floorboard. She clutched them to her stomach as she spoke. They were wet with blood.

'Huo tell me Beatrise is dead,' she said calmly, then hid her face.

Finally, at Lionel's insistence, Mr Barber pulled off the road on the outskirts of town.

'I have a few things I have to do,' he said. 'My mother, my brothers . . .'

'I'll get the pickney seen to,' said Mr Barber.

When they shook hands the old man held Lionel firmly, but then pulled him to his chest, squeezing him tight.

'Don't judge your family too harshly,' he said.

'Why not?'

Through the living-room window he can see boxes and furniture still waiting to be taken away. Round the back he finds the same in the dining room. Lionel wonders what the removal men actually took with them – the house is still full.

Deflated, he squats on the back step, running his thumb along the sharpened edge of his scimitar. It draws a thin line of blood and he sucks his thumb-tip, savouring the iron tingle on his tongue. He'd imagined finding Ben and James laughing on the drive, arms across one another's shoulders. He'd imagined powering towards them, weapon raised, letting out a mad battle cry as he advanced. He'd imagined them pleading forgiveness, on their knees, bodies quivering with fear. He'd imagined saying, 'Sorry. I'm a Replicant, I'm not capable of mercy,' before slicing their heads off, *swish*, *swosh*, with two deft strokes of his blade. He'd imagined watching their grinning mugs roll down the path, blood trailing behind them. He'd imagined a feeling of great satisfaction. Relief and revenge. This is for Mordecai, he'd shout. This is for me!

But no one is home.

After a while he lifts Buddha out of the knapsack, his body now rigid, as if a taxidermist has set him in this tragic pose. At least his face is peaceful and Lionel fancies he sees a subtle, catty smile on the old boy's furry lips. He kisses him and lays him on the patio table, one hand on the animal's haunch for a second, thinking about the life that once flowed through him. He says a prayer. Finally he walks to the bottom of the garden and begins to slash at the long grass near the greenhouse.

He cuts the old onions, now gone to seed, and pulls up the dandelions and bindweed. Despite a wintery nip he begins to sweat and he removes his shirt and works on determinedly. The white honesty – broken at angles – takes some hacking, but soon the reckless growth that Judy has allowed to overrun the place is in a dry heap. He's about to start digging Buddha's grave when a scream belts out from up near the house.

Judy, on the patio, has her hands on her cheeks, staring at Buddha. But as Lionel advances towards her she backs away with one hand up, warding him off.

'Stay away from me,' she shrieks. 'Just stay away.'

'It's fine. It's only Buddha. He died, that's all; he just died.'

Taking in his naked brown chest and his scimitar, she shrieks louder. 'You're insane. I know it. Stay away.'

'No, this? This is just a costume. Look, see . . .' He drops the weapon and rips off the Visor, blinking with the light for a moment before opening his arms. 'See, I'm not mad – it's a costume, that's all. Fancy dress.'

Judy presses her hands to her bosom. 'The police are looking for you.'

'I haven't done anything. I was angry. But I'm not any more.' Lionel hangs his head. 'James killed my cat.'

Judy glances at Buddha.

'Not Buddha. Mordecai. You remember Mordecai?'

Judy stares blankly.

'Lilith told me some things, but I didn't want to believe her. But now I remember. You have to believe me. James tried to hang me. When I was a kid.'

Judy is wide-eyed. Her whole body is shaking.

'But they hadn't tied the rope at the top so it unwound and fell down.' He laughs. 'So it was all right in the end. He could've killed me, but he didn't. Lilith thought I was going to die.'

He can hear he's babbling, but he can't seem to stop. 'And then Dad punished us – me for lying, Lilith for swearing, or biting, or something, I can't remember what she said.' He shakes his head. 'She was a fierce little thing, even back then. Hah! But it wasn't a lie. Honestly. They hated me. I understand why. I was an imposter, of course – it makes sense. But they were so cruel. You must have known.' Tears run down Lionel's cheeks and he pauses, shaking his head. 'That's what I don't understand. Why you . . .' He holds his throat and the words come out strangled. 'Why you despise me. Why you brought me all the way here from Kenya just to despise me.'

Judy shakes her head minutely, presses her lips into a tight line.

'You have to tell me. You must. It's . . . you just have to.'

Judy looks to where Lionel has been at the weeds, then she looks at her hands as if there must be something there. 'The boys have gone. They didn't want me.' She rubs her hands together. 'Ben was adamant that I should live with them, up in Blyth, but apparently Susan has had a change of heart.' She closes her eyes when she says Susan's name. 'But it's Ben who had second thoughts. I know that. He left an hour ago. I had to send the removal men away.' She touches her forehead before she continues. 'James got a cancellation flight. He'll be taking off about now, back to America.' She looks directly at Lionel and gives him a guilty smile. 'He's not very nice. I didn't do a good job there at all, did I?'

Lionel shakes his head. 'I ran into them early this morning, at Sunnyvale.'

'They mentioned it.' Judy sits on the step, looks at her hands again before clasping them at her lips. 'Your mother,' she begins, 'was my best friend. She was Jamaican, you know – or her parents were. She was beautiful.' Suddenly she's fighting back tears. 'I loved her so much. She was like a sister and when she got pregnant with you, well . . . she was mortified. She wanted you. But she wasn't married. The puritanical elements in the church would have cast her out. But I persuaded them to support her. I told them it wasn't right, or Christian, to abandon a sister like that, so far from home.' Judy pauses. 'She died three days after you were born. I was with her. But she saw you and held you. And loved you.' Judy can't go on.

'Delia Johnson?'

Judy nods.

'Why didn't you tell me? What's the big secret about adopting your best friend's child?'

Judy's face hardens. 'It turns out she wasn't my friend, after all. It turns out she was a nasty, deceitful creature, who tricked me into loving her.'

'I don't understand.'

'Delia was your mother.'

'Yes. I know but –'

'And David was your father.'

Lionel hears the words, processes them slowly. David was his natural father. He feels odd. Weak. Almost dreamy. And he leans against the wall for support, lets his head fall backwards onto the bricks.

'Good Lord,' he says hoarsely.

Judy acknowledges his shock with a pitying moan and continues. 'They'd been having an affair for two years, him sneaking off every night. I was so wrapped up with toddlers, always a nose to wipe or a mouth to feed . . .' She pauses, briefly eliciting memories of motherhood. 'And she'd come to our house and beam at me with those lights in her eyes as if the whole world was dull and she was the only bright thing in it. You understand?' Years of suppressed anger are punching through Judy's decorum. 'He loved her. He loved her and not me. And I hated him for it and I hated her for it and I hated you for it, too.' She wipes her nose with her hand. 'Every time I looked at you I saw betrayal. Can you understand that? Can you?'

'Yes.'

Sunlight burnishes the lawn and picks out the red leaves of a Japanese acer. It's as if the tree is on fire.

'I made them hate you. James and Ben.'

Lionel sits in front of her on the chilly patio. 'It's okay.'

'No, it's not.'

Tears have left a residue on her cheeks and when she looks at him Lionel is sure he has never seen anything or anyone so aggrieved. He wants to enfold her.

'We can all start again,' he says. 'You, me, Lilith. We'll support one another.'

Judy shakes her head and laughs bleakly. 'Ah, Lionel. There it is, you see.'

'It's not impossible. Families can –'

Judy interrupts him. 'I always thought you did it to punish me.'

'What?'

'Lilith says this, Lilith says that . . .' Judy screws her face and holds her head as if she might crush it. 'Every time I saw you . . . reminding me, always reminding me.'

'What?'

She studies his face. 'You really don't know, do you?'

'What?'

'The doctors said it was unlikely you'd ever remember the accident and I suppose it was my fault – sending you away, so nothing gelled. But Dr Rand said you'd gradually realize. It would all come back.'

'Realize what?'

Judy grits her teeth. 'Your sister is dead, Lionel. She's been dead for eighteen years.' The effort of saying it hijacks all her energy and she pants for a long time before flinging herself back against the patio doors. 'Oh, I can't bear it. I still can't bear it.' Her body convulses as she sobs. 'My dear sweet girl.'

'What on earth are you talking about? I saw Lilith a couple of weeks ago. She's been living in my flat.'

'Lionel, please stop.'

'We all go in the car together. We meet at her house.'

'It's just you' – she points at him, then melodramatically grasps her own bosom – 'and me in the car.'

'I don't understand why you're saying this.'

'David and I – we bought you the car, which you thoughtlessly abandon all over the county. It's in the garage now. Take a look. And Sunnyvale is our . . .' Her voice rises to a quivering high note as she corrects herself. 'My house. David bought it so you would have a soft landing after university. And you hated it,' she spits, 'and abandoned it for that gruesome flat, in that horrible street. The Sunnyvale house was never Lilith's because there is. No. Lilith. Any more.' Judy is hysterical.

'No,' he says, laughing, worried that Judy is about to have another of her fabled breakdowns. 'Calm down. This is ridiculous.' He flips open his Google device. 'I've got videos and photos and her ID on here, and her profile.' Lionel is talking at speed. He wants to show Judy proof before she loses herself completely. 'There are her friends and her job and all the people we see together.' But even as he says it he's thinking how isolated they are, how they mostly stay in the flat. How he has never really known about her job. How her only friends turned out to be gangsters, who defiled him. How George insisted that *he* had attacked him and not Lilith. 'I can't find the photos. There are hundreds. I mean, literally hundreds. This is stupid. I don't understand. I must have deleted all the files.'

'What is the likelihood of that, Lionel?' Judy is exhausted. 'I mean, really?' She holds her face.

'Hold on, hold on, hold on.' He's flicking manically through his handheld. 'Ah, SocialNet!' He raises a finger and logs into the network domain.

He hasn't accessed his profile for some time. Here's Michael Unger and Joseph Knox and Pablo and all the shops and artists he follows – but Lilith has disappeared from his feed. He searches in vain for her profile.

'It's been deleted.'

'Oh, Lionel, stop it. Please stop it.'

'George! She hit that awful nurse. He'll tell you. You were there.'

'I've seen the CCTV of you attacking George, for heaven's sake. It's all on film.'

'No. Ridiculous.' He smacks his forehead.

'God, please God. Enough!' Judy clutches her heart.

In the dining room Lionel watches as Judy uses a kitchen knife to split the tape that seals a large box. Inside are albums and papers and document wallets.

'Here.' She hands him a photograph.

Lilith – wearing a red dress, the one that twizzled – standing in front of the laburnum at Bethesda. He crumples to tears.

'And here. I'm sorry.' The letters from Aunt Rachel are neatly bundled. 'She was too sick to come back for David's funeral. These are all the ones she sent to Sunnyvale after you moved out. I've read them. They tell you everything about your mother. David – your father. Everything.' She wipes her nose. 'And here.'

Lionel balances Lilith's death certificate on his upturned hands. It's heavy. It's heavier than anything he's ever held. It weighs him down so thoroughly he sinks to the floor. But even then it's too much to bear and he lies back, the paper on his chest, squashing the breath out of him. Judy lies beside him. She doesn't bother to smooth her tweed skirt, or worry about her hair being pushed out of place. She simply lies there and they stare at the ceiling together. Lionel panting. Judy crying.

'You were inseparable. Everywhere you went she followed. I suppose she was the only one who loved you unconditionally. I can see that now.

She tried to follow you the night you ran off. I've blamed you all this time. She got lost, you see . . . or tried to find you. But you found her.'

Here it comes. The memory. Flooding in from all sides. The bridge, the cone of light picking out Lilith's body in the road, his confusion when he saw her. The rain falling in sheets and him diving through it to save her. Too late.

'We used to go to the bridge when we were sad.' The weight is unbearable. 'We used to pretend we could be whisked away.' He turns to Judy. 'Am I insane?'

She shakes her head. 'I don't know. But if you are, then I am too.'

Final Level: Game Over

The Final Level with its spells and its hack-and-slash finale is the same in all close-combat dimensions. A raid. But this one was not the usual *bish bash bosh* at the end of a Quest. This was epic.

The Big Boss – a dragon – was hugesome and exploded onto the scene flailing his great, spiked tail and spewing flames from his throat. Sallow fizzog, a lopsided eye and a ruby-stud collar all made him look quite twisted and creepy. But he reared up, showed his talons and flapped enormous, leathery wings at us – it was all we could do to stand up to the blast. The sorceress hovered about defending his foreground – tho it didn't seem necessary.

On our side: me, Mata Angelica, the Sylph (tho she was wounded), and the MauMau. Some details are scanty – my nog got a bashing – but it began with the Sylph finding my scimitar. I'd lost it when I came through the Wormhole. It had been in the Big Boss's lair all the time.

At first the raid was bog-standard. The sorceress cast spells – *kazam kallam* – while we hung back out of aggro range. Mata Angelica struck a fearsome pose, but from the crook of her mouth she said, 'We're not likely to win this one, He-Man – so let's say adieu,' and she blew me a kiss.

The Big Boss roared and the whole place shook as if all of the particles and the hadrons and quarks were slaves to his whim. 'Give me the Sylph,' he boomed.

The voice sent my heart arrhythmic, my bowel-coils attempted to let something go – but I stood fast, protecting the Sylph. The Eroticon managed a brave, blaze-of-glory salute before cracking her whip and advancing. Straight off, the Boss fired a spike that clung to her neck and she coiled like an eel to dislodge it. I sprang to her aid, but she let off a pulsar that threw the spike back at the dragon. Very dramatic.

She flick-flacked to a forward position, lithe as a gymnast, and lashed ruthlessly hard with her whip. Meanwhile, I made figures of eight with my scimitar and a few swings hit their mark.

This went on. Click after click. And then something happened. The sounds of the fight merged to an inchoate hum and all the combatants lost their discrete forms – came as one – as if a continuum was contained in all movement and everything existed at once. Time was everywhere. Everything belonged to everything else. I bashed my Visor, tho it hadn't malfunctioned. The analytic report flashed *optimum energy* and I stood utterly still while my comrades faded around me.

Every scrap of wrathful pain I'd ever felt came alive in that moment – an accumulation of hate – and I directed my wrath at the sorceress. Suddenly, great voracious beasters, twixt somatic and myth, were conjured out of my nog. Devilish real – ivories jagged as rocks – but not real. I can't say how I did it, but the sorceress whizzed off soon as she saw 'em and the creatures made for her arse as she fled. The MauMau skidded after, quite comical, tho he soon got to work with his pring-claws. Made short work of her. Once the sorceress was Void the mythical beasters dissolved, *pouff*, as quick as they came and I slumped to the floor quite bewildered.

It was the Sylph who next sprang into action. Hardcore ninja. She went for the Boss – kung-fu boxing, long-fist, crane and crake – and cracked his goolies and kicked his skull till he went down with a fabulous wallop and instantly burst into flames. It was the weirdest fight scene I'd ever been in, and we'd won with a Wispy Sylph and a nightmare buried deep in my nog. The hit-count in my Visor showed '6610' – Final Level – and should've provoked a euphoric *woohoo*, but I stayed in the dirt, quite indecorous, scrubbing through old footage of other Quests I'd been on. And I realized they were all the same. Loss. Always loss. Compatriots cruelly taken. Dan-Albwr-han's image did 3D rotation in my Visor with a legend that flashed *wisp* over and over. I heaved with the sadness.

Ensanguined and triumphant the Eroticon came skipping. 'We've done it.' She embraced me, elated. 'I can't believe it. The Sylph was the Key, after all. She had the moves to beat the Boss. Alter the game.'

'I know. She's our hero.'

'And what was that magic you pulled? Demented! The sorceress was toast.'

'My rage made the beasts come. I don't know how.'

'Who cares how? It was epic!'

As she spoke my Visor came loose, dangled from one rivet for a click and clattered to the floor. A million splinters shattered there – dazzling, reflective. My retinas burned with the blow of new light and I shielded my eyes.

I heard Mata Angelica say, 'I knew it was custom, not integral.'

When I took a peek I could see the Sylph, finally, for who she was.

Game Over.

The Send-off

A light rain sheens everyone's skin and dampens their hair as they wait for Crystal to finish her goodbyes. Michael is the only one with an umbrella, but he's using it as a walking stick instead of keeping the rain off, leaning suavely on the handle. He's had a shave and looks a little younger. Less tired. Eve links arms with him as Crystal kisses Mr Barber's cheek and thanks him for everything, for saving her life. The old man demurs, kicks a pebble on the ground.

'A'right now,' he says. 'That's enough. Mi comin' with you to the airport anyway, so you can miss me outta this goodbye. Mi cyaan bear it.'

'You did save my life,' she insists, including the whole group as she turns.

There's a ripple of polite protests as she goes round and kisses each of them for the second time. Finally she comes to Lionel.

'You are good mans,' she tells him.

Brown, not black or blue, and smaller than he imagined, with creamy folds of skin cutting across each corner, her eyes are no less compelling than the first time he fixed on them. But she's no anime character – not any more.

'Are you sure you want to go back?' He rubs the palm of his hand with his thumb, as if he can scrub out the lines of his destiny. 'You can still change your mind.'

'My mother, she move to Taiwan. She want me come home. I am on list for job. Google factory.' She shows him her new passport. 'I can be me again,' she says, pointing to her name.

'Well, good luck then, Mei-Zhen.' He's practised the pronunciation.

This beautiful girl is holding him tight in her arms as if her whole life has distilled to this moment and Lionel is remembering the first time he saw her on Milk Street, damaged and ranting. Their connection saved him, altered him at least. She will always be Crystal to him.

'You same like me, yes? Now I am *me* and you are *you*.' She holds his face, kisses him on the lips. 'You are Lionel, not Ludi.'

'I am me,' he agrees.

When the car turns at the end of the road and they've let their arms flop back to their sides after an age of waving, the three of them puff and roll their eyes.

'Well, that's that,' says Michael and heads to the house.

The place is in the process of being packed up. They're moving on, Eve and Michael, off to recruit more disciples – although they won't say where. Pema Khalsa is in custody. Security discovered five bank accounts, each containing more than half a million credits. Larissa Greenough was charged with conspiracy, but was released when immigration officials swept her modest semi and found a remote communication device inserted, subcutaneously, in her cat – a gift, the previous year, from Mrs Khalsa.

Lionel can't go back to Meddingley, or Milk Street; Huo's death has put paid to that. And, despite footage from his Visor proving he didn't kill him, Lionel has no intention of incriminating Crystal. Besides, questions remain about Grippa. There's CCTV evidence linking him to the gangster's death.

'Here's your new bio-ID,' says Michael. He passes a card and some documents from a small holdall. 'As you know, your name's Paul Johnson – nice choice. I've deleted every trace of Lionel Byrd that I can find. I've scoured every goddamn network in the Northern Hemisphere. But you know it's not failsafe, eh, buddy? Can't scrub the cloud clean once you've smeared your DNA all over it. The internet's a crazy brain. It's got secret vaults.' He flicks Lionel's lapel. 'But I reckon I've done a pretty good job of reinventing you, if I do say so myself.'

'Thank you.'

'What're you planning to do now?'

'Travel. Somewhere exotic I think.'

'Jamaica?'

'Africa perhaps.'

'I thought you turned out to be Jamaican.'

Eve interjects. 'We're all African, you know.'

'Yeah, I knew that.' Michael pulls a face. 'Hey, look, I'm gonna get on with this shit.' He points to the half-packed boxes then takes Lionel's shoulder. 'Good luck, buddy boy. You're a total fucking freak, but I like you.'

'Thank you, thank you very much.'

'And thanks, you know, for what you did, in the game.'

'You're welcome.'

The room is suddenly quiet and here's Lionel – opposite Eve – with his hands in his pockets, not knowing where to look.

'I know I deceived you.' She looks at her fingernails. 'But it wasn't *all* an act.' She looks up, takes a step towards him. 'You look kind of cool with the dreads and the beard.'

Lionel strokes thick strands back off his eyes. 'Thanks.'

'And Michael tells me you're doing well.' She gives a grave nod.

'I'm working things out. I'm good.'

'I'm glad you're good. I always knew you were *good*.'

'Yeah.'

They smile awkwardly.

'Hey,' says Eve, as if she's had an afterthought. 'You mustn't tell Michael, but I made sure our avatars weren't deleted.' She bites a nail. 'I know it could never work out in this dimension – between us, I mean. But Ludi and Mata Angelica were damn fine together, don't you think?'

The musk in her perfume clarifies as she moves in.

'Yes, they were.'

'If you're ever in Thrar' – she's close enough to walk her fingers across his chest – 'you know where to find me.'

The bridge is overgrown with brambles and the disused motorway it straddles has succumbed to the rampant progress of nature. Weeds have grown up through cracks in the macadam. The crash barriers have crumbled. A hundred metres away, in the central reservation, a vixen watches her cubs as they yap in the sun. Slowly, Lionel makes it to the centre of the cattle bridge, brambles snagging his trousers – touching him one last time before he goes. He looks out, recognizes the wide sweep of the road, diminishing to a thread in the distance. This road was once a snarling highway. Now it's peaceful.

It's not easy getting up onto the barrier; he's so tall and gangly now he's a man. But he stands on the edge like a high diver, arms stretched towards the deep blue of the sky, sun warming his face through the thick of his beard.

Woohoo.

He goes over. A swallow dive. A graceful, uninhibited arc. Into the Void. And he falls and he falls and continues to fall.

@GameAddict (#23756745): 28:9:27

It has to come to an end. You'll reach the Final
Level eventually – there's no putting it off.
And you're bereft for a while and play a few
old games – though they're never as good. But
then, thank God, they launch the new version.
CoreQuest: The Hidden Realm or something like
that. And you log in, shaking with anticipation.
And as soon as you look around you know.

You've died and gone to heaven.

A New Realm: Level 1

Gog has turned into a verdant new paradise of grasses and wild flowers and lazy streamlets. In fact, the whole Realm is popping with plantlife and colour since the game was altered.

Along the lush banks of the Nur the settlements are mud-made and primitive, yet the Krin who dwell here come out and greet me, hale fellows, every one of them.

I find him eventually. He has a mate and a sprog – a daughter – and a few modest possessions, but no more than he needs. There's a small-holding, about a hundred paces square, and a moody Heeber with swollen udders in the corner of his field.

'Stranger,' he shouts when he sees me. 'What brings an outlander to these parts? Come share some vitals. I have DumGrog.' And he winks as he offers a paw. 'I could do with some tales of far away.'

I search his fizzog for prior knowledge of me and there's none. But later, as we warm ourselves before his hearth, he says, 'Uncanny, I feel I've known you all my life.' And he hard-eyes me, all deeply searching. 'You should have a Visor, covering your eye-gems.' He makes the shape along his brow with one paw.

'You know,' I say. 'I did have a Visor once, but it fell away.'

When I leave he slaps my back and gives me a jar full of stars to light my way to camp. 'Come visit again,' he says.

'I will,' I say. 'If I'm back this way.'

He calls after me. 'The Grog has robbed me of my manners. I'm Dan-Albwr-han.' He touches his chest. 'What's your good name?'

'Lionel,' I call back.

'Fine name,' he says. 'I'll remember it.'

And we laugh and *hip hip halloo* until my jar of stars is a mere dot in the dark and he closes his door on the night.

The MauMau and the Sylph are waiting by the fire and they greet me all keenly and purrsome. The MauMau slinks up round my trunk and rubs his ear-glands right on my chin. Giant beaster catches Jigga bugs and desert shrews if there's space in his maw. He's come quite domesticated since the reconfiguration.

My new Quest: find a distant corner of the Realm. Settle there with the Sylph and the MauMau. I don't care how long it takes. I am alive now. Totally alive. And I have all the time in the world.

As we settle, the Sylph slips her mitt into mine.

'I've been wondering,' she says. 'What shall I be called?'

I smile. 'Your name's Lilith.'

'Lilith. I like that.'

She snuggles her wireframe into mine, all snoozy and happy, and my heart swells with the perfection of it all.

Acknowledgements

I would like to thank my editor, Luke Brown, for his commitment to this novel, and everyone at Tindal Street Press for their support. Special thanks to Arts Council England West Midlands for financial support; Joe Falke for sharing his game design expertise and to Amanda Smyth and Saskia Bakayoko for their insightful readings. Thanks also to Anthony Ferner, Kerry O'Grady, all my friends at Tindal Street Fiction Group and my agent, Karolina Sutton, for their thoughts and advice. Above all, my family – Orville, Joëlle and Naomi – for their love and understanding.

About the Author

Mez Packer lives in Warwickshire and is senior lecturer in interactive media at Coventry University. Her debut novel *Among Thieves* was shortlisted for the Commonwealth Writers' Prize and longlisted for the Authors' Club First Novel Award.